# The Angel's Cut

Also by Elizabeth Knox

# The Angel's Cut

# Elizabeth Knox

Victoria University Press

TE WHARE WĀNANGA O TE ŪPOKO O TE IKA A MĀUI

VICTORIA UNIVERSITY PRESS
Victoria University of Wellington
PO Box 600 Wellington
http://www.victoria.ac.nz/vup

National Library of New Zealand Cataloguing-in-Publication Data

Knox, Elizabeth.
The angel's cut / Elizabeth Knox.
ISBN 978-0-86473-600-0
I. Title.
NZ823.2—dc 22

Printed by Printlink, Wellington

*We all have one story. But what would you do after that and that and that day after day after dozens hundreds thousands and ten thousands of time?*

F Scott Fitzgerald
(from working notes for *The Last Tycoon*)

# Contents

## Acknowledgments

I'd like to thank this book's early readers, Kirsten McDougall, Bill Manhire, Natasha Fairweather and Naomi Leon. Thanks also to Bernadette Hall and the Stout Research Centre for the loan of rooms when my own room was besieged by building noise. Many thanks to my editor Linda Funnell, and—as always—my first reader, Fergus Barrowman.

# Prologue

# The English Channel

## 1917

The Zeppelin hung concealed in cloud, a layer of thick stratus with a base three thousand feet above the sea. The airship's navigator—the angel Xas—was in the control cabin, studying a map in the greenish light from the gauges, when his captain came to stand beside him. They looked out together on the ghostly country of cloud.

'Hans,' said Captain Hintersee, 'would you say that this cloud extends all the way to Dover?'

The navigator Hans Ritt was famous in the fleet, for he never lost his way. Pilots navigated using compasses, and by making dead-reckonings from roadmaps they carried. They dropped down and looked for landmarks. But Ritt seemed to know all of Europe from the air; to have it in his head. Even without a compass and in the thickest fog he always knew where north lay.

That night, over the Channel, Xas turned his eyes from the window and the gauzy white topography below to tell his captain that yes, he did think the cloud cover extended from coast to coast. Then he dropped his chin and waited. The Zeppelin captain frowned at him. 'Perhaps you should—' he began, then caught himself and modified his suggestion so that it was an order. 'Hans, I want you to take the cloud car down and take a look about.'

Xas stood straight, clicked his heels, then smiled happily, which spoiled the effect of military propriety. 'Thank you, captain,' he said, and left Hintersee's side.

He reported to the belly of the airship, where he found the cloud car ready, its attendants around it, and at the controls of the winch and its thick coiled cable.

The car was a basket made of hardwood struts covered in canvas, a streamlined cradle with a bulbous front end where an observer would sit, hunched behind a low windscreen. It was equipped with a telephone the observer used to communicate with the control cabin.

The basket was positioned above a gap in the longitudinal girders of the airship's frame. It hovered, swinging slightly. Cloud fumed through the gap.

Xas wriggled and jumped and tugged his way into a thick, fleece-lined canvas suit. He put on a helmet and gloves. Two crew members held the basket steady as he clambered through the cables that kept it level. He positioned his goggles, hunkered down, and gave the crew the thumbs up. The winch spun, the cable unwound, and the cloud car took him out of the light inside the airship, and into the wet white air.

Cloud came between him and the airship. The diffuse

patch of brightness that was the gap in its belly dimmed, then disappeared. The hum of its engines grew muffled.

Xas removed his goggles, helmet and gloves and stuffed them between his knees. He was always careful to put the protective gear on again before he returned to the ship. The gear was, like his name, a disguise he wore for the benefit of others.

He raised his hands and opened his mouth and let the air caress him. As the basket cut its way through the lower layer of cloud, its cables acquired thin white streamers of vapour. Xas ran his fingers back and forth through these dragons' whiskers, which broke and eddied like smoke rings.

The cloud car passed through the thinning vapour, and Xas looked down.

The sea was dark, but textured, its waves backlit by the faint radiance of a rainfall several miles away. Xas could see where the rain softened the air. He could see too that there were several interruptions in the sea's surface. Black strokes. Three ships, showing no light. He waited till his eyes made a further adjustment and he could spot each ship's wake, and therefore the direction they were headed.

He picked up the telephone, and put it to his ear. There was a loud click, then the electric hum of the open line. He asked Hintersee to have the men in the belly of the airship lower him a further ten feet. He said that the cloud was thicker than they'd thought. He reported that he was only just out of it. Really he hoped to relish more of the clear sky under the cloud.

The basket shivered as the winch started up again far overhead. The soft bright underside of the cloud receded, and the wind grew a little less wet. He savoured it. In a moment he would turn to his duty, but for now he swung through the dark in his own true home, the fully three-dimensional terrain of the sky.

He took a moment, then put the phone back to his ear and began to talk to his captain, to relay the bearings of the target ships.

Suddenly, a coil of vapour spun down past the cloud car. Dark spirals of turbulence appeared in the underside of the cloud some twenty feet above. Xas knew at once what was causing it. Clear air from above the layer of cloud was being forced down through it, making black vortices in the vapour, vortices formed by the tips of great wings describing high-velocity parabolas, and mixing fog and air.

Xas dropped the phone. The soft ceiling above him ruptured. A huge dark shape pierced the cloud and opened a gap through to starlight. Wings made a rushing thump in the air. Xas felt the concussions of displaced air shuddering around him.

The archangel braked his plunge, then banked against unbroken cloud, coming around in a tight loop that would bring him back to where Xas hung in the fragile cradle of the cloud car. Xas saw that the attenuated avian hands on the wrist joints of the archangel's six wings were splayed, reaching. He saw light flash on the pale palms of the archangel's two human hands. And, as the huge winged body closed on him, he saw that one of those many, avid hands was missing some fingers. It was by this mutilated hand that Xas recognised Lucifer—who had cut off his wings.

He threw himself out of the cloud car.

Looking back through his feet as he fell, Xas saw the archangel connect with the cloud car, catch hold of it, and hang swinging, hands gripping the basket, two top wings flared back and flapping furiously. He heard the cable shriek and groan. And he heard his name, for the first time in over fifty years. Lucifer shouted, '*Xas!*' and Xas closed his body into a ball. He knew he could fall faster than Lucifer could fly down. The archangel had too much surface area to race any falling, wingless creature a few thousand feet to the sea.

Xas plunged straight down, and hit the surface of the sea so hard that he rebounded once before sinking into it. He let out all the air in his lungs and stopped breathing.

It was cold and dark under the water. Far away the ships' propellers whined like bees caught behind a curtain. Xas hung below the surface and looked up through murky transparency at that surface in reverse—the gleam of light on the backs of the waves. After a moment he saw the ragged star of Lucifer's form pass above him. The sea turned momentarily smooth in the downblast of the archangel's wings. Then Lucifer banked and drove upward, disappearing in a flicker of darkness into the night sky.

# Le Crotoy, France

## 1922

Xas was the last act of the day. The sun had come out, a seven p.m. sun that sat balanced on the top of the grandstand. All afternoon the crowd had been a flowerbed of faces, hair, hats, exclamatory hands, but now, with the sun behind them, they had become a dark, tense fur of persons, a mass of exhausted nerves, and unslaked lust for catastrophe. They'd enjoyed the show, applauded the aerial acrobats—six girls who never left their perch on a biplane's top wing, but clambered over one another to make shapely filigrees of limbs against the sky. They'd laughed through clenched teeth at clowns skating back and forth along the wobbling wings of a slow, low cruising plane. They'd held their breath when the parachutists performed their bullet drops. Of the day's thrills all that was left now was the grand finale, the plane-to-plane transfer.

Xas tucked his plait into his flight suit. The huge, adenoidal voice of the Tannoy began to tell the spectators what he planned to do. He gave a wave, keeping his arms close to his sides so that no one would divine the full effect of the trick until it unfurled before them.

There were no other planes in the air. The skylarks had returned to the field and were threading the evening with song.

Xas climbed into the biplane, taking the forward seat, and gave his pilot a thumbs up. A mechanic span the propeller, hauled away the chocks, then ran around to a wingtip and turned the plane onto the airstrip. The pilot gunned the engine and they took off, banked and climbed. They levelled out and waited for the second plane to join them. Once it was in the air they settled at their different altitudes, Xas's pilot climbing to eighteen hundred feet, the other to only five hundred. The planes levelled off, then turned again to make a run past the grandstand.

Xas climbed out of the cockpit. A big drop of oil blew back from the open cowling of the engine and splattered on one lens of his goggles. He wiped at the splash with his glove, but couldn't shift, only smeared, it. He pulled his goggles off and dropped them onto his seat. He had his back to the wind and it pushed his thick bound hair into a kind of hood around his face. It was as if he'd smeared lamp black under his eyes. There was no glare. He could see everything—could even make out the expression of anxiety and disapproval on his pilot's face. Xas smiled at the man and, in a moment of mischief, unbuckled the parachute strapped to his chest and dropped it too into his empty seat. The pilot shook his head. Xas took hold of the top wing and hauled himself up onto it.

He swapped his handholds and turned around into the ram air. He felt his eyes and facial muscles stiffen in response to the pressure of the wind. Ram air made everyone grimace—everyone but him. His face lost all its pliability and settled, sculptural, angelic, as hard as a bird's beak.

Xas stood up and spread his arms. The wind caught the webs of silk and baleen between the sleeves and sides of his soaring suit. The plane leapt away from him and for a moment he floated, a dark star against a pale blue afternoon sky. Then he rolled into a somersault—followed by an apparently uncontrolled series of writhing falls. He flung his arms out again and stopped tumbling, only to swing back and forth like a leaf falling from a tree, rocking as it dropped.

This was what the crowd saw. Xas could hear them sighing and crying out. He realised that he shouldn't have abandoned his parachute so surreptitiously, but with a flourish. Then they'd be silent, and their silence would be like the skin he felt forming as he curled up once more. He closed his body, and the air closed around him.

All aerial acrobats and parachutists wore helmets so as not to be deafened by the eardrum-sucking speed of the passing wind. But Xas hung wrapped in the sound of that wind, and of the world below—all discrete and distinguishable. He was balanced on the bubble of air that people feel form under them in a freefall. For a moment he felt an invisible hand holding him up, and promising to hold him, promising that the space below him would be divided infinitely, that there was no bottom to it, because all halves *have* halves, as Zeno said.

This ecstasy lasted only seconds. Xas let the seconds go by and then he spread his arms and legs and looked down. He searched for the second plane—his target. It was below him, as it should be, and behind, as it should be. But it was too near. It was going to overshoot their rendezvous.

Xas dipped into a shallow dive, speeding ahead, gaining ten feet of forward distance while losing a hundred in height. The second plane slid by, the transparency of its propeller only twenty feet below. Xas felt a flutter on his feet and knees. It was the slipstream, an invisible churning serpent of displaced air. He knew the slipstream would pull him down before it pushed him back behind the plane, so he tilted his hips and dropped his suit's canvas fantail into the turbulence.

The slipstream flipped him. As he went over he wrenched his head around and his eyes found the nearest carbane—one of the wires between the biplane's wings. He snatched— making contact with one fingertip only. He closed that finger into a hook and was jerked forward as he simultaneously stopped falling and matched speeds with the plane. The change of direction was so sudden that he went into another somersault and crashed into the wing. The spectators howled. The plane yawed and wobbled. Xas clung on, lay still as the pilot brought the plane level. The green, shadow-filled grass was streaming by directly beneath them, and he understood that the second plane had dropped dangerously low to catch him. There was the blur of green, then the fawn dust of the rolled dirt air strip. Xas crawled back along the wing. He lowered himself into his seat in the same moment the wheels touched the ground.

The pilot taxied the plane in close to the grandstand. The crowd poured toward them. Xas clambered down and stood waiting to be congratulated on his feat. Then he saw that his first pilot was nearer than the nearest of his admirers, was coming at him, swearing, and swinging his abandoned parachute. Then he was engulfed, muffled in bodies, one pummelling him with the soft package of the chute, the others thrusting pens and flyers at him—the flyer advertising the air circus which figured him at the centre of its images, in his soaring suit and long, black braid, as '*The Daring, the Devil May Care INDIAN.*'

Later that evening Xas was sitting in a bar with the pilots, acrobats, parachutists, when a woman arrived at their table with eight glasses of Dubonnet crammed in her skinny hands. She was a light-skinned Coloured woman with high cheekbones and marcel-waved hair. She fixed her eyes on Xas and mustered words. She asked, in ungrammatical French, whether he was really an Indian?

'He's German,' someone said, 'but since the War no one is letting Germans fly in Europe.'

Someone else pulled out a chair for her. She said her name was Millie Cotton, and that she was an American. She was in France because she was learning to fly. 'Flying schools back home won't even take Coloured *men*. I'm at the Ecole d'Aviation des Frères Caudon. It's near here.'

Seven of the glasses had been claimed. The circus people were waiting for Millie to take the eighth. She didn't notice. She only stared at Xas as though hoping to somehow absorb him. 'How do you do it?' she said. 'How do you find the other plane?'

Xas's first pilot touched her arm and said, slowly, reverently, in French, 'He's a pioneer. He plans to make his mark.' Then he raised a hand and slapped it down on the tabletop so that all the empty glasses jumped and toppled.

Millie looked alarmed.

Xas explained. 'To make your mark is to fall to your death, splashing some farmer's field. He's saying I take big risks to make my mark, to finally lose my game with gravity.'

The pilot put his hand on Xas's. 'Tell her this,' he said. 'Tell her that most days the spectators can see the effort and care it takes to make a transfer from plane to plane. But today you were having too much fun.'

Xas said to Millie, in English, 'He says I was having too much fun. On other days the crowd can see the care and effort.'

Millie laughed.

He said, 'Would you like me to take you up and teach you to jump? All pilots should know how to use a parachute.'

'Yes! Would you?'

'Can you come after the show tomorrow morning?'

Millie nodded. And then she looked around the group and reverted to her halting French to tell them that, in the States, there had been law changes that had pretty much put an end to the airshows. The pilots had to fly too high, and the audiences couldn't really see the stunts any more.

Everyone made sounds of disgust. Then Xas said, to Millie, and to anyone who might give him an answer, 'Do you think that will happen here?'

First Reel

# Los Angeles

## June 27, 1929

In 1929 Xas came to Los Angeles looking for a flying job. He hung around Glendale airport, hoping something would come up, and every time a plane came in to land, or a mechanic or radio-operator punched in, the current custodian of his tale would say, 'See that pilot? Somebody up there likes him.'

He'd been flying to spot schools of tuna for the fleets out of San Pedro, when his plane went down. Its rudder line had broken, sending it into a steep dive. A tuna boat captain who'd watched the spotter's plane plunge into the sea, and who hurried to the wreck to see what came up, at first found only a few floating fragments of varnished canvas and balsawood. Then Xas surfaced still grasping the plane's joystick—which had broken off in his hand as he tried to pull up. He was alive and unhurt, and the boat's crew had regarded him with awe when he came on board, standing back as if afraid to go near him.

Xas sat in the waiting room at Glendale airport, his hand curled around the bowl of his coffee cup, and answered questions about the crack-up. And, as the day wore on, his answers became more considered. He remembered struggling out of the crumpled and disjointed wreck, leaving it sinking, its pale shape slowly growing green as it went down into the gloom, shedding air upward from every gash. He had drifted up with the bubbles, and when he reached the surface he found the stick still in his hand. He remembered looking at it, and wondering at himself. After all—he was always conscious, he had only ever slept when he was sleeping beside someone. So why had he held so hard to that piece of broken machinery?

By late afternoon Xas's musings had begun to bemuse his audience. 'I think I have an instinct to hold onto what has fallen,' he said, 'an instinct that trumps sense.' He flexed his hand, and, looking around the baffled faces, he saw one he recognised.

'Millie Cotton!' Xas was delighted. He jumped up and pulled out a chair for her.

'With a story like that it figures it's you,' Millie said. She told the flyers who'd come in with her, 'This guy is the wildest wing-walker I ever saw.' She sat down beside Xas and unfastened the buttons of her powder-blue leather flying suit to reveal the dewy skin on her collarbones.

Xas took her hand. 'I taught you to jump,' he said. 'And on the strength of that you bought me drinks for a whole week.'

'Was it really only a week?' Millie said.

'Yes. And here we are, together again—only there's Prohibition.'

The flyers who'd come in with Millie all snorted.

'Shame about that,' she said, dry. Then, 'Leastways, I have a job for you.'

It was after midnight when they drove to Santa Monica in Millie's Buick, their bellies full of steak and bootleg beer.

The Buick was new, and Millie was wearing her leather flying suit, and a white silk scarf. By her car, clothes and the way she drove—though she was far from sober—Xas was able to measure how she had shaped up as a pilot. Her driving was efficient and debonair. She watched the dark, dusty roads and handled the wheel, gear stick, clutch and brakes, her brain playing with space.

They had left the houses behind and were driving between a field of beans and a eucalyptus windbreak—big old trees planted for ironwood railway ties. Between the trees Xas saw blank, frizzled fields, still and pale in the starlight.

'We're going early,' Millie said, 'not because you have to be early for me to get you hired on, but because I want to show you something.'

Millie turned in at a gate, and parked by a hangar whose sign read 'Mutual Aircraft'. She shut off the engine and grinned at Xas, her round cheeks and oiled hair outlined by a distant column of light, its brightness grainy with the bodies of flying insects. The searchlight was aimed up at a mast, where a Zeppelin tilted at the end of her tether, nose down and aft up, a weightless silver whale in the cone of radiance.

'*Lake Werner*,' said Millie, 'isn't she a sight?' She got out of the car and walked away toward the mast. After a moment Xas saw a match lit, the flare, then the orange coal of Millie's cigarette tip coming and going.

He got out of the car and followed her. He saw that the field he walked on wasn't grass, but clumps of battered alfalfa and barley—remnants of old crops between patches of dusty hard-baked earth. He reached Millie, took her hand and pinched out her cigarette's fire. They were too near to the Zeppelin and its volatile gas.

'But I'm gasping,' Millie said, then dropped the butt and wrapped her arms around herself. 'You told me in '22 that you used to crew one of these things.' She peered up at him, waiting for more.

'I heard that my captain had to give up his Zeppelin as part of the reparations,' Xas said. 'He had to deliver it personally to a French fort in Africa, after which he travelled back home by sea and train.'

'It was a raider Zeppelin?' Millie said. 'Were you flying those raids on London?'

'I was the navigator, not the bombadier.'

'Uh-huh,' said Millie. 'So you were.'

The field around the mast was showing signs of a melee of deliveries. It looked like a village square after a market packs up—littered with broken crates, wadded paper, cabbage stalks, and an orange dented by a boot heel. There were rolls of red carpet leaning against the mast's supports, and several other incongruities, like stanchions and silk ropes, and palm trees in brass pots.

'There's a big send-off this evening,' Millie said. 'A jazz band, searchlights, well-wishers, and the Movietone news.' She nudged him. 'Do you like jazz?'

'I don't know.'

'I'll take you to some clubs.' She peered at him. 'You'll stay for a bit, won't you? There's lots of work for flyers in this town.'

Above them the airship creaked and groaned as its gas envelopes expanded—the gas slower to cool than the surrounding air. The condensation that had formed on the ship's warm sides fell in pattering drops on and around them. The airship was beginning to come level again as her crew moved ballast about. In the beam of the searchlight the whirlwind of insects rattled against her silver skin.

'She's going around the world,' said Millie. 'You must have read about it.'

'I have. But I didn't know she was here.'

Millie said that *Lake Werner* had already flown from Berlin to New York, New York to Rio, Rio to Los Angeles. She would depart Los Angeles that evening for Tokyo, then continue on to Berlin again. She took his arm. 'Let's go back to my car. We can smoke, and I can tell you about the job.'

Millie had her smoke. She slid down in her seat, her flying suit creaking against the Buick's upholstery.

'The name of the film is *Spirit*. It's about aces—a guy called Marshall and his buddies. It's set mostly in France.

I'm doing Marshall's battle stunts, in a Spad. And the director wants me to crash for him.'

'Today?'

'Yeah,' said Millie. She tossed her half-finished cigarette over the door beside her and took an inhaler out of her jacket. She closed her lips over it, huffed, coughed, and handed it to Xas. 'Benzedrine,' she said. 'It's the ticket, as they say in England.'

Xas, curious, put the inhaler's damp nozzle to his lips, pressed and sucked. To his surprise he felt the drug. His clear head opened up even more, like a summer's day dilating.

'Oh yes,' crooned Millie, looking at him. She slumped, leather squawking, along the seat and rested her head on his shoulder. She said, 'I don't want to crash the plane today.'

Her voice was quiet and confiding—but it worried Xas. He asked, 'What's up?'

She shrugged. 'Crow has till tomorrow to get all the stunts in the can. Crow's the director—Conrad Crow?'

Xas shook his head.

'The film's in trouble,' Millie said. 'The studio shifted some of the budget and asked Crow to shoot sound scenes. He has all these battles planned, and now he's having to write *dialogue* with Ray Paige. Paige is the writer. He's a lush. Crow's really pressed for time and money getting all the battle footage he needs.' Millie sat up straight, shook herself and opened the glove compartment. She had a flask in there. She took a swig and gave it to Xas. Tequila.

She continued. 'But the *real* problem is Conrad Cole. And in case I'm confusing you—yes—Connie Crow and Con Cole are two different Conrads. Anyway,' she said, 'Cole has bought up most of the planes Crow might like to use. And he claims that Paige had already sold *him* a version of *Spirit*'s story. But Cole's only playing at making a film—he's been shooting his *Flights of Angels* for two years. And, because he might want them at any time, he's hired the Red Eagles— the so-called aerial stuntmen's union. They call themselves a union, but I think any union that signs an exclusive contract has got to be more a company, hasn't it? Or just another club that won't let me join.'

'So, you think Crow will hire me because he's short of time and stunt flyers?'

'Crow would hire you on my recommendation alone. He likes me. And he's a friendly guy who likes men of action. I'm telling you that so you'll know how to treat him. Crow's friendly and sharp and straight but he's a cold-hearted bastard and don't you ever forget it.' Millie nodded at Xas, emphatic. She had the flask up to her lips and Xas could see the reflected lips lifting to kiss her real ones. Xas, watching the two sets of lips, said, 'Do you want me to crash the Spad for you?'

Millie tilted her head back and looked up at him. 'I need the money, sweetie. I just don't want to do it today.'

'How much is he offering?'

'Nine hundred. For an emergency landing on one wheel only, because the left wheel is missing. The left wing to touch enough to slam the plane around. He doesn't need me to flip it, Xas. But Marshall, the hero, ends up upside down. They've filmed his death scene already. But I guess they're doing it again, with sound.'

'Do you have any idea what this Crow will want me to do?'

'You can fly a Fokker. I recall you had one in France. Crow will want neat, nasty moves for back projection of the Fokker on Marshall's tail. We get the battle plan today. One of the other stunt flyers is bringing another Fokker, so we'll have four—which still isn't quite enough.'

They turned to stare at the airship, and the whirlwind of insects in the beam of the searchlight. A light sea breeze was blowing across the field. In the east night was separating from the black mountains, the light a pale pith between them. Millie lit up again. She told Xas about her plans. She was saving money to set up a flying school for Coloured people in Texas—her home state. She had three instructors already. Two had trained in France, like her, the other was Brazilian.

'I have a good sum set by,' she said. 'From stunt jobs, and now and then I invest a couple of hundred with a friend of mine. My friend Flora raises—say—five hundred, and I put in two, then I fly across to Cocopah or Pasqualitos and buy tequila. Flora's from Brawley, down near the border. Her uncle cuts his fence wire so these bootlegging boys we know can drive off the highway, and through his pastureland, to the edge of the desert. Flora and the boys put down kerosene in broken bottles to mark out an airstrip, then they listen for my engines and light the kerosene so I can see where to bring her in. The boys pay for my cargo. Flora and I split the money. Flora's uncle lets the boys out again onto the highway, and mends his fence. Flora pays him his cut, and we fly home.'

Millie finished, then said, 'I suppose that sounds more dangerous than flying stunts.'

'Do the bootleggers carry guns?'

'Yes. But we try not to take it personally. Besides, if we waited for help we'd be waiting forever—me and Flora. We have to play the hands we've been dealt.' Millie yawned, and stretched, and her elbows popped. She passed him the flask again. 'Are you warm enough?'

He nodded. 'So that's why your friends at Glendale sniggered when I mentioned Prohibition.'

'Yes. Because I never have to do without booze. We keep what we need, me a little, Flora a lot.'

'She's a drinker?'

Millie nodded. 'She has her reasons.'

# Venice, California

## June 27, 1929

On the same day that Millie ran into Xas at Glendale airport, Millie's friend, Flora McLeod, had a visit from an old flame.

When Gil Crow arrived at Flora's bungalow she was in her robe. Her clothes were lying, muddied, just inside the front door.

Gil kissed her, said, 'Ah, Flora—your slatternly ways,' and handed her a bottle of whisky. He went in ahead of her and began moving magazines and clothes to make room for himself on the couch. 'Though I hear your cutting room is a picture of order,' he said.

Editing film was Flora McLeod's second career. She'd first come to Hollywood in 1920, at nineteen years of age, after winning a beauty contest in Brawley, her home town. She did get to act in movies, though for her biggest role she only got to play the girl who *almost* gets the guy, a peppy girl standing at the door of a dance hall, checking her hair and waving hello. Flora photographed well, worked hard, and was fun to have on a set. She might have gone on to better roles, and the talkies could have used her sharp, clear voice. But in 1925, when she was at a costume party at the Ship Café, her boyfriend touched a cigarette to the grass skirt she was wearing. It was meant to be only a bit of mischief, but the skirt caught with a whoosh, and the flames seemed to lift Flora off the ground. Later people saw that the paint on the café ceiling was blistered and blackened in a long trail, for Flora had bolted across the room before a quick-thinking twenty-one-year-old millionaire called Conrad Cole tackled her and wrapped her in a thick velvet curtain.

When she finally got out of hospital Flora was down to four and a half stone. She went to live with an aunt in Brawley, and learned to walk again, at first with her legs apart as if to hold her in a straight course on a moving deck. She put on a little weight, but nothing would induce her to round out again, for the scarring on her hips had hardened into a kind of cutaneous belt above and below which any extra flesh would billow, and pull at every movement.

Flora might have remained with her aunt. There was some talk about turning the porch in which she was sleeping into a proper bedroom. But she saw the life she'd have, as a poor relation, a scarecrow figure who helps a little around the house, hanging out the family wash, wincing every time she has to lift her arms. She could help, and not just live on sufferance because, although they weren't close, she did get on with her aunt and uncle and young cousins. But, Flora discovered, the larger world was eager to take her back.

There had been a lot of people at that party, people who remembered what had happened with horror and pity, and were keen to do what they could for her.

The man who had caught her in the curtain was the lover of her film star friend, Avril Maye. Conrad Cole had paid for Flora's hospital room and, although he cooled on Avril—after her husband refused to give her a divorce—they parted on friendly terms, as, Flora would later discover, Cole did from many of his lovers. And, before they parted, Avril persuaded Cole to help Flora.

Cole asked the editor of his first feature film to let Flora sit in with her. Flora never knew whether to credit Cole with having recognised a talent in her. It didn't seem likely. Cole's considerable achievements seemed due entirely to his own inhuman drive, not to any ability he had to surround himself with good people. It was a fluke that he had his very good editor.

Cole's editor had been at the party, and was easily persuaded to lend 'the poor burned girl' a hand. She was willing to pass on her knowledge, and did, patiently, then passionately when she discovered that cutting film was Flora McLeod's true talent.

Flora had a feeling for editing, for handling time. She loved the editing suite. She loved the process, loved to stop and start time. She sat in with Cole's editor for the rough cut of *Desert Nights* then, when the editor argued with Cole—as people did, without knowing that they had until he failed to answer their calls—Flora sat with Cole himself, re-cutting the finished product. (Or, at least, Cole declared it finished because he was tired of it, whereas Flora saw how much more there was to do, how much better they all could have done.)

Flora was going to every movie at that time. She lived in the dark, until her inner thighs touched again without pain as she walked, and she could go out in public without looking as though she'd 'just serviced twenty-five sailors', as she'd joke. Flora began to emerge from the dark when she stopped minding what people saw when they looked at her. So that when some man who was admiring of her wit, or her heavy brown hair, would ask 'What's this?' of the polished streaks on her neck and under her jaw where the fire had licked her, she'd say, 'I have pointy petals, like an artichoke. Do you like them?'

Flora opened her visitor's bottle, and went to find clean glasses. As she did she explained to Gil that there were muddy clothes on her porch because she'd clambered into Coral Canal.

'I saw that they were filling in the canals,' said Gil.

'We wrote letters and went to meetings, and we were all put aside as Luddites,' Flora said. 'So today I went to help block the earthmoving machines.'

'You shouldn't be doing that, Flora.'

Flora paused before pouring his glass and gave him a look. Then she went on. 'When they began to shove dirt into the canal we all jumped in to scoop it out again. I found myself up to my chest, behind this churning mass of protesters. The contractors were bashing our signs with their shovels.

Meanwhile the machines went on easing fill into the water, and the lovely blue canal went grey.'

She gave Gil his glass, and lifted her own to him. 'I walked home dripping, and picking clots of cardboard off my clothes.'

They emptied their glasses. Flora filled them again, and glanced about her. For a moment she tried to cast Gil's eye—as she understood it—over her arrangements.

The kitchen door was open and she could see the dishes stacked high on the draining board. Her underwear and stockings hung on a rack winched up against the ceiling— all silk, but faded with wear, and stiff, the soap not fully rinsed out before they were draped there to dry. Most of the chairs in her house were covered with a mix of clean laundry and clothes she'd worn too few times to need a wash.

That the place was untidy inconvenienced no one but her. She still got out looking presentable, and kept herself fed. But she never had a big clean-up, only kept as much order as was required to stay on the edge of comfort, and in a state of sufficient hygiene. If she cleaned Flora knew she might get the notion to invite someone special around—to plot her own pleasure, rather than just entertain whoever turned up.

Gil and Flora had been together for just over a year a couple of years before her accident. Flora was the girl his family had approved. If he had to have an actress, Flora was better than many, a 'quiet country girl' in their estimation. But she and Gil hadn't worked. He was too much the gentleman to let her feel she'd let him down—stirred him, but not satisfied him. And he was kind, too kind to show her how disappointed he was in himself. After Flora, Gil had gone on through starlets and showgirls. He was ostensibly playing the field. But really, Flora knew, he was like one of those dreamy kids who can't concentrate, or catch a ball, the ones who volunteer to go stand in the long grass of the outfield but then still miss the fly balls. If Gil lost interest in a woman then his loss of interest explained away his problem. He could always *get* women, he was attractive, polite, well-spoken, successful. He had a string of two-reelers to his name, and a hand in several of his more famous older brother's feature films.

At that time in Hollywood there were two Conrads whose names you could bank with—Conrad Crow and Conrad Cole. Gil's brother was always arguing with his producers, and breaking contracts, but moviegoers liked his stories, which were stuffed with adventure and detailed portraits of the lives of men working in dangerous businesses—mining, logging, deep-sea fishing. Flora had cut one film for Connie Crow, and had loved working for him. She did not, however, enjoy working for her rescuer, Conrad Cole. Cole was self-financing, a king of the grand splash, and something of a star-maker, but he was difficult and litigious and there were people in the business who fervently hoped he would tire of Hollywood and go glory-seeking elsewhere.

Gil Crow was *someone* in Hollywood, he had pedigree, was always a good catch. Gil got women and, Flora guessed, did what he had with her. When they were together Gil stayed out late, drank too much and, when Flora laboured over him—with discouraging results—he always blamed the drink.

However, a year ago, Gil gave up the showgirls, and got married. His marriage had come as a great surprise to Flora. And she hadn't held out much hope for its happiness.

Flora went into the kitchen to get ice. She'd forgotten ice, had been in too much of a hurry to get that first drink down. She pushed a stack of dishes into the sink, wiped the draining board, set an ice block down and went to work with her ice pick.

It was a still, hot night and for hours the skin at the rims of all her scars had been itching. The scars didn't sweat, and the border of damp skin and dry scar was often irritated. Flora would have to wait until tomorrow for relief. This was the last of her ice. Tomorrow the iceman would bring another block, and the milkman her usual three pints. She would put the ice in a basin and pour milk over it— she would soak a sheet in the icy milk and wrap it around her hips and thighs, then lie in the hallway, the coldest part of the house, her hips on a pile of towels and her head on a cushion. No one would come to her door. The movie she was working on had stalled again. Flora didn't mind. Everyone whom Conrad Cole thought he might need was still being paid, including his editor. The other day he'd said to her, 'I take too much time over things.' He thought his fault was perfectionism, and certainly he did worry at details which Flora often thought didn't matter, and wouldn't show in the end. But this time Cole had suspended work on his film because—the papers said—he planned to travel to Europe with his movie-star fiancée, on the airship *Lake Werner*.

As Flora chipped at the ice and gathered the chips in her vacuum-sided ice bowl, she told Gil that she was off work because Cole had stopped the clock again.

And Gil told her that his wife was having an affair with Cole. 'He's—what?—twenty-five? Twenty-five and completely corrupt already,' Gil said. 'Myra read in the paper that Cole is sailing off on that airship with Sam Goldwyn's new *it* girl, and she came home crying to me. She expects me to welcome her with open arms, and woo her all over again. She expects me to *comfort* her.' Gil dropped his head into his hands and his loosened tie drooped between his thighs.

Flora put ice in his glass, poured whisky, and rattled it under his nose. He took it, said, 'You know what we are, Flora? We're *neutered*.' He raised his glass, inviting her to treat his insult gallantly.

'Why did you get married?' Flora asked.

'I was in love. I thought that would make a difference. But I can't *be* married,' Gil said. 'Love doesn't do the trick.'

'Have you—' Flora began.

'Don't start making suggestions. The only reason I'm talking to you about this is because you can't either.'

Flora recalled getting drunk and crying on Gil's shoulder. She didn't recall what she had said to him. How far she'd gone. Her trouble was that the scars were everywhere that counted.

Gil drained his glass and poured another. 'What will I do?' he mourned—he wasn't really listening to Flora, only wanted someone to drink with, and complain to. He didn't mean her to answer him. But she hated to hear him grieve. She wanted to stand up and open her robe. She wanted to be able to do that. For one lucid but self-destructive moment it occurred to Flora that because of her scars she might have to be forced a little, and that if Gil forced her maybe he could do it. When they had been together she had often suspected that his liking for her was part of his problem. She could imagine how much trouble he'd have with any woman he really loved. Flora was sure that it was better for him if he was able to treat a woman as if she was immaterial in herself. Then he could be rough and selfish and speechless.

'At least I can get out now,' Gil said. 'Out of my marriage, with my honour intact. And then—never again.' His eyes, even filmed with tears, looked mean.

'Don't challenge the future,' Flora said. She always felt provoked when men talked about honour. Gil and his brother Connie were both very big on honour.

'You're right,' Gil said. 'I shouldn't say that. I *do* want to be in love. Doesn't everyone?'

Flora said, 'I don't know.'

They inclined over the stained oak table top, mirroring each other's movements, tilting their glasses so that the light caught on the surface of the whisky and its glossy scabs of melting ice. Flora asked, 'Did you ever think to promise yourself? To say: "I can't, so I won't"?'

'You *really* can't,' he said. 'So it's easy for you to promise. Besides, Flora, you know it's more acceptable for a woman to give it up.'

Flora was angry with him for saying this, but only said, 'I have pain to remind me of any promises I've made.'

'I know. I'm sorry. And God how I wish I'd been there, Flora. I wish I'd been there to help.'

Flora shrugged. 'Cole was there. If he hadn't pulled down a curtain and caught me I'd be dead.'

'Which is why you work for him.'

'I work for him because he pays well. And *Flights of Angels* was the feature I was offered. I'd prefer to work for Connie, but he didn't seem to want me again. Do you know why?'

Gil shook his head. Then he said, 'Actually, I do. But it's unworthy.'

Flora waited.

'It was because we were filming in the Yukon. And we were hunting. It was a boy's outing and you aren't a boy.'

'Of course,' Flora said, and peered into her glass. She sighed. 'Anyway, I'll tell you, I'm glad to see the back of Cole for a while. I don't want to keep sorting through the best shots of Monty Mantery's hands.'

Gil said, with grim, delighted spite, 'So the rumours are true?'

Flora thought that any man who had been nearly in tears a moment ago about his trouble in bed shouldn't start passing judgment on any other man's masculinity. But that was men, and that was half Gil's trouble. He was ashamed of his trouble because it disturbed his sense of his own masculinity, and because other men might find out. It *was* easier for Flora to give up sex because, for her, there wasn't any great shame in it. For any woman there was perhaps chagrined enlightenment in learning at forty or so that she couldn't really expect any more to command male attention. But Flora, maimed, was to feel none of that—her injuries were an honourable withdrawal from the game.

Gil asked if Flora could get by with Cole gone to Europe.

'I am editing short subjects. Because Cole's dithering I've been moonlighting for months.'

'Come to us when you're done.'

'I will.'

Gil was working on his brother's latest film. Flora asked, 'How's *Spirit* going?'

'The studio have moved some of the budget to the new sound scenes. But we're shooting the battle schedule tomorrow at Clover Field. Dogfights mostly. Connie's having your friend Millie Cotton crash her Spad. I'm in one of the chase planes.'

'Then you should be at home, asleep,' Flora said, 'not up drinking.' She couldn't stretch far enough, so got up and came around the table to take the glass from his hand.

'All right, mother,' Gil said.

She caught him under the elbow and he got up, towering over her. Then he took his glass again and upended it to catch the last drops on his tongue. 'Flora,' he said, 'you're a good friend.'

'That's me: Flora McLeod, friend to man.'

Flora wanted to help him. To give him some advice on

parting. 'Divorce your wife and go back to the showgirls, to temporary, uncritical women.' But she wouldn't say it. Solutions were fantastical; his problem was his life. There wasn't anything honest she could offer but herself, and she had done that already, in naive self-confidence, in her beauty, almost in love. She had wasted on Gil her, as it turned out, rather limited licence to love. Besides, Gil wasn't offering her advice on what *she* could do—she, whose corset of scars prevented her even spreading her legs. Her case was hopeless. How was he to know that, though? How much had she confided when drunk? Or was it so plain, that when she went about, walked and sat, her body, once flexible and comfortable, now warned anyone who looked: *Noli me tangere*—touch me not.

Gil kissed Flora's hand and took his leave.

Flora turned back to the room and stood staring at the spot where they'd been sitting, at their glasses, the crystal clouded by grease from their lips and fingertips. The bottle was empty, her vacuum-sided ice bowl overturned, and the oak tabletop white where water had been spilled on it. She carried everything to the kitchen, wiped her table, and drank some water to down the whisky inside her. Then she went outdoors.

Flora's bungalow was at the end of a cul-de-sac and partly concealed from the road by orange trees whose branches were massed with a mix of ripe oranges and green, and aged fruit whose shrivelled skins were speckled with black mildew.

Flora went down the porch steps and into her front yard. She walked off the yellow square of the indoor light and into the dark. There were as yet no streetlights down this far. Flora stretched out her hands and felt for the spiny branches of an orange tree. She searched for a fat, slick-skinned fruit, twisted it off its stem and peeled it where she stood, dropping its rind around her bare feet. She ate, the crack at the corner of her mouth stinging. The sky was growing light in the east, and grey-grained blue. Flora licked her fingers and waited. The moon bulged on the horizon, its top edge like viscous liquid then, as it cleared the hills, it solidified and settled into a chipped circle. One night off full.

Flora watched the moon fade from gold to white. Then she went back into her house where she lay down to sleep, and to wait for the milkman, and the man with ice.

# Clover Field, Santa Monica

## June 28, 1929

At dawn Xas and Millie got out of her car to stretch their legs. They strolled over to the windbreak, set their backs against the trunk of one of the eucalyptuses, and watched the sun come up over the mountains.

A truck growled past, its tray full of milk cans. The dust it raised met the mist lifting from the field. Dust and mist hung together for a moment above the road like spectral coral then, when the dust settled, the mist was gone.

A moment later a bus arrived, stopped at the gate to the airfield to put down a parcel of newspapers, and four of the airship's crew. They made their crooked, jostling way toward the Zeppelin.

'They'll sleep,' Xas said, 'they'll sober up,' as if the wellbeing of the airship's crew was his business, as if he were an officer on the airship.

The sun seemed to switch on the crickets, for they all started up at once, calling to one another. Xas heard them as a call to prayer. He was never alone with his thoughts, but he'd taught himself not to talk to God. Yet he could no more fall wholly silent than the crickets could meet the appearance of the sun with silence. He stood still, but the grass seethed with noise. He felt God dropping over him the net of the new day, of this particular day. He felt the vivid presence, and the personal interest of God.

Then someone opened a door in one of the nearby buildings—an aircraft factory—and let the smell of hardwoods and glue out into the morning air. A man in grey overalls came across to pick up the bundle of newspapers. He waved at the two people standing in the windbreak.

Millie waved back. And then Xas did too, a fly-shooing wave, as if he was clearing the air around his head.

Four more trucks went by them, turned in at the gate and continued on toward the aerodromes.

'That's us,' said Millie. 'Come on.'

The aerodrome was surrounded by dozens of ex-Army surplus training planes. Millie explained that ex-Army pilots and others had bought these Curtiss Jennies as bargains after the war. Some were only recreational planes, but many had been turned to all sorts of uses. 'You can see how worn they are—stunt planes, modified racers, battered old barnstormers,' she said.

There were war planes among the Jennies: several Sopwiths, Spads, and three Fokkers. The covered trucks were parked by these, and were unloading cameras and camera crews. Two new closed-cabin planes, Travel Airs, flew in as Xas and Millie crossed the field. They taxied over and joined the film crew.

Xas and his friend were nearly among them all, when Millie abruptly grabbed his arm and veered away toward the airship.

Three men were standing below *Lake Werner*, their heads thrown back. They were an almost comic mismatch in size—a small Asian man between two gangly giants. The small man would gesture now and then, composing some picture in the air. The tall men stood with their hands on their hips, looking up at the ship with the appearance of climbers figuring the best way up a cliff face.

The day was warming already and *Lake Werner*'s sleek silver volume was visibly sinking, settling a little nearer the ground, the gas in her cells slower to take heat too, and now cooler than the air.

Millie hauled Xas over to the trio, and placed herself under the nose of the tallest man. 'Connie,' she said, 'this is Xas.' Then, mischievous, 'I think it's short for Texas.' She cackled, then said with a straight face, 'Xas is a stunt flyer. He used to be with an air circus in France.'

Conrad Crow was a patrician individual. His face was fresh and young but his hair was an even, luminous grey. He looked down his nose at Xas, then asked, interested rather than challenging, 'Do you have any use for a surname?'

'Just call me Xas.'

Millie chipped in again, 'Xas can fly one of the Fokkers. He used to own one.'

As if on cue a fourth Fokker wobbled to the nearest airstrip and made a clumsy, hopping landing. It slowed a little then made a slewing turn toward the other planes, taxied to them, stalled and stopped.

'Excuse me, Millie,' said Crow, and hurried away toward it.

'Sorry,' said Millie to Xas. 'He's like that.'

The other tall man, a fair-haired spit of his brother, said, 'And what is *that* like? Eh, Millie?'

'You know as well as I do,' said Millie. Then to Xas, 'This is Gil Crow. He's assistant director. And this is Jimmy Chan.'

Jimmy said, wistfully, 'I'd really like to get a camera up in the control cabin of that airship. I could get some great take-off shots.' Then he shook Xas's hand and said, sympathetically, '*My* name isn't really Jimmy. I changed it when I went to school, because it was too difficult getting people to understand that the name that came first was my family name.'

Xas said, 'I sometimes find it convenient to change my name in order to change my nationality. For instance, I found I could get a pilot's licence with a French name, not a German one.'

'Is "Xas" a French name?' said Jimmy.

And Gil said, 'Here real pilots always say "wings", not "licence"—as in "I got my wings". In case you find it convenient to blend in.'

Millie rolled her eyes and started after Crow. Jimmy, Gil and Xas followed her, Jimmy looking longingly back at *Lake Werner*.

They joined the knot of people who had surrounded the pilot and were escorting him from the Fokker to the parked trucks and—between the trucks—a businesslike thicket of cameras, campstools, people. The pilot was holding a balled-up silk scarf against his right ear. He looked ill. He was dabbing at blood coming from his ear. His friends sat him down on a camp stool. They loosened the fur collar of his canvas flying togs and tucked a towel around his neck as though they were preparing to give him a shave. They gave him water. They appeared to want to coax him into a quick recovery.

Conrad Crow hunkered down in front of the pilot, turned the man's head and looked at the ear. 'I think you've burst your eardrum, Frank.'

Frank said, 'I had an earache. I'm only here because I promised to bring the plane. It'll be missed. You have to be quick. Use it, then let me take it back.' The pilot's face was white and his hand, holding the glass, was shaking so hard that the water splashed him.

'I appreciate it, Frank. Right now someone will drive you to a doctor.' The director looked about, then nodded at someone in the group, who went to get a car.

Gil said, 'How can Cole miss one plane when he has seventy?'

'Cole knows what he owns,' said his brother. Conrad Crow was apparently unperturbed by the pilot's pallor and oozing ear. He got up and his eyes found Xas in the crowd. He stared for a long minute—then frowned. For a minute Xas could see Crow wondering what he was looking at—then the man put it out of his mind and got down to business.

Crow pointed to where, out over the sea, there was a towering white cliff of cloud, a solid-seeming mass that hung in the air, its dark base almost flat against its own black shadow. 'That cloud may not be going anywhere in a hurry, nevertheless I want everyone in the air before it disappears, or bears down on us. It's the first thing I saw when we got here. It's the kind of cloud that it usually takes a whole hot day to build. So perhaps the day will pack up on us come afternoon. Meanwhile, that cloud is a Godsend. It'll help give some sense of scale to every movement in the battle. Xas—if that's your name—the first thing I'd like you to do is take Frank's Fokker and put it into a spin right up against that cloud. Can you do that?'

'That's my name,' and, 'Yes,' Xas said.

The director looked around the gathering. 'We have to do this today. We have to do *everything* today. I want Millie to crash her Spad—I'm already up to nine hundred and she still hasn't given me a firm yes.'

'I haven't given you any kind of yes, Connie.'

Crow gave Millie his full attention. He revised his offer. 'Nine fifty,' he said.

She shook her head. 'I'll fly stunts and light the smoke pots for you today, Connie. I'll crash the Spad tomorrow.'

Crow was silent a moment, looking out over their heads, serene, like a minister directing his prayer to the decoration over the door of the church. When all the talk had subsided in the group, he returned his eyes to Millie. 'Barnstormers blow in all the time here, Millie. But I like to hire the best people. People I know. I'm in a fix with this film. You know that. And my best pilot seems to have lost her nerve.'

'Sorry,' Millie said. 'But not today.'

'Even if I hire your friend?'

'No, Connie.'

'Early tomorrow, then?' Crow said, with arch sweetness. 'I'm talking about a crash you'll walk away from without a broken fingernail. I'm not talking about a big spectacle. Just something that will *do* with the right shots around it. I'm not Cole, after all. I'm not going to leave in footage with real deaths.'

The pilot with the bleeding ear spoke up suddenly. He said, 'I think I'm good to go.' He sounded gloomy, but gallant.

'No you're not, Frank,' said Crow, and clapped his hands and pointed down at the man, meaning 'someone get this guy out of here for me'. 'But thanks,' he said.

Frank's appointed minder helped him up and led him over to a car. Its engine was running. Frank paused, looked back over his shoulder and said, to Millie, 'Will you get that Fokker back to Mines for me?'

'Sure,' Millie said.

Crow lifted his voice to recall everyone's attention. 'I'll go over the plans once more with all the flyers, and the crews in the chase planes.' He placed his hand on his brother's shoulder. 'Gil is in charge once I go. I have to hunt up Paige this afternoon and write dialogue.'

Various people made noises of sympathetic exasperation.

'We'll re-shoot Marshall's death scene with sound tomorrow, so might as well do it in the wreck. Did you get that, Millie? The *wreck*.'

'Nine hundred,' said Millie, 'and I'll supply you with a wreck tomorrow morning.'

'Okay. But remember I don't need you to flip it, Millie. I need Marshall upside down, but we can flip it with wires. Between the crash and flipped plane we can cut away to the crash team running from the hangar.'

'You might get lucky. I might flip it anyway,' Millie said.

'Try not to,' said Crow. Then he said, 'Have I got everyone's attention?'

Everyone made noises of affirmation and encouragement, the whole group moving closer together as if to protect and warm the director. Xas found himself shuffling in, pressed by bodies, feeling their eagerness and loyalty.

Crow said, 'Jimmy has it in his head to get some shots from the control cabin of that airborne luxury liner. I know it doesn't sail till eight this evening.'

'The newspapers say "aloft for the sunset",' said Gil.

'So our plan is to go over there now and make friendly overtures to the captain about him watching some of the shoot.'

'As if he'll see anything when we're out by Redondo Beach,' said Gil.

'Well, he's not to know that,' said his brother. 'And ten to one he's sentimental about fighter pilots.'

'And you're not, of course,' said Gil, teasing.

'I'm not sentimental about anything.'

Gil said, 'Jimmy and I will go make overtures. We have some German.'

'Take Carol.' Crow put his hand on the silky crown of the woman who had been standing beside him. She was very pretty. 'Carol will butter them up.'

Gil, Jimmy, and the director's secretary walked off. The rest of the team surrounded the plan table. For the next forty minutes Crow talked the pilots through their stunts. For some of it—Crow said—they were just to get up in the sky and dogfight, chase about keeping one another in sight. 'The fighters will be filmed by both chase planes, from above and below together. Then alone from behind and in front for later back-projection—especially shots of the Fokker on Marshall's tail.'

The chase planes were closed-cabin six-seaters. They were going up with four men in each, and equipment. The stunt flyers sat in to hear what the director had to say to the cameramen. Xas picked up new words. He wondered what it would all look like when it was put together, the dogfight, the cockpit shots of 'Marshall' before the swinging shape of a hunting enemy plane, black blood blowing from his mouth. He wondered if they meant to film only against the towering cloud and clear sky, for how could straight Californian roads and right angle intersections double for the landscape of France? Xas wondered—but didn't interrupt to ask questions. He watched, all the while feeling his attention dilate. He was enchanted by the accord in the group; how, though Crow was in charge, everyone contributed. He got the feeling that this group wasn't just full of old hands, but was, as a group, itself an old hand.

Someone passed around sandwiches and coffee.

Then, 'Oh, goody,' said Crow. He put his coffee cup down, drew himself up to his full imposing height, and strode out to meet Gil, Jimmy, Carol, and a group of men in dark blue uniforms. The last of these was just stepping off the zigzag stair of the mast. A square, bearded figure, his uniform bright with silver braid and buttons—the captain of *Lake Werner*. For a moment the captain stood, rocking from foot to foot, testing the lack of give in the ground. When he did this, Xas recognised him. It was his captain. Hintersee.

At around four the slight breeze that had been blowing all day began to fall. The thunderhead still hung over the bay, its shape now degraded by the hot rising afternoon air. Xas's stunts were done. Millie was up again in her Spad, with smoke pots, playing at being wounded. The big chase planes had joined her.

Crow had left his brother completely in charge of the second round of the day's shoot. He said that the writer, Ray Paige, would be up and sober—he and Ray better get to work on that dialogue. As Gil climbed into his Travel Air again Crow warned, 'Careful of your turns,' and walked off toward the Mutual Aircraft hangar where he'd parked his car.

Jimmy Chan discussed his signals with the pilots he'd lined up for his 'take-off' shots. Then he turned to Xas and said, 'Would you help me carry my camera up the mast?'

Xas didn't really want to go into the airship, but couldn't see how he could explain his reluctance. After all, he could hardly claim to be afraid of heights.

He and Jimmy carried the camera up the zigzag stairs. Xas volunteered to be on the downhill side, since he was stronger. Jimmy stopped to catch his breath at the top, then they clambered across the gangway from the mast into the airship's control cabin.

One of *Lake Werner*'s officers came over and said, 'You are going to have to be quick, Mr Chan. The ground crew will soon arrive. We have borrowed one hundred men from your Navy to grapple the airship down so that our passengers can come aboard as though walking into a night club. These are not people who'd take kindly to having to scale the mast.'

'I promise to be as quick as I can,' Jimmy said.

'Your stunt planes have been too far away to watch without the aid of field glasses,' said the officer, with a faintly accusing air.

Within the next few minutes, as Jimmy set up his shots, the Navy riggers arrived. For the moment they seemed content to sit on and around their trucks.

Xas looked down from the control cabin and saw that there was a platform already in place, covered in red carpet and festooned with bunting. It had a rail made of bronze stanchions threaded with red silk guide ropes. There was a red carpet running up to the platform, flanked by potted palms and the flags of the republics, Weimar and the United States. From above, the platform looked like a hotel lobby during a political convention, only parked in a field of self-seeded barley and alfalfa. *Lake Werner*'s flattered passengers would, once they were aloft, be able to see for themselves how notional the ceremony of their send-off really was.

Jimmy began filming, while several curious Germans hovered around him.

Captain Hintersee appeared beside Xas. He took Xas's arm, and spoke to him in German. 'When I saw you before among the stunt flyers I wasn't sure, but now—' Hintersee shook his head, apparently stunned. Then, '*Who are you?*' he said.

Xas realised that, in fact, he'd been waiting for his captain, that when he'd agreed to help Jimmy it wasn't just because he hadn't been able to make an excuse.

Hintersee led Xas away from the control cabin. Xas was compliant, waiting on the resources of the moment, for the moment to crack open and reveal a secret compartment and its tools: facility, goodwill, concord. And then it did, and Xas saw what he could say. He answered Hintersee in German. 'August Hintersee,' he said, 'I believe that my brother, Hans Ritt, was under your command?'

'Yes. Yes, of course, you are Hans's brother.' Hintersee sounded at once relieved and dubious.

Xas's jaw was sore—which surprised him. He tried to relax it. He thought: 'Living with these apes is making an ape of me.'

Hintersee retained his arm. He said, 'Please join me for coffee. I'd like to talk to you.' His voice rose at the end of his sentence. He was asking Xas for a name. 'Herr Ritt,' he added, when a name wasn't forthcoming.

Once, Xas's beloved, Sobran, had made a list of names the angel could use. 'By rotations,' Sobran had said, 'a new name every twenty-five years, at least.' It was a kind of game the man and angel played, the man imagining what lasting influence he might have on the angel and inventing things, like a calendar of aliases. But the game was meant also to remind the angel to behave himself. Not to double back on a dead identity. Not to break in on the hearths of those who live in the shelter of time.

Hintersee conducted Xas to a table on the promenade deck. They were shortly followed there by a steward carrying a coffee pot and cups on a tray. The captain had the steward pour the coffee.

For a few minutes Hintersee let Xas sit and look at the view.

The Santa Monica Mountains weren't visible from the promenade deck's angled windows, only the airfield as far as the eucalyptus lining Pico Boulevard. The deck was built for taking in views from the air. *Lake Werner*'s designers hadn't wanted her passengers to keep a constant eye on the weather, as those in the control cabin did.

'Our meeting is a very happy accident, it seems to me,' said Hintersee. 'For I hope you will be able to help me solve a puzzle that has troubled me for years.'

Hintersee was bearded. By tradition all airship officers were, and many of the men too, which in wartime had been a departure from the rules of any other service, where only officers wore whiskers and non-coms might be permitted a moustache at most. A beard helped to keep an airship man warm. It is cold at eleven thousand feet and, unlike planes, airships stayed up for days.

Xas looked at Hintersee and saw a sombre, watchful man with a thick, glossy black beard. He saw that his captain had aged well, but was nevertheless greatly altered. Hintersee seemed grim and formal—very different from the man who had commanded the raider Zeppelin. It was as if that man had been folded up very small, like a letter a rejected lover folds and pokes into a corner of a wallet. Perhaps—Xas thought—his captain was the kind of man on whom loss makes a greater impression than any happiness before or after. Hintersee had *Lake Werner*, but remembered his lost airship. And he remembered his navigator, Hans Ritt, a young man of whom he was fond, and who had fallen from the cloud car.

'This is most welcome, thank you,' Xas said to his captain, and lifted his cup in salute.

Hintersee said the coffee was his own private blend. Then, 'We have some time, Herr Ritt. So—if you please—let me tell you what happened to your brother.'

On a night in 1917—said Hintersee—when there was a fog over the English Channel, his navigator, Hans Ritt, was lowered down in the cloud car to see if he could spot any ships. 'We were in luck that night,' Hintersee said. 'There were three ships, showing no light, but visible to Hans, who had excellent night-vision. Hans calculated their positions, and began to relay the information via the telephone line that linked the cloud car to the control cabin. I had the receiver to my ear. I was above Hans in the cabin, with five other men.'

Xas fixed his gaze on the coffee in his cup, its diminishing circle of black. He tilted it back and forth so that it caught the light and flashed like a signal lamp.

'The line was open,' Hintersee said, 'so I heard everything that happened to the occupant of the cloud car.'

Xas looked up from his cup to his captain. 'Oh, Hell,' he said. From the moment the fog had ruptured he hadn't given the phone a thought.

'Good. I have your full attention,' Hintersee said. 'Yes—the line was open. And there was *someone else there*.'

Xas shook his head.

'Yes,' Hintersee said, insistent. He must have read Xas's look as disbelief. He asked, 'Did you never speak to any of the men who were in the control cabin that night? We all came through the war. Weren't you curious to hear from any of us? It surprises me that Hans's own brother didn't have enough curiosity to seek out those men and ask them what had happened.'

Xas didn't say anything.

'Hans stopped speaking,' continued Hintersee. 'It was abrupt. He had begun to give us the bearings of our targets. But then he just stopped and said, "*No*." It didn't seem connected to his calculations. He wasn't saying, "No, I'm mistaken, there are four ships, not three." It wasn't anything like that. When I heard him say "No" I didn't feel *myself* addressed—and, after all, I was the man on the other end of the phone line, the only person Hans should be talking to. But, "No," Hans said, not to me. And then we in the control cabin felt a faint jolt as he jumped from the cloud car.'

Hintersee stopped and studied Xas's face. 'You're angry,' he said. 'Are you angry because I'm representing your brother's death as a suicide?'

'No,' Xas said.

'But you *are* angry. I can see that you are.' Hintersee waited for a response and, when he didn't get one, he simply went on with the story.

'The cable jolted faintly as Hans jumped, then, a moment later, it jerked again and swung as though something had struck the cloud car. A shock went through the ship. The cable made a ringing noise, as though it was taking a greater weight. And then I heard the other person—the person who was there with Hans.'

'*No*,' Xas said—in a perfect imitation of Hintersee's lost Hans—a blunt refusal.

Hintersee went on. 'The person who spoke after Hans had jumped—*that* person addressed someone else again. I was listening, but I knew then, and know now, that it wasn't to *me* that he spoke.' Hintersee considered Xas's face. 'How do I know that?' he said, as though Xas had asked. 'I know by what he said. Do you want to know what he said?'

'No,' Xas said again. He wanted to get up, but found he couldn't move.

'He said: "He won't speak to me." That's what I heard as the cable swung back and forth beneath the belly of the airship as though something heavy were clinging to the cloud car. He said: "See what he does to avoid speaking to me?" His voice was indescribable—'

'How could you understand him?' Xas said. 'Was he speaking German? Why would he speak German?'

'I think it wasn't German. And I have no idea how I was able to understand him. If I were to describe the voice I would only be able to say that it was commanding—and comprehensible,' said Hintersee. 'He finished speaking and the cloud car lurched violently. It was as if something sprang away from the car and, relieved of a weight, the basket rebounded on its cable. It was all over in a moment. My officers were shouting at me. They wanted to know what was happening, what I'd heard. I couldn't even begin to explain. I ordered the cloud car winched up. And when it appeared it was empty.'

Hintersee sat, his hands folded behind his coffee cup, and looked at Xas. Who didn't say anything.

Hintersee checked his watch.

Xas took note of this and said, 'You don't want to push your departure time.'

Hintersee signalled the steward. He said, 'Fetch the officer of the watch.'

The steward went away through one of the narrow doors in the salon's wall, which was decorated with a frieze on the theme of the romance of travel—steamer trunks, paper streamers, and women with bobbed hair and long blowing scarves. Xas stared at the frieze till the door opened again to admit the officer of the watch.

Hintersee said to the officer, 'Would you please get those riggers on the job.'

While Hintersee gave his orders, Xas steeled himself to wait the man out. Any moment now Hintersee would realise that he had told a mad story, and that Hans's brother would no longer meet his eyes. Xas resolved to stay silent, and let the man's self-consciousness well up and cover everything over again.

But that wasn't what happened. Once the officer left, Hintersee returned his attention to Xas and began to eulogise. 'Hans wasn't ambitious,' he said, 'but things came to him in the same way that this sugar cube——' He picked one up between his thumb and forefinger and touched its bottom face to the surface of his coffee. The cube darkened with an audible hiss. 'In the same way that sugar absorbs liquid, Hans could touch things and take them up.'

Xas turned away from the man. Hintersee's expression hurt him. That look of love and regret. He faced the window and, for a moment, was dazzled by reflected light. The sun had reappeared. In descending its disc had been eclipsed for some time by the lower slopes of the thunderhead over the sea. Out again now, the sun was reflecting from the ground below the airship, ground whitened by the uniforms of the Navy riggers, who were deployed on the airship's six anchor lines, pulling with gloves and grapnels. The officer of the watch was giving orders, standing well back and signalling with his bright gloved hands. *Lake Werner* began to sink. Its shadow appeared in the crowns of the distant eucalyptus; a horizon of shadow, like an inverted hill.

Even through his pain and confusion Xas could feel the wonder airships always inspired in him. *Lake Werner* had the appearance of solidity, cast a huge geometrical shadow, but was being managed in the air like a grappled cloud.

Hintersee reached across the table and touched Xas's hand. 'Have you anything to say?' he said. 'Have you understood what I've been telling you?'

Xas looked into the man's eyes—alert eyes, a familiar bright blue. He said, 'What is there to understand?'

'Everything.' Hintersee tightened his grip. 'Please tell me what *you* think happened.'

Xas waited. The air itself seemed to shrink back from him, so that, apart from the hand gripping his, he was sitting in a shell of nothingness. After a minute of this nothingness he said, 'Hans Ritt was attacked by an angel.' He said it to put the past behind him—Hans Ritt and his few human attachments. And what happened to Hans Ritt; the archangel he had fled, the hitherto unknown consultation over his falling form, only one side of it audible to the man listening in on the control cabin phone.

Hintersee huffed out a breath. He pulled his collar away from his throat. 'Why would an *angel* attack Hans?' His eyes filled with tears, which Xas supposed might be tears of indignation.

Xas said, without any expression, 'Do you remember how Hans didn't like anyone to touch his back?' Then he looked away from Hintersee again to watch *Lake Werner*'s shadow settle nearer the ground. He saw that the Navy riggers had paused in their work and were all looking in the same direction, away from the officer in charge of the operation—who was also looking away—all of them turning toward the hangars, where the crash alarm had sounded.

Hintersee and Xas stood up together, then stooped and peered out the tops of the promenade deck windows.

They saw two fire trucks burst out of one of the hangars, followed by a knot of men, who scattered as though propelled from a shotgun muzzle. The running men were all looking up at something beyond the field, behind the airship. The trucks continued on to the west-facing airstrip, but the men all ran to a standstill, some stopping with their palms flat to the tops of their heads, as though protecting their skulls or submitting to an arrest. They looked appalled.

Hintersee and Xas exchanged a look. Then they hurried around to the other side of the gallery, and its west-facing windows.

As Xas stooped again to look out the downward-angled window he felt his captain delicately and deliberately place a hand on his back. Beneath his clothes, the layers of leather and cotton, his feathers compressed and rustled—the down that lined the deep channels of scars where his wings once joined his body. Xas heard Hintersee draw a sharp breath at the sensation. Or possibly the man was reacting to what they were looking at.

There was smoke over the sea, a clot several thousand feet up, from which a light rain of sparkling debris drifted down. There was a trail of smoke that twisted in descent from the point of the crash—a midair collision. A number of planes, tiny at this distance, were patrolling a point on the sea, out over Redondo Beach, where the trail touched—the place where an aircraft had entered the water.

The airfield's fire appliances were parked either side of the west-facing strip—just waiting. The riggers finished positioning the airship at the platform and tethered it to its anchors, then they gathered on the west side of the ship with the men from the hangars, and stood, eyes shaded from the lowering sun and their shadows stretched out on the turf.

The officer Hintersee had sent to oversee the riggers reappeared in the salon. 'Do you suppose there's anything we can do, captain?' he asked.

One by one the stunt planes came in to land. First one of the Spads, then a Sopwith. Some of the planes shut down their engines on approach, landed and rolled to the end of the airstrip to get out of the way as quickly as possible. Xas waited till he saw Millie bring in her Spad, then he stepped away from Hintersee, whose hand slid from his back.

News cameras had arrived. They had come to film the celebration of the embarkation, and *Lake Werner*'s departure, its society pages passengers, the jazz band, the spectacle of it all. Now they shouldered their cameras and ran toward the stunt pilots, whose planes had taxied into a little cluster, some with their engines still running as though they planned to go up again. A few of them had sprinted from their planes to the hangars—to the radio box, around which the ground crew had gathered. They were all listening for news.

Hintersee looked at his officer. 'Would you go and ask if we can assist in any way.'

The man clicked his heels and went off.

'I should join them,' Xas said.

Hintersee said, 'You should take a moment to explain yourself to me.'

Xas stared. Perhaps he was trying to stare Hintersee down. He didn't understand what he was trying to do. Eventually he said, 'I never even *think* about what you want me to explain. My mind says "No" and jumps ship. Hans was attacked by an angel because he was an angel.'

'Hans!' said Hintersee. '*You're* Hans. You're the man I lost.'

Xas took his captain's hand. He felt his skin chilling Hintersee's rather than warming it. He had isolated himself so thoroughly that nothing could be impressed upon him, neither warmth nor pity. He said, 'Captain, you're an airman, like me. Like me you know there's nothing but grief on the ground. Have you ever been able to tell that story? Anyone who tells that story sounds mad. Do you want people to think you're mad?' Xas drew the man closer to him and said, 'You've told *me* now. And that has to be enough.'

'You jumped,' Hintersee said.

'That isn't your business. I jumped, but it isn't as if I'm a deserter.'

Hintersee was pale, the contrast between his skin and hair so pronounced that his hair and beard looked like a black balaclava. Xas found that he wasn't just holding his captain's hand, he was holding Hintersee up. The man was faint—from Xas's implied threats as well as the workings of his own powerful feelings. Xas held his gaze. 'Don't expose me,' he said. 'All you need is to *know*. You don't need to tell anyone.'

As he said this, pressing his point with his gaze and his grip, Xas realised that he wanted the option to stay where he was for a time—Los Angeles, where he'd just happened to find himself.

Xas lowered Hintersee into a chair. He drew his cuff down over his hand and dabbed at the man's tears.

'I need to pray,' Hintersee said. 'That's what I need.'

Xas snatched his hand back, and straightened abruptly.

Hintersee lunged forward and grabbed his sleeve. 'Wait,' he said. 'I think you *are* a deserter. An angel visited you, and you didn't stop to hear him.'

'We're finished,' Xas said, refusing anything further. Then he walked away.

He walked away, but with the feeling that he wasn't going far and, try as he might, he was going *somewhere* after all.

When he'd lost his wings, and his lover, Xas had gone on not as people do in their grief, but unimpeded, like a high altitude weather system, full of ice. Forty years after Sobran's death the Wright brothers made their flight, and though there were people who said flying machines were only a novelty, others kept building them. In 1909, at the Great Week of Aviation in Rheims, Xas had begged and bargained for a five-minute joyride. He went up, and was separated from his shadow. He felt that separation as the end to a long endured pain. For a short time his suffering was three hundred feet below him in the grainfields, the grandstands, the mud. He had found his way to Friedrichshafen and the Zeppelin factory in order to live in the air. For the last twenty years, that had been his only purpose. He may have jumped ship, but he found the air circus, and the French war films. He found his job flying mail and supplies in South America, and his job spotting schools of tuna. But it seemed to him now that each of his flights was shorter than the one before, and he could feel something pushing up against his persistence. He could feel a barrier before him like a great body with bones of thunder. And—as he stepped down from *Lake Werner* onto the carpeted platform and walked away between the incongruous silk ropes and potted palms—a song started up in his head. It was one of the songs he and his brothers would sing when they weren't singing God's praises. A song about the air: '*What does it take to turn a wind? Mountains. Or another wind.*'

The Travel Air camera planes had collided. They were flying over the bay at five thousand feet, into the sun. They were flying at the same level, chasing Millie's smoking Spad. One plane had veered toward the other. Their wingtips touched, one spun around and slammed into the other. Both went down, tangled, and on fire.

Millie had looked back to check her smoke trail. She saw the point of impact above her, a patch of smoke and below it a scarf of sparkling debris. She looked all about her like an owl, checked for clear air, then winged-over and turned back. She saw the planes falling. Saw them smash into the water.

Everyone on the Pacific Coast Highway saw the crash. Fishermen saw it, and rushed to the spot. Two bodies came up right away.

The boats were still out there, but it was night. The Navy was on its way, but it was night. Conrad Crow was out on the water with the searchers, but there wasn't any more anyone could do.

Xas sat with Millie in her Buick. It was dusky where they were parked, but the coloured lights and camera flashes and band music reached them from where *Lake Werner* was having its ceremonious send-off. Millie smoked cigarette after cigarette and, now and then, held her hands out in front of her to see whether they'd stopped shaking. She kept saying, 'It was the camera crew—not one of us. I was feeling spooked, and it turned out I was right. But I was right without getting it right.'

'I heard Crow say to his brother, "Careful of your turns",' Xas reminded her. 'People can read the possibilities of danger without it ever reaching the level of rationality. There was no evident reason to be afraid.'

Millie tossed her head. '*Evidence,*' she said. 'At least I know it's not you who's the Jonah, because you're lucky.'

'Jonah wasn't a Jonah.'

She said, 'Hold out your hands.' When she saw that they had no tremor she said, 'You didn't know them.' Then, 'Would you fly Cole's Fokker back to Mines for me?'

'Yes.'

She told Xas how to get to the other airfield, told him to follow the coast south and count the piers. She told him where he would have to turn inland.

When the moon came up they got out of the Buick. They walked across the field to the dark shape of the Fokker. Millie spun the propeller for him. He taxied out to the west-facing strip and took off.

# Venice, and Mines Field

## June 29, 1929

Thirst woke Flora before dawn. She felt that she had been on a two-day drinking binge. In fact, she *had* been drinking for two days, but with an intervening night of sleep— without which she'd be far the worse for wear.

Flora's drinking was opportunistic—she drank when there was something to drink. If the booze didn't come easily she didn't bother. She would keep only a little of her share of the Jose Cuervo Millie brought up from Mexico four or five times a year. Flora put up part of the cash to buy the liquor. For each hundred she staked she could earn up to five. She owned her house, and those closest to her understood that it was paid for as much by bootlegging as editing film.

Flora's drinking and criminal activities had, like her job and injuries, moved her further into the world of hard-living, enterprising men. Prohibition was in full force, but beating the revenuers had become both big business and a national sport. Everyone Flora knew drank too much, but since they weren't supposed to be drinking at all there were no guidelines as to what constituted too much. People finished bottles rather than carry them, or they carried flasks as their fathers and grandfathers might have carried guns. Flora knew dozens of other amateur criminals; those who, like her, smuggled mainly to supply their friends. For instance, Gil, while scouting locations in Mexico on his brother's yacht, brought booze up from Tijuana. Sometimes it seemed to Flora, whose grandfather had come to California after gold and ended up herding sheep in the Imperial Valley, that these adventurers—pilots, filmmakers, smugglers—had all found another frontier. The sky was the West, and movies were the West, and Mexico, though south, was West too. Flora always felt alive and whole when she was standing in the dark desert listening for the engines of Millie's plane. She had lost so much, and her life perhaps mattered less to her, but, as a trade-off, she was comfortable with things that would formerly have terrified her—her desert vigil, her drinking binges, herself alone in her house, on a hot night, with the windows open to any breeze, drunk and without apprehension asleep on the window seat, only the lace curtains between her and the man standing on her porch, unknotting his tie.

That morning Flora lay for a minute or two, feeling groggy and parched. Then she thought: 'Someone has been here.' The room smelled of whisky, tequila, and sour milk—and of some man's cologne. Flora touched her damp, naked chest and found something coiled there—a silky ribbon. She picked it up and squinted at it. The ribbon was a black silk bow tie.

Had Cole looked in on her before flying off on *Lake Werner*? But Cole wouldn't call in at Flora's house just to say so long. He'd only come if he wanted something from her, something urgent and work-related. Cole wasn't exactly Flora's friend, but, of the few people who might come to her house late and find her drugged with drink and in her icy compress of milk-soaked sheets, only Cole would let on that he'd seen her. He had left his tie as a calling card on an earlier occasion (and a note on the pad on her porch that she only ever checked when she came in). He perhaps meant to be polite. Cole was more mannerly than diplomatic because, in fact, diplomacy actually demanded that he go away without letting on he'd seen her.

Flora wasn't really disturbed by Cole's visit. He was an oddball, a creature of habit who was also perverse and unpredictable. He was, for instance, capable of revising in an instant whom he loved, but not his preference for canned peaches over any other fruit. Flora sometimes thought that she was perhaps the only person about whom Cole had any enduring protective feelings.

While she ran herself a bath Flora checked the notepad on her porch. She found a note in her employer's dashing and elegant hand. She saw that he had pulled off three pages—sheets faded by light and dimpled by damp—before he found one neat enough to receive his writing. Cole wrote that he wanted her to start work on a new cut that day. He told her where she could find him. When she got up—

he wrote—she was to hurry over to Mines Field. And could she bring sandwiches? *Turkey or chicken,* he wrote, *not beef, beef gets stuck in my teeth. It's too chewy. And no tomato, because it wets the bread. And have them put any beetroot in the middle between the meat slices so it won't make the butter pink.*

'Jesus,' Flora muttered, and ripped the note off her pad.

When it was still dark Xas landed at Mines. He climbed out of the cockpit, and down the ladder of the Fokker's canted-back wings. He left the plane parked facing other ranked aircraft as if they were soldiers and it their drill sergeant, and headed toward several rectangles of yellow light. As he came nearer he saw that the lit room was a lounge-cum-office, with desks and swivel chairs, sofas and coffee tables. It was by far the most humanly inviting place in that vast blue twilight. There was a man at a radio, another man pacing back and forth before the glass inset in the top of the door Xas meant to go through—to go through and say: *'I've just returned the Fokker Frank flew out yesterday. Frank is at St Mary's.'*

If Xas had had something in his hand, something to return—if he'd come with more than the Fokker and news to deliver—he'd have gone on into the lit room.

But instead as he was heading over to the office, he passed a hangar. In the nearest corner of the hangar's big opening he saw a solitary light, a lamp suspended over a trestle table. The lamp cast light down in a cone within which bugs were flying in tight spirals, circling the cord of the light switch. The lamp illuminated plans lying on the table, and a figure stooped over them. Xas did notice the person, but what made him pause and turn toward the hangar was what he glimpsed beyond the veil of downcast radiance. There was a sleek shape in the partly illuminated space: a plane with an aluminium fuselage, a body that looked all-of-a-piece, and as silky as the silver nitrate dope that coated *Lake Werner*'s outer fabric.

Xas went in to take a closer look. He walked right by the person at the table and stopped beside the plane. He stroked its fuselage and traced the flat rivets that stitched its seams.

The plane had a high tail, and two torpedo-like ailerons at the ends of its wings. The metal frame and glass panes of its cockpit were the only things that interrupted its whittled smoothness. It looked as if it had been dipped in a river Xas knew—a river in Hell—and was still wet with that river's mercury.

Xas moved around the aircraft, continuing to caress it, slipping his fingers into one of the gills that let out engine exhaust, and peering behind the propeller, trying to see something of the engine. He said, without looking at the person at the plan table, 'Is it built for speed or distance?' The plane had been made to break records—that much was clear to Xas. But he hadn't heard of it, hadn't seen its picture in a newspaper, so it perhaps wasn't yet finished.

The figure under the light didn't reply.

Xas squatted to pat the plane's wheels as though it were a horse and he was checking how sound its knees were. Then he turned around, trying to put all his questions in some order.

The man under the light was young. He had glossy brown hair parted on the side, but with a floppy boyish forelock that clearly required more hair cream than he was prepared to use.

Xas got up and went toward the table and the man suddenly switched out the light. 'I don't know you,' he said. He looked away from Xas when he said it, and began adjusting his pencils and slide rule so that they lined up with the top edge of the plan.

'I brought back the Fokker Frank flew out of here yesterday. Frank couldn't himself because he had a problem with his ear.'

The man scowled down at the plans. He tugged at one earlobe then said, 'I *don't* have any problem with my ears—I just don't *know* you.'

'He's deaf,' Xas thought, 'more than a little—and refusing to admit it.'

He moved around the table so that he stood beside the man, who glanced at him sidelong from under his eyelashes, then turned the plans face down on the table.

'That's a beautiful plane,' Xas said. 'Is it built for speed or distance?' He spoke clearly, and inclined closer.

The man turned his head all the way across his own shoulder, giving the angel his better ear.

Xas moved around behind the man, to get at that ear. He repeated his question again, and was finally answered.

The man spoke slowly and quietly, his words in batches rather than sentences, as though they were peas he was shelling into a bowl before him for, as he delivered his information, he seemed to set something aside, the casing of each thought. After a moment Xas began to wonder whether what he was setting aside was *himself*. The man seemed so deeply interested in what he was talking about that, when he answered, he apparently hadn't any urge to *own*, wasn't proud of what he knew and what he had done.

'This aircraft didn't handle well with a bigger engine, the engine we wanted to put into it. We were aiming for speed. *Distance* is probably the greatest challenge, because the true future of aviation is in delivering mail and passengers—not its use in warfare, despite what you'll hear.' He went on, 'You see, the two problems that have to be solved for long-distance flight are fuel and altitude. This plane has a skin that offers as little resistance to air as possible. We first tested it in a scale model in the variable density wind-tunnel at Langley. That went well. It has a water-cooled engine, so we've been able to close its engine in. The engine cowling reduces drag. That works for speed, but, like flying at altitude, it also works for distance, for fuel economy.' He paused. 'Can you follow what I'm saying?'

Xas nodded. The man gave a little stiff, unwilling smile. More a spasm than a smile. He went on, 'The higher up you can take a plane, the less resistance there is, and the less fuel you have to carry. But a pilot still has to breathe. We tried carrying bottled oxygen. We took her up to twenty-five thousand feet, and tried to do without oxygen for a time, to conserve it. But if you stop sucking on the tube, while it isn't in your mouth and warmed, condensation from breath that's already accumulated in the tube freezes and blocks it. So, if you've left off the oxygen until you're desperate and dizzy, there's a danger you'll find the tube blocked and you'll have to do something drastic like biting the tube in two below the ice. *Then* you're left with a short tube and have to keep your head down throughout the rest of the flight, which is mighty uncomfortable. Anyhow—we solved that problem by installing a small heater in the cockpit. Which, unfortunately, means more weight.' He shrugged.

Xas said that creatures with wings had trouble flying at high altitudes because there was *less* resistance, less air for their wings to clutch on the downbeat.

The man leaned nearer. 'Did you say "creatures with wings"? What creatures? Bats? Bugs? But you mean birds.'

Xas didn't acknowledge the peculiarity in his wording, though it had led this proud deaf man to question what he thought he'd heard and Xas had the impression that this wasn't something he did very often. He said, 'When geese fly at altitude they go in a V formation, the strongest one going first and the rest benefiting from its and the others' turbulence.'

'I didn't know that.' The man seemed genuinely interested. 'At higher altitudes even a propeller will run out of air. But we haven't reached that limit yet. We don't yet know how high we can go—what the actual atmospheric limits are. The object now is to fly as high as possible in order to fly as far as possible, in the lightest possible craft, that uses the least possible fuel. So you see—it's all about possibility. This aircraft's engine is modified to run on tetra-ethyl-lead, which doesn't freeze. Now—' he said '—a bird on a long journey must refuel as it goes. It catches its dinner. Right?' He kept his head inclined toward Xas, eyeing him sidelong. 'By the way, why did you say "creatures with wings"? Are you some kind of foreigner?'

'I said *birds*. Birds can fly enormous distances close above the sea. That's one way they conserve energy. The air moves slower over the sea. An albatross gets lift at the crest of each wave, on the slower, denser air there, then dives into accelerating air along the troughs of waves. It can go like that, sharply up, then slowly sliding down, for thousands of miles.' Xas tried to explain what he knew about albatrosses, what he'd seen when he had travelled among them, riding down the air before the dark blue, foam-streaked faces of the Southern Ocean's towering waves. He knew another trick for long-distance flight, but couldn't explain it to the man, since it was only available to angels. An angel, invulnerable, could find a storm cell and rise inside it, up among the lightning and giant hailstones then, with an extra effort, escape the top and fly away in a long shallow glide, letting down over tens of thousands of feet, and thousands of miles.

The man said, 'Sometimes I have impractical dreams in which I try to design an aircraft that can make the same minute adjustments to the air that a bird's body can.'

Xas noticed that this was the first time he had volunteered the personal pronoun in relation to these experiences of flight. He'd talked of problems having to be solved or having been solved without once saying 'I'. Xas hadn't been able to tell if he was a designer, engineer, or test pilot. Now he thought perhaps the man was all three.

'I'll tell you why,' the man went on. 'Why I have my impractical dreams. Have you ever made a parachute jump?'

Xas nodded. As 'The Indian' he'd had to wear a parachute to perform his soaring stunts. His fellow wing-walkers would have thought it very odd if he'd trusted to skill and timing alone, and there had been times when he'd missed and had to pull the ripcord.

'I've jumped too,' the man said. 'A parachute gives you unimpeded views. But it's only a slow fall, not flight. To fly, to depend on the air without an engine, I got near to that only once. It was the very first time I went up, when I was only four. This was how it happened. My father and I were out driving when we saw some men down on one of the flat flood meadows by the river. They had a big man-kite up in the air. I hadn't yet seen an airplane—this was only a few years after Kitty Hawk. Daddy drove us down to have a look and the men asked if I wanted to sit on the kite. They winched it down. It came down rock steady. There was a strong, even wind blowing, with no gusts. I wanted to try going up, but didn't think Daddy would let me. But he did—though he made me promise it would never get back to Mama. The men lifted me up into the kite—there was a seat on it—and let out the line again. I guess I was only fifteen feet up at most, but there was nothing underneath me. A car with good suspension can bounce you about, but this was different. I was being buffeted and jostled very *softly*. It wasn't like rocking in turbulence in a plane. In a plane you feel you're the pivot. Either you, or the engine. And it wasn't like a balloon or a dirigible. I've never felt anything like that kite. And I remember looking down on Daddy and the other men, all grinning like crazy. And then I saw our shadow—my shadow inside the kite's—and I remember thinking how funny. How funny that we weren't attached at the feet, me and my shadow. Then Daddy put his arms up for me and the men fetched me down again.' At the end of the story the man put up his arms, mimicking his father's suppressed anxiety at their separation. 'Daddy was an old man then; he and I never had much fun together, but we had one or two secrets, about the things he let me do without our having to campaign at Mama. Mama was one of those women who know everything is dangerous.'

Things at night were no less visible than they were in the daylight to the angel, only coloured differently, a world of many shades of darkness from luminous to inky. The man's eyes, his thick eyelashes, his mouth, all were variations on darkness. Xas could see him clearly, but he still seemed obscure—obscure and unfathomable. Xas was closer to the man than he'd been to almost anyone in a long while; close enough to smell the ketones on his breath and know that he'd gone without food for too long. It wasn't a pleasant smell, but it was very human and, blowing in Xas's face, this scent, and faintly moist breath, seemed as powerful in their way as the ram air into which he used to lean when he was wing-walking.

The man added, 'Mama was always a stickler for neatness. She would dress me, then ask me to check myself in the mirror, where I'd find myself looking the way she wanted me to look, not that I cared then—I was too young to care. But my reflection never impressed me as *me*. When I went up in the man-kite I recognised myself by my shadow.'

Xas inhaled sharply. He felt breathless. He said, in wonder, 'Is that what *people* feel on first leaving the ground? They feel it too? A separation from their shadow?' This was a revelation.

'I'm not *people*,' the man said. 'Not *folk*. I have no idea what folk feel.' He had kept one arm up after miming his father's eagerness to hold him. He had hooked a finger into the cord of the lamp. Now he gave it a tug, and the light went on.

Xas and he looked at one another.

Xas felt his own face softening with concentration. Everything receded from him but the face before him, in which he read recognition, not of *himself*, but of the mutuality of what was happening.

Something was happening. The man looked wondering and resigned. Time slowed, then came to a stop. It stood still so that they could both look at it. They looked into each other's eyes and saw time. Or at least, Xas did. He saw time together, and time apart.

Then the man opened his mouth and pressed the tip of his tongue to the back of his top teeth and thrust his lower jaw out a little. It was the expression of someone who is conscious of some action he must perform with his mouth—but who can't decide what. He chose speech. 'This airfield belongs to the county. So do the roads around it. But the surrounding farmland—much of that belongs to me now. I've been buying it up. I'm going to buy a small airline and fly it out of here.'

Xas laughed. 'Why tell me that?'

'You look important,' the man said. 'There's something important about you.' He took a step closer.

Xas could feel breath stirring the hair at his hairline.

The man pulled a face, then plucked at the grubby collar of Xas's borrowed flying togs.

Xas realised that he felt encumbered, and wanted out of those togs, to be free of their thick legs and stuffed underarms. He felt like a pantomime bear.

The man laughed, in a poorly-tuned, unpractised way. 'All right,' he said, 'let's see what you have in there. Let's see who you are.' And he began to tackle the clasps of the togs.

Xas laughed too, surprised. Then they were both laughing and wrestling with the top layer of Xas's clothing, till the flight coveralls were off his arms and flapping around his waist. The man took Xas by his shoulders and appraised his leather jacket. Then he let go and unbuttoned the top of his own overalls. He was wearing a white dress shirt, without a tie. He tapped the shirt's starched front, then waved a hand at a black jacket that was hung to cover a telephone on the wall by the door. Xas recognised the thing as a phone because its receiver dangled out from the bottom of the jacket, trumpet down and off the hook. 'I was supposed to be at a fancy send-off tonight. My own. I was going to Europe with Miss Kay North.' He named a famous actress, and Xas knew that the man was still trying to impress him. 'We were to sail on the *Lake Werner*.'

'You missed your boat,' Xas said.

'I've been to Europe already.'

Xas wondered whether the famous actress had embarked alone, or would storm in any minute now to slap this man's face and throw a ring at him. Xas could see her doing that, having seen her do it in a movie.

'Tell me why you're here again?' the man asked. 'Now that we've finished horsing around.' He regarded Xas from under the fringes of his eyelashes.

'I wasn't aware we had finished. And does it matter why I'm here?' Xas said. 'Let's say we missed the same boat. We're *not in* the same boat.'

'Are we in the water together then?' the man asked. Then he said, 'We'd better hold tight.' He didn't say it in a bold or insinuating way—he simply said it. Then he put his arms around Xas. His face was young, excitable, domineering. 'You like to play,' he said. 'I can tell you like to play. You have a dangerous look. It would be better if you were famous. If you were famous you'd be careful to be careful. As it is I'm going to have to make you make promises.'

'*Make* me make promises?' Xas was amused. He moved his arms up so that he was holding on too—feeling skin, warm under the linen dress shirt. 'Shall I tell you again how I came to be here?'

'I can wait.' The man moved his mouth very gradually toward Xas's. Their eyes locked till the man's gaze lost its focus and Xas was left staring into the mysterious animal darkness inside his pupils. The man put his lips against Xas's, just rested them there, motionless, his starved breath blowing into the angel's mouth. Then his lips moved. 'But I can't wait,' he said. The tip of his tongue touched Xas's and they were kissing.

Xas put everything into the kiss. He said *Yes* in his mind, in his native language—but not aloud, not to God. He had a memory then, of flying under thick cloud in the dark of the moon, deviating back and forth, winding to follow the smell of river water, a smell like a wavering green curtain thousands of feet up in the air. This remembered river smell charmed Xas to move away onto a course that wasn't his own. He was kissing, he'd let go of his bearings, bewitched by something both behind and before the kiss, the mouth that bit through the icy oxygen tube, and the story of a boy who first recognised himself from the air, in his discrete shadow. 'I will follow this,' Xas thought, in rapture, 'I will follow this.'

The moment that the stuff in the angel's saliva hit his nervous system the man gasped and his whole body hardened and his lips flooded with heat. There was no distance between them then, for all their differences.

The lamp was swinging, then the fuse in its bulb broke with a sharp musical noise, and the shade clattered. The ground was soft, and there were too many confounded clothes, big buttons and small, and a cummerbund with hooks and eyes hidden in its pleats.

Xas had forgotten what it was like to take hold of someone avid, himself avid. He trembled and felt clumsy. His spit worked its magic—'*une puissante potion d'amour*'—as his one true love had said. But the angel had forgotten how careful and exact he had to be. He was fumbling, palsied with pleasure and lack of practice, and by his fear of being too strong, till the man's human hand gathered him and held them together, and moved, and mingled their wetness. The man's other arm, braced against the floor, held his body above the angel's, so that there was enough space between their bodies for them to press their foreheads together and look down the length of themselves, at what their hands were doing, and at their skins, damp and lustrous in the blue pre-dawn light. 'Not so fast,' the man breathed, though he was in charge, then, 'Oh, you're so beautiful!' He kissed Xas and then stopped what he was doing and pulled the angel over so that Xas lay on top of him. Even in his eagerness he registered how easy it was to move Xas. People always noticed, whenever they by chance took his weight, that Xas weighed half what any human of an equivalent size did. 'There's nothing to you,' the man panted. Then he tried to slip his arms into Xas's opened clothes, to put his arms around him and hold him close. Xas remembered his back, and took the hands and kissed them, tasting their sweet mixed chlorophylls—and machine oil. The oil made his throat catch. He swallowed several times and the man rested the heel of his hand against his throat. He said, softly, 'You're not very substantial, but I think you must be—someone.'

Xas coughed. 'Why have you stopped? Please,' he said. 'Please.'

'I hope I can trust you,' the man said, and caught Xas's hands and held them still.

Xas was astonished at this show of self-control. 'I promise I won't—' he began, but broke off. 'What do I promise?

What are you worried about? What should I do or not do? Should I promise not to embarrass you? To be discreet? To keep out of sight?' Then, wanting to pledge everything, he said simply: 'I promise.'

'You promise easily.' He stroked Xas's throat with his palm, then his cheek with his knuckles. He said, 'I get the impression you could cause me trouble. I wasn't thinking of my public life. I always close the door on what I don't like—what I don't like at all, or don't like any more. But it's like you and I are in a room together already. One of my darkened rooms.'

Xas opened his mouth to answer this, but couldn't. He was moved beyond his intelligence. He felt something closing around him, something like the warmth of a room from which all light has been excluded. He left his mouth open to taste what the man had said. Then he kissed the man, and kissed him. Then, after a moment, he stopped and thought to ask the man *why* he hadn't sailed with the actress.

'I did think I might want to marry her, so I had everything arranged. Then I thought I might *not* want to—I might prefer to work on breaking records. I decided that I'm not in a hurry with anything else.'

'What else?' Xas stroked the lobe of the good ear.

But the man's gaze had moved to take in the body above him, and his face stopped looking clever and turned blank and greedy again. 'Are you really like this?' he said, nonsensically.

'What else?' Xas said again, hungry to learn who this person was.

The man made a noise of exasperated delight and seemed about to answer when Xas heard someone whistling. The whistling was a tuneful, carrying rendition of a popular song.

The man was watching his face. He lifted his own head to listen. He frowned in concentration. 'Is someone coming?'

'Yes. Whistling.'

The man scrambled up. Xas followed. They began fastening buttons. They were laughing, wasting time looking at each other instead of attending to what they were doing.

Xas saw the woman first, crossing the field, against a blue and mushroom pink sky—the sun wasn't up yet. She was wearing a fox stole and a cloche hat, which framed the long, pale oval of her face. Her dress was cut on the bias, a thin fabric that showed her hollow thighs and the round bosses of her hip bones as she walked. She was carrying a brown paper bag. She came into the hangar and stopped, raised an eyebrow at the two of them, and set the paper bag down on the trestle table.

'It's only Flora,' the man said, breathless.

Flora had dressed and got out of the house when it was still dark. She had a danish and coffee at Albert's, while the baking shift made Cole's sandwiches with the day's first bread. The sun was just below the horizon when she crossed the bridge over the mire the county had made of Coral Canal. The oil rigs lining Trolley Way stood against the pre-dawn sky like black latticework.

At Mines Flora parked her car and went toward the hangar that housed Cole's experimental distance racer.

The morning was so still that the airfield felt like a soundstage. Flora pursed her lips and began to whistle, and her tune floated away from her and seemed to echo against the pale shell of the twilight.

When she came to the hangar door Flora saw that Cole had his back to her and was buttoning his shirt. His hair was tousled and he was laughing his disconcerting, shiftless giggle. When he laughed, Cole looked his age, which was twenty-five. He seemed big, gangling and coltish.

The man Cole was with was even younger, but was at that moment more composed and in better order. His hair was neat, cropped, and a velvety black, and, as soon as he saw Flora, he stopped trying to tidy himself, as if not wanting to draw further attention to the opened layers of his *burrowed in* clothes. He only ran a hand across his mouth and stood still. So still, it was as though he was attempting to vanish. It was something that Flora had only ever seen wild animals do.

She put the paper bag of sandwiches down on Cole's plans. She said to her employer, 'Here's your very particular order.' She flicked it with a finger.

Cole fell on the bag and rummaged in it. He took a sandwich and stuffed it into his mouth then groaned with pleasure. 'Have a sandwich,' he said to Flora, around his sandwich. Then, 'This is Flora,' to the other man.

Flora had only recently begun to understand the broad prejudices of Cole's promiscuity. He liked mechanics, carpenters and suchlike—young men, hungry, poorly educated, pliant, and in California in oversupply. The movie stars whom Cole wooed and loved and lavished his attention on might, in the end, be interchangeable, but these others, these semi-literate nobodies, were *disposable*. The stars had Cole's goodwill, gifts, free publicity, his interest in their careers. The mechanics and carpenters were generally taken up, turned to use, and sacked. Flora was rather surprised Cole had introduced her—surprised that he'd done anything to acknowledge the presence of this person.

Flora didn't want to look at the guy. She wanted to spare him any further embarrassment. And herself, too.

'Flora McLeod,' Cole added after a pause, speaking around his sandwich. 'She's editing my film.'

'Cutting-room Flora,' said the young man, softly. It took Flora a moment to realise he'd made a pun, and one that seemed aimed to claim her attention more than entertain Cole.

She had been carrying Cole's bow tie balled in her first. She opened her hand and it unravelled. She smoothed its length between her fingers and put it on the table. She did so pointedly, as though Cole were *her* lover. She did it to warn the man, then looked at him to see what he made of it.

'I don't know this guy's name,' Cole said, to Flora. He sounded delighted.

'Let me think about that for a moment,' said the man.

'I don't even know what he's doing here,' Cole said, laughing still.

The young man said, 'Yesterday Frank somebody flew one of your Fokkers out of here. He burst his eardrum and had to put down elsewhere. I believe he's at St Mary's hospital. I promised to return the plane.'

Cole had been listening, looking keen and meek, and lip-reading, Flora realised. She had scarcely ever seen Cole showing such a need to know what was being said to him. But then, when he had understood, his face stiffened. He finished chewing, swallowed, and said, 'Elsewhere, you say? But I know that St Mary's is in Santa Monica, and that Clover Field is where Conrad Crow is shooting stunts for his little film. My Fokker has been at Clover Field, hasn't it? Being used by Crow—isn't that right? I hope you don't take me for a fool.'

Flora reached in the paper sack, pulled a sandwich in half, then, after some thought, into quarters. She was always watching her weight, hated it when her belt of unyielding scar tissue tightened even a little around her hips. She nibbled the sandwich and looked from Cole to the man. She felt sorry for him, though relieved to find that he was a pilot—better than a mechanic, better able to defend himself against Cole's fresh-faced mad Roman emperor act.

Flora might have felt sorry for the young man, but she gave him up for lost. She had known Cole for some time, had seen him being generous one moment and brutal the next, bashful then tyrannical, anxious then overpowering. She stayed in the hangar only because she knew her presence might mitigate the degree of humiliation to which the young man would be subjected. She had long ago divined that things went worse for people who displeased Cole when there were no witnesses.

Cole was saying how the writer Ray Paige had told him a story some years back, that he had used as a basis for his film *Flights of Angels*. 'The story is about some aces. Paige let me buy it. But Paige has been working on Crow's film and he reckons he's reusing *his* story. But I bought the story, so it's mine. Because I'm in no hurry to finish *Flights of Angels* they think they can do that. *Crow* thinks he can do that to me.'

There was something odd here. Not in the situation—Cole scoring, undressing some stranger, then, later, dressing him down—but in the figure, the stranger. Flora was looking straight at him now, but she couldn't seem to see him properly, beyond generalities. She saw black hair, radiant pallor, a slender male figure of a little under six foot whose clothes were out of order, shirt half buttoned, jacket open, thick canvas-and-fleece flying togs half off and hanging around his waist. Flora saw a pilot—a step up from the mechanics, but still just a guy, some careless, venal, star-struck guy. Flora realised that he was possibly as pretty as any of Cole's movie stars. But—Flora blinked—there was something *wrong* with him, or with her eyes. She couldn't seem to see him properly, as though her eyes were failing and she was peering through a spot of blur. As if someone had buttoned up her pupils with glass buttons. She was having some optical difficulty, but only with the man, not with the rest of her field of vision. For a second he seemed about to spill, to pour out of the edges of his body. It was as if he had something bright hidden behind him.

She shook her head, shut her eyes and said, 'Have you decided what your name is?'

'Xas,' said the young man. 'It's short for Texas.'

'I'll call you Tex, then,' said Cole.

'Will you.'

Flora opened her eyes. 'Are you from Texas?' she said, 'like Cole?'

'No one is from Texas like Cole,' said Cole. 'The boys at my school back East used to call me Tex. I didn't like it.'

'He likes to be called Mr Cole,' said Flora.

'And I likes to be called Xas.'

Cole found the remainder of a sandwich in his hand, frowned at it, then threw it away. Then he advanced on Xas and offered his hand. 'Nice to have met you,' he said.

Flora looked away. Her mouth was dry. She didn't want to see what Xas made of this dismissal. When she looked back she saw that he was walking away from them. He hadn't said anything.

'He got the message,' Cole said to her.

Flora asked, 'What was the message?'

'Well—I can hardly say that no friend of Crow's is a friend of mine, can I, since *you're* a friend of Crow's. But that guy must know the rules. Those people always know the rules.'

'Oh, they do, do they?' Flora said, then, 'I can't believe you left him to hoof it.'

'I admit I would have liked to have finished with him.'

'You did just finish with him.'

Cole looked at her sly and sidelong and said, 'Honey, you know what I mean.'

Flora laughed. She'd interrupted them. 'Sorry,' she said, 'but you're the one who called for sandwiches.' She could predict, watching Cole's routine of yawns and tendon-popping stretches, that he was going to ask her to drive him to the studio. He'd say, 'Someone can collect my car later.' He could have asked the young man to deliver his car wherever he wanted it taken. He could have given the guy something to do—but no, not after he'd detected contamination by Conrad Crow.

'I'm ready to work, but too tired to drive,' Cole said. He stretched again. 'Frank Flynn is out of my film, and out of the Red Eagles.' He seemed to bask in his own malice.

'Make a note, Miss McLeod,' said Flora, biting.

'Flora, honey, there's no profit in feeling sympathy for stupid people.'

'Frank only took a chance for a friend. And that guy said Frank was in hospital, for Christ's sake.'

'Frank should choose his friends better.' Cole put his hand under Flora's elbow and walked her to her car. She disapproved of him but, despite that, was moved by his warmth, the sidelong look he gave her, his eyes black with unsated sex and sated anger. The smell of his body made her flush, all over, till her scars began to crawl and itch. Cole's own smell, of starch and expensive hair oil and the metal of machinery, had an overlay of something new, like the smell of cold, wet air that comes into an open cockpit when a plane flies through cloud.

Minutes later, when they saw Xas ahead of them walking at the edge of the unsealed road, Flora began to slow.

Cole said, 'Don't you dare.'

She sped up again, and they rattled past, raising dust.

*

An hour later, at the studio, someone with a sad, watchful face handed Flora a newspaper, then, while she was still staring blankly at the headline, and photo, they told her what had happened to Gil Crow.

# The piers, Forest Lawn Cemetery, and Sunset Boulevard

## July, 1929

Ocean Park Boulevard and the piers: Lick, Venice, and Santa Monica. It was midsummer, and everything was open late. By night all the structures were outlined in green, pink, and white lights. Ferris wheels were dew-dropped webs, and the rollercoasters were silvery tangles. On still nights the stretches of sand between the piers weren't long enough for anyone to be out of range of the noise: the steamy thunder of a calliope, laughter, and thrilled screaming.

By day, sun umbrellas covered the beaches like a carpet of button mushrooms. The sea was full of slick, bobbing heads. The piers smelled of tomato sauce and fried onions, ice-cream, hot tar and fresh paint. They were so crowded that people brushed up against one another under the monstrous coloured and carved facades of rides and bathhouses, theatres and noodle houses and ballrooms, every building bulging with tumorous decoration, and creatures, like the blue serpent wound around the door of Dragon Gorge. Everything and everybody was crowded up against the ocean in a way that made the open space of the sea beyond the city look like a closed window at the back of a long dusty room.

Xas, going about among the summer crowds, discovered to his surprise that he was fully visible again. Over the years he had managed to grow a repellent shell made of apparent preoccupation and purpose, and actual independence and indifference. His shell announced to the world 'My looks deceive you,' and 'There's no pleasing me.' It had formed gradually, and was, by the summer of 1929, as perfect as a pearl. But it seemed to have disappeared overnight, and Xas found that, instead, he was wandering around inside a fragrant bubble. He could smell the fried onions and tomato sauce, the sauerkraut and soda and cider, but if he turned his head toward his own shoulder, or held his hands to his face, he smelled Conrad Cole, he smelled hunger and hair cream, starch and laundry soap, machine oil and sexual fluids. It drove him mad, and his madness seemed to give off its own light. People turned toward him, looked, and didn't look away. They made eyes. He stank of unfulfilled longing, so got offers. He was asked if he wanted company. He was plied with drinks and cigarettes. He was bumped against, breathed on, pressed, and once his mouth was touched tenderly and boldly by a woman who, like him, seemed haunted by some focused longing.

Xas kept moving. He went on directly *away*. Away from Mines Field. He didn't know what else to do. He was in the kind of panic only angels experience—fear, accompanied by smooth, kinetic, self-preserving retreat.

The last time he'd felt anything like this, it was *real*, a cultivated emotion that arose from admiration, troubles endured and shared, and ground lost and found. It was true love, and his love was worthy. Xas kept telling himself that angels don't simply ignite. He tried to call to mind things that would put him off what he found himself wanting. He remembered Conrad Crow saying: 'I'm not Cole; I don't leave in the footage with deaths.' He gave himself a stern talking-to while walking unhurriedly away through carnival nights and the white haze of late June, and early July days, in the crowds, his feet in the water, and the sleeves of his jacket knotted around his waist.

On the second day, when he had to seek shelter from all the attention, he went in among the forest of the piles of Lick Pier.

The man who found him had cigarettes in the pocket of his shirt, a pocket with a torn corner. His shirt was unbuttoned to his sternum, his skin was tan, his lips scabbed with white scales of sunburn. He said, 'I have a bottle.' He said, 'My room is only a block back from the beach.'

Xas looked at this person and thought: 'I've been here.'

After his wings were cut off he spent much of the following winter wrapped in a blanket and crouching in a corner of the Soldiers' Gallery in Château Vully. (His lover, Sobran, had often slept at Vully, although his own home was only two miles off.) Xas had crouched, still and silent, till Sobran, exhausted by his grief, threw him out into the snow.

After that Xas went away, he wandered and, for a long time, he let anyone who wanted to have him have him, as if their use could somehow make him disappear. During that time he wasn't ever taken up and tended to. Instead his misery attracted a certain kind of person, those not frightened by an abject, unresisting, resilient being. The kind of person blind to the glaring contradiction of a someone who would put up with anything, yet stick at something trivial—like never removing their shirt. Xas had come to hate those people, and they had allowed him to sink into hatred for everything, for himself and the man he loved, for God and Lucifer—his Maker, and the general he had followed. He hated those who took him up and *took* him—and there was no end of them.

Among the thick shadowy piles of Lick Pier Xas looked at the face of the man making an offer. 'I've been here,' he thought, 'and this is just this. I don't want this.'

A wave washed over his bare feet. He was carrying his boots tucked in his armpits. He said to the man, 'No.'

The man moved nearer and put his hand on Xas's hip. He said, 'Why not?'

'I'm kidding myself,' Xas said.

The mist of tension and speculation cleared for a moment and the man looked at Xas properly. 'All right,' he said, 'I won't bother you then.' He backed off, disappointed, but decent.

Xas went on the rides, burning the money he'd earned flying stunts in Crow's film. He returned to each pier's rollercoaster again and again, stirred and soothed by the tattoo of rattles as the cars went up, clacking over joins, their couplings ringing, then the roar down, the rushing tumult of bangs and screams. After a few days he found himself riding only on the Hi-Boy rollercoaster at Ocean Park Pier. He rode it over and over, dropped and tossed on switchbacks, and flung around bends, deafened by shrieking. Xas rode and watched the patterns of other riders, the patterns of the rollercoaster's use. At one bend, where the track sent the cars curving out abruptly toward the bay, then snatched them back, he'd raise his arms over his head to let his upper body go with the momentum, straining against the safety bar.

The angel plotted, fixed on a quiet time, then got a seat in the last carriage, at the back, and alone. He knew that he was being antisocial, that if anyone saw what he was planning to do they'd be alarmed. He might set off searches and rescues and—since he'd returned to the ride many times—talk of an elaborate suicide. But Xas felt that he needed to do something to shake himself out of those apparently indelible sensations: Cole's smell on his skin, Cole's voice in his ear, phantoms of Cole's hands still handling him.

He had decided it must only be *sensation* he was after, some powerful sensation, the inward storm of skin on skin, the dependence of one body on another, desire and wakefulness, and desire and sleepiness, the sweet hour afterward where the lovers seem to fall through warm mist. The angel remembered it all exactly and wanted it again. But he was, he told himself, only craving a sensation he'd wantonly attached to Cole, to the smells, sounds, textures and temperatures personal only to Cole. Cole was coming between him and his memories of love. Real love. It was wrong, and false. Cole's body odour must only be a fixed idea, a fetish, not a new shrine.

'I should forget it,' Xas thought. 'After all, I must remember that, for years, all I've wanted is to live in the air. I've gone looking for flight, not for pilots or aircraft designers. I wanted to be severed from my own shadow, not to touch anyone.' He told himself that it was only that Cole had spoken so eloquently of flight and he'd fallen for Cole's talk. 'I should just have kept him talking,' Xas thought. He believed that he could choose what sensations would enslave him. There were no white water rapids between Long Beach and Santa Monica, and no hurricanes that midsummer, so he was forced to choose the Hi-Boy rollercoaster. He would choose to undo his belt and stand up as the car hit that sharpest seaward bend. After that everything would be all right again. His senses would be restored to him, clean and empty.

Xas was in the last car. He hoped no one was watching. The rollercoaster was ramming up and down against the dazzle of the setting sun and, he hoped, his body would show only as a floating flake of soot in all that fire. He unclasped his belt and stood up and, instead of being jerked to the left and snatched down into the next dip, the floor of the car punched the soles of his feet and he flew out in an arc, hundreds of feet up. The first catapulting force began to weaken; gravity touched and tested him, and then took his weight. His flight slowed to a fall, then his fall sped up and he plummeted into the water twenty feet from the end of the pier.

Xas swam to shore, causing a bit of a stir coming out of the water fully dressed and in a flying jacket. One drunk yelled, 'Hey! Look! It's one of those drowned pilots!' Xas realised the man meant somebody from Crow's crashed Travel Airs. He trudged, squelching, up the beach and climbed steps to the concrete and timber strip that went on along the shore. He turned north into the haze. As he walked under the hissing palms, the breeze dried his shirt and pants. His boots stayed wet, and water seeped from their eyelets at each step.

Xas felt smug. He imagined his own ghost, like a movie ghost, a double exposure Xas, still riding the Hi-Boy. He'd flung himself out of that person, had left that person's hungry skin. If he looked back he was sure he'd see, in the dusk, that susceptible self still riding in the last car, shining, a lantern of hallucinatory memory, the afterglow of his encounter with Cole.

He walked along the shore for an hour. Above his head strings of lightbulbs swung and bounced in the breeze.

Xas eventually found his way back to the steakhouse near Glendale airport where he'd gone with Millie. He began to haunt the place and, several days later, they managed to reconnect.

Millie kept Xas close, and took him about with her. When she went home to wash and change her clothes, he'd wait in her car, parked outside the building where she lived, a Coloured-only boarding house.

She'd hurry upstairs and be back out within half an hour. 'I don't need a bed when I'm not sleeping anyway,' she'd say.

She was drinking at all hours and hitting her Benzedrine inhaler hard. There were several used canisters rolling about in the back seat. Xas drank and took hits of Benzedrine with her, and the city seemed to dry out around them, its colours dull under clouds as fine as fish scales.

Millie took Xas to jazz clubs. First she sent him on his own into Sebastian's Cotton Club, where the musicians were black and the clientele white. Then, at around two in the morning he'd hook up with her again down in Watts, at the Château or Villa Venice supper clubs, where they'd mingle with movie stars and listen to black and white musicians jamming together. And if Millie was still on the upward slope of a bout of Benzedrine they'd move on to one of the speakeasies or breakfast clubs.

July wore on another week and the bodies were recovered from the submerged Travel Airs of the six men who hadn't managed to jump before the tangled planes hit the sea.

Xas went with Millie to Gil Crow's funeral. Or, rather, she pulled down the half veil on her hat, and walked up to the graveside, while he stayed to mind her car.

The car was parked in the shade of a pepper tree against the kerb of a curving road in a cemetery that, from the fresh state of the stones and green sod, appeared to be growing as rapidly as the boomtown whose citizens it buried. The cemetery looked a little like a set after the carpenters had finished, before the art department had gone through painting moss and mildew, time and twilight.

The grave and coffin were obscured from his sight by a bulwark of floral tributes and black-clad bodies. He spotted Conrad Crow's grey hair, his bowed head. The crying was subdued, and from where Xas waited he could hear only the murmured eulogy, then the prayer of commitment. The speaker was more careful than solemn, he seemed to stop and start.

Above Xas the pepper tree fidgeted, the wind puffing up its green plumes. The lawns had been watered that morning and the verges were still seeping, the road's pink-tinged paving dark at its edges, as though scorched.

Flora was surprised to see that Gil's wife, Myra, hadn't attended his funeral. The actress was sequestered, the columnists said—and under a doctor's care. The studio was protecting its asset.

The studio had sent two huge wreaths, towers of white gardenias, that stood at the head and foot of the grave. Gil's tall man's coffin lay between them like the span of a suspension bridge. The floral tributes seemed to shoulder the minister aside. He stood at one corner of the baize-lined hole to perform his rites, flicking his aspergillum awkwardly so that some drops of holy water landed on Flora's shoes.

Flora watched the crowd. Apart from Gil's parents, it was largely a movie business crowd. Since Gil was Myra's husband and Connie's brother there was some politics in the tears. Some of the sorrow was for show, and so was some of the composure. Monroe Stahr was at the graveside, a man both Gil and Connie had made films for. Connie had picked a fight with Stahr to get out of contract, so the man, while looking appropriately sombre, still managed to favour Connie with a look that suggested it was the *better* Crow they were burying. Because Myra wasn't present her friends weren't crying, but merely dabbing their eyes. These women might have wept, but lacked the right cue. Edna, Connie's fragile wife, was there, doped-up and trembling. Ray Paige was there, sober, and knuckling water out from under his eyes. And at the back of the crowd, brushed and polished, were the stunt pilots, all looking as though they'd rather not be there, most of them having long ago forgone all ceremony of mourning. Many were veterans of the war, and others had worked on the early airmail carriers—on airlines that, at times, had lost up to ninety pilots in eighteen months in planes downed by storms, lightning strikes, mountains, iced wings, engine trouble, or thick fog. The pilots had attended too many funerals. Still, they were regarding Gil's coffin with expressions of settled shock. It was the scale of the loss that had surprised them—eight men, in a moment, in one wreck, no seasoned seat-of-the-pants pilots, but camera crews, men with—for Christ's sakes—*insurance policies.*

Flora caught Millie's eye and nodded, then continued to take stock of the crowd. It seemed that this was the way she could best cope—by keeping her eyes moving from face to face.

Flora hated public gatherings as thoroughly as she loved her house at the end of the street and edge of a waste ground, and her cramped and dark cutting room. Crowds made her uncomfortable. She'd been that way since her accident. Yet, as she stood through the service, forced to contemplate this particular crowd, Flora suddenly realised what it was about crowds that she didn't like. The mass of faces forced her to search for one face, one in particular. And it wasn't the face of the man in the coffin that Flora found herself looking out for. No—she was looking for the face of another old boyfriend, the man who had touched his cigarette to the hem of her grass skirt. Flora suddenly understood that, for years, she'd had her eye out for John Weber. Not because the sight of him would make her fearful—after all, John had been an even-tempered man, often drunk and silly, but only once to devastating effect. At the time of her accident Flora hadn't even realised who it was who'd set her skirt on fire. John hadn't visited her in the hospital, and she hadn't seen him since. She had no idea where he was now, or how he'd paid for what he'd done to her. She remembered that there had been a charge considered, assault, later downgraded to a misdemeanour. In the hospital there was once a bitter exchange over her bed between her friend Avril and Conrad Cole about what John Weber deserved. Flora had a vague memory of the argument, of Avril's tears and Cole's vehemence. But after that no one mentioned the man in her presence again.

Standing over the coffin of the man she'd most cared for and thinking about the man who had hurt her most, Flora began to feel that there was something curiously wrong with her life. Something odd, and misshapen. Her injury and her burden of pain couldn't entirely account for her sense of having holes in her story. It was as though her life had a bad director and an inexperienced cameraman, a combination that always meant a lack of 'coverage' of the film's scenes. If a scene was badly covered, filmed in too few takes, then an editor might find herself with too little film to work with. Poor coverage meant that it was hard to make a story make sense, or flow. At that moment, at Gil's graveside, Flora's story didn't make sense to her—even with this soundtrack, from *The Book of Common Prayer*. She should know where the man who maimed her was, and what had become of him.

Flora stared at Gil's coffin and saw her own face and other faces reflected on the curve of the casket's lacquered lid, all stretched and draped like a sheet of soft, pale pastry.

The service ended. The sexton and another man operated a mechanism that winched the coffin down into the grave. A hymn was sung. The crowd thinned and reformed around the chief mourners.

Flora went back down to Jimmy Chan's car—she'd come with him. She took her bags from the back seat. Her handbag, and the canvas satchel holding a can of film. Flora waited while cars filled, and pulled out, and drove away, and the throng by the grave thinned further. She kept her eye on Crow, who took his mother's and father's arms and escorted them to their car, leaving them in the care of his wife and sister.

Jimmy came back to his car and Flora thanked him for the lift and told him she'd take the trolley home. Then she went to intercept Crow, who was standing looking after his departing relatives, perched on the kerb, his big feet in his stiff shoes seesawing, like a twelve-year-old playing with the possibility of a fall. Flora said his name and he turned to her, startled, and stepped off the kerb. She took his hand and he stooped to kiss her cheek.

'I know your film's in trouble,' she said, but didn't say that Gil had detailed its trouble when he came to see her the night before he was killed. Flora didn't know whether Crow knew about Myra's affair. If not she didn't want to be the one to tell him.

'I've lost my whole second unit,' Crow said. 'The way things are now it won't be released. The studio is patching every film it has with dialogue. They even have title-writers on it—writing terrible stuff.'

Flora handed Crow her bag. He took it, puzzled, then when he felt the shape of the canister through the cloth his eyes widened.

Flora said, 'Altogether there's six minutes in there. Dog fighting footage, all solid stuff, but nothing really distinguished. You can cut it in with what you have.'

'Cole doesn't know anything about this, I'm guessing.'

'No,' Flora said. 'It's up to you what to do with it, Connie.'

'Thank you,' Crow said. He took her hand again and they stood together for a time, holding hands and standing at an angle to one another as if leaving an opening, an invitation for some other person to join them. Above them the pepper tree puffed up like a bird letting air in under its feathers.

Crow said, 'Myra is at San Simeon with her buddy Marian. I'm going up there to establish the facts about her "tenuous health". I guess I'm hoping for the sort of good news the studio won't necessarily like. Anyway, I want to talk to her before the studio offers her a doctor and "a simple solution". I don't know how she's feeling. She and Gil were in trouble.'

'Yes, I know,' Flora said. 'So do you really think she's pregnant?'

Crow shrugged, said, 'Come and see me sometime soon,' and released her hand.

Flora went down toward the cemetery gates, walking along the now broken line of cars. She saw Millie ahead of her and called out. Millie stopped and they stood with their hat brims touching while Flora lit a cigarette from the fiery tip of Millie's.

Flora said, 'What do you say to a trip down to Brawley? I'm working only one day in five. Cole's re-shooting every scene with the girl in it.'

'Yeah, I heard he sacked Miss Jensen.'

'He had to. It turned out that when she opened her mouth she sounded like a cow lost in a mossy tunnel. He's got someone else, someone much better.'

'He's burning celluloid while he learns,' Millie said. Then, 'I'd like to go, Flora, but I won't have my stake till I'm finished for Crow. I promised myself never to touch my savings.'

Flora remembered that Millie was saving up to establish her Coloured flight school. She said, 'I'll stake you. After all, you do the flying.'

They reached Millie's car and Flora saw who was in it.

'This is Xas,' said Millie. 'It's short for exasperating. Xas, this is my friend Flora.' Millie leaned on her car door and frowned at Flora, her forehead puckered into four perfectly even ripples. 'I don't know how long my stunt is postponed, or even if Crow is still wants me to do it. I didn't think I should ask him today.'

Xas was watching Millie. He looked as though he were waiting for something—patient and placid.

'Crow wants me to crash a plane,' Millie said, to Flora. 'I've done that kind of thing before, often. But I don't want to.'

'I can understand that,' Flora said.

'I could do it,' Xas said, as if this was what he had been waiting for.

'You might get hurt, sweetie,' Millie said.

'No,' Xas said. Then, 'Only if I meet another angel in the air.'

Flora frowned at him. She said, 'So is that what you think happened? Gil and the rest of them "met an angel in the air"?'

'No,' Xas said, thoughtful. 'I wasn't thinking about that.'

'He's very religious,' Millie said.

Flora raised an eyebrow. She remembered Xas tucking his shirt-tails back into his flight togs, which struck her as a rather unusual religious observance. She asked him, 'When you dropped the Fokker back at Mines Field, why didn't you tell me Gil had been killed?'

'I didn't know you knew him.'

'You didn't even mention an accident.'

'I didn't know you knew *any* of them. Cities are so big now I've stopped expecting people to know one another.'

'So you two have met already?' Millie sounded disappointed.

'Millie,' Xas said, 'I'd gladly do the stunt and—'

'Don't!' Millie warned.

'—give you the money.' He began by sounding eager then, suddenly, impatient. 'I'm so sick of having to pretend to have feelings about money. And I don't mean that doing the stunt for you is a way for me to show that I don't care about it, because I don't care about showing anything either.'

'You're raving,' Millie said, fond. 'Honey, stunts are my livelihood. I can't afford to be afraid. So, I'll wear a diaper and do the damn stunt. But—sweetheart—are you broke?'

Xas turned out his pockets. He had a thin stack of bills, limp and sandwiched together as though they been soaked and dried. 'The jazz clubs and rollercoasters have just about cleaned me out,' he said.

Flora said, 'Do you have enough to get us drunk?'

'Says Flora, with conciliatory self-interest.' Xas smiled at her. 'I think I have enough.'

'So—you two *have* met?' Millie wanted to hear where and how.

'At Mines,' said Flora.

'Over Cole,' said Xas. 'Flora had Cole's bow tie.'

'And Xas had Cole's attention,' said Flora. 'Briefly.'

Millie said, 'Why are you fighting?'

They said together, 'We're not.'

But they were, Flora thought. It wasn't just that he had an annoying manner, or that, at any moment, she expected to get an even more annoying explanation for his annoying manner—like, for instance, that he wrote poetry or was a devotee of Aimee Semple McPherson. Something like that, something he was proud of, and thought distinguished him from the masses. His otherworldliness irritated her. And it wasn't even consistent. In fact, it was just inconsistent enough for Flora to imagine that perhaps it wasn't an affectation. Perhaps he was simple, not a fake. Whatever—he *was* hugely exasperating. But Flora realised that some of her irritation was made up of tension. It was as if, although she expected nothing from Xas, she sensed that he somehow had the ability to cause her a sudden, serious, *personal* disappointment.

She could see him clearly now, at least. She had him in focus as she hadn't in Cole's hangar where what she could see was distorted by her expectations. She could see how he looked—white skin, dark blue eyes, a purplish sheen on his thick, close cut black hair. He looked like a star, glowing in his own key light.

Millie opened the back door of her car. She began to run through a list of places they could go to shut themselves up all day and drink. Flora knew that Millie would understand that she wouldn't want to talk about Gil. Millie wouldn't want to either; she'd lost too many flying friends over the years and, in that profession, the form was not to dwell on their losses. Millie would want her company—Flora knew—but silence on that subject. She wondered how many of the eight men Millie had known well. More than Flora, and possibly Millie knew one or two nearly as well as Flora had known Gil. But they wouldn't talk about it. And somehow it helped that the other stunt pilot—Xas—hadn't known any of them, had returned the Fokker but not carried the news, and had sat in the car during the service.

Flora climbed into the back seat.

Three hours later Millie got up from their table saying, 'I'm going to break formation. I'm going to waggle my wings and peel off. Okay?' She left.

After a few minutes Flora made a suggestion. 'Shall we go to the movies?'

'We,' said Xas, musing.

'Was that "yes" in French?'

'No, it was "we". But, *yes*, let us go to the movies.'

They came out late and stood for a time on a patch of pavement studded with glossy stars of polished, dropped chewing gum. Then the lights on the canopy went out, followed by the light in the ticket booth. Xas waited to see which way Flora would turn, and when she came out of her daze and started walking he went with her.

They had seen newsreels, Movietone footage with narration. They had watched shorts, all silent. And they had seen two features by a German working in America.

As Xas walked he thought about a scene in one film. It took place at night, on a lake, after a storm. A boat had gone down and people were searching the lake. A man leaning out from the bow of one boat, a lantern in his hand, spotted a bundle of cut reeds, a crude buoyancy device, collapsed and coming apart, afloat on otherwise empty black water.

Like poetry, stories and novels and plays, film proved to Xas that more often than not people saw as he saw, and felt as he felt. He thought about the film, and remembered Hell, its corrosive air and light, its ceaselessly milling shadows—a motion wearying to the eye and brain. He remembered how the fallen angels would shut themselves away and read, how they built all the time, like wasps, mixing mortar and shaping stones and piling them one upon another to make more rooms to house the books, to make shade and seclusion to house themselves in order to read the books. Lucifer's palace was a library, a repository of copies of every work ever copied, from papyrus scrolls, through vellum, to paper and leather, paper and cloth. The fallen angels would read the books before they dried out and crumbled. And they remembered what they read—for angels never forget anything. But in Heaven, where everyone was in bliss, even fierce archangels in fierce bliss, no one read.

As Xas walked with Flora he wondered whether films, like books, found their way into Hell. Films were copied for distribution, so might. But, Xas wondered, without a projector, how would his brothers watch one?

He was thinking about all this, to the point where he began to feel that it was his responsibility to find out what the situation was, when Flora McLeod saved him from his thoughts. She said she was sorry he'd seen *The Four Devils* in that version. 'That was its second release. With sound.' She sighed. 'You see—the silent version is a grown-up film. It's fluid and mature, and it trusts its storytelling. For instance, Charles isn't late because he's hit by a car—that's such an expedient bit of plotting! In the silent version he makes a choice. He chooses the slinky siren over the heroine—or at least a final night with the siren, one last bout of bewitched lovemaking.'

'I liked it anyway,' Xas said. 'I liked the trapeze, the Leap of Death. But I liked *Sunrise* better.'

'Oh, yes,' said Flora. 'When the wife and husband are wandering around the city together, miserable. The way they sit in that café, dazed and indifferent to other people. It's so *real*. The way she clutches the slice of cake he's bought her and cries.'

'I liked the bit when he's on his bed thinking of drowning her and he's so haunted and histrionic that he imagines the water, and it appears below him.'

'That's a lap dissolve,' said Flora. 'And then he thinks of the city girl and she's there, embracing him, ghostly, hanging under his face like his own breath.' Flora turned toward Xas as she spoke; her face blurred and bright and beautiful. Her shoes had plates on their heels, and her footsteps sounded definite, but she was only ambling along, stepping sideways each time she turned to look at him. She was walking with an odd, stiff gait. She said, 'That scene was filmed on the reservoir out at Silverlake—but it looks like Bavaria, or something.'

Xas told her that he also really liked the speckled enamel bowl on the supper table in the couple's house.

She laughed. 'Now you're down to admiring the props.'

'I'm sure some thought went into them. The speckled enamel bowl was chosen and coincidentally preserved. I love how film does that to things, how film can wind up *times* within time. If I say, as people do, that time is a river, then, since the first films, that river is carrying the larvae of countless little rivers—reels of film like time bundled-up. So, while my favourite thing I saw this evening was the bunch of reeds floating on the water, the thing I was happiest to see captured was Alfredo Cordona's *Sauf de Mort*, which I saw him perform in Peru some years ago.'

Flora asked, 'Where are you from originally?'

'Heaven.'

'Millie wasn't kidding,' Flora said, 'you are religious. I suppose you're letting me know that the important thing about you is your religious beliefs, not where you're from.'

'I do hope it turns out that my religious beliefs aren't the most important thing about me,' Xas said, then regarded Flora, waiting for further speculation.

'I've been wondering how you square your Christianity with—' Flora began, then sucked in a breath and let it out as a slow whistle. She mustered her courage. 'Well—with *Cole*,' she said. Then, in a rush, as if she wanted to prevent Xas answering her, 'And how do you square Heaven with being so darn happy that film has captured Cordona's leap of death?'

Xas chose to answer only her second question. 'I don't know what Heaven's policy is on film. Heaven may not look after film. For that matter Heaven may not look after Alfredo Cordona.'

'Isn't that up to him?'

'Yes—it's up to him whether he goes to Heaven or not. But Heaven probably won't care to preserve his desire to jump through flaming hoops one hundred and fifty feet from the sawdust of the centre ring. I don't think circus acts go to Heaven, even when circus performers do.'

Flora laughed. 'You have your own theology, don't you?'

They had reached a lighted building, a stop of the Venice short line train. There were people sitting about on wooden benches. The floor was covered in a confetti of punched paper.

Flora said, 'This is my stop.'

Several sleepy-eyed people looked up at Xas—who instinctively turned from them. He knew he always looked more like what he was to people who were alone, or to people in the early hours of the morning when—once—their ancestors would be surrendering to sleep despite the wild night noises. Over the years he had been greeted by lonely night travellers as ghost, god, and vampire. He had learned that it was always best to call out to any solitary traveller: 'God save you!' or the local equivalent. But on small groups he tended to turn his back.

Xas swung away from the seated people. Flora looked alarmed, and then she said, 'Goodnight,' and hurried to the ticket booth.

Xas realised he had spooked her. She'd seen him hide his face from the other people at her trolley stop, and she'd imagined he meant to harm her.

He left the station, crossed the gravel strip where the tracks lay and went to stand out of the light. The trolley came, the small group of late-night passengers mounted its steps and settled in its yellow-lit interior. Flora McLeod took the steps like an old and arthritic woman, her jaw clenched with suppressed pain. She was still finding a seat as the trolley pulled away and took a corner, its wheels splashing the road with white sparks.

Xas followed the trolley, walking between the tracks. The vehicle drew further ahead, a focal point in the long perspective of the boulevard, one warmer light between bright streetlamps. Then the trolley seemed to dissolve, its lights fading and dying away. A few minutes later Xas came to the place where the tracks vanished into the base of a great, dank fogbank.

He stopped walking. He thought about what he was doing. He thought: 'I am going around in circles, pursuing Conrad Cole as though God wants me to find him.' It occurred to Xas that he wasn't acting like a human *or* an angel. A human would ask Flora McLeod, Cole's editor, whether she thought Cole needed a test pilot. An angel would drop down into the man's life and make some kind of bargain.

The latter was impossible for Xas now, but he was incapable of practising ordinary human opportunism. What's more, it occurred to him that he was acting as though Cole had all the time in the world, as if he—Xas— had forgotten his hardest-learned lesson.

*

When, in 1801, Xas met his friend Apharah she was still quite young and recently widowed. Her elderly husband had taken a bride only late in life, when he was in poor health and his eyesight was failing. Apharah could read, and had a beautiful speaking voice, and her husband had wanted company, and someone to read to him. After his death, Apharah lived, solitary and secluded, in a house in Damascus. Her house had a beautiful garden.

Xas's own garden in Hell—at an altitude, sheltered by two spurs of rock, and enclosed in a dome of glass as dark as flaked obsidian—had growing conditions similar to those of the gardens of Damascus. The Damascus gardens were walled, had fountains, were filled with plants that weren't too thirsty. Xas had, over some hundreds of years, developed the habit of dropping in on those gardens to get ideas for his own. And to steal plants.

Over the years most of the people he met, he met because he was stealing for his garden. An Irish monk, Niall, had caught the angel trying to carry off one of his beehives. Xas had wanted the bees for pollination, but it turned out that the hive was too heavy for him to carry. When he dropped it the bees swarmed and the angel had to stoop on Niall and use his wings to shelter the man from the swarm. Niall later gave Xas a newly established hive of a more manageable size.

A Polish baron had shot at Xas when he caught the angel pulling pieces of flowering vine off his castle walls. Xas took the man's gun and returned it only after it had passed through the hands of every angel in Hell. For some time thereafter the fallen angels had sent Xas out after other novelties, so that for several decades he would enter at upper windows to steal whatever took his fancy: clockwork toys and clever tools, weapons and scientific apparatus, hand mirrors, hair brushes, wigs, walking sticks, spectacles and false teeth.

On that night in 1801, a night with a full moon, when Xas first flew over Apharah's garden, he saw what looked like a white star suspended in a pool as black as oil. It was a waterlily. He decided to break roots from the plant once it had finished blooming, and see if he could get it to grow in the pool in his own garden. The following full moon when he returned he was so focused on his thievery that he didn't see or hear or smell the woman sitting in a dark alcove in her garden wall. He didn't know she was there till she spoke up, proposing, in her lovely calm voice, that he *pay* for what he was taking. As payment Apharah suggested he sing to her— then she objected to his choice of music, and insisted on teaching him her favourite song. She detained him with searches through songbooks, comparisons between different versions of the song, a singing lesson, and a history lesson. She treated him as she had the peddlers invited into her father's harem—as though he were a novelty, but quite legitimately there for her entertainment. She bossed Xas about, and he decided he liked her. Of course he came back, but, being an angel, he forgot to come back with sufficient regularity. Once, when a whole year had elapsed between his visits, Apharah met him with tears and reproaches. She'd missed him. She was worried about him. She valued his visits.

After that she seemed to set out to find some way to have Xas learn to experience time as people do. She said to him: 'It might be good for you to pace out a human life. But—' she said, 'that is a poor analogy for someone who hasn't ever had to measure a stretch of ground by *walking* across it. Rather, let me say that it might be good for you if, next time you happen to meet someone who interests you, you make an arrangement to meet them again, on the same day and in the same place the following year.'

Xas said, 'Or *every* year.'

'Yes, but,' she said, 'perhaps every year of a life is too much of an undertaking, even for an angel.'

Shortly after Apharah made her suggestion, when Xas was on a flight from Denmark to a certain salt dome in Turkey (the passage into and out of Hell) he stopped to take a rest. He was carrying a rose bush. It was heavy, its roots intact and wrapped in damp sackcloth. He'd been flying at a low altitude so the plant wouldn't ice over. But at a low altitude the atmosphere was thicker, and it was heavy going, so he stopped to rest on the crest of a rolling rise near the Saône River, in a vineyard. It was night, the moon fat, but waning. As Xas sat there, a young man appeared from the low stone house at the foot of the slope. The man was carrying two wine bottles. He wore patched woollen trousers, a linen tunic, and clogs. Before he left the yard he set the bottles down on a bench and used a knife to ease out their corks. He left his knife on the bench, replaced one cork, and came up the slope stopping now and then to throw back his head and swig from the open bottle. He drank the wine as though it were water, drank with capacity and appetite. Halfway up the slope he sat down with his back to the angel and finished the bottle, then moaned, dropped it, put his head in his hands and dug his fingers into the roots of his hair so that it seemed to flood out under his hands like a gushing wound he was trying to stem. Xas watched this—the young man, drunk, and in a rapture of demonstrative misery. Xas enjoyed watching the man, and so didn't move when he climbed to his feet again and continued toward the ridge. When the man finally noticed Xas, he didn't believe his eyes. He came on, frowning and peering and waiting for the angel to disappear or turn into something ordinary. Then his face turned white, as though the moon had suddenly rushed closer to the hillside. Xas saw that he would fall and jumped up to catch him. The man was unexpectedly heavy—his blood full, not foam like an angel's—his bones as dense as hardwood, and full too, of greasy animal goodness. Xas caught the man and was carried down with him so that they lay together. The bottle and Xas's rose bush rolled a little way down the slope and stopped. Xas sat and cradled the man and waited for him to wake up.

When he did wake the man told the angel his troubles—just blurted them all out. Xas gave him counsel (bad, as it turned out), and then he had the man—Sobran—promise to meet him again the following year, and every year after that, and made the same promise himself.

And so Xas learned to measure time by Sobran's life. By the time of Sobran's death at seventy-three, Xas was living from year to year. He had lost his wings, was on the ground, and knew what miles were. There were morning and evening hours, there were days and weeks, and he could make no real progress any more against the spin of the earth.

There was time. And, in time, there were the weeks after Sobran's death which the angel spent in an attic room in a house near the walls of Beaune, a room with a window, a bed, a chair, a candlestick. In those weeks Xas wanted time to be gone too. He waited for time to go, and willed it to go, until he felt that he almost understood how that might be accomplished—an end to time. But he went out of the room and nearly the first thing he encountered in the street made him gain substance again, a substance that might be only curiosity, the curiosity that now led him about, led him to enthusiasms he could pace out, could *live*, as he had lived Sobran's life.

Xas made a choice. He chose to surrender to his latest enthusiasm—the talk of an aircraft designer, and the taste of the mouth that talked. He followed the edge of the fogbank toward the ocean. He crossed streets and sandlots and another trolley line. He passed over a drain with an inch of green scum floating on its surface. When he reached the coast he followed it up to the pier where, more than a week before, Millie had told him to turn inland. He turned inland. Eventually he found the unsealed road along which he had walked away from Mines Field. He jumped over a fence— concealed in fog now and free to move as he could. He crossed a field between the shapes of the planes. It was like passing through a segment of a time, twelve years back. Some airfield in Europe, an airfield that hadn't ever existed, where a Sopwith Camel might be found standing in the shelter of a Gotha bomber. (Except Xas saw that the bomber wasn't a Gotha, only a Sikorsky in costume.)

Xas located the hangar and stood for a moment peering up at the roof above one end wall. He crouched back on his heels and rocked from foot to foot while staring at the place he was aiming for. He made his leap—thirty feet up—and clamped on to the roof with both hands. His boots skittered on the plate iron and he slammed stomach-first against the steep slope. He held on and hauled himself up, hand-over-hand, and scrabbling with his toes.

The hangar's hollow interior boomed. A light went on nearby in the fog. Xas swarmed up, reached the apex of the roof and flattened his body against the metal. Someone came across the field sweeping the beam of a torch back and forth through the fog. They rattled the lock on the hangar door, stalked around the building, checked the lock again, then went away.

Later, much later, when he had some covering noise—a plane taking off—Xas pulled a bolt from the roof and worked it around in its own hole to increase the hole's size. He looked down on darkness and a hint of silver—Cole's experimental plane.

He stayed on the roof. He lay in wait like a tiger at a waterhole.

*

Cole said, 'Close that door.' He said, 'You have rust on your shirt.' He said, 'You smell of the open air.'

Later, when they were leaving the hangar, Cole paused before the two deep prints in the damp turf, the marks the angel's feet had made when he jumped down from the roof. Cole regarded the prints with savvy scientific intelligence. He pressed his own heels into the ground beside the marks. 'There was an accident,' he said, 'and they chose not to tell me.'

Xas asked who 'they' were.

'The people who work for me. People I expect to keep me fully informed.'

'I'd like to work for you,' Xas said.

'So that's what you want? What you came here for?'

Xas went closer to Cole, who stepped away so that Xas's hand only brushed his shirt.

'I'd like to be of some use,' Xas said.

'We'll see. You can drive, presumably? That would be good right now. Suddenly I'm very tired.'

'That happens,' Xas said. 'And nosebleeds,' he added. He eyed the man. He could still see Cole, his racked joy, his reddened skin. He wondered how Cole could be so selective with the evidence of his senses. Cole's body knew a great deal, seemed bathed in an aura of his many conquests—but he lived in his head.

'I have work to do,' Cole said. 'You can drive. You can get me there.'

# Burbank

## August, 1929

Three weeks after Gil's funeral Flora was back at work in her editing suite.

She was expecting Cole that day but was surprised when he arrived with Xas. They came in talking aeronautical engineering. Flora heard Xas saying something about 'torsional weakness' before the squeak of the screen door covered the rest.

Flora got up, unkinked her back and moved her stool to make room for her employer. Xas backed into the shadows, stepping gingerly in the spaces of clear floor between curled shavings of celluloid. As he did he finished what he was saying. 'When I began my descent I noticed that the fabric on the wings got a kind of sheen on it. I didn't like that. I'd like to take it up again and test it in incremental dives.'

Cole said, 'We'll see.' Then he said to Flora, 'You got my note?'

Cole had sent Flora a note saying he wanted her to wait for him before she took a look at Monday's rushes. She leaned over and began sorting through a stack of film cans till she found the one she wanted. She took out the film and threaded her projector.

This particular scene had been shot fifteen times—though that was quite a small number for Cole. When Flora studied the rushes she at first thought she was looking at a double exposure. Monty Mantery's face filled most of the frame. The actor's hair was plastered to his damp skin, his neck beaded with sweat and arched as his head thrashed about and seemed to scoop a deep hole for itself in his white hospital pillow.

Flora had viewed the scene before, she was sure. Cole had shot it just like this, and she thought he must only have re-shot to add ambient sound—which would be crazy since music would work better anyway.

Months before she and Cole had discussed how this footage of Monty's thrashing head must be inter-cut with shots of a page of his sweetheart's letter. The letter where his sweetheart lets him know that she's decided to marry someone else. Monty's character is injured, lying in a crowded ward of a French hospital. Cole had taken a great deal of trouble over the ward itself and Flora understood that the detailed, bustling scene was supposed to resolve into a montage of Monty's face and ink on a page. She had said to Cole at the time, 'We can all see that he is in a fever and is being persecuted by her words in a feverish dream, but none of that is as interesting as the hospital. You might have to do away with the hospital, Con. At the moment the contrast between the busy ward and the fever and letter just punctures the film. It puts a hole in its spell. It's the rhythm that's wrong. At this point cross-cutting like you want to will make the film feel like a car wobbling along on a flat tyre.'

At the time Cole had seemed to take in Flora's comments—but that was months ago now, before Kay North, and Myra, and before he replaced his female lead. Flora looked at this apparently new footage of Monty's sweat-soaked squirming head and hoped that she wouldn't have to repeat her objections. And then she saw that the footage was entirely new. For, as she watched, brilliant, sparkling white letters began to form as though in the air above the perspiring face. '*Dear Adam*,' Flora read. It was the beginning of Monty's sweetheart's letter. The words hung, bright, and smoking blackly. And then the magical writing went on, the text appeared, blazed, then blackened. Of the fifteen takes five were of the beginning of the letter, five its devastating line '*we can never be together*', and the final five of the sweetheart's signature. The footage was simple, expressive, and quite unlike anything Cole had done before.

Flora said, 'This looks German.' Then she asked Cole which of the five takes he wanted to use. She wound the film back to run it again, saying that she assumed he was wanting to use one of each. '"Dear Adam" and "never together" and "your Sally". "Your Sally" as she brushes him off. Your new girl does look like someone who might do that.'

'Jensen was a herbivore; Jean's a carnivore,' said Cole.

For the next hour Flora ran the film back and forth and made marks on the edges of the frames. She got the nod and began to cut, dropping curls of discarded film around her feet. She glued the final footage together, wiped her tacky fingertips, and wound the film in again. She and Cole peered together into the light.

'That's good,' he said, when they'd run it several times. Then he explained what he'd done. 'We set up a sheet of glass between Monty and the camera and then wrote on the glass with a mixture of gelatine and gunpowder. We wanted the letters to look like a burning fuse. We had to keep wiping the glass clean and starting again. But really—in the end—the most difficult thing was finding a paintbrush that made a flat stroke like a fountain pen.'

From the back of the room Xas said, 'We found a man in Chinatown with calligraphy brushes. I think the hardest thing was to make the mix work. It had to have enough gunpowder grains to burn in solid, lingering lines, but not so much that we could see the letters before they were lit. But, as you can see, "Dear Adam" and "we can never be together" and "Yours, Sally" all start beyond the edge of the frame as if the girl writes with big flourishes. We couldn't do anything about that.'

'But that only makes the effect more suggestive of a fuse,' Cole said.

Flora noticed that Cole and Xas were leaning toward each other as they spoke, that Xas already had the habit of addressing himself to Cole's good ear, and that—more surprisingly—Cole inclined toward Xas as though he were intent on hearing what Xas had to say.

'So you're pleased with it?' Cole said.

Flora was sure Cole was speaking to Xas, not her.

Xas didn't seem quite so sure, and nobody answered Cole's question. Instead Xas said, 'Are you going to let me take that plane up again and try some incremental dives?'

'Just because you're curious?'

'I'm *involved*.'

'Ah—' said Cole. 'Involvement.' He seemed to be issuing some kind of caution. 'Maybe *I* should take the plane up. You can always tag along.'

'And lie behind you in the fuselage taking notes while you shout at me over your shoulder?'

'That's all that's on offer right now.'

'Okay,' said Xas.

Cole turned back to Flora and said there were other people he had to see in the studio. 'I'll leave you to it,' he said. He got up and pushed through the screen door. Flora listened to her employer lope down the two flights, his steps shaking her shack so that the stacked film cans rattled.

Flora waited till he'd gone, then went outside to have a cigarette. Xas followed her and sat on the steps.

'When he said he was leaving me to it are you sure he meant to leave you too?' Flora said.

Xas patted the step next to him. Flora felt that she wasn't being invited to sit because he wanted her beside him. She thought he was testing her, looking for the cause of her stiff gait, as though she were an experimental aircraft he wanted to take up and subject to 'incremental dives'. Flora didn't move. She tapped her cigarette on the rail, scattering ash into the air. She said, 'I keep finding myself thinking,

"What's this guy's story?" But please don't feel you need to tell me. I'm scared you'll start quoting verse, or the wisdom of Aimee Semple McPherson.'

Xas said, 'I don't know who she is.' Then he apparently decided to pick up on the conversation they'd been having, weeks before, as they walked to Flora's trolley stop. 'What would *you* most like to see on film?'

That was easy. 'My grandmother after church talking to her cronies. My grandmother, who raised me.'

'Is she still alive?'

'She died before the war.'

'Then you see what I mean.'

'So we're back to the speckled enamel bowl, and what film is able to preserve,' Flora said. 'If you're really interested in my opinion, and not just making a point, perhaps you should ask me whether what I want to see on film has sound or is silent.'

'I know you don't like sound,' Xas said. 'But I don't really understand why.'

Flora told him that her first talkie was *Tenderloin*, with Dolores Costello and Conrad Nagel. 'I sat there listening to the dialogue, and was embarrassed. It was as if the people sitting beside me in the cinema had caught me eavesdropping. It was all too intimate. Besides, Dolly and Nagel kept saying dim things in a dopey way. So—bad acting is one reason I don't like sound. Another is that the studios are putting so much money into sound that it's making them too investment-minded about the films they want to make. I can see a time when it'll become harder and harder for anyone to freelance in this town. I'm starting to feel that if I don't attach myself to a particular director I'll wind up pinned down in one studio—having to edit every film only one way.'

'If that happens then Conrad Crow would be the one to choose,' Xas said.

'You worked for him for a single day and you picked that?'

'People hang on his every word. He's autocratic, but not grandiose. He's having fun. And he's slippery, which is interesting in itself.'

Flora was fascinated. This young man had read her friend very quickly, and very well. She wondered what he thought of Cole. Surely he mustn't be seeing clearly there. She decided to ask him: 'And what do you make of Cole?'

'I don't understand him. But you mean as a director?'

'Directing film is just something Cole's doing, I think,' Flora said. 'He's extremely able. But I haven't worked out yet what he is naturally—playboy, director, inventor—apart from being someone who does things that would terrify just about anyone else. Professional and personal things. Cole sometimes acts as though he has no imagination, but he does. I've known him for some time and *I* can't work him out. It's like trying to learn a river. You might get a stretch of it figured, and then it changes on you. Cole has fixed habits, though. For instance, he doesn't like beef in his sandwiches. He's predictable in that way. But, with most people you can say that their habits are like landmarks in the country of their characters; you can't with Cole. If he was a character in a film and you were watching him behave you might be able to think, "If he does *that* then he's *this* kind of person." But I've been watching Cole for ages, and as far as I can see he's not coherent.'

Flora finished talking and lit another cigarette from the end of her first. She wondered, would Xas take this warning? Which was how she'd meant it.

He was looking at up at her, his face in full sunlight. His expression was open and alert—but she couldn't read him at all. She could tell that his alertness was a combination of excellent health and intelligence, but couldn't tell whether his openness was simplicity or a kind of faithful courage. She wanted to know—suddenly needed to know—so she asked him whether he'd understood what she was saying.

'Cole is complicated,' he said.

'I'm saying he might be crazy, and you should be careful of him.'

'I try to be careful with everyone.'

'I said "of" not "with". Be careful *of* Cole.' Flora stubbed out her half-finished cigarette on the handrail and flicked it into the lane. The shadow of the nearest soundstage was climbing her two-storey shack. Flora thought that, if she stood a moment more, sober, without a smoke in her hand, then she'd have to admit to herself that she was doing more that passing time with this person. Cole had left them together, and for a short while Flora had felt as if she and Xas were Cole's retainers, left to themselves after receiving their orders. They were both doing things for Cole. That was their only connection. And Millie. But Flora kept feeling that she wasn't just passing time. She felt she needed to know why this person sitting on the step at her feet and looking up at her had a quality of attention that was quite unlike anything she had experienced before. What had happened to him to make him able to focus on things with such vivid patience?

The shadow had reached the step where he was sitting. He stood up and leaned on the rail opposite her.

Flora said, 'All right, I'll play your game. What would *you* most like to see on film?'

He began to stroke the mesh of the screen door. It didn't rasp but made a soft, breathy singing under his fingertips, as though it were being rubbed with silk. He said, 'I'd like to point the camera and microphone at a person or a group of people, and ask them questions. That's what I'd like to see—a film of people answering questions.'

'What kind of questions? And what kind of people.'

'Anyone. And before you started filming you'd have to find out something about them first. You could ask about their job, or family, or hometown. You could ask about their health. Anything. Keep the camera rolling—then keep the film forever. Keep what God won't.'

Flora was startled. She blinked at him.

He went on. 'You could put the camera on a couple of eighty-five-year-old veterans of Shiloh, for instance.'

'Hang on,' said Flora. 'What won't God keep?'

Xas said, 'God doesn't keep bodies—bodies and all their faults. Let's start with that. After all, I'm only talking about what it would be good to have on film. The bodies of people, and the voices of those bodies. Can I give you an example? Can I tell you a story?' He waited for permission, and began to speak only when Flora gave him a nod.

'I lived for a time in Burgundy in the town Beaune, near the ramparts, where I had an attic room. This was after my friend, Sobran Jodeau, died. Actually everything *since* then has been after his death. Sometimes things happen like that. You find yourself living not really in the world any more, but in another sorry place called Afterward.'

Flora touched her dress and, beneath that, her girdle of scarred skin. She nodded again, mute.

'I had a room with a candle, a table, a chair,' he said, then finished his sentence in a rush, 'a room with rot-riddled beams, and a tiny arched window looking out over the street. I remember sitting in that room determined that it should be my whole universe, as though, if I were responsible for only a tiny territory, I could somehow take control of time there. Because, you see, it was time that took my friend from me.'

Flora said gently, 'But then you had to go out to get something to eat.'

'No, I didn't. But I frightened myself. That's why I left the room. Anyway—this isn't a story about how I frightened myself, this is a story about what should be on film.

'There was a school near my room. At intervals I could hear the children out in its yard. They sounded very wild to me. The first thing I did when I finally left my room was to go past the school and stop at its gate to have a look at these wild-sounding children. I was only idly curious, but I stayed at the gate because they were beautiful. Children of all sizes, in faded, patched uniforms—apparently ordinary children, but every one of them was graceful and amazingly alive. I realised that they were deaf, and were communicating by looking at one another and gesturing. I watched one boy trying to impose his plan of action on some others; trying to convince them to play the game his way, arguing his case without making any articulate sound. I found myself wanting to do what he suggested, whatever he suggested. I would have obeyed any of them—they were so forcefully expressive.

'So,' he said, 'that's what I'd like to see on film—deaf children at play. In Heaven those children's hearing would be restored to them, even if they were born deaf. So they'd lose their particular beauty along with that language of gestures.'

Flora stared at Xas for a long while in silence. The silence was like the balance of something—the remainder of his story. The story that extended on either side of his observation, and the peculiar theology he'd chosen to draw from it. There was the history of his friendship with his dead friend—Sobran Jodeau—who was what to him? And there was whatever he chose to do after he left the gate of the school for deaf children, whatever it was that brought him, eventually, to the door of her editing suite.

The sun was still shining on the distant Verdugo Mountains, and on the cylinder of the studio's water tower, but the roofs of the soundstages were saw-tooth shadows.

After a long while Flora found herself simply saying 'Yes' to Xas. Surprised by the sound of her own voice she collected her wits and decided to make her 'Yes' pertain to something. 'That's a good idea,' she said. 'Someone should do that.' Then she asked him what he was up to—apart from helping Cole with fire-effects.

'I did some work on Millie's plane—she lets me take it up. And I've flown one of Cole's experimental aircraft. Not his racer, but one with a big brute of an engine and six propellers. And I found the new public library. I spend time there reading. There are people I see every time I go, they are the regulars. I'm the *new* regular.' He smiled happily. 'The other day a boy talked to me for two whole hours about L Frank Baum, and not just *The Wizard of Oz*, which is the one he says, scornfully, everyone knows. He's a funny kid, everything he says seems to come from far off, as if he doesn't belong in the solar system but is just coming around with his enthusiasms like a comet in its halo of ice. In fact, he reminds me of a relative of mine.' Xas shook his head, then said, 'I like libraries because I used to live in a kind of library.' Then he dropped his head and murmured, 'It'll take me forever to catch up.'

'On your reading?'

'Yes. I can't take books out because I don't have a library card. I can't get one without a local address.' He looked up again and smiled, and this time the smile was sly. 'Though perhaps I could use your address.'

Flora saw that Xas had finally asked a question to which she could properly attach her 'Yes'. She fished in her pocket and found a scrap of paper and the greasy pencil she used to mark film. She wrote out her address and gave it to him. She let him know where she lived, having completely forgotten how he'd frightened her by turning his face away from the people gathered at her trolley stop.

Before leaving the studio for the day, Flora went to visit her film star friend, Avril. The warning light was off at the soundstage door so she let herself in. Flora wasn't used to soundstages, hadn't visited any of the sets for the re-shoots for *Flights of Angels*. It wasn't her practice to sit in on the shooting of any film she was editing. She thought it better that she only dealt with the footage she got, so that she could discover for herself how best to find the story in what was filmed, unconstrained by any familiarity with the director's dealing with the actors.

Flora was used to the sets of silent films, in which she and Avril had worked together. Sets lit by crackling carbon arc lamps, and filled with noise. The sounds of production people bustling about beyond the live area, carpenters sawing and hammering, sewing machines clattering, all kinds of talk, and the director yelling directions—'You see him! Now fix your hair. Wave hello, honey! A big wave! You're worried you won't get his attention'—voice raised over the mood music.

The set of Avril's latest film was baking under incandescent lights. It was bright and silent.

Someone closed the door behind Flora, stepped up to her and put their finger to their lips.

Avril was sitting straight-backed on an ottoman, her skin was velvety with powder and shone pinkish under a tower of piled platinum hair. The director was talking to the men in the mixing booth. He came out and found his seat. He was visible—but barely. Beyond the border of yellow key lights the crew appeared as shades of the living. They were signing to one another, and moving in a gliding ghostly way, or standing frozen and watchful like deer at the edge of an open glade.

The director murmured some instructions to Avril and the other actor, who was standing at a casement behind her. Then he asked for silence. Flora heard, '*Rolling*'—then the bang of the clapper. A second later Avril began to speak, clear and distinct, her bearing composed and head raised regally, all for the benefit of the microphone in the fruit bowl on the table before her.

They did ten takes, then waited for the verdict from the mixing booth. Finally the sound men seemed satisfied and Avril came to life and swept off the set and toward her dressing room. Flora intercepted her.

Avril took Flora's hands and kissed her. Her rigid eyelashes scratched for a second at Flora's cheek. Flora followed her friend to the dressing room and sat beside her while her hairpiece was carefully detached and her make-up removed. They talked into the mirror, Flora feeling moved as Avril's face slowly emerged, brighter than all its bright artifice.

Avril complained mildly that the director really was a bit of a dope, expecting her and the other actors to have these conversations in cavernous sets hunched over things like the fruitbowl—which was all very well and good but he never thought to have them, say, hunched over a radio, or a bassinet with a baby in it, or any of the sorts of things people do actually gather around. 'I just keep telling myself that I'm paying for my new swimming pool,' Avril finished. She thanked her dresser and sent her away. Then she leaned into the mirror to make up her face for the street. 'Anyway, darling, what's up? Is Con still tinkering?'

'Actually, he's making some progress.'

'And is it really all off with Kay North?'

'No. Kay's still on the back burner,' Flora hesitated, then took a deep breath and said, 'Avril, I want to ask you about something.'

Avril met her gaze in the mirror and nodded.

'John Weber,' Flora said. 'Whatever became of him?'

'Remember how Con tried to browbeat you into pressing charges and pursuing damages? I'm amazed he ever forgave you for not taking his advice.'

'I remember very little of that. I was on morphine, and everything seemed to go on forever.'

'Do you remember the lawyer Con presented you with in hospital?'

Flora shook her head.

'I convinced the lawyer to let you be. Con was furious with me. I think he took what happened to you personally. The shock of it. He had the presence of mind to pull down that curtain and wrap it around you, but the whole thing was mortally shocking to him. He wasn't eating, and he'd gone right off sex. I think he wanted his own revenge on Weber.'

'But I wouldn't press charges.'

'That's right. And Con gave up the whole idea of legal redress.'

'So what happened to Weber?'

Avril shook her head. 'He must have left town.'

The women peered into the mirror at each other's faces, Avril apparently waiting for another question. Finally Flora asked it. 'You don't suppose Con did something to John?'

Avril nodded faintly, but said, 'I don't know.'

# The Mojave Desert

## September, 1929

Cole in the cockpit was an impediment between Xas and the sky. Xas's boots and elbows were braced against the frame of the fuselage, and he had one hand resting on his notebook, pressing its pages flat. His parachute pack was a heavy lump in the small of his back. He peered over Cole's shoulder at the constricted skyscape, the fresh, unfolding clouds, and felt resentful.

They had flown up to ten thousand feet, in order to discover the aircraft's utmost viable angle of dive. They would try its limits, and somewhere in the shimmering space around them they would find the place in which the plane would pass, and its pilot would ease back, or in which it would break and fail.

Once they were above the clouds Cole banked away from the sun and bought the nose of the plane down in a very shallow dive. He turned his head to relay the readings on his instruments. Then he brought the plane back into level flight for a moment, before pushing it into a steeper dive.

This process went on for some time. The plane inscribed a wavering graph in the air. Cole called out the figures, and Xas wrote them in his notebook, while listening as the wind hammered the fuselage like a storm of wings.

Cole brought the plane up and level for the eleventh time, then pushed the stick forward. This time he turned his head quickly to report a vibration, a tremor in the stick and pedals. Beyond Cole's head Xas caught sight of a little bit of the horizon, the solid floor to their world of air.

The engine missed, coughed, missed again.

'It's the fuel line,' Xas shouted.

Then the engine fell silent.

'Let's hope it's only an airlock,' Cole called, his voice loud now. 'Brace yourself—I'm going to roll her.'

The plane was using a gravity flow fuel system, and they both knew that sending it into a roll might shift any air bubble in the fuel line.

Xas saw that the propeller had spun to a stop. It hung before their faces, a dead thing. He scrambled forward till he was right at Cole's shoulder. In the unnatural silence of the glide he heard his dropped pencil rolling forward.

Cole waited till they passed through a cloud layer, its buffeting gloom. They came out and saw a small town below them in the desert—buildings like a scattering of white ash. They sank toward it in a slow glide.

Cole turned to Xas again, so close that he was breathing into his face. 'I said brace yourself.'

Xas jammed his feet, elbows and hands against the fuselage once more.

Cole pumped the throttle and pushed the stick over. The plane went into a roll. The desert turned above it, the solid world making an outline around the open sky between cloud and horizon, their corridor of air. The engine spluttered and started, the propeller becoming transparent once more.

The abrupt change in airspeed made the plane's tail kick up, and the aircraft jerked into a dive at an angle Cole would normally have worked his way up to only gradually, after hours of tests.

The plane gave a lurch. Xas heard a wrenching noise and thump behind him, then the plane plunged into a steep dive, its engine roaring. It rammed downward, faster than falling. Xas saw Cole hauling back on the stick—to absolutely no effect. The plane wouldn't flatten out. Its nose dropped further. It was driving downwards. The horizon rocked in Cole's window, then swung above them, receding above their heads. For a moment the aircraft hung inverted, then it continued to roll, and went into a spin.

Cole let go of the controls and reached up to release the roof. He slid it back. He tried to climb out of the cockpit. Xas watched him struggle. The slipstream was creating a suction that held Cole in place.

Xas doubled up and began to punch at the fabric of the plane. He made a hole and the suction relented. He looked up again to see Cole clamber from the cockpit—then be snatched out of sight.

The plane was spinning so fast now that it was generating its own gravitational pull. Xas was pressed in place against the fuselage. With a great effort he dragged himself over the seat and into the cockpit—then out into the air. The slipstream grabbed hold of him and ripped him away from the aircraft.

Xas tumbled on down, faster than falling, still moving at the speed of the plane's dive, the sky and desert alternately swooping over him. The plane was below him now, moving faster than he was. Xas saw that the tip of one of its wings was gone, and most of its tail. One wing had broken off and carried the tail away with it.

The angel could see Cole a little above him—for Xas been carried further down with the falling plane. Cole was lying spread-eagled on the air, trying to slow his fall to a speed at which he could risk opening his parachute without its splitting.

Xas too stretched out his arms and legs and lay on the air. Then he lifted one arm and dropped the other, banked, accelerated, and slid sideways for a time. He moved away from Cole, till he judged they were level. Then he made the practised adjustments of his body to steer himself through the air, back to Cole. He used his innate abilities, and those he'd learned wing-walking. He dropped down beside Cole, and wheeled to face the man.

Cole looked up at him. His eyes were slits and his cheeks rippling.

Xas seized Cole's hands, and for six long seconds they dropped together, the sum of the surface area of their two spread-eagled bodies helping to slow their fall. Then Xas pushed away and signalled, *'Pull your cord.'* He didn't pull his own till he saw Cole's parachute open and hold.

Someone spotted the smoke from the wreck and came to check.

It was a store owner, who gave them a ride in his truck to the nearest phone, which was at his place—a silvered timber ranch house with one gas pump and a barn converted to a repair shop, standing by themselves at the junction of two unsealed desert roads.

Cole and Xas sat on the porch of the repair shop and drank Coke. People kept coming by, ostensibly to fetch things from the store, really to look these downed pilots over, and to get their story.

The man's wife came and joined them on the porch. She had a bowl of apples, a colander and peeler. She sat on a step and peeled her apples. Cole moved from the rocking chair to the step below her, where he sat fishing long strips of peel from her apron and eating them. She was startled, but charmed. She promised him a piece of the pie once it was done. 'And you'd like coffee, I expect,' she said, then went off again into the dark indoors.

Cole accepted his coffee in a cup with a chipped rim. He sipped and Xas watched him checking the chip with the tip of his tongue. This, for a man who was frightened of infection, was flirting with danger.

When Cole had finished his coffee, he joined the owner, who was bent over the engine of a car.

It got quiet. Gradually the folks who'd come looking for news all departed. The mechanic's wife was indoors baking. The only sound was an intermittent murmuring talk between Cole and the mechanic, and the rattle of the man's wrench on a bolt. After a time the smell of hot pastry and sugar, cinnamon and apples drifted out into the open air. The desert instantly blotted up the scented steam. The woman came out and called to her husband and Cole. 'You should wash up now!' She turned a nervous smile Xas's way, where he was sitting, his back against the wall of the store and hugging his knees. She said, 'I guess you have to collect yourself after falling out of the air like that.' Then, 'Hadn't you better wash up too?' She spoke gently as if, when she looked at him, she saw the queasy fright of someone who has had a brush with mortality.

Xas joined Cole at the outdoor tap. Cole was scrubbing engine oil out of the crosshatching of scratches on his fingertips with a bar of greyed soap. He passed Xas the soap and said, 'Bill was just telling me he has too much work for one man.'

Xas glanced at the mechanic—Bill—then back at Cole.

Cole dried his hands and threw Xas the damp towel. He strolled back up on to the porch. The woman brought out three plates of pie, drizzled with condensed milk. Cole set to with appetite, and polished off the pie in less than a minute. He put his plate down, rested one foot on the rail and straightened his long leg to tilt his chair back. He said to the woman, 'Bill tells me you could do with some help.'

She nodded. 'My brother used to be with us. But he moved out to the coast, and got a job on a drilling crew.'

'Is this your own business, Bill?' Cole asked the mechanic.

'It is. It's not much, but at least I'm working for myself. Joan's brother is working for a wage. His employer will make money if the well comes in, but my brother-in-law only takes his wages home.'

'Well—there's not much wrong with working for a wage,' Cole said. 'It has advantages, like not having to make all the decisions.'

The mechanic nodded. 'True.'

Cole said, 'Sometimes I think the ideal life would be simpler than the one I have. I think it might be better to follow someone else's lead, to work with my hands, to live someplace quiet, where it's possible to know everyone, and know them well. Those folks who came to take a look at us—you knew every one of them, didn't you Bill?'

'I guess I did. This isn't the highway here, so we don't get too many people just passing by.'

Cole nodded, a slow, sage gesture. 'I kind of like that idea. No strangers. And waking up every day with a pretty clear idea of what that day will bring. And making do with plans that don't need any hard push of will power. Maybe even dealing with things you could trust to come true exactly as you expect them to.' He turned to the woman, who had been frowning at him with a sort of suspicious amazement, but blushed and smiled when he looked at her. He said, 'Take this pie, for instance. It's delicious, Joan, but I bet it's made to a simple recipe.'

'Flour, sugar, shortening, salt, cinnamon and apple,' she said. 'It's about as plain as can be.'

'And if you get all the measurements right it turns out just the way you expect it to?'

'So long as you remember to take it out on time,' said the woman, who wasn't about to oversimplify her pie in order to illustrate Cole's homily.

Cole flexed his knee and rocked his tilted chair back and forth. 'There are many different things I could choose to do with my life,' he said. 'So I sometimes wonder: why don't I choose something simple? Something clear of complications.' He looked at Xas. 'What do you think about the idea of getting a job, and being an ordinary guy?'

'Of you getting a job and being ordinary? Or of me doing it?'

The mechanic and his wife exchanged a glance.

Xas went on. 'For now I more or less get up every day and see what I can fix, who I can help. But that's finding work, rather than having a job. Should I have a job?'

Cole dropped his chair back on all fours. He asked Joan where her brother had lived when he was working there.

'Ed lived over the workshop.'

'Could you show my friend where Ed lived?' Cole asked.

'Sure,' she said, puzzled. Then to Xas, 'If you'd like to follow me.'

Xas got up and followed her. She kept looking back over her shoulder at Cole as they crossed the yard and went through the door of the workshop. They skirted the edge of a grease pit. She stopped at the foot of a steep staircase, and said, 'There. You can go on up if you like.'

Xas climbed the stairs. He found a room in the roof,

a room with a pitched ceiling, one window, and an iron bedstead. The mattress was doubled up on the rusty bedsprings. Xas put a hand on the mattress and felt rustling lumps inside it. It was stuffed with corn husks. He listened to the dry stirring under his hand, and the faint hot shimmer of sound from the world beyond the small window in the gable.

It was the kind of room in which someone might wait for time to stop.

Xas went back down the stairs.

The mechanic's wife said, 'Why does your boss want my husband to offer you a job?'

'Is that what he wants?'

She reflected a moment, then nodded. 'As I see it.'

Xas looked at his feet and didn't say anything.

'Was it your fault that the plane went down?'

Xas shook his head.

She gave his arm a light tap. 'Is he firing you?'

Xas sighed. 'I believe he is thinking of "the simple life" for himself. He sent me to check out the room because he's used to asking people to do those things for him. At the moment I think he's worried about how things will turn out, with his planes, his film, his girlfriends. He's trying to imagine how easy it would be to walk away from everything, like he walked away from the wrecked plane.'

'So he's not mad at you?' She sounded relieved.

'I don't know. I have such a lot of trouble figuring him out. He was so proud of himself for keeping his head—and his eye on the nearest road as he was falling. But since he jumped before the plane hit, he still doesn't really know what it's like to walk away from a wreck. He hasn't walked away. He's scared, so tries to tell himself he could be a motor mechanic instead of Conrad Cole. He could live "the simple life". And he thinks I'll show my true colours if he says he wants to stay here and get his hands dirty and do a decent day's work for a decent day's wage. He thinks—' Xas suddenly took a good look at the person he was talking to and shut up.

The woman had pressed her hand under her throat. 'Me and Bill don't have to stay here either, you know. We could sell out. Bill could go and work for the oilmen, too. But this is a pretty good business. And our lives aren't simple. *We're* not simple.' She gave a fierce laugh. 'Ordinary, yes, but not simple.' She turned away from Xas and ambled toward the grease pit, kicking her slip-on shoes a little ahead of her toes at every step then stepping into them as though they were footholds, and she was climbing something. 'We'd better go back,' she said, over her shoulder. 'Bill might wonder just what I'm showing you.' She laughed again.

They walked out into the sunlight. She shaded her eyes and peered at her husband and Cole on the porch. 'Look at them,' she said. 'Bill's happy. He knows your boss is a big shot. Bill doesn't ever look at my movie magazines—but once I tell him exactly who your boss is he'll be full for weeks about how he had Conrad Cole give him a hand.' She pushed her hair back and scowled at Xas. 'I guess it's okay for Mr Cole to dream about all the different lives he could look into, but most of us have just the one, and some of us really feel it.'

'Do you feel that? Your one life?'

'Yes. Don't you?'

Xas felt a little dizzy, a little crazy. He said, '*There's* a question.'

It had hadn't really occurred to Xas that he was as liable to make or avoid choices as any of the people he met. He didn't like to think about this, so instead he found himself defending Cole. 'Cole tells stories. It's natural for him to put himself into other people's shoes.'

'You think?' The woman looked about, at the serrated horizon, the distant Sierras, the scribbles of shade under the creosote bushes, the smoke of dust raised by a car passing on an intersecting road. She looked about at her life.

'Cole's only thinking about fame,' Xas added. 'Fame is his difficulty.'

The woman looked at him again, with a keen, knowing look. 'And what's your difficulty?' she asked.

He pointed with his chin at Cole, who was head down again in the workings of the car. 'He is, for now.'

'Getting you to check out Ed's room—that wasn't nice.'

'He isn't,' Xas said.

As they came up to the store Cole took his head out from under the hood. 'Much obliged, Joan,' he said. Then to Xas, 'So, what do you think?'

'Have you made that phone call yet?'

For a long, silent moment they eyed one another. Then Cole picked up a rag and wiped his hands. 'We could stay here.'

Bill glanced at his wife, dismay and confusion in his eyes. He coughed loudly.

Cole held up a hand.

The mechanic went pink and subsided.

'Why stay?' Xas said.

'Why not?'

Xas closed his eyes. 'Con, I did promise not to cause you any trouble.'

'Can't you just answer my question?'

'All right,' Xas said, he opened his eyes again, feeling combative. 'You're playing a game.'

'With you?'

'With me, and with possibility. But the plane only cracked up because the engine was too strong for its wings. That's what happened. The wings couldn't take a dive at that angle, and that speed. That's all that happened.'

'I nearly got us killed,' Cole said, flatly.

'And so we should stay here and live over the workshop?' Xas waited. He rolled his shoulders, troubled by the sense-memory of wings mantled above his head. The pupils of his eyes expanded, reacting to an imaginary shadow. 'Con,' he said, 'if you'd actually take me on as a test pilot you'd be paying me to take risks. That would be more straightforward. Then you wouldn't have to think, "I nearly got us killed."'

Cole bridled. 'I was going to pay you for the work you've done. You don't need to worry about that.'

'I wasn't worried about payment, or anything else. I wanted to see for myself whether the wings would hold. And the risks people take aren't any of my business. I was just there with you.' Xas studied Cole's face, trying to see whether the man was calmed or mollified by any of this.

Joan went to her husband, took him by the hand and led him away indoors. Her sense of timing was wonderful, because it was at that moment that Cole lost his temper.

'You're like a bloody dog!' he yelled. 'I have to read lips! You don't, but you're always watching me as if you can't follow what's going on. As if you're a dumb animal!'

Xas pointed at the store, the darkness behind the grey gauze of its screen door. 'Go make your phone call,' he said.

Cole's face was tight and suspicious.

'Look,' said Xas, in a gentler tone. 'You're having a reaction to a risk you took that went bad. You should call for a car and get yourself somewhere safe and familiar. The bed over the workshop—neither of us would find it very comfortable.'

Cole came up to him and gripped his arm. He said, softly, 'I'm having a hell of a time getting you into any bed. If you puffed up and talked about your manhood I could say to myself, "Okay, I'll only make use of this guy's brains." But you don't jump when I touch you.' He ran his hand down Xas's arm and curled Xas's loose fingers within his own tight fist. 'I don't understand it,' he said. 'I thought maybe you'd get sentimental, like a girl, if I offered to give something up.'

'Your life?'

Cole shrugged. 'You're right—I am just playing.' He went indoors to make his postponed call.

The sun was so bright that its disc sat in the blue surrounded by a halo of pale grey. A wind came, dropping down between the lonely store and the mountains to stroke the desert. Miles away there was dust on the air, though it was still and silent at the intersection of the two scratch roads.

Xas turned his face up and stared at the sun. He thought, 'I disturb him. He therefore supposes I'm the cause of his trouble.'

The angel entertained this icy thought, with his face and wide-open eyes turned to the source of the near ninety-degree heat. He considered Cole's feelings, and put them aside. He put his own feelings aside. He said, to himself (and also to God, to Whom for a moment he forgot he was refusing to speak), 'All I want from that man is to be allowed to follow his thinking.' He dropped his gaze, and his eyes found the place, miles off, where a thread of oily smoke was still going up from the wrecked plane. Then, for an instant, he was engulfed in the vivid patience, the impersonal benevolence, and the personal affection of his Father. He was reminded: '*You followed Lucifer in order to follow his thinking.*'

A moment later Cole reappeared and said, 'What are you doing on the ground?'

'I'm having a temper tantrum,' Xas said.

'A very quiet one.'

'They're the worst sort. Did you make that call?'

'Yes. You can stop policing me.'

'I will. I think policing is pernicious. No one should police anyone.'

Cole came and stood over him, hands on his hips. 'I reckon I prefer the police to keep on. We don't want anarchy.'

'Oh, don't we?' said Xas.

'Come on, get up. Before Joan comes out here and thinks I've knocked you down.' Cole gave Xas his hand and helped him to his feet.

A couple of hours later Cole and Xas said so long to the mechanic and his wife and got into the car Cole had summoned. They rode back to the city. When they were on Van Ness, near Inglewood, Cole turned to Xas and asked, polite and cool, 'Where can I drop you?'

# Burbank and Venice

## November, 1929

Flora was leaving the studio at the end of her day. As she came out the gates and turned toward the nearest trolley stop she caught sight of Millie's car through the usual cluster of autograph hunters. The Buick was parked across the road, Millie sitting in the front seat, her head down on the wheel.

Flora crossed the road.

Millie had a cut on her scalp, under her hair. Her face was striped with blood, and her good linen suit jacket splattered with it.

Flora said, 'Millie?' and touched her friend's back.

Without raising her head Millie shook it, smearing the wheel. Flora walked around the car and got in beside her. She lifted Millie's head and parted her sticky hair to look for the cut. Cuts—she saw, none of them very long, and all only oozing now.

'What happened?' Flora said. She looked about and saw

they were being watched; observed and avoided. 'How long have you been parked here?' she asked.

Again Millie shook her head.

Flora fished in her pockets for a handkerchief. She found one, and luckily it was clean. She placed it in Millie's hand and set the hand against the lacerations. 'You hold that,' she said. Again she looked around. What was *wrong* with these people? The autograph hunters were only sometimes glancing their way, mostly they kept their eyes on the road beyond the studio gate guardhouse. As Flora watched they began to stir and huddle forward. The guard came out of his booth and made a positively biblical gesture toward the crowd, as if holding them back by force of will.

The car coming toward the gates was unprepossessing, battered, but Flora recognised it as Cole's. While spending millions on his film, Cole was too cheap to buy himself a new car.

Xas was behind the wheel, Cole beside him, wearing cheaters and slumped down in the seat.

Flora stood up and began to wave her arms. She saw the men turn her way. Xas stopped Cole's car between the studio gates. Cole stiffened, turned to him, and barked something. There was a short exchange. Flora watched Cole bristle and become agitated while Xas responded, calmly, patiently. Then Xas flicked his shoulders, an odd expressive gesture of abrupt leave-taking. He got out of the car and, before he'd even closed its door, Cole had slid over to the wheel, freed the brakes and hit the accelerator. He barely missed the gate guard, and did brush one autograph hunter, who reeled, but kept his feet.

Xas came across to Flora and Millie. He got in the driver's side and eased Millie out from under the wheel. He started the car, pulled out and drove away.

'Watts?' he said.

'No, let's take her to my place.' Flora gave Xas directions and then took Millie's free hand and closed her own about its tacky fingers.

They got Millie home and sat her down in the living room. Flora went to find a clean towel, a bandage, and iodine. She discovered she was out of iodine, which she used to paint her scars when they split.

When she came back to the living room with a towel and bowl of warm water, Xas said to her, 'It's money.'

Millie had volunteered this much to him. She was crying now, her hands over her face.

Money didn't explain the injury, unless Millie had been robbed.

Flora asked Xas if he'd please go out to a drugstore on the shore and get some iodine. Then she called him back when he headed for the front door. 'No, it's quickest to go out the back gate and follow the sand track through the waste lot,' she said. 'I used to go that way all the time. You can see which way to head once you've crossed the stream. The tops of the phoenix palms are visible.'

Xas left.

Flora wet the towel, wrung it out, and began to wipe the blood from Millie's hair. After a time Millie began to talk.

She said that she'd heard there was trouble at her bank. When she got there the doors were locked. 'Chained from the inside,' she said. 'They were all cowering in there, the cashiers back in the cages, the manager at his office door. A bunch of men with green eyeshades—those bank people who've always been so friendly and respectful.'

Millie said that a crowd had collected on the bank's steps and people began to push. 'They didn't mean to break the windows. We couldn't get in anyway. There were bars. But in the press someone lost their balance and put out an arm and pushed it through the bars and into the glass. The whole window came down mostly in one piece like a guillotine. I caught a few little bits that sprinkled down after.'

Millie had finished crying. She had her head bowed so that Flora could clean the cuts under her hair. Flora couldn't see her face.

'The bank people were shouting that our money wasn't there any more. They'd had all our money, but they went bust. I don't understand how that works.'

'I don't either,' Flora said. She'd read a little about the bank failures back East, and had only thought, complacently, that all her own money was in her house and car. She still had an old bank account from the time she'd had a mortgage, but she doubted there was anything in it. Having a bank account would be too much like planning a life. For the first time it occurred to Flora that her lack of direction, often a cause of shame, was at times like these something of a blessing. People with aims and dreams were in danger.

'It's all gone,' Millie said. 'What am I going to tell my friends in Texas?'

Xas returned after thirty minutes. He had a bottle of iodine in his pocket, and a ginger kitten cradled in his arms. The kitten was a very dark red, with definite bands of cream on his tail, big ears, big feet, and an eager, goofy expression.

Flora took the iodine, diluted it, and began to paint Millie's cuts. She said to Xas, 'Millie's bank went bust. There was a disturbance and someone broke a window.'

Xas didn't say anything. He put the kitten down—a big kitten, or young cat really. It minced over to the doorframe, went on tiptoes and smooched. It was a little unsteady on its feet. Xas said, 'I found him by the stream. Someone has had a go at his balls. Possibly a tomcat. He has been a mess there, but is getting better already.'

'I don't want a cat,' Flora said. 'You can take him home with you.'

'I'm not living anywhere.'

'What do you do with yourself when you're not with Cole?'

Xas didn't answer.

Millie said she'd like to lie down. Flora conducted her friend to the better of her two spare rooms and spread a rug on the bare mattress. She asked Millie if she wanted anything. Millie shook her head, winced, covered her eyes.

Flora went out and pulled the bedroom door to.

Xas was in the kitchen boiling the jug. The kitten was by the back door, hunched over a saucer of milk, his sharp shoulder blades making pale stars in his thick fur.

Flora watched Xas make tea. She repeated Millie's story in full. Then she said, 'Cole was in a hurry. I guess he didn't want to get involved.'

'He said, "It's just some shine having the vapours."'

'Well,' said Flora, flatly. 'And what do you think of that? I mean, doesn't it make you think something more than what it's so far been convenient for you to think?'

'Convenience doesn't come into it, Flora.'

He sounded sad, and a little disappointed in her, as well as Cole. But she liked it when he used her name.

'I was in love once,' he said, 'and it made me feel human.'

He brought the pot to the table and sat down. The cat had finished the milk and polished the saucer. It sniffed all around the plate then looked up at Xas, eyes glowing. It jumped up onto the chair between Xas and Flora, misjudging its leap and bashing its head on the bottom of the table. Flora laughed. Then she patted the cat to apologise for laughing. The cat's fur was thick and soft, and as she stroked it Flora raised a scent of sage and rosemary, and clean earth. 'He smells good,' she said.

'It was the first thing I noticed. Actually, I smelled him before he spoke to me—that perfume. It's like a kind of magic he has.' Xas smiled at the cat, then looked up at Flora. 'Why should I have to attach myself to a good person, anyway? Why not a bad person?'

'So you do think Cole's bad?'

Xas shook his head, then said, 'He's not good.'

They watched the cat wash. He was an energetic and fastidious groomer, but his balance wasn't very good.

'This cat is clumsy,' Flora said. She was enchanted. The fur on his spine was a rich auburn. His muzzle was almost round. His eyes were wide, hopeful, good-natured. 'Okay,' Flora said to the cat, 'you can stay.' She looked up at Xas, who was there, but absenting himself in silence. He seemed to have a trick of making himself difficult to see. She said, 'You might as well, too, for the time being.'

# Venice

## November–December, 1929

X as fixed Flora's roof, climbed up into the ceiling and lay on his back to settle the wavy rows of tiles back into place by pressing them with his hands and feet. He replaced all the rusted wire that held the tiles in place—then came down after a whole day under the roof, covered in sticky black dust, and with fingers scored by stripes of rust. He spent half an hour at the basin with a scrubbing brush, and even after that his hands looked as though they had been hennaed, like those of the Indian dancers Flora had once seen.

'Why didn't you wear gloves? I could have found some.'

Xas only shrugged and went to the window seat and his pile of library books.

Every other day he caught the trolley into the city and changed his books. He always used the short cut. Flora couldn't, for she was too stiff and uncertain on her feet for the scrambling it required. From the trolley line along the shore, he would get off at a certain stop and walk through the shallow built-up strip of stores and houses, then across a waste lot. Flora had explained the empty land. 'There's a plan at the county offices for a highway. This land is set aside for part of that highway. It's what is called "a paper road"—a road that exists only on paper.'

All the backyards of Flora's street opened onto the paper road, sandhills stilled by pasture, lupins, and wild mustard, by leggy plumbago where it was moist and, where it was dry, by creeping succulents, and beds of orange poppies. The land was divided by a tidal stream, and crisscrossed by sandy tracks. In one place the stream spread an apron of water to make a marsh, where ducks nested. Horses were sometimes grazed on the pasture below the thickets of live oak and white alder on the higher ground on the far side of the stream. And in the fall—Flora said—people from the properties along her street would go out with pails to gather berries. And sometimes, she said, when she looked out her kitchen window she would glimpse the vivid chestnut and vermilion plumage of an Asian pheasant, for, at the turn of the century, someone had released breeding pairs of pheasant and grouse and quail. Only the quail and pheasant had flourished.

Xas came and went by Flora's back gate. He contrived never to be in the house at mealtimes. She was left to suppose he went out to one of the cheap eateries along Windward Avenue. Sometimes Millie would catch him before he went, and give him money to buy her cigarettes. On those occasions he'd always arrive home with Millie's smokes, and her change.

When Xas had finished settling the roof tiles, he borrowed a ladder from one of Flora's neighbours and replaced some of her guttering. He cleared the drains, then cut the long grass in her backyard—kept cutting it, so that after a couple of months it looked likely to submit to his discipline and turn into a lawn again. He set up an outdoor clothes line. He lifted the sod in a rectangular patch in the newly reformed lawn and spent a few days preparing the soil with a compost of seaweed he hauled from the beach in sacks. And then, when it got cooler, he began to turn up with plants—mostly flowering annuals. He gathered seeds by pulling seed heads off the plants in other people's gardens. He'd do this when Flora and he were walking together from her trolley stop. He'd sit at her dining table sorting the pods from the lint in his pants pockets, putting them into piles on sheets of paper, and fending off the cat, O'Brien, who kept fishing for full pods as well as the emptied ones he was allowed to play with.

Flora watched Xas. She picked up O'Brien and put him on the floor. 'Seeds are a spring job,' she said. 'I'm a country girl. I know these things.'

'I want to be ready. I'll package these up for now. And I'm collecting tin cans too. I don't want to be scratching about looking for something to use as seed trays when the time comes.'

'So you'll still be here in the spring?'

'If you tell me to go away, I will.' He looked up as he said this and she tried to read his expression—got lost for a moment just looking at him. Then her heart clenched into a knot, as hard as the scars on her hips. 'I'm not supporting you,' she said.

'Of course not.'

Flora stamped her foot. 'I wasn't saying that I *refuse* to support you. What I mean is that you're doing all these things for me—mending my roof, mowing my lawn—and you're living on next-to-nothing; on whatever Cole gives you. And you don't actually have any agreement with him about money, do you? He just sometimes gives you something.'

'I only need a little, Flora. For the new guttering. For cat food. To put petrol in your car or Millie's when I borrow them. For the clubs.'

Xas was still going to jazz clubs with Millie. He liked his friend's company, but it seemed to take him a while to decide what he thought about the music.

Their nights would often start at the Apex on Central Avenue, where they listened to Ivie Andersen, a young singer with an eerily pure voice. Xas took to the singing before he made up his mind about the music. Then, one evening, he and Millie came back and he was on fire with enthusiasm. He sat at Flora's dining table twisting his short hair into little points and talking—practically panting with excitement about 'simple tunes and interesting textures, like a great talker shooting the breeze'. After that he and Millie began to turn on Flora's radio every evening at seven to listen to the late broadcast from Radio City Music Hall. They'd talk for hours about the Duke.

Flora felt a little jealous of Millie, and stepped up her campaign of taking Xas to any screening she could find of the films she loved. She showed him Murnau's *The Last Laugh*, Dreyer's *Joan of Arc*, Abel Gance's *Napoleon*, Lang's *Metropolis*, Weine. She was surprised by how little he'd seen.

'I saw *Metropolis* in Peru,' he said, when she asked him, as they were stepping out to the movies one evening. Her making suggestions of films she knew were showing and he must see.

'But you're German!' Flora said. 'You must have seen *Caligari*, and *Dr Faustus* and *The Last Laugh* too.'

'Someone in Le Crotoy told Millie I was German. But I only lived there for ten years.'

'You're not German by birth?'

'No.'

'Then what name did you put in your library card?'

'Why wouldn't I put Xas?'

'It's only a nickname.'

'All right—I put the name that's on my pilot's licence. My French pilot's licence.'

'Which is?'

'Jodeau.'

'But isn't Jodeau the name of your friend who died?'

'Yes.'

'So—Xas?'

'Yes?'

'Why am I calling you Xas?'

'It's my name.' He mused. 'Someday I'd like a document with my name on it.' He was smiling, cheerful, then suddenly his step faltered and he put a hand to his side.

Flora touched his shoulder.

'No,' he said. 'A human document, like a driver's licence, or a library card.'

Flora thought: 'He's not speaking to me.' But there was no one else near them. She said, 'Are you all right?'

He nodded and they walked on. He put out his hand and twisted the dried head off a poppy hanging over a garden fence.

'Does that hurt you?' Flora said.

He put his hand in his pocket and said, 'What?'

'Your side. You sometimes clutch at it, as if it hurts.'

Xas didn't answer.

'I think you have scars, like I do,' she said, and pointed at the place he'd touched.

'Yours give you a lot of trouble. Mine don't,' said Xas. 'That's why I fixed your roof. I wasn't trying to get you to ask me to stay. I just couldn't see you climbing up there.'

'I have enough money to *pay* someone to fix my roof. I'm not helpless. And I didn't think it was necessary to see to those tiles just yet—though I do appreciate it.'

'When the wind blew from the sea the tiles sounded like the streets of Paris after the coup d'état—the same loud stony clanking.'

'What?' Flora said again, then laughed because he was laughing. 'What does Cole think when you come over all whimsical like that?'

'When I'm with Cole I mostly just listen.'

'I bet you do.' Flora had put in quite a bit of time listening to Cole's tyrannous bouts of talk.

Xas gave Flora his hand to help her up the steps of the trolley. As he did he said, so casually that it was almost insinuating, 'I meant the coup d'état in 1851. Someone I knew was there and told me about it. About how the loosened cobbles made the street like a riverbed. The citizens kept prising them up to throw at the soldiers—then someone would put them back.' He handed Flora along the aisle and onto a bench. 'It works,' he said.

Flora told him he sounded like a defensive screenwriter. '"It works." Honestly!'

'I wasn't in Paris myself in 1851,' he said. 'I know that wouldn't work.'

'Needless to say,' said Flora, then giggled again, startled into it by his own sudden, pretty, wild laugh.

'No,' he said, through his laughter. 'Paul reported the sound of the loose cobbles. Paul de Valday, the Comte du Vully.'

'Oo la la!' said Flora, waiting for the rest of the story of his encounter with the aristocracy, or with history, whichever it was to be.

'I was in Damascus at the time,' he said.

Flora kept giggling. She looked around her and saw they were attracting attention—attention but not disapproval; people were smiling at them.

'Oh, all right, I'll play. What were you doing in Damascus when Paul what's-it told you about the cobbles?'

'No. I heard Paul's story later. I was in Damascus at the time of the coup d'état. I was trying to find out what had happened to my friend, Apharah Al-Khirnig.'

'Who was what?' Flora asked, wondering how long he could keep his game going, and how exotic his answers would become.

'Apharah was a cultivated and wealthy widow.'

'And what *had* happened to her?'

'I found her grave and put flowers on it. Waterlilies, which wouldn't have lasted long. Then I went to Scotland. Then back to France. Then to Turkey.'

'To another dark-eyed widow?'

'There's a salt dome in Turkey that is the gate to Hell.'

Flora nodded sagely. 'Naturally. And you wanted to scout out Hell before having to go there yourself. In due course.'

'I found a copper pipeline leading from an evaporation pond and disappearing into the ground at the salt dome. The pipe had been laid to convey water into Hell.'

'That's sensible,' Flora said. 'I don't imagine Hell has any water.'

He looked mildly chastened. 'I don't know why I never thought of a pipeline myself. I *carried* water. I suppose I must have wanted things to be difficult.'

'Xas—are you trying to prove to me that you can act?'

He shook his head. 'Why would I do that?'

She brushed his shoulder with her ear. 'I have connections in this town, you know.'

That night, late, after the bright layers of images from the three films they'd seen had loosened and lifted from his thoughts, Xas was able to think about his 'game' with Flora. He'd just followed a line of truth. He'd let himself speak openly. But it wasn't play. He was shocked at how right it had felt, and then how sad it was that it couldn't change anything. He had wanted to tell Flora. To tell her in order to imagine his life going on like this—with him lying in his narrow bed in the slightly damp back bedroom of Flora's house, his hands behind his head, listening to light rain tick on the secure roof tiles. Flora was in her room, asleep, with O'Brien curled in the crook of her knees. Millie was out at a club but would probably be back soon. And his lover, Cole, was in easy reach, but not actually there, which was more restful. Xas knew his desire to stay put wasn't about being at a convenient proximity to Cole. It was about Millie, in a mild way. But, really, it was about Flora, and her house. Xas simply felt that he'd like to stay. 'Stay here, rest here, recover here,' he thought, almost in prayer, but trying not to pray. He knew that what he wanted wasn't possible. But it was nice to have discovered what he wanted. That he wanted something at all. And that what he wanted was a good thing, not a bad thing.

# Château Marmont

## January, 1930

Cole had given up the house he'd been renting and had found a more secluded and better managed bolthole, a room on the ground floor of the newest apartment block on Sunset Boulevard.

Xas hadn't been to Cole's house, the man always wanted to meet somewhere else—at the studio gates, an airfield, or a street corner at a certain time. But when he shifted into a ground floor room off the garden of Château Marmont, Cole seemed to feel it was time to set some rules.

Cole was waiting for Xas at a door in the garden wall. He stood aside, but as he did so, said, 'I don't want you coming here unless you're invited.'

The sitting room of Cole's apartment had silk rugs on its tiled floor, soft furniture, and low light. The curtains were closed, the room dusky. Light was pooled on a polished wood sideboard under a Tiffany lamp. There was another lamp on a low table between two settees. The surface of the table was covered in glossy photographs—publicity shots of actresses. The photos were laid out in overlapping rows, as though Cole had been playing patience with them.

Cole sat back down in his place, before the photographs, and frowned at a full glass of milk on the corner of the table. The glass had a paper circle on top of it. Cole picked up the glass and passed it to Xas. 'Throw that out.'

Xas carried the glass to the small kitchen. He poured the milk away and rinsed the glass, passing his hands back and forth through the stained sunlight shining in the dark blue glass that framed the clear panes of the kitchen's windows. As he moved his hands through the blue light, the veins in their backs appeared and disappeared. He stood there for some time, running water, mesmerised by the sight of his own hands being more or less human.

'What are you doing?' Cole said. 'Come here and look at my list.'

Cole had a list of items and their prices—his planned spending on the opening of his film. 'I've wired a copy to my business manager. He called me yesterday to tell me to be a little more careful of my spending. "For an indefinite period," he said. Seems I took a hit with the rest of the market. He's had to lay some people off. It'll be all right though. This country runs on gasoline. Anyway—I'm cutting back. So I'll keep on running my current car, and I won't get married.'

'Were you planning to?'

'Yes.'

'To?'

'Kay. Or maybe Myra. I think perhaps I should marry Myra. But, anyway, I made it clear to my manager that, no matter what, I'm committed to making a big splash with the premiere. He's an old stick-in-the-mud. He reckons I'm only planning to throw some kind of big party, but this film's opening has to be an occasion, it has to say that the movie has arrived, and that it's unparalleled.' Cole turned the list so that Xas could read it: *stunt planes, coloured smoke pots, klieg lights, arc lamps, jazz bands, vaudeville acts, lilies, roses …*

Xas looked at the list, then up at Cole. 'You called me and asked me to come over. What did you have in mind?'

Cole flicked back his cuff. 'My watch has stopped.'

Cole had recently given Xas a watch of his own. It had been in heavy rain a couple of times, but was still working. Xas told Cole the time.

The man reset his watch and wound it.

'You asked me over to get the correct time?' Xas said.

'I haven't seen you since you jumped out of my car at the studio gates.'

'To help Millie.'

'And you're mad at me for not helping? I don't see why. You know where I draw the line. I don't expect to be entangled in your life. We're not *affianced*.' Cole paused, and seemed to consider Xas's silence—a silence perhaps striking even to someone hard of hearing.

Xas said, 'Millie was saving to establish a Coloured flight school. Her bank went bust. She imagined her money was still there, in its vault, because she'd carried cash into the building, dollar by dollar. Actually, you know, that's how I assumed banks worked—they kept people's money, took it and stored it, like wine in a wine cellar.'

Cole began to laugh, and kept on till he had to wipe his eyes. 'And you're so slick with a slide rule! How can you understand math, but not money? And what do you do with your money, given your naivety about banks?'

'I spend it,' Xas said. 'I fritter it away on clubs and booze and downpipes.'

'Did you say downpipes?'

'Yes. I fixed Flora's guttering.'

The man studied Xas through narrowed eyes. 'Why are you always so helpful?' he asked. 'Not just to me but to—all sorts.'

And Xas found himself answering with a kind of desperate impatience, 'I have to live with people.'

But Cole was going on, developing some point. 'I'm more choosy. I like *talented* people,' he said. 'I recognise that, although you're a nobody, you're quite talented. For instance, you're analytical—you noticed the torsional weakness of the wings of my plane.' He gestured at the photos on the table before them. 'And you are beautiful. Didn't you notice that when you came in I was looking from you to these publicity shots, making comparisons? You never seem to be looking at me when I'm looking at you, unless we're like this, face to face.'

'I get alongside you, Con, so I can speak into your good ear.' Xas looked down at his own hands, then sidelong at Cole's, the fine-grained skin, faintly roped with veins, light tan, with slightly too long, but very clean fingernails. Xas wanted those hands touching him. He wanted not to have anything to hide. Cole's curiosity about what he did with his money was unusual. Usually Cole and he would work on whatever problem Cole was playing with in his mind. Xas had helped Cole with the film, as some kind of technician. He'd helped test aircraft. He'd chauffeured Cole about, fetched sandwiches, making sure they were made to the correct prescription. He'd listened to Cole's plans.

It had been good. Xas had walked into the fogbank to follow Cole's thinking, and it had been good. He'd watched Cole set up his dinners with actresses, watched him go out pressed and perfumed and *premeditated*—and once or twice Cole would turn to him and kiss him like someone stuffing their mouth while talking. The kisses happened, then the talking resumed and Xas hadn't had to answer any awkward questions.

Now here he was, sitting in a curtained, dimly lit room, feeling tired. He sighed. 'All right,' he said, 'I'm a nobody. Good to get that established.'

'You're not making the best of yourself.' Cole said.

But Xas had stopped listening, for, in that moment, he'd remembered that, though he was a nobody, he did have means. He had the means to help Millie. He had money of a sort. All he had to do was to find a valley near a lake in the Californian Sierras, and the split apple rock into which he had dropped his only real earthly possession—a rope of perfectly matched black pearls.

Fifty years before he had been caught in a forest fire. The blaze had jumped from one ridge to another, torn sails of flame separating from the wave of fire cresting hundreds of feet high. The flames were behind him, then before him—emptying the valley of air. His mule dropped to its knees and rolled onto its side, kicking. The fire was cacophonous, but still Xas could hear the rasping hitch the animal made as it tried to suck breath in a vacuum. And he heard a bright smash from the saddlebags, where he kept the photographs he'd taken on his trip across the Rockies. His mule was finished. His camera and the fifty glass plate photographs were too bulky to save. But he remembered his pearls, took them off, wrapped them in his shirt, and dropped the bundle into a deep crack in a boulder split like an apple. After that he walked on through the flame's agonising but ineffectual heat, held upright in blinding, billowing transparency, almost afloat on the fire's twisting updrafts. He emerged on a smoking hillside, naked but for his charred leather belt, and smeared with ash. He didn't go back when the valley cooled. He didn't try to retrieve his pearls, because he wasn't ready to discover he'd lost them.

The pearls had once belonged to Lucifer, who had worn them to demonstrate—in a way that his indestructible body could not—that he was above discomfort, above the fire, living in the shade and insulation of his book-filled fortress. All angels are indestructible, and if they are also proud they must keep something perishable close to them and declare: 'I mean to keep this.'

With this recollection came a feeling of ash coating his skin. Xas remembered, and felt his empty, superficial self drifting up like feathers of ash on a forest fire's thermals.

'You're smiling again,' Cole said, bemused. Then, 'Can you do something for me?' Xas heard the springs in the sofa creak as Cole moved. 'Come here now,' Cole said.

Again Xas was taken in by everything: Cole's thick oiled hair, the strength of his hands, and the flushed, furred lobe of his good ear.

They were kissing, but something was wrong.

'I don't do this with people like you,' Cole whispered. 'So you have to do what I want.'

Xas found himself in a horror of puzzlement. Somehow Cole didn't smell or taste right. He had a smell like dry mouse droppings at the back of a cupboard.

'Take your shirt off,' Cole whispered. 'Turn over,' he said. 'You can't always keep your back against the bed.'

Xas made a soft noise, somewhere between laughter and distress. 'I'm sorry,' he said. 'But I have lines I draw, just like you.'

Cole paused. He asked, 'Is there something you're hiding? Something *wrong* with you?'

'Yes.'

'Something freakish? Or something like Flora?'

Xas saw an opportunity to distract the man. He said, 'What exactly happened to Flora?'

'She can tell you, if she wants. What happened to you?'

Xas was silent.

'Is it ugly?'

Xas stirred and murmured, 'Yes.'

'I don't want to press you,' Cole said. 'And I don't want

to see. I don't like ugly things. But you would tell me if it was something contagious?' Cole must have had some fear pushing him to go on, for he added, confidingly, 'I've been feeling off-colour lately.'

Without thinking, Xas said, 'I think you *are* sick.'

'Why do you think that?'

'You smell different.'

Xas had hoped to distract Cole, but was a little alarmed at how successful he was. 'You didn't answer my question,' Cole said. 'You didn't tell me whether or not it was contagious.'

Xas put his mouth against Cole's good ear. 'No,' he said, then touched the lobe with his tongue. 'It's an injury, not a disease.'

'Good,' Cole said. His voice was tight. Then, 'I'm not sick,' he added.

In the early hours of the morning, Cole was restless, and exhausted, and talkative still. He wanted to try out more ideas. But everything he said let Xas know that Cole thought he was angling for something—permanent employment, a salary. Xas listened, and ran his hands through the man's thick, slick hair, while Cole kept trying to interview him.

'Come on, then,' Cole said. 'Why don't you try to impress me—without unbuttoning your shirt.' He peered at Xas, his head reared back on the pillow. 'Hasn't that been your aim all along—to impress me?'

When Xas didn't respond Cole went on. 'I think you are one of those people who can only answer questions, like the clever boys at my prep school. You can't think what to say, given a broad charter.' He stroked Xas's face. 'But you're better than that, too, aren't you? You have your beauty, and your facility—your way of turning out to be good at things.'

'Con,' Xas said, 'what do you imagine I want? Do you think I do this,' he kissed Cole, 'in hopes of a position, or income?' He stroked the man's chest; felt both Cole's heart and his own beating in the tips of his fingers. 'I'm interested in your life, and what you'll do with it.'

Cole sat up abruptly, and curled his arms around his crooked knees. He said, 'For now why don't you go get us some more ice. I'm going to take another shower.'

And Xas thought: 'I've said what he wanted me to say.'


Cole opened the door of the room for Xas as someone opens the door for a bee that has wandered indoors in the hope that it will find its way out again. And then, once Xas had put on his boots and laced them up, Cole had another idea. He decided to make an offer. Of money. 'Before I wire my list of expenses to my business manager I'm of a mind to add a few thousand "miscellaneous".' He winked.

Xas came and leaned in the doorframe opposite the man. It was January, crisp in the mornings, but only cold when it rained, which it did with modest infrequency. The sun was out. The bougainvillea had opened, and its colour warmed the air.

Cole said, 'If you had ten thousand dollars to invest, now, when businesses are closing down all over and almost everyone has retrenched their spending, where would you put it? That's my question for you. And don't tell me you'd give it to that Coloured girl.'

'You want to see if I have vision, don't you?' Xas said. 'Because that's what you're proud of in yourself.'

'With just ten thousand you'd have to have a lot of vision. With most of the exciting industries it's better to have real money and to spread the investment.'

'Sound recording. Aviation. Movies,' Xas said. 'I know. I have your list even if I don't have your vision—or any real money. But I can think of one safe business, somewhere I could put the whole ten thousand.'

'Safe? Even now?'

'In a growing city.'

'Construction,' Cole said, and shrugged. 'But growth will slow for quite some time. And there's oil exploration—overall a great business, but chancy.'

'You can test me if you want to, Cole, but you'll have to trust me, and be patient about the results.'

'I'll think about it. I'd better not make the ten thousand a whole sum or my manager will say, "This doesn't look like a total of several miscellaneous items." So we'll say nine thousand and change.' He inclined toward Xas and rubbed his hands together. He took a careful look out into the garden to check that no one could see, then kissed Xas again—beginning the kiss proprietary but finishing with the pressure of true possession. He broke off and breathed at Xas, 'You're *my* miscellaneous.'

# Flora's paper road

## January, 1930

On a dank, late January evening, Xas was on his way back to Flora's. It was after dark, and foggy when he got off the trolley at the stop along the Venice shore. He left the beach by an alley between a pool hall and a chop suey house, then passed the little lean-to where a man worked mending sewing machines, and another shack that had a butter churn standing by its door—no one ever seemed to be home there. He reached the start of the sandhills.

The track from the shore to Flora's back gate was fringed by orange poppies, their bells pinched closed in the damp air. In the dips by the path the tangles of bushes were reefs where fog clung like seaweed. When Xas passed a flat stretch of rushes and wet sod, he could hear a soft quacking conversation, but couldn't see the ducks. He found the stile that took him over a fence, where the track went along for a while beside a brackish waterway. Xas crossed the water balancing on a sewer pipe. The pipe's rusting iron was wrapped in tarred cloth, and sticky beneath his boot soles.

On the other side the track continued along by a stand of low, matted live oak. When the trees came to an end, Xas was out in the open, surrounded by blind white mist, with no landmarks in view, only the track leading him on. Up and down it went, a course of cold sand. The fog had set its surface, but the sand was dry underneath and Xas's footprints showed behind him as white splashes on the dark grey path.

Xas didn't hear the archangel coming, for his wings were silent, mist lubricating each feather. The archangel dropped down out of the air as stealthy as an owl. He knocked Xas over and pinned him on the ground.

'Ha!' he breathed, a satisfied predatory noise, then added, offhand, 'I wasn't actually looking for you.'

'Then perhaps you don't need to sit on me,' Xas said.

Lucifer extended one thin finger of a wing hand and scratched Xas's neck. Xas felt the archangel's nail tear his skin. He felt the bright, frightening pain of damage—something he'd not experienced for a very long time—not since he'd woken up in the Soldiers' Gallery of Château Vully to find his wings had been cut off.

Lucifer put his mouth by Xas's ear and said, 'He feels that,' as solemnly, savagely happy as a tiger delaying his kill by making sport of his prey.

Xas wasn't sure whether Lucifer was talking to God about him, or to him about God.

When—some twenty-five hundred years before—God and Lucifer had signed him, and made their treaty, they had agreed to split both the price and benefits of his freedom, which is to say that Lucifer got the benefits and God the price. '*Xas can go freely,*' the treaty said. '*Lucifer shall have his pleasures and God his pains.*' Xas had very little idea why they chose to tie themselves to him in that way, though perhaps it was to keep each other honest, for, if Lucifer had the pleasures of his freedom then Lucifer wouldn't interfere with him, and if God shared his pains, then God would protect him. Xas had believed that was the idea—until the day he lost his wings. (The treaty had a third clause: *Only when Xas is with Lucifer will Lucifer be with God.* But Xas didn't like to think about that.)

The archangel abruptly rolled over onto his back and lifted Xas above him, holding the angel by throat, wrists and ankles. As Lucifer went over, Xas heard his wings hiss and clatter, his plaits and pearls sliding from his neck and shoulders. He looked down at the terrible scars on Lucifer's chest, partly hidden by the gleaming ropes of his jewels and hair. Xas noticed that the archangel had a residue of salt in his ears, and salt on his bare arms. Xas knew, of course, that Lucifer had come from Hell to earth through the salt dome in Turkey, Hell's only gate. Then Xas was immersed in the cloud of the archangel's bodily perfume—a resinous scent of apple, ozone, and lightning—and he lost all the strength in his muscles. He found that he couldn't take his eyes off the glassy points of the archangel's canine teeth, just visible between his relaxed lips.

There is nothing more appalling and paralysing in nature than an archangel. Archangels have no natural enemies. Xas knew that this archangel wasn't the most dangerous, wasn't the great champion of Heaven—but he was brilliant, and princely, and playful, and full of the malice of misery.

Lucifer looked at Xas with distaste. He said, 'What *are* you wearing?' Then, 'You smell,' then, 'What do you smell of?' Thoughtful.

'Cologne,' Xas said. He'd been with Cole, and hadn't washed. He smelled of Cole, of sweat, cologne, and the mousy smell of Cole's infection.

Lucifer said, 'Listen,' then was quiet as though they were both supposed to be listening to God.

'No,' Xas said, refusing again.

'*No*,' Lucifer mimicked, and moved the angel back and forth above him as fathers fly their babies. Xas had always liked the look of that. He knew that parents only did it to make their babies laugh and—instinctively—to rock their infants' senses of space, motion and position into health and capability. But to him it had always looked as if those parents were saying to Heaven: '*I hold this happiness between me and You,*' and, if they were, then that was instinct too, the instinct humans must have, despite all their ideas about a just and loving God, to preserve themselves from that God's unloving love of perfection, His exacting beneficence.

'Why would I be looking for you,' Lucifer said, 'when I have nothing to say to God?' He repeated, in exactly the same tone, 'I have nothing to say to You,' this time addressing God. He pushed himself up off the ground using one set of wings. The sand billowed up around them. He landed on his feet and let go his multiple grip, keeping hold of Xas with only the hand on one top wing. He stretched his wing high over his head so that Xas dangled by one ankle.

Xas's jacket flopped over his head, and Lucifer shook him till coins dropped out of his pockets.

Xas had had enough. He contracted his stomach muscles, bent his spine, whipped up and grabbed the hand clamped to his ankle. He closed his teeth on it. He bit down till he broke the downy skin, and the sinew in the archangel's hand creaked, and the archangel's blood spilled into his mouth. Xas sank his teeth into Lucifer—and learned something new.

Archangels may have no natural enemies but, it turned out, Lucifer had a remarkable array of defences. There was no reason—no divine design evident in the fact that Xas's spit on the permeable surfaces of human mucosa—men's mouths, women's mouths and vulvas—could make men stiff and responsive, and women wet and responsive. Why would God have made an angel like that? And why would God have made the blood of an archangel, who had no natural enemies, so toxic?

Xas's mouth began to burn, then his vision blurred and he became breathless. He opened his teeth and let go. The muscles of his jaw and neck stiffened, then locked in a spasm. Foam filled his mouth and nose and burst from them.

Lucifer dropped him.

Xas thrashed about on the ground. The half moons of his own eye sockets eclipsed his vision, then he saw red, and a roaring filled his head.

*

It was Millie who found him. She was coming home from the Villa Venice, making her way in the pre-dawn dark. She'd nearly reached Flora's back gate when a noise made her stop. She couldn't make any sense of the soft scuffles and thumps or the sound of breath bubbling through froth. Whatever it was that was making the strange noises lay in a hollow before the last rise in the track that branched off the main way and terminated at Flora's gate. The hollow was shadowy and, Millie later said, all she could make out was motion, a frenzied thrashing that seemed to form a knot of clearer air in the mist there. Whatever it was, Millie knew she'd have to go past it in order to get to the house.

She edged down the hill, shading her eyes from the streaks of light shining through the gaps between the plank palings of the fence. (Flora, knowing that both Millie and Xas came the back way, had left the light on in the kitchen.) A clot of kicked-up sand hit her leg and she broke into a run, jumped over the place and scrambled up the slope. At the fence she stopped and looked back. In the lines of light shining between the palings she saw that was it Xas. It was at that moment Millie heard the sound of one of her own records, Duke Ellington's 'Black Beauty'. Flora was at home. Millie hauled open the gate and ran to the house.

Flora brought a blanket and they threw it over Xas and pinned his flailing limbs by lying on him. 'No, let me do it,' said Millie, who was worried about Flora's scars.

'I'm down here now. Did you know he had fits, Millie?'

Millie shook her head.

Flora, who was close to Xas's face, saw that the foam streaming from his nose and mouth was tinged pink—but a little less so than the smears on his hair or the puddle of foam around his head. She hoped that the blood was only from a bitten tongue, and that the bleeding was easing. The foam gave off a fiery resinous perfume. 'Has he poisoned himself?' Flora said.

Millie looked about for a bottle or a pill box. 'Maybe he's snake-bit,' she said.

'I can't help you carry him,' said Flora. 'Sorry.'

'Once he's quieter we can roll him onto the blanket and drag him in,' said Millie.

'Jesus—what *is* that?' said Flora. The resinous smell alone made her heart pound and her mouth fill with metallic saliva. It wasn't unpleasant, but somehow terribly alarming.

There were pauses now between Xas's spasms. Millie let go one of his hands to retrieve a dollar note that was sticking out from a flattened spray of lupin. 'There's money all over the place,' she said.

Flora touched Xas's face, felt the wet foam, then snatched back her hand and wiped it on her shirt. Her fingers throbbed as though she had brushed against the ruffled stingers trailing below the sail of a Portuguese Man-of-War. She told herself that the sensation must be imaginary, but her fingers continued to smart.

Millie got off Xas and helped Flora up. 'He's still breathing,' she said, and Flora supposed that her friend had been thinking the same thing she had, that Xas might succumb completely to whatever this was. Millie continued, 'My cousin was bitten by a rattler. But it wasn't like this.' She caught up the blanket and spread it beside Xas's trembling form. 'Though I suppose this might be the beginning of the paralysis,' she said, uncertain.

'We need a doctor. Let's get him to my car.' Flora gave Millie a shove. 'You roll him onto the blanket. I'm sure I can help you drag him.'

Millie did as she was told, while Flora went on, speaking faster all the time. 'He can't have meant to kill himself. He just got out another big stack of library books. And he just restocked my cupboards.'

Millie said, 'Restocking your cupboards might be his way of taking care of you, seeing to you before going out into the wasteland to drink lye.'

'This isn't lye.'

'Poison. You know what I mean.' Millie added, 'I knew a guy who drank lye. It burned his insides out.'

The women each took a corner of the blanket and pulled Xas's now inert body slowly up the slope to the gate, through it, across the lawn and into the light of the spider web encrusted lamp above Flora's back door. There Millie crouched and searched Xas's legs for a bite, for puncture marks in the fabric of his trousers.

'He has a gash on his cheek,' Flora said, and then realised that she'd never seen a scratch on him, or a bruise, or any kind of blemish.

'There is a mark on his ankle too,' Millie reported. 'Like a rope burn, as if he's been tied.'

'His wrists are all right,' Flora said. 'There's no marks of any kind on them.'

'So it's not bloody Cole,' Millie said.

Flora started to laugh. She laughed at Millie's vehemence, and because they both knew what she meant. And she laughed in a kind of wry distress because she understood that all this time she had been expecting to see signs on her friend's body of Conrad Cole's passionate ill-use.

Millie carefully turned Xas's head. She slipped her fingers into his mouth to check his tongue.

'Careful.' Flora didn't know how to warn her friend about the foam.

Millie gingerly pushed two fingers and a thumb between Xas's teeth. His cheeks stretched as Millie's fingers probed his mouth. It seemed that Millie wasn't stung, as Flora had been, though she did say, 'This frothy stuff tickles like sodium bicarb.'

Flora had a thought then that maybe Xas was faking. Perhaps he'd staged all this. Maybe this was all-of-a-piece with his odd habitual altruism, his strange stories, his manic busyness. With considerable difficulty, Flora got down on her knees. Millie put out a hand to help, then reminded, 'We should get him to a doctor.'

Flora slapped Xas hard across one wet cheek. The moisture had an oily, acidic feel to it, but stung her palm no more now than the slap itself did. 'Stop it,' Flora whispered, and slapped him again, backhand this time.

'Okay. Enough,' Millie said. 'You're reminding me of a teacher I had who was always slapping me when I couldn't stop coughing. He can't help it, you know.'

'He's putting it on.' Flora was determined. She hit him again.

He moaned. It was an enormously satisfying sound and, hearing it, Flora felt masterful, faintly amorous and, for an instant, completely free of pain. It was as though by doing violence to him she was passing on her chronic pain, handing it up to some vast, engulfing, anodyne being. She had an image of herself as a child in church, sitting beside her grandmother, exempt from everything but keeping still, taking the collection plate from a person at the head of the pew and passing it on to Grandma without having to put anything in it herself. She started to cry. She sobbed, 'Stop faking,' and punctuated it with another slap.

'Flora!' Millie was shocked.

And then Xas spoke. He said something. Flora didn't hear what it was. She seemed to lose her sense of continuity. She had meant to hit him again. She saw that her hand was raised, frozen, up by her head. The blood on her palm was so red it looked independently alive, as though it might any moment coalesce from a smear into a drop, then harden into something living, like a beetle perhaps, a red beetle, that would fly away, leaving her hand wiped clean.

Millie had her own hands over her ears and her shoulders raised as if to defend herself against a very loud sound.

'I've gone deaf,' Flora said—and heard herself saying it.

'Jesus,' said Millie. 'What was that? What did he say? Was that really just him speaking?'

Xas was trying to lift his head, his eyelids fluttering. A line of white showed beneath his thick lashes, his consciousness as far away and threatening as lightning on the horizon. Millie stooped again to stroke his head. 'Honey,' she said, 'what happened?'

Xas wouldn't let the women put him in Flora's car. He held onto the door, wedged himself there. They tried to prise his hands free, but weren't able to. Finally he managed to say, 'No.'

Millie helped him to sit on the running board.

'It's over,' he said.

'Was it a fit?'

He peered at her, his head still wobbling on his neck.

'Epilepsy?' Flora said. That would figure—epilepsy and religiosity, like some character in Dostoevsky.

Xas nodded. It looked like capitulation rather than assent. Of course he wouldn't have wanted them to know he was an epileptic. Flora thought of his pilot's licence and things began to make sense—Xas had fits and hid the fact because he didn't want to lose his licence. All the disproportionately alarming events of the last hour instantly became much less scary.

'We thought you'd been bitten by a snake,' Millie said.

Xas laughed, then said, 'Sorry.'

Flora wanted to kiss him, despite the sand and muck on his face. Millie did kiss him, planted one on the top of his cropped, velvety head.

'Flora, can I borrow your car?' Xas asked.

'And how does this relate to your fit?'

'It doesn't—unless you're worried I'll crash it.'

'Don't.'

'It's only for a few days.'

'Why do you want to borrow my car?'

'I'm just reverting to my last constructive thought before—before my fit. I've been planning for a few weeks to ask whether I could borrow your car and go see if I can find something I lost somewhere, some time ago.'

Something, somewhere, some time ago. Xas's obscurity seemed to Flora as much a part of him as his occasional strange literal-mindedness.

'Say yes, Flora,' Millie said. Then, to Xas, 'Or— sweetie—you could borrow my car.'

'Flora's is more beaten up—in case I do have another fit,' he said and gave Flora a weak but teasing smile.

'Don't,' she said again.

Millie put her hand under his arm and helped him up. 'Come inside,' she said, 'and let us put you to bed.'

# Los Angeles

## February, 1930

X as had Flora's car, so Millie offered to drive Flora over to Culver City where she had a meeting with Crow about his next film. Millie dropped Flora at the studio gates and she walked unmolested through a clutch of autograph hunters and onto the lot.

Crow was waiting in the writers' suite with Wylie White, a playwright turned screenwriter. When Flora arrived Wylie informed her gloomily that he and Crow were having a quarrel. He said, 'Crow is expounding his ideas.'

'I do not expound,' said Crow and whipped his feet off Wylie's desk, preparatory to jumping up and taking charge of the room by towering over its occupants and furniture.

Flora glanced at the open stove door and spotted the bottle Wylie kept hidden there. She found a glass, wiped it, and poured herself a whisky.

Crow decided not to get up, after all, only pulled the

chair Flora had her hand on nearer to him before she sat. He said, 'Wylie and I are talking about dialogue.'

'Crow's taken my screenplay and scribbled all over its facing pages. If we record all his dialogue our film will be as long as *Greed* before they cut it.'

'It will if the dialogue is spoken by someone like Johnny Swanson.' Crow named a fading star. 'Swanson, intoning, and gazing into the air beyond the camera as if he's dazzled by footlights. He cultivated that look on stage, and his stagey voice to go with it.'

Flora interrupted. 'Connie, I thought you despised sound.'

'For one thing it's against my philosophy to despise the inevitable,' said Crow. And Flora wondered why it was that all the men in her life had to have philosophies. 'For another, what I really disliked was having to do things over in *Spirit*. The strain on the budget.' Crow threw his long arms wide as if to gather in a scoop of the room. 'I love talk,' he said. 'Apart from learning to fly, big-game fishing, watching my own horses compete down at Agua Caliente, and being in bed with a beautiful woman, most of the real excitement of my life has taken place in conversations. Film talk should be like that, *big*, stuffed with substance.'

Wylie picked up the dog-eared pages, and waved them about. 'This isn't substance! This is characterisation!'

'That's the substance I care about! Jokes! Bitching! Flirtation! Bullying! How people *behave* and what it says about them.' Crow leapt up, lunged at the stove, grabbed the bottle, and filled his glass. He didn't offer it to

Wylie, but turned to Flora with a smile and a courteous indrawing of all his limbs and asked her if she wanted a refill. She did.

'No one talks like this!' Wylie shouted, still waving the pages.

'Are you proposing that people in films speak like the man in the street?'

'Connie, this is a movie, not Shakespeare!'

'Ah, Shakespeare—the only excuse we have not to talk like the man in the street. If it ain't Shakespeare it had better be Joe Blow.' Crow turned to Flora again. 'I ask you—do you think that you talk like the man in the street?'

'No. But I'm the woman in the street.'

'See!' Crow gave a hoot. '*That's* dialogue!'

Wylie threw down the screenplay. 'No, dammit, that's conversation.'

Crow began pummelling the writer's desk. Several of Wylie's pencils jumped out of the jar he kept them in and rolled away.

'Two things!' Crow yelled. 'One: "I'm the woman in the street" is an idea. An idea about the world. Two: if she says "I'm the woman in the street" to draw the attention of her interlocutor to the fact of her sex, then *sex* is involved—because she's gently reminding the man that she's a girl. She is also reminding the audience that she's the girl in relation to the man. The audience is always present, so is always being addressed by characters in movies!'

Flora reflected that Crow couldn't have drunk too much if he could still pronounce 'interlocutor'. But then Crow was one of those people who disprove arguments based on 'what people actually say'.

'She was addressing *you*, Connie,' Wylie muttered, sly and satisfied.

Crow looked flummoxed and stalled, then he glanced at Flora. She raised her glass to toast him. Crow said, gravely, 'Thank you, Flora. Believe me, I haven't forgotten you're a girl.'

'Can I have a look at the screenplay?' Flora said.

Wylie tossed it to her. She fumbled her catch and the pages exploded into a flapping mess around her. Flora picked up the one page left on her lap. Crow's additions were long, and very funny. She said, 'How do you expect the actors——?' then stopped, on catching a gleam of triumph behind Wylie's round spectacles.

Crow said, 'People in talkies are talking slower than people actually do. Is that natural? But, anyway, should we appeal to what's natural, or to what's right? What will *seem* right.'

Wylie butted in. 'Stahr says——'

'If you quote me Monroe Stahr I shall thump you, Wylie,' Crow said. Then, to Flora, 'It's all style, see? Movies are artifice. So why not have actors speak faster than people do?'

'They won't be heard, Connie.'

'I say they will. If the human brain can manage a dogfight, then it can manage to sit in a cinema listening to people talking at sixty miles per hour.'

'Okay,' said Flora, 'that seems reasonable.'

Wylie said, 'Thurston does not need to start his speech barking "No!" seven times. It sounds like he's on Benzedrine—I mean, as if *he* is, not just *you*, Connie.'

'Dick will know how to do it—like a big, gorgeous, good-natured bully. "No, no, no, no, no, no, no." Touching the girl at the same time.' To demonstrate Crow placed a hand on Flora's forearm and leaned toward her, looking at her brow rather than into her eyes. 'No, no, no, no, no, no, no,' he said, then, 'See?'

Wylie got up and gathered some pages off the floor. He looked at them, disgusted. 'Here's two pages of yak and only one direction, "He watches her fiddle with cutlery".'

'It speaks volumes,' said Crow.

Flora said, 'Wouldn't it be better if it read, "He watches her fiddle with his utensils"?'

Crow laughed.

'Get out of here, both of you,' Wylie said. 'Leave me the bottle.'

Flora remained sitting for a minute, only raised one foot as Crow picked up and reassembled the screenplay. 'I'm getting this typed up, as it is,' Crow said to Wylie. 'And we'll try it that way.' He gave Flora his hand and helped her out of her chair. As they went out he said to the writer, 'And Wylie, stay away from Stahr. I'll deal with Stahr.'

They went down the steps. Flora said, 'I'll stop in at the commissary and see who's there.'

'How's your friend?'

'Which of my friends?'

'That man you're living with.'

Flora frowned. 'I'm not living with him, he's just—living with me.'

'Hmmm,' said Crow. Then, 'Is that addressed to me?'

'Don't, Connie.'

'Don't what?'

'Don't flirt with me.'

'All right.' He squeezed her hand and kissed her on the hair.

'Did you call me in just to witness an argument?'

He said, 'I wouldn't have won it if you hadn't witnessed it.'

'No, I guess not,' she said. It was true that Crow was always more assertive with a female in his audience.

They walked along for a little time in a slow traffic of cars, and costumed figures on bicycles, and alongside one piece of scenery on wheels, a tropical beach backdrop that still reeked of turpentine.

Flora said, 'Why do you ask about Xas?'

'I'm just curious. He's living with you. Gil would have been curious about that too. So I guess I'm acting as Gil's proxy.'

'Xas is sleeping with Conrad Cole.'

'I've heard that too. But that's a big club, Flora. Living with you is a little more exclusive, wouldn't you say?'

'It isn't significant, Connie.'

'Sure, sure,' said Crow then kissed her once more when they reached the place where they were to part ways.


A couple of days later Flora sat in on a studio screening of *Flights of Angels*. Afterward Cole asked her to wait, he wanted to speak to her. She braced herself for the usual bad news, that he'd like her to cut the movie again, just when they had a date for its first screening, and it was opening in theatres countrywide—and how much time did Cole think it took to make hundreds of prints?

Flora remained in her seat as the screening room emptied. Cole went out with the studio people and didn't come back for a whole twenty minutes. Flora had given him up and was putting her coat on when he reappeared. He loped down the aisle and began to pace before the blank screen. He paused for a moment, and glanced up at the projectionist's booth. Flora looked back too, saw the lights go out. And, as though this was a cue, 'Where is Xas?' Cole said.

Flora was surprised and didn't immediately answer.

'Come on!' Cole said.

'He borrowed my car for some business of his own.'

'I gave him money,' Cole said, as if this followed on from her statement.

Flora waited for more. She knew Cole had been paying Xas, but wondered if he'd finally paid him off.

Cole began to bite his thumb.

'How much money did you give him?' Flora felt that she was throwing him her question as, in a film, someone might use a belt or branch or jacket to pull another person out of quicksand. 'How much?' was a question that would keep Cole talking.

It worked. Cole took his thumb out of his mouth—its nail bloody at the quick. 'Ten thousand,' he said. Then,

'Everybody has ambition.' He began to pace again. 'Even layabout Gus at the gas station has ambition.'

Flora nodded in encouragement.

Cole said, 'I can't be near anyone I can't trust.'

Flora watched her employer, wary. 'Sorry,' she said, 'I have a bit of a hangover. I'm not following you. Do you mean that you can't trust Xas because he's not ambitious? Or because he is?'

Cole looked bewildered for a second, then simply continued. 'I'm not saying I need people to jump through hoops for me, only to be fully attentive to my needs.'

'Wasn't he?' Flora asked, but Cole didn't seem to hear her.

'That's just what I happen to ask. That's my requirement. That's not unreasonable, is it?' Cole planted his feet and glared at Flora. She was very glad that there was a row of seats between them. She nodded faintly and Cole went on. 'Do you have any idea how many people I have on my payroll? Thousands. Paying people is straightforward. I'm a straightforward person. Anyone who thinks that it's too much trouble being paid, and being accountable, can just walk away.'

'So—you're saying Xas has walked away? From you? Because he took offence when you paid him?'

Cole put one knee on the seat in front of Flora, and loomed. 'He said to me: "Whatever you want, Cole. Whatever you say." He said I could put my foot on his neck.'

Flora didn't have any trouble believing this. Xas was fearless, and immune to indignity, and there was *something wrong with him*. Flora gnawed her lip, then finally voiced this thought. 'There's something wrong with him, Con.'

Cole stared at her. The muscles in his jaw bunched and jumped. 'I know. And I don't buy his "circus freak" line. He only wants to make me think of carnivals because carnivals move on. That's what he's done. He got what he wanted, and gave himself a way out.'

Flora said, 'What do you mean "circus freak"?'

'He says he has something wrong with him. Something congenital. That's why he won't take off his shirt.'

Flora said she'd thought Xas was only shy. 'Or something,' she added, uncertain.

'I should have known better!' Cole shouted suddenly. He turned away from Flora to face the screen. He clenched his fists and threw his arms wide. For a moment he held this pent-up, beseeching, histrionic pose.

'Con,' Flora said. 'Xas was ill. The other night he had some kind of fit. Maybe that has something to do with wherever he's got to.'

Cole dropped his arms and rounded on her. 'I know he's sick. And *I'm* sick. And that's why he's made himself scarce.'

Flora frowned at him.

Cole said, under his breath, 'They're always the filthy ones.'

Flora understood what Cole meant. 'The filthy ones' were the men Cole slept with—his secret liaisons. Flora guessed that Cole had picked up a dose from who knew where—possibly even Xas, though Xas's fit hadn't been at all suggestive of venereal disease, except maybe tertiary syphilis in its end stage.

Flora stood, with her usual difficulty, and sidled out of the row. She went up to her employer and closed her hands about his upper arms.

He stared down at her hands and trembled like an overtaxed racehorse.

'Con, dear,' she said. She walked him backward and sat him down. She would have liked to crouch at his feet, but wasn't able to.

'Let's not quarrel,' Cole said.

'We're not quarrelling. You're upset.' She took his hands gently, mindful of the scabs where he'd gnawed the skin from the sides of his fingers—one of this insanely fastidious man's several unclean habits, like his fondness for sex with strange men. She asked, 'Have you seen a doctor?'

'Yes,' Cole said.

'Are you being treated?'

'Yes.'

'Have you talked to Myra? Jean? Kay? Or, for that matter, Monty?'

'It's not them. They all have ambition.'

'Ambition doesn't make anyone immune to venereal disease.'

'It's him. He's to blame,' Cole said. Then, very bleak, 'Where is he?'

'He'll be back. He's not about to steal my car.'

Cole nodded. 'That's true.' He looked a little calmer. Then he changed the subject. 'The film is splendid, I think,' he said, with serene self-belief.

'Yes,' Flora said, and stroked the backs of his hands.

'And it's done with. And the well fills up from behind. There's always something for me to do next. But—Flora—it's not always *good* that flows in when a project has gone.'

'I know. You just have to be more patient.'

'And *you're* drinking too much,' he added.

'All right,' she said, to humour him, and because she was touched. Though, come to think of it, she could really do with a drink right now. She said, 'When Xas returns my car I'll send him straight to you.'

Cole nodded. Then his eyes wandered and he dropped his head. A moment later he lifted a hand, very slowly, as though he were pushing it up through syrup, not air. He gestured for her to leave him.

Xas came back after eight days. He brought Flora and Millie rock candy from some beauty spot up in the Sierras. Millie insisted they celebrate his return over Flora's protests that one week's absence didn't make him a prodigal son. Millie couldn't be discouraged. Having lost all her savings she was now spending every cent she made.

They went out to eat on Santa Monica Pier. Millie and Flora ordered a pot of tea with their meal then decanted the contents of their hip flasks into their teacups. Millie got Flora talking about her few years acting, and about how she was never the girl who got the man. Then, tipsy, Flora moved in an apparently natural progression from never getting the man in movies to talking about Crow's shortcomings. Connie was a braggart, she complained. He was never satisfied with his real achievements. 'He's always making up big boastful lies,' she said, swinging her cup as though conducting an invisible orchestra, her fingers slippery with spilled tequila. 'For instance—he makes this wonderful film then has to say he came up with the whole story though I know for a fact that he lifted it from a magazine.'

'Flora, honey,' said Millie, 'you always said that it would be a relief not to be working for Mr Cole, so why are you complaining now you've hooked up with Connie?'

Flora gave Millie a hooded-eyed look. She found her purse, her pillbox, and popped a couple of Nembutal into her mouth, washing them down with her last swallow of tequila. Then she leaned across the table to whisper mushily, 'Can we go to Mexico soon?'

'Sure,' said Millie.

'You might as well start trying to build up capital again,' Flora went on.

Millie's face went still and remote. She leaned back in her chair and cast her gaze down. 'Let's just plan to top up our supply. You get in touch with those boys of yours.'

Flora promised to call the bootleggers. 'You can come too,' she said to Xas, who shook his head, and began, 'No, I'm thinking—'

'Cole needs him,' Millie interrupted, salaciously drawing out 'needs'. She made cupping and kneading gestures. Then, 'Are you going to eat that?' She pointed to the cake in front of Xas, then took it without waiting for his answer.

Though she was intoxicated Flora had noticed that when she asked Xas if he'd fly down to Mexico with them and he'd begun to make his excuses it appeared he was about to go on to say not just why he couldn't do it, but why he wouldn't be there at all. Flora had laughed at Millie's teasing, the vulgarity of which was a relief to her because whenever she considered what Cole might believe he wanted from Xas it worried her terribly. Xas and Cole pressing one another's bodies—that was normal. Flora actually liked to imagine that, instead of helplessly imagining them—those two strange and strenuous people—apart, and surrounded by vast gulfs of empty space, as though they were falling from a ditched plane. Xas had shaken his head, said, 'No, I'm thinking—' when Millie interrupted to tease him. 'He's thinking of leaving,' Flora had thought. Now she took a deep breath and attempted to speak clearly. 'Xas, what are you planning?'

'Flora asks with drunken solemnity,' said Xas. 'I don't make plans. I only let time go by.'

She waved a finger back and forth beneath his nose. 'You're planning something.'

'Well—I need to find a good appraiser.'

'Huh?' said Millie.

'I have some jewellery I need valued.'

'Can't Cole help you with that?'

'Cole recycles his diamonds whenever the girls throw them back in his face. Sometimes he even asks for them back. But he never sells them. There are always more girls to woo.'

'How many diamonds are we talking about?' said Millie, bemused.

Xas shrugged. 'They're just tools to him.'

'So you haven't counted them?' Millie said, and all her dimples appeared. 'Though you're the one who gets to polish Cole's tools.'

Flora had an idle sideways thought that if actors spoke their lines very quickly then it might be possible to get these sorts of jokes past the censors' exhausted attention.

'I have something I want valued so I can sell it for its full worth,' Xas said. 'I don't need a fence. I want someone who can appraise jewellery.'

'I'll find you an appraiser,' Flora said.

Without getting up Millie moved her chair around the table in a series of little hops till she was sitting right beside Xas. 'Can we see your diamond, honey?'

'Was it a *diamond* Cole gave you?' Flora was surprised. She wished she wasn't quite so drunk. 'He did say he paid you. But I thought he only gave diamonds to actresses.'

'Cole gave me money and made me promise to invest it. It was a kind of test, I think.'

Millie asked, 'How much money?'

'Nine and a half thousand.'

Millie said, 'So there's no diamond.' She sounded disappointed.

Xas got up to reach deep in one pocket of his wide-legged pants. 'No. But I have these.' He produced a wad of dusty cloth and sat back down. He peeled apart layers of fragile cotton and Flora recognised cuffs and buttonholes, and that the rag was a very old shirt. Then the two women were looking down into this dusty nest at a clutch of large, lustrous pearls. Black pearls, with a nacreous sheen, both lilac and green—no—blue too, Flora saw, and pink, and creamy gold, the colours like ripples of oil running on gloomy pond water.

Millie moaned in admiration.

Flora thought the pearls looked real, but asked anyway. 'They must be worth—' she said, but couldn't think of a figure. She sensed a little flurry in the tables beside theirs and looked up to see all the craning heads and amazed, avaricious faces. 'You're causing a stir,' she said.

'I'm not. They are,' Xas said, and gathered the pearls into the dusty shirt once more and stuffed them back into his pants pockets.

'Are those really yours?' Millie said.

'A relative of mine gave them to a friend of mine. Before my friend died she gave them back to me. She never did wear them. Agnes, her daughter-in-law, wore them once or twice but for most of that time they were shut up in a bank vault.'

Flora took note that there was only one name in this little narrative, and it wasn't the name of his 'relative'.

'You've been carrying these around?' Millie said.

Xas smiled at her. 'I used to wear them, but for some time now they've been stashed in a safe place.' He put his hand on the back of hers, didn't just pat it, but began to play with her fingers.

Flora kicked him under the table. The restaurant wasn't segregated, but it was terribly unwise for him to start winding his fingers with Millie's in any public place. He looked at Flora, wide-eyed, but didn't release Millie's hand.

He clearly didn't see why he should. But Millie remembered herself and retrieved her hand and gave Flora a look that seemed to warn—don't say anything, don't do anything to spoil his unworldliness. 'Let's get out of here,' she said.

Flora offered to get the cheque then had to deliver a little lecture to her friends on the importance of learning to accept gifts graciously, speaking a little more pointedly to Millie, because she knew that Xas was planning to give Millie the money from the sale of those preposterous pearls. 'Then he's going to leave us,' Flora thought, as she counted out coins at the cashier's desk. 'He's going to make his extravagant gesture, acquit himself of our care, and leave us.'

Millie had them drop her off at a club on Central Avenue. Flora drove back to Venice, and parked with one wheel pushed up against her already unstable fence. Xas got out of the car and went up to the porch, where he waited facing her door. He didn't have his key. She called him back. He came down the steps and into the moonlight.

'Give me those pearls,' she said.

He put his hand in his pocket and produced the rag bundle, and offered it to her. She unwrapped it on his open palm. She studied the shirt with its dust-starched creases, its grandpa collar and its holes for collar studs. The shirt was like something from a studio's costume department, something an actor would wear in a western.

Flora stepped closer to Xas and eased his jacket off one shoulder and arm. He transferred the wrapped pearls from one hand to the other to let her remove his jacket altogether.

It dropped behind him on the path. While Flora did this she said to him, 'Shhh. Stay still. Do this for me.' He did oblige her; he remained passive. She said, 'I'm not going to do anything bad. I'll keep asking you as I go.' She looked up at him and met his serious, alert expression. She said, 'I'm going to undo this button.' She touched the button at the base of his throat. She unfastened it. 'I'm going to undo another three.'

'You've been talking to Cole,' Xas said.

'About what?' Flora's spread the top of his shirt to uncover his collarbones. She ran her fingertips along one and then the other. His collarbones were like lines drawn under something for emphasis, under two words, like 'touch me'.

'Shirts,' Xas said. He was standing with his head level, but eyes lowered, eyeing her, aloof and hawkish. Flora lifted the pearls out of the rag in his hand. They were warm. She raised her arms—her scars shrieking at her—and slipped the string over his head. The pearls settled with weighty kissing noises. 'Three more buttons,' she said. She undid these slowly, and slowly eased his shirt open so that she could see the whole rope, the curve of its end only an inch above his navel. She didn't touch his skin again or uncover his shoulders. She knew he wouldn't let her, that he was shy, or frightened about people seeing his body—possibly only women, though he didn't seem at all wary of women in any other way.

Flora stepped back and looked at him. Against his white skin his nipples were a shade that might be found on the mouth of one of the very best porcelain dolls, a pink that was perfect, pretty, almost inorganic.

Regarding him Flora was as moved as she expected to be, but what moved her was knowledge, a cool intellectual acknowledgement of his extraordinary beauty. Dammed up behind that was something that astonished her, a catastrophe of feeling that wasn't tenderness or infatuation or lust or even love. For Flora knew she loved Xas, that she'd come to love him without being afraid of what would happen to her if she did. If he went she'd grieve, she knew that. But the suspended feeling wasn't love, or fear of loss, it was something else, something she wasn't equipped to feel because—mad thought—people never felt it: a powerful, fatal feeling of responsibility, as if just being near to him involved her in something that mattered. Something that mattered and no one ever spared a thought to, like air, like the breathable gas that wrapped the world.

Flora said to him, 'You don't make sense. And I have feelings about you that don't make sense.'

A look of distress appeared on his face and the pearls suddenly belonged to someone else, someone who could never wear that look.

'You're going to leave,' she said.

'I have to.'

'Did he do something?'

'Do you mean Cole?'

Flora nodded.

'No.' Xas's mouth was twitching at one corner. 'I—I only have to find someplace else to live. But—but it can be in Los Angeles. And I can still come around—sometimes—and—and—'

He was stammering. Flora wanted to put her arms around him but didn't dare to when he was showing so much skin.

'—and fix things,' he finished.

'Do you see me as a responsibility? Like your old mother or something?'

'Flora!' He sounded agonised and jittery. He wrapped his arms around himself, sealing his skin and the pearls away under his shirt. Flora saw that his cuffs and collar were grey with grime and that his hands were dirty. There was red clay under his fingernails as though he'd been digging. As though the pearls had been buried somewhere and he'd dug them up and driven back to Los Angeles and hadn't thought to wash the dirt off his hands. She said, 'Do you expect me to say, "Go with my blessing"?'

'I'd like to stay, Flora, but I can't.'

'Is this about Cole?'

Xas shook his head.

'Do you know that Cole has a dose of the clap?'

'I thought it might be that. He smells of mice. Mouse droppings in the back of a cupboard.'

'He thinks you gave it to him.'

Xas sighed and said, 'I shouldn't have given in to Cole. I shouldn't have wanted to give in.'

'What you should do is see a doctor.' Flora turned away, hesitated, then asked him why he was washing his hands of Millie. 'I know you mean to pay her off with the price of those pearls.'

'I'm not paying her off.'

'I think you are,' Flora said, 'I think you've picked up more than the clap from Cole.' As she went up her path she said over her shoulder, 'I'll look into appraisers for you first thing tomorrow.' Then, 'Don't leave that jacket lying where I'll trip over it.'

Flora went into her bedroom and closed the door. She took off her hat and fluffed her hair. She sat down at her vanity table and peered at her own reflection. She tried to see herself—whatever it was that inspired people to confide in her, then keep her at arm's length.

The day before she had been on a long drive with Crow. They'd run into each other at the apartment of a friend, near Griffith Park. When they left together Crow asked her to go with him to Pasadena. He was visiting his wife, who was in Las Encinas sanatorium. He said to Flora that he didn't mind the drive out, but disliked the drive back. He'd often find himself at the racetrack instead of the studio. 'But I can't go today because I'm dodging a bookie.'

As he got older, Crow, always an undemonstrative man, had become more taciturn and businesslike. This little insight into his domestic and financial troubles was a great concession, Flora thought, to her and their old friendship. Throughout the trip, as they drove from Griffith Park through Burbank and on past the airports to Pasadena, and while she waited for Crow in a tea shop near the sanatorium, Flora had felt a *future* in the outing, in Crow's confidence in her, and his desire for her company.

Now she saw she'd been wrong. It was just that there was something about her. Something half-dead. Crow had given her his heart to weigh, as if she was that Egyptian god—Anubis, was it?—who weighed and measured hearts. Xas was doing something similar. Sometimes Flora felt he was handing himself over to her, but only to work on, not to keep. She felt that he'd finished with himself and it was now her job to make something of him, reassemble him in some order that made sense, and played cleanly, as a film would once she'd finished cutting it.

# Mines Field

## Late February, 1930

When Xas checked in with Cole from a phone box in the Breakers Beach Club, Cole said, 'I'm having a problem with a Bristol I want to use for the flyover at the premiere. I'm taking it up to check it out. Would you like to go with me?'

And Xas said, 'Sure,' and arranged to meet Cole that afternoon at Mines. He went home to change his clothes, and caught the trolley.

He and Cole put on thick flying togs, for the Bristol was an open cockpit two-seater. They took off from Mines and climbed into the cold air at eight thousand feet. Cole mushed up through a loop, took the plane gently over, its engine missing and catching the way Bristol engines sometimes did. Xas thought it sounded just fine.

Cole glanced back and signalled 'hold on'—for the Bristol had no seat belts. Xas clamped his hands on his seat. Cole tilted the Bristol into a shallow dive and pushed the stick over gradually. The plane began to spin. The solid part of the world became a barrel and they shot along a chute of air aiming at open sky. They flew out over the water, spinning still, the Pacific a tubular blue solidity whose sides they seemed to swipe as they went by. Then Cole put the plane into a slow bank from inverted, up and over, and they were flying level.

There was a haze on the sea, plumping out its normally notched surface. The ocean looked vertical, not horizontal, the distances robbed of distance, and the horizon a knife-edge.

Xas relaxed now that Cole had finished his aerobatics, and let go of the sides of his seat. He looked back at the city, in its depression, and under cloud like fungus, not white, but stained with smoke and car exhaust.

Cole turned again to look at Xas and smiled with a kind of merry intensity the angel hadn't seen before. Cole signalled to him to look forward, to enjoy the view.

Xas looked and saw nothing much—only Catalina off to the right in ripples of tide as though it had just been dropped there and was still making waves. Other than that there was only open water and open air ahead.

# Los Angeles

## February–September, 1930

Xas had gone one morning to see the appraiser Flora had found for him. He'd said he was hooking up later with Cole at Mines. Then he hadn't come back.

Days went by. Then weeks.

Millie kept expecting him. When she went out to the Apex Club she would leave notes to tell him where he could find her.

Flora tried to tell Millie that she thought that possibly they'd seen the last of him—but Millie would only purse her lips and shake her head.

Flora tried to contact Cole. But Cole was incommunicado, though Flora was cutting trailers for *Flights of Angels*, and had messages from him, delivered by one of the many anonymous people he now had working for him.

Cole's hermitage was still his room at Château Marmont. Owing to the Depression and a lack of investors the apartment building had become a hotel, and Cole had simply stayed on. The hotel management confirmed for Flora that, yes, Cole was in, and meals were delivered to him, and empty plates removed, but his curtains were always shut fast. When, in late March, Flora finally took her selection of trailers to the hotel, she sent a message in with them: 'Have you seen Xas?' To which Cole made no reply.

Xas's presence had altered Flora's house, not just its emotional temperature but, it seemed, its material existence, so that after a time, although Flora stopped waiting for him to return, the house itself seemed to. His cleaning and mending owned him. The house seemed to shine with reflections of his attention as much as with its floor polish and new paint. It seemed intent on keeping faith, as Millie was.

Millie did wait for Xas, and nightly renewed her notes saying where she'd be. She asked after him at every airfield in Los Angeles. But Millie had her own plans to keep faith with. She had to recoup her lost seed money. So, in May, she sold her car and bought a two-year-old, closed-cabin Velie Monocoupe, and entered the San Francisco to Hawaii air race. The race had a thirty-thousand-dollar purse and, unlike the Powder Puff Derby—a competion for women pilots flown out of Clover Field—San Francisco to Hawaii wasn't whites only.

The day Millie flew out to San Francisco, Flora was the only person at Clover Field to see her off.

They stood for a time in the shade of the Monocoupe's wing, Millie sweating in her powder-blue flying suit. She was saying, 'Even with all the new navigational instruments it's a risky course. I'm hooking up with my Navy man in San Francisco, but, as it turns out, he isn't going to be much use. His maps are all nautical, and show the Pacific from sea level.'

Flora took her friend's hand. 'Can't you find someone better?'

'It's too late for that,' Millie said. 'This is my chance. I have to take it.' She kissed Flora, opened the plane's door and stepped up into the cabin. Then she turned back and said, 'Besides, you know who I wanted.'

Flora nodded.

'He *lived* in the air,' Millie said. 'And he was the nicest man I ever knew.'

Flora nodded again but didn't reciprocate—it didn't seem quite the right way to speak about Xas.

'He wouldn't lose his way,' Millie added.

'If you think you're going to get lost, then you shouldn't fly,' Flora said. 'You know, I'm pretty sure Xas was trying to sell those pearls of his to pay for your flying school. He might have managed it. He might turn up tomorrow with all the money you need.'

Millie shook her head. 'No one is that nice. Not even him. And, Flora, this is a change of tune for you. You haven't exactly kept a light burning for him. You tried to talk to Cole—then you just let the matter drop. Instead you've been working, and rushing about, and hitting the bottle—'

Flora interrupted. 'Millie, I think those pearls were stolen. And perhaps by trying to sell them he brought trouble on himself and had to leave.'

Millie's eyes filled with tears. 'Then what good was it for him to be so generous and naive—and not be here when I need him?'

'If he turns up in the next couple of days I'll send you a wire and put him on a train.'

Millie's face got a faint glow of hope. 'Thanks,' she said, 'maybe that'll happen.' Before fastening the cabin door, she added, 'Take care of yourself, honey, will you? Just ease off a bit.'

Flora said, yes, she would, and they closed the door together. Flora checked its handle then stepped away. Millie took her seat in the cockpit, and waved. Flora turned back to her car which was parked just behind the farthest row of battered Jennies. She heard the Monocoupe's engine start, but didn't look again till Millie had taxied away.

Flora had been drinking heavily throughout March and April, but by the end of May, after Millie had gone, she was drinking to stay drunk—all the time a little foggy, ill, anaesthetised. Drunk, Flora was confident confiding in people whose opinions didn't matter to her, but whose attention was sustaining. When she drank and hadn't any other appetite, she would feel smug rather than excited when Crow's cameraman Pete Zarvas drove her home from some place where there had been dancing and she'd not danced. He'd stop by her gate and wouldn't invite himself in, but would unbutton her shirt and touch his tongue to her nipples while she massaged him through his open fly. He'd do all the twisting about to position himself. She could just sit up straight with her head resting on the back of the seat and move only her hand. Flora knew that Pete looked on her as some kind of aperitif, for afterward he'd go out and spend time with some other more flexible and demanding woman. He never offered to do anything more to Flora, and she never asked, but when she went indoors with his spit still on her breasts, drying in small tugs that kept her nipples stiff, she'd feel appreciated and attractive.

When Flora drank she never wholly sobered up. All her sleep was drunken semi-consciousness. She'd go to work feeling poisoned and fragile and not have enough energy to join in Crow's brainstorming sessions until she was really moved and interested.

Crow was making a film for the studio from a screenplay by a writer recruited from the women's pages of *Harper's*, at the same time as planning his comedy with Wylie. Crow had told Flora that the *Harper's* women's screenplay was desperately sentimental—but it was all he had been offered after *Spirit*. Though audiences had liked *Spirit*, the film had run over budget, and the plane crash hadn't helped. Crow asked Flora, 'Would you please find me something for this Helen Hope to do?' Helen Hope was the eponymous heroine of the screenplay. The magazine story had been vague about Helen's 'charity work', but the film would have to put the character somewhere. Crow said, 'She needs some concrete occupation to give her all the moral currency she's supposed to have. She needs manifest good works. Vic Fleming would have had her conducting choirs of orphans—but that's not my style.'

Flora would sit brainstorming with Crow and others, silent at first, nursing her now chronic hangover, until something was said that provoked her to speak. She'd join in the talk, and enjoy the sound of her own voice—rough and reluctant. She'd enjoy the sharp things she'd say, words distilled by impatience down to essentials. Though she could never sound like the men with their sulks and enthusiasms and perpetual pleasurable tussles for dominance, Flora nevertheless thought that she managed to sound like a pithy sibyl, the voice out of the ground of a hibernating oracle.

Drunk, Flora felt invulnerable, insular, and abandoned, all at once. And, so long as she kept clean, and kept to time, she felt she didn't have to be in any other way civilised, or rational, or ever to feel she was waiting for something better.

Crow had developed a habit of giving Flora news about his private life as though offering an apology. His wife came back from her latest rest cure and they bought another house. He told Flora about it—saying he really did think he was doing the right thing there. Then he purchased another couple of racehorses. He drove Flora out to his stable to see them—saying, 'I know you think it's a frivolous hobby.' He talked to Flora about his fears for his wife's health. Flora was fragile and irascible and Crow was careful with her, but chose to share these things. In her sour hangovers Flora felt these confidences as a power she had over her friend. She enjoyed it. It was something. Something better than the silence of nobody else in her house.

*

Flora was never to know for sure what happened to her friend Millie Cotton. But what she imagined was this:

Millie and her retired Navy navigator lost their way. Perhaps it was night. The navigator pored over maps in the weak light of the cockpit. In later years Flora would dream about that little capsule of radiance carrying those two souls in the huge darkness over the ocean. As it got light they maybe dropped down to look for islands, or ships. They ran low on fuel. They ran out of time.

Of the seventeen planes that set out from San Francisco to Hawaii, only nine made it. Some pilots ditched and were rescued. One wreck was found. Three planes, including Millie's, disappeared altogether.

There was a memorial service. Flora attended. And Conrad Crow. And Millie's old landlady and some of her fellow tenants from Watts. And jazz club patrons, musicians, a couple of bootleggers, and Millie's old boyfriend from Texas—one of the men she'd hoped to go in with on the flying school. All the Powder Puff Derby flyers were there too as a kind of honour guard: Margaret and the two Ruths, Clem, Amy, Amelia, Phoebe, May, Marvel, Claire, Edith and Vera.

Flora sobbed helplessly all the way through the service—for Millie, and for all the things Millie had asked of the world and of her life, hopes that should have been reasonable, and within the reach of her hard work and daring.

When she came in from the service the first thing Flora saw was Xas's library books lying in a dusty pile on the window seat. She went straight back out again, returned them, and paid his fines.

A month or so after Millie's memorial service, Flora stopped drinking. She didn't decide to, or intend to, but, one day, she had a task that took too much time for her to get to the day's first drink.

It was the day she packed up Millie's belongings. In the early afternoon she sat on the sling-backed single bed in Millie's room and looked at how little there was. She thought, 'This shouldn't take me long.' But each of Millie's possessions asked her to stop and look and acknowledge it. Flora remembered everything—this scarf, that hat, this pair of shoes. She could even see what was missing, the few things Millie had with her when she left for San Francisco. Millie had always been careful with money, and each of her purchases had been a considered one. They were good things, and well cared for. The shoes were stuffed with balled newspaper, the clothes hung on padded hangers. There were mothballs in the wardrobe, with a clove-studded orange pomander. Flora could remember Millie making the pomander one evening while they listened to the radio. Looking at her friend's tidy room it seemed to Flora that all this thought and order and care should have been a charm against what had happened.

When Flora did eventually get up from the bed she only pottered about for an hour picking up and caressing this and that, saying hello to Millie's belongings, then placing them back where they belonged—where Millie had put them.

Finally she left the bedroom and wandered around the rest of the house. She opened the drawers and wardrobe in the damp back room and looked again at Xas's few anonymous things. She had already gone through pockets and shaken books. There was nothing. All Xas's things had to say was that he hadn't meant to stay.

Flora went around the rest of her house. Her room, the living room, bathroom and kitchen. In the kitchen the shelves were lined—Xas had done that—but the dust had begun to settle again. The rooms were once again cluttered. It was the house of someone who didn't live with her eyes open. Sure, she could keep her eyes open in the dark, cutting film, watching artificial scenes set, and artificial acts repeated over and over. She could look for the best *take*. But she couldn't pay attention to her own house. It was dingy, disorderly. To Flora it looked as if she wasn't even in occupation—of the house, or her life. She hadn't any plans. *Millie* had had plans. Millie had had a use for herself.

Flora stood in her drab, slovenly kitchen and whispered, 'She should be alive.' Then she went out and sat on the back step, where she was joined by O'Brien, who flopped down beside her to clean his rich fur—the only cared for thing at her address.

It was late afternoon by the time Flora drove over to Millie's old apartment building on Vermont Avenue in Watts to give Millie's former neighbour her gramophone and discs. The neighbour asked Flora to stay for dinner, and because Flora ate, the food confounded her craving for alcohol. The following morning, for the first time in months, Flora didn't feel unwell. That afternoon, instead of sitting down with Pete and Wylie and other drinking buddies, Flora made a little experiment: she ran away from her craving. She drove out to Malibu and sat on some weathered steps that went down to the sand. It was late September and most of the brightly painted shacks were shut up and the shore almost empty. Flora smoked and thought about Gil and Millie and Xas. And while she sat there it seemed that some other Flora, a woman who had been doggedly trailing her for months, maybe years, finally caught up and sat down where she was sitting, slipping into her sore body, providing it with an extra notch of contrast, or wash of colour. She was joined on the steps by the Flora to whom things had mattered more.

The sun went at its usual fall time, though it seemed earlier. Flora drove home. She went into her kitchen. She picked up a dry glass from the draining board. It wasn't much later than she usually started drinking, and she did feel that there wasn't really any great harm in starting. But, nevertheless, she replaced the glass and opened a packet of crackers instead. She was a little curious about how she'd feel the following morning. Would she feel any better? How much improvement was possible? Flora had forgotten how it felt to be wholly well. She couldn't expect to discover *that*, since she was still strapped into her cilice of scars, and even if it turned out that her body was after all a whole habitable world, the pain of her scars was still that world's equator. But Flora was curious. If, the following morning, she felt better, then perhaps her interior would become bigger, and some part of her would at least be further from the pain.

She put away her last unopened tequila, conserving not just the bottle itself, but also the option of a steep descent into what drink gave her, stimulated self-forgetting, sensual relaxation, sensuous numbness and vertigo. That ongoing twilight could remain an option, a last thing to turn to.

Instead, Flora ate crackers and a withered orange and made a shopping list:

*bread*
*butter*
*cookies*
*tomatoes*
*beans*
*bacon*

—before her imagination failed her.

She went to bed sober.

The next day she noticed that her stomach was flatter—it had been swollen—and that the scarred skin on her belly wasn't pulling so much.

Over the following weeks Flora rediscovered lucidity. Initially there were times when she felt she was eighteen again, fresh and full of energy. But that didn't last. Sobriety wasn't like the promises of the Prohibitionist preachers she remembered hearing when she was a girl in Brawley. She found herself living in relation to a reality no more real than her drunken one. It was just new to her. She missed her old life: the muddle, the self-righteous ire, the pleasurable spite of her drunken self. She missed her own infantile blundering. She had a little less pain, and far more fear of it. She missed never having to choose. Pete had touched her, but she hadn't had to say, 'Yes, *you*.' The old life was simple; she was hungry and she drank, she was heated and she drank. There were no better choices, and there was no better time. The world was in soft focus and Flora was surrounded by objects and faces that radiated light. And when she passed out, her bed was made of balloons, and nothing that touched her touched heavily.

Sober for five weeks, lucid, dull, Flora found her focal length had altered. Before her now was a long vista, with a vanishing point. She found herself in her life, in time that had an end to it. Time to get serious.

# Cahuenga Building, Hollywood Boulevard

## October, 1930

The new, sober Flora found the time to dig out the address of the appraiser to whom she'd sent Xas. She drove to a building on Hollywood Boulevard, and took the elevators to the fourth floor.

The appraiser was a manufacturing jeweller, the best on the coast. Flora spoke to a receptionist behind a steel grille. The receptionist pressed a button and let Flora into the showroom, a room with thick carpet, and very modern, recessed downlighting. There were more lights in glass cases, illuminating diamond necklaces, bracelets, and rings. Among the diamonds were plump and oily pearls.

Flora took a seat in a gilded chair and waited. She picked up a *Photoplay* and flicked through it. She found a portrait of Cole's new star, and stills from *Flights of Angels*. She remembered the scenes of the stills as stopped frames in her editing machine. She had spent so long on the film, and it had receded so quickly. Flora stared and tried to imagine it all as history, instead of merely last month's news. She found that mattered to her. She felt her life with its new long perspectives might one day feel finished, and *thought through* like Cole's film, rather than just made of moments like the sweepings from the floor beneath her editing bench.

'Miss McLeod?'

The jeweller was a neat person in a double-breasted suit that made his shoulders too wide for his height. He introduced himself—'I'm Mr Green'—and took Flora's hand, retaining it as he sat beside her. She could see he was worried because he didn't know who she was. Whose wife, whose girlfriend—though she was unescorted, and not pretty enough.

Flora said, 'I sent a friend to you several months ago. He wanted to get a valuation on some pearls, and possibly to sell them. Black pearls.'

Flora actually saw the man's hair bristle as his scalp tightened. It was one of those expressions that looked as much like disgust as surprise. She went on, 'What I want to know is, if my friend did sell the pearls, whether he ever collected his money?'

'Miss McLeod—this friend of yours, was he a good friend?'

'Were the pearls stolen?'

'Why would you say that?'

'He didn't own anything.'

The man scratched his ear. 'I still have them,' he said. 'Your friend, Mr Jodeau, struck me as very confident, very candid in his manner. He didn't act like someone selling stolen goods. He wasn't in any great hurry either. I did say to him that a pearl rope like that must have some provenance. Each one of those pearls would have been a remarkable find, a once-in-a-lifetime find.' The jeweller waited, watching Flora while this sank in. He said, 'They're not cultured. I used an X-ray to check the material at their cores. They are wild South Sea Island pearls, perfectly matched, and an extremely rare true black.'

Flora understood that she was being made to appreciate some enormity, some professional miracle.

'Pieces like that have *names*,' he said.

'Did it?'

Green shook his head. 'No. After some research I found that the only pearl rope answering its description was the subject of a disputatious insurance claim, and an old family quarrel. The families involved were French—so I suppose the pearls were originally Tahitian. The family Lettelier made the insurance claim on the death in 1876 of one Baron Lettelier. The Baron's wife, Aurora de Valday, had died the year before. The pearls had belonged to her. The Baron had insured them with Lloyd's of London in 1845, which is actually too early for Tahitian pearls, though they *must* be Tahitian. The insurance claim was made because the pearl rope wasn't found among the Baron's effects. The Baroness Lettelier never wore them, though her daughter-in-law the Comtesse du Vully wore them at court in 1857, where the Empress Eugénie admired them. Vully is a château on the banks of the Saône river, in Burgundy. It makes one of the world's most famous wines. Lettelier was Aurora de Valday's second husband, the Comte du Vully was her son by her first marriage.' Green paused and shrugged. 'Anyway, the Comte's and Baron's families fell out over the pearl rope. The Comtesse du Vully insisted that she had returned the rope to her mother-in-law. The Baron's heirs said she hadn't. All I can establish for sure is that the rope hasn't been seen since 1857.'

Flora was a little disgusted by this tale of cupidity—these families squabbling about treasure none of them had seen for twenty years (unless of course the pearls, never worn, were only gloated over in private). She remembered how the rope had looked against her friend's skin, and how he had crossed his arms to close his shirt. She remembered the beauty of the pearls, and his beauty, and the shame in his posture. Thinking of this, Flora wasn't surprised to hear what the jeweller said next.

He said, 'The pearls were supposed to carry a curse.' He blushed. They had a little laugh together. Then he said, 'Your friend did offer a vague account of how they came into his possession. He said that a relative of his gave them to a friend of his, who later returned them to him.'

Flora nodded. 'That's more or less what he said to me, too. So it's his relative who is the thief.'

'I don't know. The way he said "relative" I felt I was listening to someone refer to London as "a city in England". Possibly the Jodeaus are related to the Letteliers or de Valdays?' Green touched Flora's gloved hand again and asked. 'Where is Mr Jodeau now?'

'I don't know.'

'He didn't come back to see what I'd offer. Possibly he realised that questions would be asked.'

That was it, of course. Xas had disappeared because he tried to sell something he, or someone he knew, had stolen, then realised later that he couldn't just cash in something so unique and not have to prove ownership. His naivety was staggering.

'I can't sell the rope,' the jeweller said. 'If Lloyd's had paid on the claim, Lloyd's would own it. But Lloyd's didn't pay. And I have no idea who owns it.'

'Dead people,' Flora said, 'and their dead children and grandchildren.'

'I'm trying to obtain an address for the present Comte du Vully—if there is such a person.'

'Good luck with that.'

'Your friend gave the rope to me wrapped in a rotting shirt.'

'Did he?' Flora said, darkly amused. Xas hadn't even bothered to conceal the fact the pearls and their packaging had been freshly dug up.

Green blushed from throat to hairline. His mouth worked. He seemed to want to say something more, but was having trouble with it. Flora caught his eye and saw dread there. She waited.

'I cleaned them,' the jeweller said. 'Then I thought I should restring them. They were strung without knots between each pearl. Very bad practice. But—' He stopped and silence seemed to arc above them like an unstable stone roof. He finally said, 'I found I couldn't cut the string.'

Flora was silent.

He went on, his voice shaking. 'It wouldn't cut, though it was only the thickness of a fine hair—a single strand of black hair. I tried with a sharp knife, and scissors, and using real force. I scratched one of the pearls.' He was pale now, and sweat had started on his forehead. Flora was beginning to worry about the state of his mind, with all this talk of curses and strings that wouldn't cut. But he collected himself with a deep breath and a series of little shudders. 'That isn't something I can expect you to believe unless you try it yourself. And I suggest you don't.' He was quiet for a moment, then, before Flora had thought what to say, he went on. 'You'd think that all that was required of a fact was that it be demonstrable. That, if a fact was demonstrable, it would be an honourable fact.'

Flora didn't say anything. She felt lost.

'It's not true,' the jeweller said, earnest.

'No,' said Flora. She decided that it was better to agree with him. She glanced away from his moist, unhappy face at all the rich stock glimmering in the glass cases. There was no sign of disorder anywhere, or of any dishonourable facts.

'What kind of man was your friend?'

Flora thought: hard-working, able, poetic, practical, sad, unworldly, complicated, flighty, speedy, stopped, restless, remote... She shook her head. 'He was a mass of contradictions. He was a stunt flyer. He talked about Heaven as if he'd been there. Sometimes he liked to quote Huidobro, a Chilean poet. I only remember the line: "A shady bed in the whirlwind of mysteries."' Flora wanted to add, 'I felt safe with him. Safe, and stimulated at the same time.' But strangers didn't say things like that to one another even in the world where one of them supposes he's discovered that some strings can't be cut. Flora got up. 'Thank you, anyway,' she said.

'Let me know if he comes back.'

Flora shook her head, meaning that she thought Xas wouldn't, not refusing to pass on any news that he had.

Green said, 'I won't contact the police, I promise. I'm sure this is all just an old family matter.'

# Santa Monica

## November, 1930

A letter came for Xas. It was from Madill Brothers funeral home.

'*Dear Mr Jodeau,*' it began. '*Here is our annual report. You will see that after the initial outlay of fitting the new premises in Pasadena, and the purchase of another hearse, our earnings now have a healthy margin.*'

Flora went to visit these Madill Brothers, taking the letter with her. She found Doug Madill behind the premises, wearing a rubber apron and washing his new hearse. Flora stood clear of a froth-edged puddle and held up the letter. 'I'm sorry I opened it,' she said. 'He's gone with no forwarding address.'

Doug Madill shut off the hose.

'I'm his landlady,' Flora said.

Doug Madill looked worried, perhaps thinking he might be liable for rent owing.

'I only want to know what's happened to him,' Flora said.

'All I'm able to do is follow any clues I have about what he was doing before he vanished.'

The sun came out. It slowly warmed and dried the man's rubber apron so that, as they stood there and Douglas Madill explained what 'Mr Jodeau' was to him, the air filled with some sweet chemical scent.

The Madill family had been in the funeral business for seventy years, forty on the coast. Doug and his brother had wanted to open a branch in Pasadena. Mr Jodeau turned up one day at Madill Brothers in Santa Monica, and said he had some money to invest. 'He said his employer and he had been talking about the Crash and investments and his employer had given him a certain sum of money to invest— and not to lose. Mr Jodeau was very clear about that. He didn't have to have astonishing returns, he said, only a safe investment.'

'He decided a funeral home was a safe investment?'

'Yes,' said the funeral director. 'He said to me, "Business is never slow."'

Flora laughed, then apologised for laughing.

'That's quite all right, Miss. That isn't the whole story, of course. There are always times of retrenchment, and plenty of people learn not to pay more for a funeral than they can afford. And there's competition. I told your friend all this.'

'But the population is growing.'

'Exactly.'

'He did have a practical streak.'

'He has nine thousand five hundred dollars invested. I'm instructed to keep reinvesting his dividends.'

Flora thanked Mr Madill. He asked her whether he should keep sending those reports to her address.

'Yes. And let me know if you hear from him.'

'Likewise.'

Flora left him polishing the hearse's black flanks.

# Venice

December, 1930–February, 1931

Flora got herself a telephone. But every morning, for weeks after, she would still check the notepad that hung in her porch. She'd given out her number to all her friends and acquaintances, but still imagined there might be some who'd forget and, stopping by, would leave a message out of habit. *'Called by at 8 p.m., Pete.'* or *'Darling, where are you? Avril.'* There were sometimes notes—but not from Pete, who hadn't bothered to pursue Flora's company once her drinking and hand jobs dried up together. And not from Avril, who had her own phones, a black one in her hall that her maid answered, and a white one in her white satin bedroom.

One morning Flora stepped out in her robe to look among the orange tree leaves for any fruit remaining and not too wizened to juice. All the oranges were shrunken and leathery. Flora went back to the house snipping the air in front of her with her scissors as though she were a dignitary invited to open a succession of bridges. She saw that there was a note on the pad hanging from her door jamb.

*Dear Occupant*
*What has become of the person who was living in your*
*house with you?*

The writing was an even and attractive copperplate, but there was something foreign and unpractised about the wording of the note.

Flora took the pencil off its string, carried it inside, sharpened it, reattached it to its string and wrote an answer.

*Do you mean Millie? Or Xas? Please leave a name and address*
*or phone number so that I can let you know. Or call me.*

And she left her number.

The following morning there was another note. It had arrived after Flora came home at ten and retired at midnight, but before seven-thirty when she got up. She hadn't heard any footsteps on the tarred tin of the porch flooring.

*I don't mean any Millie. I mean the other. Where is he?*

It annoyed Flora that this correspondent hadn't complied with her instructions and left a name and address, or dropped a dime and made a call. Xas had vanished and she was mourning him and this person wanted something for nothing, it seemed to her.

Flora spitefully removed the pencil and pad from her porch. If this person was so keen to ask her questions they could turn up at a reasonable hour and knock on her door.

The following morning Flora stepped out, dressed, on her way to Culver City and the studio. She put her foot on a large sheet of canvas that had been spread before her door. The canvas was striped, a sun-faded pink and cream, and still had zinc poles at either end of it. It looked like an awning from one of the cafés on Venice Beach. There was writing on the awning, in charcoal.

*Surely we can come to some agreement. You tell me what I*
*want to know in exchange for what you might like to know.*
*Tit for tat.*

Once she had recovered enough to move, Flora bundled up the canvas, which smelled of apples, so might once have belonged to a fruit shop. She put it in her car. A mile from her house she pulled up to throw it into a canal.

Flora was rattled. She didn't want to go home. She spent the hours of darkness—too long, because it was winter—in a movie house, then one of Millie's clubs on Central Avenue. She drank a little and came home very tired, her ears buzzing, to find that her unknown correspondent had, this time, come equipped with paper. There was one sheet, apparently the endpaper of a book, because it was marbled on one side, made of linen, and crumpled at the edges as though it had been carried pressed not quite flat. As Flora picked it up she noticed that it, too, smelled of apples—and the scent washing has when it's been dried in the wind and sun. That smell reminded Flora of something, something other than clean air and laundry, but she couldn't exactly remember what.

The note read:

*I should warn you that I have no sense of the ridiculous. Don't go on to do the next things—keep watch, or post armed friends. I have no notion what resources you might have, little notion of who you are, or what to expect of you— but I do know that I'll pursue you, my only lead, with as much patience as I can muster, which is more than almost anyone else. Please take me up on my kind offer while it's still on the table.*

Flora took the page inside and called Cole. She was told he wasn't taking calls. She left a message, said that someone was asking questions about Xas's whereabouts. 'Tell Cole I'm frightened for myself,' Flora said to the flunky, then, as soon as she hung up, regretted having added 'for myself' since Cole would surely be more motivated by fright he could feel as his own. All day she waited for the phone to ring, then, exhausted by anticipation, she finally wrote a note, left it and the pad on her porch, and went out.

Her note read:

*If you call* in person *at a reasonable hour I will tell you the little I know. But I believe that Conrad Cole may have been the last one to see Xas.*

Again Flora went out and stayed out—in a hotel room with Pete. She came home the following afternoon, hung over, with two bloody fissures in the thick scarred skin on her hips. She limped up onto her porch and looked blearily at another note, which said:

*Who is Conrad Cole?*

Flora was astonished. Who the hell would ask 'Who is Conrad Cole'? Con was famous nationwide, almost worldwide—millionaire, playboy, inventor, and the producer and director of Hollywood's most expensive film to date. Flora stood for a long time staring at the note, then went indoors, climbed into bed fully clothed and fell asleep.

When she woke, O'Brien was smooching her chin and purring his anxious purr, the one that had a kind of soft whistle in it. Flora's head was sore, but clear. She'd woken with a very vivid memory of Xas. Of just one of the inexplicable habits he'd had. He used to leave the house when it was raining heavily, and she'd once seen him standing in the waste ground, maybe a quarter-mile away, his naked body a streak of almost phosphorescent brightness in the rain-smudged, grass-greened dunes. He was washing himself. He'd taken a bar of soap out with him. He never used her bath, her shower with its rust-dimpled rose—no— he went where no one could get a good look at him and let the rain clean him.

Flora lay, patting her cat and promising him food *any minute now*. She couldn't get the picture out of her head. 'Why?' she thought. 'Why did he do that?'

Though there were no more notes, Flora was haunted by what she'd written herself—that, as far as she knew, Cole really was the last person to see Xas. She had a suspicion, not much more than an itch. It was as if something she hadn't fully recognised had managed to find another way to present itself to her.

Late at night, and upon waking, if her mind didn't conjure Xas, out on the paper road in the rain, it mysteriously presented her with Cole, beside her hospital bed, all those years ago. Cole speaking to Avril, in a low, vehement voice, about John Weber, the man who'd set fire to her grass skirt. Flora would remember Cole and Avril standing together over her tented, iodine-stained body, arguing, Cole's voice full of boyish indignation. He kept saying, over and over, that John should be made to pay. That anyone who injures another must be *made to pay*.

Flora would wake in the small hours, disturbed by O'Brien's usual comings and goings, and instead of dropping off again would come fully awake, her heart pounding, her mind fixed on that memory of Cole.

Finally, unable to put it out of her head, Flora went to visit him at Château Marmont.

Flora waited for a time in the hotel bar, before being led into the garden and pointed the way to Cole's door. It was open. Cole was lying on the couch, which seemed afloat in a sea of paper. The room was dusty, and smelled rancid, but Cole was clean. He was in a robe, his hair wet from the shower. Flora saw he hadn't rinsed all the suds from his ears.

He asked her to close the door, then sat up and made a sweeping gesture over the piled papers. 'Look at all this. All these people making bids for my attention—finally prepared to acknowledge what I can do.'

Flora took a seat, though she'd not been invited to.

Cole picked up a screenplay and began to tell her about it. She couldn't make out whether he was feeling enthusiastic, or only demonstrating how well he understood the story. She listened and tried not to show too much interest for fear that her own vague intentions would have their legs knocked out from under them by his torrent of talk. Gradually, over a number of hours, and by flattering reminiscence, she managed to get him onto the subject of how he'd saved her life. Then onto the subject of John Weber. And in the course of his reminiscing Flora became inspired. She suddenly understood what she must ask him; where her own secretive mind had been leading her.

'A while ago I was talking to Avril about Weber,' she said. 'About how, once I came back to town after my convalescence, I was always a little frightened that I might run into him. But I needn't have worried, since he'd disappeared. Later I got to wondering whether *you* had anything to do with his going away. No matter what other people might have thought *I* always understood that you were capable of extraordinary decisiveness.'

Cole blushed. He looked momentarily smug. Then he seemed to think of something else, and his eyes flickered and their focus moved beyond her.

Flora went on, as if she hadn't had any sign from him she could take as an answer. 'It wasn't just that I lost sight of John. He seemed to vanish. Did you pay him off, Con?'

The room was silent for a moment, absolutely silent and exclusive, with not a sound from the other rooms, or the street beyond the garden wall. Flora watched as Cole's smugness won out. He began to explain. 'When you were in hospital we found that Weber had made himself scarce. Avril supposed that you wouldn't notice, or wouldn't want to be reminded of him. But I thought that if it was me, I'd mind very much one day. I do understand that it wasn't as if Weber had you in his power when he did what he did. I understand that he was careless and you were merely combustible. But what he did to you was about as terrible as anything I ever saw. You were lying in that hospital covered in bandages, and the doctors were just waiting for an infection to set in. We could all tell they didn't give much for your chances.' He broke off, then blurted, 'Did I tell you that my mama died of blood poisoning? That's what your doctors thought would happen to you—blood poisoning, then kidney failure. When you were in hospital it was apparently enough for Avril to put on a mask and gown and *pose herself* at your bedside. But I wasn't about to stand by and watch anything like that again.'

'You paid for my room and my treatment, Con,' Flora said. 'You caught me in the curtain. No one would have expected you to stand watch at my sickbed.'

Cole looked at her blankly.

'So—what about Weber? Did he ever show his face at the hospital?'

'No. He skipped town. I hired detectives who tracked him to San Francisco. I flew up there to find him and told him what Avril was doing and what he should do. How he should be with you. I offered to fly him back. I'd taken my two-seater Curtiss float plane. It was a favourite of mine back then, when I still thought of true flight as being out in the open air. Anyway, I took my Curtiss, so I guess I knew what I meant to do.'

'Which was what?'

'I flew him out over the sea.' Cole took several deep breaths, his eyes went hazy. 'When we were well out I grabbed the sides of the cockpit, pushed the stick over with my knees, and the plane rolled. The cockpit was open, and the seats had no belts. Weber fell out.'

Flora sat very still. She had a terrible suspicion that this was what had happened to Xas. Cole supposed that Xas had given him clap so he dropped him out of a plane into the sea.

In a moment she'd begin to cry. She could feel the tears coming. It wasn't just her eyes, or the bones of her face that felt the imminence of the tears, it was her whole body, as if she might begin to blister as she had when burned, and, from every inch of her, shed tears.

Cole was still talking. 'I thought it through,' he said, in a reasonable, explanatory way. 'When Weber touched his cigarette to your skirt you can bet *he* hadn't thought anything through. I had to do something decisive. I wasn't going to sit around waiting for you to die—because of what had happened with Mama. When Mama became sick they sent for me at school. My school was in Boston; she was in Houston. I spent two days on a train. She tried to stay alive to see me, but wasn't conscious when I got there. They had tucked her in up to her neck. They presented her to me like that, like a monument of herself. When they left us alone I fished her hand out from under the covers and saw that her fingers were black. She was black and mottled all the way up her arm. The first flying lesson I ever took was because of those two days on the train. So—of course I couldn't wait to see whether you'd die.'

Flora put her fingers to her temples and pressed. She shook her head.

'I don't expect you to thank me,' Cole said, 'but I am glad you know now.'

They sat facing each other but with their heads turned like cats paused mid-scrap to measure their respective importances. Then Flora began to sob.

'Flora?' Cole was astonished.

Flora opened her purse. She took out a handkerchief and then just held it. She glared at Cole through her streaming eyes. She said, 'He wasn't yours. He was mine.'

'He was a waster,' Cole said, frowning at her.

'*He was wonderful!*' she shouted.

Cole went pale. 'Oh,' he said.

Flora got up and ran out of his room. She moved as fast as she could, hampered by her scars. She had to get out. Out of that moment, that hour—but it had its hooks in her. Cole came after her, caught up as she was fumbling with the catch of the garden gate. 'Flora,' he said, 'Flora.' Just her name, pleading.

Flora wrestled the bolt back. She jabbed her elbow into Cole's sternum, pulled the gate open and fled out onto Sunset.

Though Cole had confessed, if only sidelong, Flora had no proof. She was in a rage of grief, but powerless to act on what she knew. Who could she go to for help, or even sympathy? Who would care now, but her? Because, in the end, what was Xas? He was a thief, he was shiftless and unreliable and lived under aliases and had left nothing behind him.

After several sleepless nights and drained days all Flora could think to do was to leave a note on the pad on her porch. She wrote to her mysterious correspondent. She wrote that Xas was dead. And that Conrad Cole had killed him. She wrote that she had no proof, and that her heart was broken.

For over a week the note stayed where it was, slowly curling in the damp air. Then one morning it had gone, and in its place, Flora found this. This list:

*Four facts about angels.*

*1. Angels are indestructible. An angel can only be injured by another angel.*

*2. Angels are animals not spirits. (The separation of the spiritual and mundane, and the notion that angels are spirits, only dates back to the Lateran Council of 1215.) Angels are*

*warm-blooded animals, but have no oesophagus, duodenum,*
*stomach, small or large intestine, no anus, no need to eat, and*
*no genitals. (Except for the one angel who is a copy of a*
*particular human being—though since God added wings He*
*might have considered subtracting other appendages as a*
*matter of balance.)*

*3. Fallen angels are not demons.*

*4. God made angels. Angels are, broadly speaking, copies of*
*humans, whom God did not make.*

Two days after she'd received this insane and taunting
message, Flora had a call from the jeweller. Green told her
that he'd had a response to the queries he'd made through
Lloyds of London. The present Comte du Vully had written
to him requesting a full description of the pearls, their
number, size, and colour. Green complied, and three weeks
later he received a wire saying that one Henri de Valday was
coming to America to claim the pearls. De Valday would
arrive in New York on the fifteenth of March, and would be
in Los Angeles eight days later. Green said, 'Would you like
to be present when I speak to him, Miss McLeod?'

Flora said yes, she would.

'And have you heard from your friend?'

'No,' Flora said, and that she knew now that she wouldn't
be hearing from him. 'He got into trouble. People bore him
ill will. I guess there was something provoking about him.'

'I hope you're not in danger!' Green was concerned.

'No. All I suffered was spite. Harmless, pointless spite.'

'I'm very sorry to hear it. Are you all right now?'

Flora reassured the jeweller that, if she wasn't yet, she soon would be. She hoped she was telling him the truth. She felt so low. Whoever it was who'd coaxed the truth out of her—the truth about what Cole had done—had only mocked her trust and her grief.

'I'll let you know when M. de Valday arrives.'

'Thank you.'

# Cahuenga Building, Hollywood Boulevard

## March, 1931

Flora had been sitting for some time by herself among the gleaming display cases when Green and M. de Valday arrived. They'd been out to lunch. Green had grease on his chin, and a look of happy triumph in his eyes. He introduced Flora, then told her that he'd been very daring and had taken de Valday to a little delicatessen nearby, whose specialty was avocado sliced on rye and dressed with olive oil, lemon juice, salt and pepper.

Henri de Valday was in his early thirties, a slight, energetic man with a pockmarked face and warm hazel eyes. When Green finished describing their lunch de Valday kissed his fingertips—a gesture Flora had always thought a property of film, not life. He added, in perfect English, 'And at last I forgot to shake my head over the absence of wine at the table.' He took Flora's hand. 'So, you are the friend of this Jodeau?'

Green led them to his office, a room even more hushed and exclusive than the showroom. De Valday and Flora sat side by side on a sofa. Green went to a wall safe, and came back with a blue velvet box, which he set on the coffee table before the Frenchman. The jeweller then perched on the edge of his desk.

De Valday opened the box. His face went soft and sombre. He lifted the pearls from the box and wrapped them around one hand. As they moved they made their distinctive heavy kissing noises.

'You see,' said Green. 'Priceless is not a word I use lightly or lazily.'

De Valday looked up at Flora through his eyelashes. 'Jodeau is not a common name. Before I left home I spoke to our neighbours, the family Jodeau. They couldn't think who this person might be, although, of course, they are a large family, and spread far and wide. M. Green tells me you have no idea how your friend came by the pearls.'

'None,' said Flora.

'The Jodeaus of Aluze are still in partnership with my family. Vully's only Grande Cru is made of Jodeau grapes— and hence its name, *Château Vully l'Ange du Cru Jodeau*—'the angel of the soil of Jodeau'.'

Green leaned forward, eager. 'Would you please tell Miss McLeod about that? Tell her what you told me.'

De Valday smiled. He coiled the pearls in his lap and made a steeple of his fingers. 'In the cellars of the Château are the two barrels in which our only Grande Cru matures. Two barrels, because the wine is pressed from grapes from one slope only, a stony south-facing slope above the villa of the family Jodeau. There are vines growing right to the walls of the house—the soil is that good, that blessed. The barrels in which the wine matures are very old. I have seen myself the bill of lading for their delivery, which is pasted into the Château's account book for the year of 1838.

'There is, in my family, a story told about these barrels. A legend. Though it is a legend with an addendum I regard as truth, since I myself heard my grandfather swear to it.'

Flora liked the man's 'I myself', and the caressing gesture that went with the words—he'd stroked his own sternum with the tips of his fingers.

'The legend is this: that the Château's vintner, Sobran Jodeau, my great-great-grandfather, ordered the barrels, which were very large, and were built by a cooper on site in Vully's old cellar. Before they were finally sealed, a bundle was deposited in each barrel. Large silk-wrapped bundles. There was a rumour in the district that the winemaker had used the barrels to conceal the evidence of some crime. And there was other talk—for these country people were at that time not Christian in any civil sense—that the bundles were some kind of talisman, an offering to St Lawrence, the patron of winemakers.' De Valday gave a simultaneous shrug of eyebrows and shoulders to show Flora what he thought of these theories. She didn't respond. She didn't like to intervene with questions. She didn't know what to ask. What to ask about 'Sobran'—the name of Xas's dead lover and, apparently, this man's distant ancestor.

'There is another story. The family story. And that is this: that what Sobran Jodeau concealed in the barrels were what gave the wine its name. What lay beneath the silk wrappings of each bundle was the severed wing of an *angel*. M. Jodeau himself apparently never had anything to say on the subject, though his wife, my great-great-grandmother, would say quite readily that it was true, that the bundles were wings and that she'd had some part in cutting them off. However, another of my great-great-grandmothers, on the de Valday side, Aurora, the Baroness Lettelier, used to spit with fury whenever anyone repeated Madame Jodeau's remarks. Of course I should say that there was no love lost between the Baroness and Madame Jodeau, the Baroness having been for many years Sobran Jodeau's lover.'

De Valday made a graceful, dismissive gesture. 'So much for that. It's a good story—a colourful story—a pretty legend my brother the Comte would like to print on our wine labels. But what I will tell you next is what I must regard as true.

'The Angel of the Soil of Jodeau is a great wine, and one that has always had a heavenly consistency. There are variations, naturally. There are vintages. But for all its faintly altering points of interest, for all that comes to the wine from different seasons and changes in the soil, there is a *spirit* in the wine, a divine quality, and the family opens a bottle whenever anyone is ill.

'Because the wine is so consistent, the methods of its making have never altered, and the barrels are never opened. They are filled and emptied. The Château's practice of reverence toward "The Angels"—as the barrels are called—is regarded by the neighbourhood as simply a sensible superstition.

'However, when my grandfather was a boy the Château employed a winemaker from outside the district and, during his tenure, it happened that there appeared a discernible clouding in the wine drawn from Angel One.

'On the winemaker's prompting the family decided to take a look in that barrel.

'The job of scrubbing plaques of tannin from the timbers of a barrel usually falls to a boy—someone old enough to follow simple instructions, but small enough to fit through the aperture in the top of the barrel. It is a dark job, though someone will be posed at the opening with a lamp. It is a suffocating job, because the wood of an empty barrel is impregnated with wine and the barrel full of fumes.

'My grandfather was eight years of age when he was lowered into Angel One. He had scrubbed other barrels, so was prepared for the darkness and the smothering perfume of the wood. The perfume was as strong as ever, he said, but different. The barrel was warm, he said, but there was something cold to the smell in there. My grandfather said that the family didn't tell him to get on with the usual job—chipping at the staves—instead they wanted to know what was in there. My grandfather said he could hear the winemaker too, but the way in which the winemaker asked what was in the barrel was quite different from the way his father and uncles and cousins were asking, for, after all, the winemaker was only looking for the cause of a pollution.

'Grandfather shuffled about in the silt at the bottom of the barrel. He explored its damp curving walls with his fingers. He moved out of the light. Then he touched something—wet, slimy fabric. He called out to tell his father and uncles. He said what he'd found. Then he heard the winemaker ordering him to "Get that mess out of there!" Then, at once, there was a chorus of other voices countermanding the winemaker, asking my grandfather to just "pull at the cloth".

'My grandfather got a grip on the cloth and pulled. He ignored the quarrel outside. He gathered two handfuls of material and shook the bundle till the cloth was free. Then he carried what he had in his hands to the hole and handed a wine-stained mess of disintegrating silk up to his uncle. He heard the winemaker say, "Is that all of it?" and answered that no, he'd only pulled the silk free from another mass. Then he shuffled back out of the light, through the encapsulated warmth of fermentation, and closer to that strange, powerful cold odour.

'And what my grandfather said he touched then, and tried to lift, was a damp mass of feathers. He hauled the mass over to the light and that's when he, and his uncle above him, saw the wing.

'The wing was white—grandfather said—and there was wine *on* the feathers but not staining them. Small beads of wine sat on the feathers like crystals of water on the back of a duck.'

De Valday paused and leaned back in his chair. 'The family sent the winemaker away—dismissing him on the spot. Then they opened the other "Angel" and lowered my grandfather into it and had him remove the wine-ruined silk from the other wing. The wings were unwrapped, and left in the barrels. Then the barrels were sealed and haven't been opened since.'

De Valday looked at Flora with the look of someone who knows he's told a good story and is more interested in its being appreciated than believed. Green caught Flora's eye and made a gesture, less a nod than a spasm of enthusiasm. 'What do you think?' he said.

For a moment she wasn't able to think anything. Her mind only blazed, painlessly, as though she were freshly on fire. And then she remembered Xas's figure, glimpsed through her kitchen window, out on the paper road in the rain, white skin whiter still in patches like mist floating below high, even cloud. She thought of the brief, taunting correspondence she'd had, and the startling unworldliness of the person who'd written the notes. She thought of an awning torn from a shop front and used as notepaper, of the stealth it would take to have spread that canvas at her door, for the crackling tarred tin on her veranda had given nothing away. She remembered Xas saying that the pearls had belonged to a relative of his. And she thought that, of course, that relative had wings—*still* had wings—and had dropped down out of the sky above her house to ask after Xas.

Flora didn't answer Green, she only put out her hand for the pearls. Henri de Valday poured them into her palm. She stretched the rope out taut and gave it several sharp, strenuous tugs, so that the pearls vibrated, singing. The string held; it had no give.

'Careful,' de Valday said. He retrieved the pearls from Flora, and shook an admonishing finger at her.

Flora apologised. Then she said to Green, 'I wanted to see for myself.' But what she was thinking was: '*Angels are indestructible.*'

# Balboa Yacht Club

## March, 1931

When Flora hailed Crow's boat he appeared on deck and gave her his hand to steady her as she stepped aboard. Then she was pulled into a hug and, for a moment, her face was against his cotton sweater with its smell of soap and expensive whisky. She took a deep breath. He set her away from him and frowned. 'You look hungover,' he said, then, mischievously, 'Would you like a drink?' She declined, and he went down into the galley to make his own and talked to her as he did about her cut of *Haywire*, the film he had shot on the side of *Helen Hope* with his own money and some siphoned from the studio's official project.

Flora listened to his voice and the noises from the marina, water lapping against the hull, and the clack of hawsers against masts. She looked over the side at the deep green water in the lee of the boat. She tried to imagine Xas's fall from Cole's plane. She found she couldn't visualise the fall itself so instead conjured an image of Xas surfacing from water like this, bubble-blistered seawater streaming off his upturned face. He would look for Cole's plane, far off, dwindling in the sky. Flora imagined the expression on his face, a look she'd seen often but had never understood, an alert and deeply thoughtful look, that she now knew meant he was trying to fathom some human feeling he had never felt himself—Cole's vengeful spite.

Crow came up from below and gave Flora a cup of coffee. He had remembered how she liked it. He sat beside her. 'Edna is out of hospital,' he said, his voice now low and confiding.

Crow's wife had had another month-long stay in a private clinic. It was general knowledge that she suffered from bad nerves, and bouts of unhappiness when she would lapse into a silence and inactivity so profound that she eventually needed to be washed and fed, put to bed and got up, moved from garden to dayroom to her own room like a pale, poseable mannequin.

'She's much better,' Crow reported. 'She's always better when she's pregnant.'

Despite herself Flora sighed. It was true that Edna was better when she was pregnant. But she had suffered her most serious breakdowns in the months following the delivery of each child. Besides, Flora had thought that Crow had finally decided to divorce his wife. Crow wasn't so much tired of his marriage as worn out by all the alarms and discouragements of living with someone who couldn't seem to find any durable happiness in herself. And then there was Carol, Crow's secretary. Carol and Crow had been lovers for three years now and, as far as Flora knew, Crow had been faithful to Carol—excepting Edna, obviously, since Edna was pregnant again.

'I suppose you think I'm hopeless,' Crow said.

'I did think that there was only Carol now. You and she are always together.'

'Edna and I have twelve years of marriage and three children in common. We once knew all the same people. We're connected, and all our connections would have to be cut.'

Flora thought that Edna was like one of Crow's heroines—was possibly their model—a fatefully sad, tired, and touching person. The heroines of his films loved consolation. They liked to fall asleep with their heads on the heroes' shoulders. After *nothing*—a narrative nothing that wasn't to do with censorship, and all the new entrenchments in the rules of decency for film. No—they would fall asleep after no lovemaking, after nothing more than an offer of understanding. Was it any wonder Crow was having trouble with the crusading Helen Hope?

Flora opened her mouth to begin saying what she'd come to say, that she had solved Crow's problem with that film, that she'd found a charitable occupation for Miss Hope, something that would film beautifully and add interest to the movie. She was about to speak when Crow said, 'You should be careful yourself.'

Flora looked at him and lifted an eyebrow.

'I don't have any objections to Pete *per se*, but you should be careful nevertheless.'

'Pete sometimes sees me home. It's meaningless, Connie.'

'Pete couldn't spend five minutes alone with an attractive woman without handling her.'

'And he's welcome,' Flora said, defiantly. 'There's no harm in it. I'm surprised you even know about it, that anyone's bothered to tell you.'

Crow blushed. 'Flora, I'm not worried about your reputation, I'm worried about your health.'

Flora understood then that Crow knew more about her then he was entitled to. Drunk, she had confided in Gil, and Gil had passed on what she'd said to his brother. But Connie had no business knowing, and she didn't want him looking at her and seeing someone neutered by an injury. She said, 'I'm touched by your concern,' cool. 'But it's none of your business.'

Crow made a soothing motion, patting the air between them. They were quiet for some time after that. There was no sound but the lapping of the slightly oily water against the hull, the wooden bells of the hawsers, and a crackling of ice cubes in Crow's whisky. 'So, Flora,' Crow said, finally, 'to what do I owe the honour of this visit?'

'I finally thought of something for Helen Hope to do, to be *seen* doing. Something that will play well.'

'Good! I just had a spat with Stahr about bloody *Helen Hope*. He knows I'm dawdling, but not that I've made a whole other film. Anyway, he told me I was just a technician, and I told him he was only a businessman. And fortunately that was the end of it—in our mutual understanding that we're both too honest to imagine ourselves as visionaries and artists.'

'My idea should work,' Flora said. 'Then perhaps the businessman will stop breathing down your neck.'

# Intermission

# Berlin

## August, 1931

One day, after the shoot had wrapped but before the film was shown—*Kameradschaft*, the film on which he'd worked as a carpenter, then as a pyrotechnician—Xas received Flora's message.

He'd spent the day in a beer hall. The beer halls were inviting, he thought, a novelty anyway. It seemed to him that Germans had lately turned into Russians—all of a sudden they were extravagantly sentimental, in public at least, and liable to jump up to make speeches and sing songs. All the zealotry and sentimentality at his table was about the job they'd done. Everyone was making promises. He was promised more work. There had to be more work for, they said, a man with such a feeling for fire.

Xas spent all afternoon drinking his share of beer till his innards were sloshing, and listening, puzzled and muzzy, to the speeches. He joined in the singing, and forgot to moderate his voice so that everyone in his vicinity eventually stopped singing themselves to stare at him in astonishment. He was quiet after that, and only listened— making a conscious attempt to assimilate the changes in the city he had supposed he knew. Finally, when the sentimentality began to seem a little sinister, he got up and went out into the day, using the banister to haul himself up the stairs—so drunk that his balance was impaired.

Outside there were more inebriated people sprawled on benches built around the trunks of old linden trees. But beyond the plaza Xas found a quiet street, where families strolled in the evening air, and bathers lounged on the banks of the river while boats glided by, rowed with vigorous but silent synchronicity. The angel found a urinal and pissed not urine but beer, with only a little of its alcohol and sugar subtracted from its mix, then went on his way feeling lighter but still light-headed.

He was passing a cinema when a poster in its box office caught his eye: 'Monroe Stahr presents *Helen Hope*, a film by Conrad Crow.' There was a picture of Franchot Tone and some actress with eyebrows like two fairytale bridges.

Xas bought a ticket. He sat through half of another feature film, and a selection of shorts—a strike by sailors in the Royal Navy, Scotland; bank riots in Düsseldorf— and then the film started, and Xas took note of Flora's name on the credits.

The heroine, Helen Hope, after a run of man and money trouble, found shape and direction in her flighty life by teaching painting at a school for deaf children. Whole minutes of the film were without dialogue, and seemed silent, made for the eye only, despite the music and the sounds of hands clapping, or rubber balls bouncing on pavement. The film ended with an embrace on the front steps of the school. Helen Hope and her man were holding hands—or, still not quite in accord, still resisting one another—their hands came together as if to say, 'Stay, and argue with me.' As they came together the school doors opened and the pupils spilled out for recess. One boy, Helen's tough-guy favourite, noticed the vestigial embrace. He grabbed at his friends, then began to flap his arms to get their attention. Then his flapping turned into the universal gesture for 'come back'. 'Come back' he signalled to the other children, and then looked up at the couple. His face grew brilliant with delight. He had caught them kissing. The camera didn't show the kiss, only the boy's delight, and his signalling hand growing still and going up to touch his own mouth.

Xas, sitting in the dark, thought, 'How like Crow not to show the kiss. Not to satisfy us in any ordinary way.' He was entranced, he was admiring—but these were cold reactions. After all, he had taken in the other thing, that Flora McLeod had got her friend Crow to film what he, Xas, had told her he'd like to see filmed, and had used that deaf child's vivid face and graceful hands to call him back to her.

He had new clothes, a silk shirt and flannel trousers, a pale grey jacket and hat—a fedora, at a time when many other men had adopted Tyrolean hats with little feather cockades. Then again, young men were also wearing lederhosen. Xas didn't know quite what to think of this adoption of peasant costume by clerks, students, and city folk. It wasn't yet a wholesale adoption, but there was something in it more fervent than faddish. It puzzled him. He didn't like it, and he wasn't going to do it.

The angel arrived at the Hintersee country house looking respectable in his new clothes, if a little rumpled from the train and cab ride. Frau Hintersee took him off the maid who'd opened the door to him, and conducted him through the house and out onto the long lawn that sloped down to a canal, where her husband, August, had his narrow boat.

She explained, 'August likes to keep out of the way of the young people. They were all here this summer, our nieces and nephews as well as our own children. It can be very noisy. August says he needs quiet because he's writing a book, but I see no sign of it. He reads. I think that's all he does.'

The canal was a vivid green, and black where the willows dabbled their long fronds into their shadows. The water was still, disturbed only by tiny spasms of insects touching-down or taking-off or stepping across the water on their hair-like legs.

As Frau Hintersee and Xas neared the gangplank she waved to her husband, who was sitting in a deckchair in the shade behind the wheelhouse. August had his shoes off and an open book resting on the slope of his belly. He looked up at them— and didn't wave, or move. Frau Hintersee stayed on the riverbank, and watched her guest step across the gangplank. Then she turned away and trudged back up the slope.

Xas leaned on the rail at the back of the barge. There was about ten feet separating him and the man in the deck chair.

He took off his hat and brushed his hair back—he was wearing it long on top now, and it fell forward unless he oiled it, and he often didn't oil it because it was so thick it took too much oil. 'I feel I should be standing, hat in hand,' he said.

Hintersee only stared.

'I want to say that I regret the way I acted when we met last,' Xas said, 'and that I've now learned that the policies I made for myself about how to treat people don't work. That if I act in a certain way at the outset—if I smile, share a beer, show affection, mend a roof—I can't then just say "no".'

'You threatened me,' Hintersee said at last.

'Not *with* anything,' Xas protested. Then he gave Hintersee his name and spelled it. He did this as though it was a great concession. 'What happened in 1917 haunted you,' Xas said. 'And it was reasonable for you to want to understand it. But I didn't want to discuss it any more than I wanted to hear then—in 1917—what the *malalak* had to say to me.' He used the Hebrew word for messenger. He said, 'Sooner or later one of Them is going to try to explain Himself to me. God—or Lucifer. But though there may be a reason why my wings were cut off, a reason for doing it, and for letting it be done, the reason is nothing compared to the act. The world of the act is a different one from the world of the reason.'

'After you jumped from the observer's car,' Hintersee said, 'and after what I overheard, nothing we were doing made the sense it had. I lost my stomach for the fight. I lost interest in my men. I felt I had a new duty to—to the mystery of what had happened. It seemed to me we were all wasting years staring through gun sights instead of looking into——' He trailed off.

The hinges and canvas of Hintersee's chair creaked as he dismounted from it. His book dropped onto the deck. He put one foot out of the wheelhouse shade then lifted it again immediately, its sole striped with soft tar from the deck's caulking. 'What do you think God wants from us?' he asked Xas.

'I don't know.'

'Do you think He wants us to better ourselves?'

'God thinks you are all automatically improved by dying after a blameless life.'

'Shouldn't we want better for ourselves? For instance, a society free of poverty and degeneracy?'

Xas shrugged.

'You mustn't just shrug!' his captain said, chiding.

'Sorry,' Xas said. 'I'm sure God approves of improvements. But should people be wondering what God wants of them?'

Hintersee looked surprised, but not scandalised. Then he looked thoughtful. 'The world could be more like Heaven,' he said.

'I suppose it could,' Xas agreed, mildly. He got up and joined the man in the shade, stood beside him for a moment, then leaned on him, as a dog leans on its master's leg.

Hintersee put an arm around Xas, as much to maintain his balance as to show affection. Then Hintersee was conquered by the smell of the angel's body. Xas smelled of the air up high; air without any obstacles. The man breathed deeply. They were standing hip to hip, and Hintersee tilted his head so that his temple touched Xas's. He heard Xas's voice, both in the air and through the bones of their skulls. Xas sounded gentle, ingenuous, submissive. He said, 'I hear *Lake Werner* is crossing the Atlantic again next month.'

Second Reel

# Los Angeles, and a spa in the Sierras

## October, 1931

Flora was very busy cutting films for the studio. In May Stahr had called her into his office to say how much he admired her cut of *Helen Hope*. He told her that he was aware she had more than an editor's hand in the film. The studio had some top-end films in production and he wanted Flora to edit them. 'You can be a kind of backstop for our directors. Not all of them need one, but I'm going to be a lot more confident knowing you're on the job.'

On a cool day in October Flora was, as usual, in her editing suite, when the first of the day's unscheduled visitors appeared. Carol, Crow's script girl and girlfriend, stood holding the screen door open with her body and asked for Flora's help. 'With Gil gone I don't know who to turn to. This shouldn't even be my business. I've already called Connie five times. I would have had Edna's sister call, but I don't want to risk him repeating to her any of the things he said to me.'

Carol told Flora that Crow's wife was at Cedars of Lebanon, committed by her own doctor, and that the new baby, Francis, was at another hospital, Sisters of Mercy. Carol hadn't been able to get a straight story from Edna's sister. 'She tracked me down, never mind that she clearly knows what I really am to Connie. She made me promise to get him back to town as soon as possible. But she wouldn't let me have any details about what had happened. That family are unalterably Brahman, steeped in dignity.'

'Do you have any guesses?' Flora said. 'Could Edna have harmed the baby?'

'Possibly. Anyway, I called the Grand Hotel and spoke to Connie. But I was sent in unarmed, as it were.'

'Wait,' said Flora, 'why aren't you with Connie? He always takes you. You got to go to Mexico and Alaska.'

Carol said, 'Well, this time I wasn't admitted to the sacred circle of two.' She pulled a face.

Everyone who knew Crow and Cole was very surprised when, on finally meeting, the two men not only hit it off but began taking Crow's show-off Italian car out for long drives in the desert; long drives where they'd stop the car, and sit on the running board in the shade and desert silence, and talk, Crow unembarrassed by having to shout to make himself heard—for Cole was now partly deaf in his 'good' ear too—and Cole apparently happy to be the recipient of the older man's advice and friendly patronage.

'It's not the old boys-club stuff,' Carol said. 'I was in on that. I was counted "a sport". This time there's just the three of them up at the spa, and Wylie for a week only. Connie said to me that they hoped to hack out a whole screenplay. He's more excited about this film he's doing with Cole than he has been about any other. He said to me that it's "serious". As if everything before wasn't.'

'They've given each other permission to think dark thoughts,' Flora said. 'And maybe the film will be all they hope, if Connie can temper Cole's grandiosity, and Cole can soften Connie's bravado.'

Carol said, 'I told Connie that I wouldn't have disturbed him unless it was a matter of vital importance. And he said that everything with Edna was always a matter of vital importance, and that Edna's universe consisted of herself, her suffering, and a ticking clock. That's what he said. I asked him why he'd imagine I was exaggerating—why the mistress would wring her hands over the wife's troubles.' Carol paused and her eyes swam.

Flora got up and gave Carol her handkerchief. Carol's was sodden and balled in her fist.

'Sorry,' Carol said, and dabbed her eyes. 'I don't want to tell you what he said. But it appears he's made up his mind to cut both of us loose—wife and mistress.'

Flora put her hand on Carol's arm. The woman gave her a weak, brave little smile. She said, 'I'd rather not think about it. When he gets like this, trying to work out what he's doing is like sitting up in the road to try to work out the make and model of the car that's just run you down.'

'How can I help?'

'You could call him. So that he knows it's not just me. I would've got Edna's sister on to it, but I don't want to be responsible for his saying something irrevocable.'

'What if he asks me for my source of information?'

'Does it matter? Oh—Flora—you'll think of something!'

There was no phone in Flora's editing shack, so they locked up and went down to the nearest—a box by the commissary. They waited for a girl in black tights, a bow tie and tails, to finish her call. Eventually the girl retrieved her chewing gum from the booth's doorjamb, popped it back into her mouth, smirked at them, and trotted off. They crammed into the booth together and once Flora had the operator, Carol recited the hotel's number.

Crow wasn't in his room. Flora asked the man at the hotel's front desk to page him. She actually heard the bellhop recede into a certain kind of sound scheme—hollow marble, hushed emptiness, thin mountain air—calling 'Phone call for Mr Crow!' She wondered aloud, 'Are there so many guests this late in the year that he has to call?' She hadn't thought the spa was a fashionable place. After many minutes she heard footfalls, and a murmured exchange, then the desk clerk came back on the line to say, apologetically, that Mr Crow wasn't accepting calls.

'Oh for God's sake!' Flora said in exasperation. She didn't hear the desk clerk's response because at that moment she was distracted by the sound of knuckles rapping on the glass by her head. She turned, irritated, ready to ask whoever it was 'what's your rush?' And saw the white grin, bright skin and dark blue rain-washed evening gaze of Xas—the angel, of course, *the angel*, how had she not seen it before? She jostled Carol out of the way and burst from the phone booth. She threw her arms around Xas, who laughed. Flora pressed her face into his neck and opened her mouth to gulp his cold cloud odour.

'You wanted me?' he said, still laughing.

Of course Flora saw her chance—Xas was back, and if she kept him busy he'd stay involved, but she wouldn't immediately have to face the difficult talk that was, no doubt, ahead of them.

Flora took Carol and Xas to the commissary, where they had coffee and she explained, with Carol's help, how Crow must be persuaded to come back to town and to his wife, but was now avoiding their calls. Then Flora explained how Crow and Cole had become friends—that Cole had dropped his case against Crow, the one about who'd owned Ray Paige's story—and, when they'd eventually chanced to be in the same place, Cole had admired Crow's Isotta Fraschini and Crow had offered to let Cole drive it. 'And now they're planning a film, writing a screenplay with Wylie White—holed-up in a little spa town in the Sierras, near where you went that time you borrowed my car.'

Then Carol said to Xas, 'If you know your way about up there, perhaps you'll go with Flora? Can you do that, Flora?' she added. 'I know Crow thinks better of you than almost anyone. And, actually, so does Cole, so it's unlikely he'll be offended by you barging in on them. Or only a little offended. If you turn up they won't automatically think "female interference".'

'Hmmm,' said Flora, sensing an insult in Carol's compliment. Then she said, all right, she'd go, and she put her hand on Xas's. 'And my friend can keep me company.'

They took Carol's car, a new Chrysler Imperial. During the drive they talked about Millie. Xas said he'd read about the disastrous San Francisco to Hawaii race in a magazine, months afterward.

Flora told him how Millie had been afraid of getting lost. 'Then so many of the planes did. She did say that if you were with her she'd be sure to find her way.'

Xas said, 'I never imagined she was so desperate about the money.'

'That flying school was her life's dream.'

'I should have been there. I had a plan to help her, but it was a stupid one.'

Flora watched him. She saw regret, and grief too, but grief perhaps without a clear object or occasion, as if he'd already put whatever he felt about Millie's death where he put similar regrets and losses. She thought, 'He has some place inside him that's a memorial not to people he cared for who've gone, but to the inevitability of their being gone.' Flora saw this, and it made her angry. He should be feeling *guilty* too. He had let Millie down.

She said, 'When you say you should have been there, what do you mean?'

He glanced at her, then returned his eyes to the road. 'I just drifted into our friendship,' he said, 'as if I'd only set down somewhere for a breather. I never got around to feeling properly responsible for her.'

'So that's what you feel,' Flora said, flat. 'Responsible.' She wanted him to know that it wasn't enough.

'Ah—what I *feel*. I feel I should have been there. I should have known she was in trouble, should have reached her in time, caught her as she fell, plucked her up from the water, or kept her company till the searchers came. I should have been there like the sun and the stars. Like God.'

They were quiet for a time after that. Then Xas began to tell her a little about what had happened to him. He didn't say why he'd disappeared, but told her where he'd been. He talked about Berlin and *Kameradschaft*. He told her how he'd got to the States, to New Jersey, aboard the airship *Lake Werner*. He took one hand off the wheel to fish in his jacket and pull out a passport. He handed it to Flora. The passport was issued that year to one Christoph Hintersee. The photo was of Xas. He said, 'My captain had a young cousin who'd died. We used the cousin's papers to get a passport. And here I am.'

'For how long?'

He glanced at her, at the road, then back at her. 'Fix a period,' he said.

'Watch where you're going,' she reminded him.

He returned his eyes to the road. He said, 'Make a bargain. Extract a promise.' The wind coming over the top of the roadster's windshield was patting at the thick, long, oiled hair on his crown. He looked confident and careless. But it seemed to Flora that there was something cold at the bottom of this gallantry of his, and that all of it—his confidence, coldness, and carelessness—wasn't directed at her, but at himself, his aimlessness. She thought: 'This is what he does. He picks his moment, and offers up his life.' If he'd thought to do this for Millie then things would have turned out differently.

Flora said, 'I'm not playing any games.'

He looked disappointed.

After another few miles she said, 'Cole will be surprised to see you.'

They slowed and turned on to Kaiser Pass Road.

'Yes,' Xas said.

Later, as they drove through a small grassy valley in a saddle between ranges and began to climb again, they passed another car. It was the first vehicle they'd seen for half an hour. It roared past them, engines throbbing, its chrome and paintwork bristling with light.

'That's Connie's car,' Flora said. The driver was wearing cheaters, a scarf and cap, and Flora wasn't sure who it was. 'Connie would recognise Carol's car, surely.'

'It was Cole,' Xas said. He pulled over, left the engine idling and turned to her. 'I'm getting out here.'

She seized his arm. 'This is the middle of nowhere,' she said.

'Good,' said Xas. He brushed her off and got out.

'What are you going to do?' Flora was afraid—for Cole.

'You go on and talk to Crow,' Xas said. 'While Cole and I have a tender reunion. You don't want to deprive us of our tender reunion, do you?'

'He thinks you're dead,' Flora said.

Xas smiled, stepped away from the car, and waved her on.


It was November and the Grand Hotel was empty of guests and grandeur. The spa town had been fashionable before the War, and people did still come in summer to enjoy the swimming holes in the river. This last year there had been fewer family parties. Jobs were scarce, and ageing cars needed nursing on the climb up into the mountains. The rented cottages on the terrace across the river were all shut up early, and looked a little battered. Fallen leaves were piled in the avenues of the public gardens, the merry-go-round was shuttered and padlocked, the kiosk's louvres already sealed by thickening spider webs. Mornings, the spa town's walls and trees were pink and gold, but both colours were greyed by dryness and a whole summer's worth of dust not yet rinsed away by fall rain. It hadn't rained, but the air was damp all morning and again when the sun went, which it did twice, declining in a shallow fall behind a near ridge, then behind another farther off. The sun was gone for forty minutes, only to reappear for a quarter-hour in the V between the peaks, its light pinched and concentrated so that, coming through the branches of the Californian hazels below the hotel terrace, it made shadows of leaves that were sharp-edged, but distilled in density, ghostly and dilute. This second sunset probed into the rooms of the west-facing

Grand Hotel so that its handful of guests could see what the insufficient radiance of the smeared crystal chandeliers otherwise disguised: the fabric on armchairs polished by grime, dust softening the folds of once cheerful yellow curtains, and the white leather on the lobby's loveseats burned brown by years of contact with acidic human skin.

For several weeks now only the hotel's ground floor had been open. At times the few guests would feel like Beauty in the fairytale, waited on by invisible servants. In the dining room all the tables were draped, but only as many as necessary set for breakfast. There was never anyone in sight, but staff would appear, alerted to the guests' movements by the talkative parquet floors. Over the years the piles of the hotel had sunk, and in the long perspective from the dining room, across a lobby and into the vast sitting room with its six fireplaces, the floor undulated in waves, and creaked and squawked when crossed. The hotel was quiet, but it was impossible for its guests to go about quietly.

Not that the guests did. The two movie people were often animated over their work. They worked all day, on the terrace, their white-painted wicker chairs pulled together so that their knees nearly touched. They were tall men, and one was hard of hearing. On the marble-topped table beside them were papers—the screenplay they were working on—a typewriter, an ashtray for the one who smoked, whisky in one jug and iced water in another for the one who always liked to fix his own drinks. They were often silent for hours, but then noisy in friendly dispute. One would jump up and act something out in an effort to persuade the other, while the other would just talk—the younger one, with the shy, hypnotic voice. One went to the grotto sometimes and took the waters, the other didn't, and was very careful about his diet. They both vanished for long drives, the younger man driving although it was the older man's car. They were Hollywood people, the younger more famous, the older easier to deal with, and more easily pleased. No one bothered to eavesdrop on them, for there was no news in their friendship or their mutual industry. But there was an air they had of being involved in something of momentous importance. As the weeks went by a kind of tenderness entered into their discussions—a tenderness directed not toward each other, but perhaps to the promise in the pages piled up between them.

For one week of the three they were joined by another man, a gnarled and waspish Southerner. When he was with them the whisky was put away and didn't reappear till the final night of his stay, and, the following afternoon, they carried him out to a cab, handed over a hundred-dollar bill and sent him off straight to Sacramento, where he was to board the *Twentieth Century*. The older man was overheard saying, 'He'll be sober by Chicago.' To which the younger replied, laughing, 'Sober enough to order a drink.'

After the writer left, the hotel made enquiries about its guests' intentions, for it was usually around this date that the maitre d' took over the cook's duties for the hotel's handful of winter visitors. The staff were told that the two intended to be there for only another week, and that they didn't expect anyone to join them.

*

A still afternoon. The sun was warm and low, the air hazy. The entire reduced population of the spa town heard the roadster before seeing it, climbing the slope on the far side of the river toward the viaduct. The road was illuminated in yellow light from the trees and the car's white paint looked cream. The dead leaves on the road hopped along after the car's back wheels, seeming to float on static over the road's surface, galvanised, and living again. The car crossed the river. It drove slowly up the terraces between the guesthouses, passed the spa where a few old people—thin haired, swollen-legged—were walking arm in arm, limping between the grotto and park benches, carrying glasses of the spa's piss-coloured water. The car passed the other hotel guests—all four of them sitting on a horseshoe-shaped stone bench with their bellies in their laps. The roadster roared up the driveway, and parked below the hotel's steps.

Crow was by himself on the terrace, with jugs and teacups, papers and typewriter before him.

Flora turned off the engine and stepped out onto the drive. Its white grit crunched under her feet. She went up the steps. The tiles on the terrace were uneven, some were loose. They made a musical tinkling under her shoes.

'Flora,' Crow said, pleased and exasperated. He was smiling and a little flushed, with drink and combativeness. 'Carol sent you. Don't deny it,' he said. 'Look—I'll join my wife's drama when I'm good and ready, and not before.'

Flora took a seat. She lifted the covers on the jugs. One held whisky, the other iced water. She poured herself a small neat whisky. 'I don't see how you can be angry at Carol. She's not acting on her own behalf. What would she have to gain by encouraging you to rush to your wife's side?'

'I'd arrive in the middle of the mess, and have to confront how irrevocable Edna's problems are. That's what she'd gain.'

'Oh,' said Flora, and made a mental note not to try to argue motivation with Crow again.

'What I'm doing here is important.'

'That's why Cole's dashing about in your Isotta Fraschini. We passed him on the road.'

'We? That's Carol's car—where is she? Did you drop her across the river? Nothing is open over there. Or only the gas station.'

Flora ignored this. 'Did Carol tell you that the baby is at Sisters of Mercy?'

'He's unharmed. I called the hospital myself.'

'Unharmed and unloved,' Flora said. 'Edna apparently refuses to see him.'

'What gross sentimental exaggeration!' Crow said. 'I scarcely know the little thing. He's hardly lying there, at eight weeks old, saying, "Where's my father?"'

Flora couldn't think of anything else to say. She looked out at the woods, a forest of redwoods and white fir that girdled the lower slopes of the mountains above the river. The sun was low, the air misty. It was the kind of season, in the kind of country, that feels like a last resort; like time emptying out, and the world winding down.

Crow said, 'Carol has bought into all Edna's troubles because, by being sympathetic to my wife's plight, she can feel better about the fact she has never had from me the full pledge of time and attention she imagines she wants. No wonder she thought better of facing me herself.'

'*Imagines* she wants!' Flora repeated, incredulous. 'Why be sceptical about Carol's needs if you're never going to answer them? And I didn't come with Carol, I came with Xas.'

Crow looked shocked and angry. 'He's reappeared? You must be delighted.'

'Inexpressibly.'

'So, you came with Cole's handmaiden, but Carol sent you.'

'She asked me to come. But, Connie, I agree with Carol. I think you should come back to town.'

Crow's face went stiff with a resolve made mostly of spite. 'And what makes you suppose I'd care what you think?'

'I don't have to consider that, Connie. I have your confidence. And Cole's too. You do know, don't you, that all sorts of people come to me asking advice on how to handle you both? The two imperial characters. I know that can all change in an instant if I offend you—or alarm him. But don't imagine that I'm going to let my peace of mind depend on being careful of your feelings. I've got bigger fish to fry.'

'Oh have you?' Crow said, scornful.

'Go on, just say it,' she said. '"Oh have you? You invalid, you spinster."'

Crow looked startled, then laughed. He got up and told her he'd go pack his bags, adding as he went, 'You old sourpuss!'

The sun declined, and the meadow gradually took on a mythical bathed-in-honey look. As Xas waited, a red-tailed hawk dropped down to the road's rutted surface to perch on a bloody mammalian smear. It planted its claws and dipped its beak to tear off a strip of furry skin.

There was another hawk, near the forest, hanging like a kite on the breeze and scanning the meadow, head down and talons ready. The air directly above the meadow was fizzing with minute insects, and looked like soda water. Beyond the meadow a grove of redwoods stood in their blue reservoir of shadow.

The Isotta Fraschini's return was first announced by a smoke of dust above the trees hiding the last downward curves of the pass. Then Xas heard the engine and, finally, the flinty roar of wheels displacing gravel. The car appeared, moving fast, and practically ploughing the surface of the unsealed road.

The hawk, its beak buried deep in piled viscera, didn't notice the car until it was too late. It had only just raised its wings when Cole's left front tyre caught it and spun it under the car. Cole braked and skidded to a stop some fifty feet on. The car's comet tail of dust caught it up and rolled over it. The car was partly obscured from Xas's sight. He did see Cole stand up and look back to where the hawk lay, one wing beating uselessly, the other plastered to the road. Its mate had veered away from the forest. It began to circle and call. Cole sat down again, clasped the steering wheel and was for a time motionless, frozen. Then he covered his face with his hands.

Xas had had his talons ready too—ready for Cole—but witnessing this private moment of humble culpability, he abandoned the plans he had and went back to waiting on the resources of the moment, as usual. He walked to the car, opened its passenger door, and got in beside Cole. Cole dropped his hands and looked at him. Cole's face was already drawn and pale and, like his clothes and the car's upholstery, powdered by dust.

Xas could see that Cole thought he was seeing a ghost— or having a vision somehow connected to the dying hawk and its distressed mate.

The wounded bird was perhaps dead now, though the steady wind lifted and flourished the wing that wasn't maimed. The other hawk alighted next to its mate, and swivelled its head, checking with either eye as though hoping for a different report from one or the other.

Xas got out again, walked around the car and opened the driver's door. He said, 'Slide over. I'll drive.' He got in and edged Cole over with his body. Cole complied. He was limp and pale.

Xas released the handbrake, gunned the engine and put the car in gear. They drove off. Cole turned to look after the dead hawk and its grieving mate, and Xas thought, or hoped, that perhaps Cole was watching for the mangled bird to lift itself out of the mix of offal and its own blood and fly away—restored—followed by its mate, faith restored. The landscape would then put itself back in better order. It would become less beautiful. It would stop looking like a place with a story to tell or a lesson to teach. Instead it would be like the moment when the curtains come down on the final act of a tragedy and everyone on stage gets up and falls into line for the applause. That's what Xas hoped— that the world had altered for Cole when he climbed into Cole's car. That the world was momentarily unmasked. It had pulled off its death mask and was taking its bow. Xas hoped Cole might see that—what was *also* true. It was true that time wouldn't stop, or run backward. But it was also true that there were things indigestible to time and that those things—even if they were neutral or trivial—could never have the life crushed out of them.

Xas slowed at the river before the spa. There was a one lane bridge and he stopped to let another car go by. It was Carol's Imperial. Crow was driving. Flora waved as the Imperial accelerated past them and Crow gave Cole a salute, a droll gesture that seemed to say, 'Look at me— taken in hand.'

Cole stared, then wrenched his door open and jumped out of the car. He ran up the slope and into the forest.

Xas pulled off the road, got out, and went after him.

Cole ran deep into the forest. Xas followed, but didn't attempt to catch him up. They passed through a sheltered grove of sequoias. The forest was silent, and scented— tangerines with an edge of camphor. There was a sheen of water in the air between the trees. Xas noticed that Cole's breath made more steam than his own.

The man stopped where the slope became steep. He flung himself back against the heavily grooved trunk of a cedar, breathing hard.

It was a forest with myriad, no-particular paths leading on from where they were. Xas glanced up at the confluence of cedar branches above his head and saw how they made a pattern against the sky like frost stars framing a windowpane on an icy day.

Cole rested on the tree trunk with his hands behind his back, his throat exposed, his posture suggesting simultaneously that he was looking for an escape, and that if he found one he wouldn't take it. When Xas came close Cole reached out and snatched Xas toward him, stepping out of the way at the last minute so that they changed places. Xas found his own back to the tree trunk. He had a second in which to try to read Cole's expression. Cole's face was white, and his eyes seemed to give onto a black gas filling the inside of his head. Cole pressed Xas into the tree, one knee pushing between Xas's legs.

Cole said, 'You're dead.' He spoke, and his misty breath filled the space between their faces. Xas had forgotten to breathe himself. A leaf fell beside them, spiralling down, reversing its spin twice in its tumble. 'Or did I only imagine it?' Cole said.

Xas could taste the whisky fumes in Cole's breath. He began to breathe again and vapour mingled between their mouths.

Cole released Xas's arms and slammed his hands against the angel's abdomen, under his ribs. His fingernails dug into

Xas's skin without breaking it. 'What do I have to do?' Cole whispered. 'What does it take?' He moved one hand to seize a fistful of the long hair on Xas's crown, and yanked his head back so that it bashed against the tree trunk, and bits of bark rained down into his collar. Cole thrust his hand up under Xas's shirt, scattering buttons. He pressed his mouth against Xas's, not exactly kissing but grinding and wiping. He caught the side of Xas's jaw between his teeth and bit down so hard that his own jaw joint clunked. He chewed at Xas's throat, and chin, and collarbone, as though drilling for blood. He attacked Xas with his teeth, tongue, lips—and his weight, hauled him away from the tree against which they were both braced, then dropped on him. Cole's hand, wound into Xas's hair, thrust into the loam, as though he meant to plant the angel, press his hair into the earth like something that might be encouraged to take root.

Xas didn't resist, not even to hide what he'd hidden with dedication for nearly one hundred years. He didn't stop Cole when the man grappled him over onto his stomach. Xas felt his shirt tear, and his jacket was pushed up over his head so that he was in the dark. His face was buried in the springy needles. His nostrils were full of the smell of fermented resin and rot. Cole stopped ripping at him, and made a fussy, impatient, inarticulate, but intelligent sound. He reached under Xas to unbuckle his belt. The cold air touched where Cole wasn't touching—Cole's hot skin, and scratchy clothes. Cole made another sound, a moan of mingled shock and rage and joy as he found what he wasn't immediately looking for, but what moved him. He thrust his hands into the pelt of feathers on Xas's back, feathers that covered the mounds of muscle and knobs of vertebra, and filled the long twisted seams of the old scars. As Cole's hands ran over the feathers they bent and popped straight again with a sound similar to the one dough makes when a baker pounds it down after it has proved, and kneads the bubbles out.

Cole said, 'Oh God what are you?' and didn't wait for an answer. He was in tears, and trembling, but he was hard. 'You can kill me,' he said. It was a promise. A dedication. He kept repeating it as his hands slid, their blades scraping Xas's only partly unfastened trousers down around his thighs. 'You can kill me,' Cole sobbed as he pushed one hand under Xas's pelvis to raise it and part his legs.

Xas lay still. He didn't try to protect himself from any of the man's harmless offers of harm—or homage—he wasn't able to tell which it was. It didn't matter; harm or homage, he deserved both. He let it happen. He'd think about what it meant some other time. He took the touches, the force, the knowledge. He stayed pliant in the grip of the elbow locked against his throat, and under Cole's weight and the precipitate dry then slippery pushing that couldn't split his skin or tear his muscles. Xas listened to Cole's self-annihilating chant. He took what hurt but couldn't harm him. It was better than being dropped out of a plane into the sea. It was more personal. And afterward they weren't so far apart.

They lay still on the churned ground. Their bodies were clotted with damp bark. They had dug down in their thrashing to where nets of white mould grew in the rotting needles. The forest was hushed. Then a gust of wind came and leaves rained down from a black oak up the slope. The leaves were dry, and solid enough to click as they hit the branches and boles of other trees. But theirs was a kind of weightless solidity, and the angel hearing the sound they made thought something—something about himself, akin to the thought he'd had all those years ago in the deathly seclusion of that house by the walls of Beaune, where he'd felt time stop. Then Cole kissed his shoulder, and the thought vanished. Cole's tongue was warm and his lips were cold. Cole's hands were abraded, red and raw. He slid one under Xas's head, his palm cupping the angel's cheek, and slipped the tip of his thumb into Xas's mouth.

It was twilight when they arrived back at the hotel. They climbed the steps to the terrace, going slowly, as if they were both injured. Cole trembled whenever he paused. Xas put an arm around the man to support him indoors. He waved away a concerned bellhop.

Cole straightened and looked about him. The bellhop saw his chance and pounced, passing Cole a note. Cole handed the folded paper to Xas.

The note was from Crow. *'I'm sorry, Con,'* it read. *'I had to leave with Flora. My wife's illness requires my attention.'*

Cole found his voice. 'I'll keep Mr Crow's room for my friend here,' he told the bellhop. He walked on and Xas followed. The parquet crackled and gave and kept on reacting to the pressure of their steps long after they had passed over it. When they were in the dingy hallway outside Cole's door Xas could still hear the floor gossiping away to itself.

Cole couldn't fit his key into the lock. Xas pulled his hand away and took the key. He opened the door and pushed the man through it. Inside Cole turned and caught him. They closed the door with their clasping bodies and leaned on it together. Cole put his mouth against Xas's ear. 'You won't die,' he whispered. 'You won't get sick. And you won't ask for anything.'

Xas breathed deeply, took sustenance from Cole's smell. They pressed their gritty faces together. Despite all the heat of the last hour the angel felt he was being told a story, one that began with extravagant formality, as though spoken in the proper Parisian French Sobran's friend Aurora had used. '*This is how the day ran——*' she would say. Xas felt he had paused in the middle of doing something practical, like digging a ditch, and was leaning on a spade listening with quizzical attention to someone better than him tell a story as though building a memorial.

'You won't die,' Cole said again. 'You won't fall sick. There's nothing you need that I can give you.'

'I *would* like to lie down,' Xas said. He pushed Cole to persuade him to move. The man moved, but didn't release him. They shuffled clumsily across the room, Cole holding Xas's collar bunched in his hands, his head lowered so that the flat of his forehead was against Xas's. The back of the angel's legs hit the edge of the bed and they fell together, rolled onto the coverlet, wound together. Cole held Xas tightly, exerting so much force that his limbs trembled. He kept talking in bursts. 'I remember you offered to tell me how you came to be at Mines Field that night,' he said. 'It was one of those fairytale offers, a *test*, like the crone at the well, or the talking bird in the apple tree. You were telling me to listen, you were telling me that there was something I might need to know before I did to you what I wanted to do.'

Xas said, 'Don't talk about tests.' What Cole was saying seemed to carry some kind of infection inside it. It made him feel the way he fancied an illness might. He had never imagined there were things *he* needed to know. What needs did he have? He'd only come back to Los Angeles to humour Flora. She'd been resourceful. She deserved to have her resourcefulness rewarded. What needs did he have? He used to carry a parachute only out of respect for his fellow wing-walkers. The only thing people could do to hurt him was die. Not that they did it to hurt him. In the hangar at Mines Field he'd said to Cole, 'Shall I tell you how I came here?', meaning, 'Shall I tell you how I have you at an advantage?'

Cole kissed Xas's neck. He was laughing, softly, mirthfully. 'You won't die, but you are an animal. You enjoy being an animal, a gasping, shaking, writhing, slick, greedy little animal! Is it any wonder I thought you were filthy? You made me do things. Made me *want* to. You're *all wrong*. Your skin never shows anything. I bit you and hit you, but does it show?'

Cole's breath was hot on Xas's throat. His voice was hoarse. 'It's as if a light is licking you clean all the time. What *is* that?' Cole froze, thinking, then raised his head and peered, his eyes mad. '*Who* is that?' He seemed inquisitive, rather than distressed. He dropped his head again and kissed

Xas's shoulder. 'I can dirty you, and you won't ever spoil. You can be kept clean forever. Think about that. Think what it must mean to me, what value I'd put on it.'

Some of this was spoken into Xas's mouth. Cole pulled back once more to look into his eyes. 'I'm looking forward to this,' Cole said, and his own eyes were wide, looking forward with happy ferocity, rather than fear. He set his mouth against the angel's again, his lips split and swollen by their violence, and caressed Xas's undamaged mouth with light, grazing kisses. He removed Xas's shirt, and stroked the angel's chest and shoulders, till his fingers once more wandered into the hairline of white down. 'You had wings,' Cole said. 'You were some kind of angel. But now you're a wreck. You're salvage. You don't belong to anybody.'

There was a window open, and one of the mountain flies had come in. The fly bumbled about vaguely and alighted on Xas's hand, immaterial, as though it were already its own dried corpse. Xas shook his hand, and then slipped it under Cole's shirt. The small of Cole's back was slippery with sweat. Xas said, 'Maybe, like a wreck, whoever raises me will own me.'

'It's very dark, but I can still see you,' Cole said, wondering.

And it was true, there was next to no light in the room, but the flesh Cole was stroking caught what there was and gleamed like the top side of a cloud under starlight.

'You can be the light for me when I close my door on the light,' Cole said.

'Yes,' said Xas. 'I can be that. A light in your sovereign darkness.'

# Venice

## November, 1931

Three weeks went by before Xas walked back through Flora's front door. It was early Sunday evening, and Flora was washing her smalls at her bathroom basin while listening to the wireless, a broadcast from Radio City Music Hall in New York. Millie had taught Flora to appreciate the East to West time difference, and the fact that the Coloured musicians who only got to play late in New York, were broadcast at a perfect time for listeners on the West Coast. Flora was tapping her feet to a tune when she heard the latch rattle. She called out 'Hello?' then dried her hands and put her head around the door.

Xas was standing in front of the radio, listening to the trumpet solo. He said, 'That's Cootie Williams.'

'I should have known it was you. You know, most people sing out when they arrive. They say, "Hello, it's me."'

'Hello,' said Xas, 'it's me.' He peered at her, searchingly.

'Your bag and parcel are in your room.'

'I left them here before I went to the studio,' he said. 'I still had my key.'

'When you left you must have had only your key, and the clothes on your back.'

He went past her, into the bedroom at the back of the house. She switched off the radio and heard him unzip his bag. He reappeared with a suit on a hanger and went into the bathroom, saying, 'This has been folded for weeks. Steam sometimes works.' The shower went on. He crossed the hall again and emerged with a brown paper parcel, which he put into her hands.

The parcel held a white silk shawl embroidered with red roses and tangles of green thorns. He said, 'There was a Czech woman who lived off my courtyard in Berlin, and did fine embroidery.'

'Thank you,' Flora said. She wrapped the shawl around her.

He reached out and freed her hair, spread it on her shoulders.

'I'm thinking of cutting it,' she said. 'I've resisted a bob for ages, but I'm so busy these days, and it's such a lot of trouble to take care of.'

'I can perhaps make a difference to your busyness. Not that that's a plea for your hair.' He went back to the bathroom and shut off the shower.

She raised her voice to say, 'So, you're going to start mending, cleaning, and cooking again?'

He re-emerged. 'Do you mind?'

Flora was surprised to find herself feeling awkward, and a little repulsed, not by anger or dislike, but as if they were magnets that had come into oppositional contact. 'No,' she said, then, 'How is Cole?'

Xas raised one eyebrow, and turned his head from her.

Flora felt dismissed. She drifted away into her kitchen and began making coffee. She called out to ask him if he wanted something to eat. There was a delay in his response, not absent-minded or impolite but, she felt, one that was supposed to allow for her to revise her invitation. Then, 'No thank you,' he said.

He must know she'd guessed that Cole had tried to kill him. Cole must have given away at least that much. Was he waiting for her to say something?

She put the workings in her percolator, then changed her mind about coffee and left the element beneath the pot unlit. 'I take it you saw *Helen Hope*?'

'Yes. Thank you.'

'For the deaf children?'

'Yes. Thank you for remembering. For making the effort. For asking me to come back.'

'You're welcome,' she said.

'That Helen Hope was a little like you,' Xas said.

Flora came out of her kitchen and glared at him. 'You're kidding! That do-gooder?'

'Up till now all Crow's heroines have been fatalistic, exhausted and asexual. I was never sure if they were his ideal woman, or a portrait of someone he loved.'

'They're like his wife. Or his idea of her.'

'Helen was a little like you,' he said again.

'So you keep saying.'

'Though you've always been fatalistic, Flora, so that's no change.'

'That's what I let everyone think,' she said, dry. 'Actually I have a plan. Or I'm open to the possibility of one.'

They were standing a little apart, and there was anger in their interaction, Flora felt, though she knew she was very glad to see him. *She* wasn't angry; so maybe it was him. She asked, 'Are you angry at me?'

'What reason would I have?'

Flora flushed and looked away. She began to babble. 'I've put you in the wrong room. It's always damp in there. You'd be better off in the other.'

'Millie's,' he said.

'Yes. I just put you back where you were before. I wasn't thinking.'

'I'll move my bag,' he said. He stood and gazed at her for a long time, then went to the bedroom where he could be heard stuffing the clothes he'd taken out of his bag back into it. He crossed the hall to the room Millie had occupied for the months they had all lived together. Flora listened to the sound of drawers slide in and out and his too-soft footfalls moving back and forth across the room. He reappeared and asked her for a bar of soap to grease the sides of a stuck drawer.

When he came back after seeing to the drawer he settled on her window seat. He said, 'You look uncomfortable.' He pushed up the sash, then lay down and folded his hands on his chest.

'I'm fine,' Flora snapped. 'You're being evasive. I asked you about Cole.'

'Cole isn't representative, is he?'

This remark puzzled Flora. It wasn't at all what she'd expected. She said, 'In what way?'

'He's unrepresentative of *people*. When we first met he said to me, "I'm not *people*. Not *folk*". But at the time I only thought he was boasting about his talent.'

'Cole's odd, through and through,' said Flora.

'His only interest in things is in how they concern *him*. Is a thing useful to him, or is it a threat.'

'Uh-huh,' said Flora, and then got stuck herself. An application of dry soap would be no help to her.

Xas said, 'We talked about the trouble we had. How he couldn't figure me out and started telling himself stories in which I was poisonous and a liability. We talked. My explanation—or my demonstration of it—cleared things up some. But he didn't ask me any questions. When we were back in town and on his home territory I thought he'd feel safer. I tried then to tell him a little about myself and he just sat in silence, smirking, as if what I was saying was an imposition, or painful in some way. As if he was being very forbearing and I was being gauche. So I shut up. Then, as soon as he was comfortable again he did what he always does, he started to talk about what he was up to. His plans.'

'Which are?'

'He owns all the farm land around the golf course next to Mines Field. The county wants his land to build a bigger airfield. He stands to make a lot of money. He wants to buy an airline. It's on his to-do list.'

'Oh,' said Flora, who had thought Cole's plans might have been influenced by the momentous things Xas had told him. 'That must have been discouraging for you,' she said.

'It was horrible. It wasn't as if he disbelieved me. It was just that the me I was revealing to him—and offering him some custodianship of—was irrelevant to the point of non-existence.'

'What was it you told him?' Flora asked.

Xas reached with his foot for the cord of the bamboo blind. He caught it between his toes and pulled it out so that the blind rattled down, releasing all the dust caught between its slats.

Flora went to him, tapped his legs to get him to make room, and settled, supported in the curve of his body. She said, 'Are you ever going to tell me?' She picked up his hand.

'Cole likes to have sex with me. So, I can make it up to him. I can make up in that way for what I am. For the impenetrable, stony, irrelevance of what I am.'

'Look at me,' Flora said. He did. His expression was a little bleak, but mostly blank. She said, 'You just told me that Cole wasn't representative. Maybe I am. You can tell *me* anything. I have faith in you. I know you're good.'

This last remark provoked a look of pain. It was faint and fleeting, but Flora saw it. Xas made a companionable, noncommittal noise, and his voice was even lovelier without words, and when his mouth was closed. Flora stroked his silky hair. 'Sorry,' she said. 'But you should trust me.'

Flora thought, 'Is he sparing me?' And she thought, 'Am I testing him?' Finally she thought, 'Is this any way to behave?'

# Venice, and the Wilshire Country Club

## January, 1932

A couple of months after he'd moved back into Flora's house, Xas was coming home one morning, at around three. He'd been with Cole, and hadn't showered. He was tacky, reeking, sated, but depressed. He'd caught the streetcar that came up Pacific Avenue, not the one that stopped on the Venice shore. He was taking the long way home, thinking.

He was on a dark stretch of road, at a point equidistant between two streetlights, when he heard the whistle of wind through long pinions. Without looking back, he dropped down onto the tarmac.

Lucifer swooped, and missed him. Didn't just miss, but miscalculated. As Xas dropped, Lucifer followed him down.

An eagle that lands on a rabbit uses its momentum to carry the rabbit away. It dives, drives its talons through furry skin into flesh, then lifts off again. Lucifer must have aimed to do something like that—seize Xas and push off from gravity by vaulting up from the springy divot of the angel's upright body, taking that body with him. But Xas ducked, and Lucifer extended his reach, and, because angels always had the lazy habit of not troubling too much to correct movements that might result in collisions—for collisions, though painful, never had ongoing consequences—when Lucifer's snatch missed he was too low, and going too fast, to correct his position. The tips of his long top wings came into contact with the ground, and he flipped and tumbled, limbs thumping the tarmac, pinions popping, a momentous tangle of flesh and feathers.

The archangel skidded and rolled the whole length of road to the next streetlight.

As for Xas—Xas had ducked only from reflex. He hadn't a hope of eluding his brother. He straightened and continued along the road, his shadow preceding him, for a car had appeared behind him.

The archangel was sorting himself out. He rose, unfurled his wings and flexed them gently.

The car's brakes squealed and its headlights slewed away. It stopped, slant on to the kerb. Its driver emerged and stood in a patch of radiance from a street lamp, eyes shaded with one hand, peering.

It was a quiet street. On its left the houses backed onto a canal. Beside Xas was a hedge with an arched opening, a white-painted gate, and a sign advertising the services of a piano teacher. For a desperate moment the angel imagined that, beyond that gate, there might be somewhere to hide.

But Lucifer simply stood waiting, and Xas came on, step by hesitant step.

When he was finally within reach, Lucifer seized Xas under his arms, crouched, and sprang away from the ground. Xas looked down past his helpless, dangling feet to watch the road recede, an illuminated strip of smooth tarmac. He saw the greenish flares of lawns, torched by houselights, the glossy black thread of the canal, the beachfront and boardwalk, the crowns of phoenix palms. He saw shop awnings, strings of coloured lights, lamps on ships moored off the coast. He saw the wasteland smeared with the thick shadows of live oak windbreaks, bright water flashing in its reed beds. He saw the peninsula, the oilfields' glow, the oatmeal-textured, weed-choked waterways. The flat tarpaper roof of a church passed beneath them, a pledge written there, meant to be read by God, or by pilots flying inland: *Christ the Lord is King.*

Lucifer didn't move his grip to take hold of Xas with any of his wing hands, even when he caught an updraft and was gliding, only steering himself by tilting the flight feathers of his top wings, the others spread out around him. The archangel's glide was slow, he almost floated rather than flew, and still he kept Xas at arm's length, carrying him as gingerly as a small child might a kitten.

Xas's hands were free, though, and he took hold of what he could reach, as if in fear of falling. He wrapped one hand around the steely striated muscle above the archangel's right elbow; the other grabbed a hank of Lucifer's gritty, knotted hair.

Not a word passed between them. It was silent in the air, the wind in the archangel's feathers making just enough noise to mask any sounds rising from the world below. They hung above the Hollywood Hills until Lucifer chose where to land, where he perhaps judged they might be undisturbed. He began to descend and Xas made out patches of green, like blankets pulled as taut as trampolines between regularly placed lights. He saw velvety grass lawns and woolly green treetops, the warm scales of terracotta tiled roofs, two opalescent illuminated swimming pools and, further from the buildings, dark lawns under the humped mists of sprinkler spray. Xas wasn't sure at the time where it was they came down. Later he worked out that they had landed on a green at the Wilshire Country Club.

The archangel dropped Xas a moment before touching down himself. Xas's boots made deep prints on the soaked green. They stayed where they landed, neither of them moving to get out from under the veil of sprinklers. The water beaded on the archangel's wings, then began to run in rivulets. It tapped on Xas's dry jacket, till the leather grew sodden and heavy. They faced one another—and God was there too, in the faintly lit mists, the ticking sounds the turf made as it drank, the sizzle of spray.

Lucifer said, 'You've given up taking your short cut.'

'I've been away, why should I take up all my old habits?'

'You've resumed living with your friend, that woman, and sleeping with some man—is it Conrad Cole?—the man whose smell is all over you. The only thing you've given up is your short cut.'

Xas's wet rattails dripped onto his nose. 'I've expected this,' he said. 'I've been waiting. Flora told me that someone had asked after me. Someone who left her anonymous notes, including one message inscribed on an awning torn from a shop front.'

Lucifer smiled, and Xas imagined running away across the squelching ground. He saw himself doing it. He would disappear beyond the lights around the arena of the green. The trees surrounding the green were elms, tall, though they had looked low from the air. There was a stable somewhere nearby, for Xas heard a horse whicker, and another answer it. Dignity didn't matter between him and God. So he would run, he'd pick up his feet and go. Perhaps the horses were housed in a stone building, behind doors with strong bolts. Perhaps their stalls were narrow and deep; too deep for an archangel to reach into.

Lucifer waited, his wings silvered by running water, calm, and beautiful with some kind of surety more personal and permanent to him in that moment even than the presence of his Father. 'There's something I want to ask you, Xas,' he said.

'All right. Go on. Get it over with,' Xas said.

The archangel said, 'I want to know why *you* think I cut off your wings.'

'I'll tell you, then you'll lie to me.'

Lucifer's forehead creased with perplexity. 'I know you've immersed yourself in the local traditions, but is it really necessary for you to go so far as to suppose I always lie?' Then, 'Ask me why I cut off your wings.'

'You cut off my wings so that Sobran could keep me,' Xas said. 'That's what you told him. And God let you do it because I'd offended Him. My lack of chastity was blasphemous. Because I'm a copy—a copy of that other one.'

'Ah,' said Lucifer, then he smiled and said, 'Since you're still being unchaste perhaps I should cut off something else.'

Xas's body remained motionless in the steady chilling spray, but his mind seemed to sidle away. He didn't want to think about why They'd chosen to maim him—God and Lucifer. He must find something to say to stop Lucifer telling him.

He removed his jacket and tossed it out of the range of the sprinklers. The drops began to soak his cotton shirt, so that a transparency seeped from his shoulders down. He said, 'Whatever reasons you had, I don't know how relevant they are now. You see, once my wings had gone, and I was on earth all the time, for maybe forty years things went on as they always had, then, gradually, many new things began to appear. For instance, there were multiple copies of books, and mass-produced clothes—the sorts of stuff manufactured by speedy machinery. So—say—a new zinc bucket would weigh less than an old wooden one, and could carry more apples, so the wooden bucket wasn't mended and was finally thrown away.'

'I'm being patient,' Lucifer said, 'but I'm missing your point. To go with your wood versus zinc analogy—God might seem to disappear, but would be growing again somewhere like the timber for a wooden bucket. He's always there, whatever shape He takes.'

'I don't mean that,' Xas said, 'though it's an interesting thought.' He heard the horses again, whickering nervously to one another. They reminded him of something he'd noticed. He said, 'There were five years in which the hundreds of thousands of horses in Paris reduced in number to only a few hundred, because of automobiles. I lived through all those different disappearances and changes, and I kept changing too, even after that first alteration.'

Lucifer frowned at him. 'Are you trying to say that your wings weren't *taken* but simply disappeared, like the Parisian horses? That there was no violence, only an "alteration"?'

Xas was silent.

'Are you trying to say that since the world has moved on, in effect you're no longer the one whose wings were cut off?'

Xas said, 'I know and feel many new things now. Nothing wonderful or exclusive. But what I feel is like—well—my shirt.'

'You feel like your shirt?' Lucifer said. His mouth stayed a little open. His face relaxed completely and Xas was distracted by a hitherto unnoticed family resemblance. Lucifer looked like Michael.

Xas shook his head to clear it. He touched the fully transparent material under his collar, which was showing the dark cartilage of its celluloid stiffening. 'This is a shirt, the same as other shirts,' he said, 'and the library books waiting for me on Flora's window seat are the same books that are in many other hands. Scarcely anything is made specially any more—books copied for one reader, a shirt tailored for one body. Nothing I've learned lately is *special*, but it was bound to make other stuff vanish, as horses vanished from the streets of Paris.'

Lucifer said, 'Are you saying that you're going to start forgetting things, including what happened to you? Including how it felt to fly? Angels don't forget. This is all wishful thinking, Xas. If God is a horse He's also an automobile, and you can't make either of us vanish or recede merely by filling yourself with what this overproducing world has to offer.'

'Vanish,' Xas echoed, softly, as if performing a rather wistful exorcism.

Lucifer dropped his chin again, and again the tension drained away from his face. He no longer looked at all formidable. He said, 'Why did I cut off your wings?'

'What is it you want? To confess?' Xas asked. 'Or to exonerate God?'

'I'd do *that*?' Lucifer took a few steps toward him, came close enough for Xas to be able to distinguish the noises the water made dripping from his wings and the sprinklers. 'Why won't you answer God,' Lucifer said, puzzled, 'when He's speaking to you?'

'God can't make me hear Him.'

Lucifer looked intensely interested. 'How long has that been going on?'

'None of your business,' Xas said.

A man had appeared at the edge of the green. A greenkeeper possibly, come to shut off the sprinklers. The man was watching them—seeing a six-winged angel in conversation with a smaller human figure. The man was peering about him, perhaps looking for the camera crew. His as yet unrewarded search was probably the only thing keeping him conscious and mobile and able to finish what he'd come out to do. He stooped to a tap and wound it, shutting off the water.

The turf ticked, and silence seem to drift down over Xas in a series of diaphanous layers, each more muffling than the last.

Lucifer turned to regard the man, who was fortunately far enough away not to suffer the blow of the archangel's attention. He said, musing, 'Why is it that just having something to do makes them so brave?' He seemed not to expect an answer—even from God—for he simply went on, 'Can you really not hear Him?'

'I really can't.'

Lucifer's lips parted again, and this time Xas could read the look. Lucifer looked impressed, and avid. He came closer.

Xas took several steps back.

The archangel came to a stop, but said, 'I was holding you before. If I intended to hurt you I would have already.'

'*You cut off my wings!*' Xas roared. The world turned a soft shade of red. He jumped at Lucifer, intending to tear at that body with his fingers and feet—and his teeth, even knowing what would happen. He'd do it. He'd bathe in his brother's toxic blood.

But Lucifer took a step back and Xas's fingertips brushed squeaking down a stretch of slippery feathers. Xas sprawled on the turf. For a second Lucifer's bare feet were before his face, just out of his reach, then Xas saw the toes splay, and press hard into the grass, raising mud. All six of Lucifer's wings swept down, so that Xas lay for a second inside a dark tent of feathered muscle. Then there was a loud crack and sheets of water leapt off the ground to follow the retreating momentous gravity of the archangel's body as he tore himself off the earth.

The water dropped back down and lay quiet as water should. Xas rolled onto his back to watch the archangel vanish into the darkness. Out of the corner of his eye he saw the greenkeeper keel over in a faint. The sound of the archangel's wing beats receded, grew faint, faded away. Xas lay for a few minutes on the sodden ground. Then he got up, retrieved his jacket, and set out walking away from the hills, toward the sea.

For Flora getting out of bed was a process. First she'd throw off her covers, using only her arms, and keeping her back firmly against the mattress. She'd roll to the edge of the bed and drop her feet onto the floor. Then she'd straighten her arms to move her torso off the bed. Each morning she would accomplish this series of manoeuvres with as little movement in her hips as possible. And still her scars pulled.

That morning, after a fog had rolled over the house and a chill set in, Flora made her usual efforts to get out of bed. She put on her robe and slippers and scuffed her way to the kitchen to make tea and toast.

Once she'd settled at the table with her toast and a wedge of fresh, sweating butter on her plate, O'Brien jumped up beside her and sat at her elbow as she ate, his eyes turned modestly aside—as falsely nonchalant as begging cats are. He couldn't be hungry, for there was still some ground beef in his plate. Xas must have come in near enough to O'Brien's breakfast time for the cat to be able to convince him that his need was genuine.

Flora finished chewing and paused to listen to the house. The bed Xas was now using—Millie's—was in better shape than the other, but still creaked whenever he moved. Not that he often moved. Flora suspected that when he got into bed, for the few hours he'd spend there, he'd lie awake and motionless, often reading.

Flora listened, and heard nothing. She called, 'Xas?'

The bed creaked. A moment later he came into the kitchen, barefoot, but fully clothed. His leather jacket was dark and damp, his shirt clinging to his chest and stomach.

Flora stared at him. O'Brien seized his moment, and the remnant of her butter, and carried it off under the table.

Xas was dishevelled, and his face seemed different, unguarded. It was his mouth. Flora had always thought his mouth was his most alien and unused feature—though he talked and laughed, and though, Flora knew, Cole had uses for those smooth, rosy lips.

Xas regarded her for a moment, then removed his jacket and dropped it on the floor. He drew out a chair and straddled it, his back to her. Then he pulled his shirt off over his head. The revealed feathers hissed, crackled, then settled. They were soft, sleek, and of supernatural whiteness. They coated his muscles, and lay close to his skin, only grew unevenly in the channels of scars—each shaped like the letter 'J', one a mirror of the other.

Flora touched his back. The feathers were warm and animal. 'They're beautiful,' she said.

'This isn't a whole body,' he said.

'I do understand that.' She took hold of his shoulder and tried to turn him.

He obligingly got up and sat down again the right way around. She was sorry to lose sight of the feathers, but at least could study the alteration in his face.

The change was sorrow, and surrender too. Somehow, he was putting himself in her hands—which was what, she realised, she wanted him to do. She said, 'If I don't seem surprised, this is the reason. A man came to claim your pearls. One Henri de Valday, from Château Vully, in France. He told the jeweller and me a story about his family's great wine. He said that, in the barrels in which the wine begins its life, there were angel wings, one wing in each barrel. His grandfather claimed to have seen them. In Henri de Valday's story about how the wings came to be in the barrels there was a winemaker with your name—Jodeau—the name on your pilot's licence, the name you gave the Madill Brothers.'

Xas kept his eyes cast down. Flora longed for him to look up at her. She touched his cheek. 'What kind of angel were you?'

'I'm still an angel.'

'But before this.' Her hands described a feathery flourish in the emptiness over his shoulders.

'I don't know how to answer that. I can't think where to start. I don't want to leave things out. With my lover, Sobran, I kept leaving things out. For decades I left out the salient fact that I came from Hell, not Heaven.'

Flora was silent a moment, managing that first shock: '*Hell, not Heaven.*' Then she mustered her courage and said, 'Start anywhere. I'm an editor, I can cut it together. Start in Hell, if you like.'

So, without pausing even to acknowledge her next poorly suppressed gasp of astonishment, Xas told her his story, beginning with the start of the calendar, the place where history commenced again in positive numbers.

'Just after the Crucifixion Christ came to preach to the souls in Hell—as the doctrine says. We fallen angels hung about to listen and I noticed that He looked like me. He had vestigial signs of injuries, some wear on His youth, and a chipped front tooth, but He looked like me.

'I thought about that for a long while before daring to ask God about it. And, while I was thinking, I began to make my garden.

'You see—I had a garden in Hell. I'm sure it's there still, in its mountain valley, under glass whitened within by condensation. In my garden I grew trees and flowering vines, shrubs and ferns, and everything was softly dark in the unsteady light that shone through the dome, of fire reflected on the summits of the surrounding mountains, and the wavering greens and purples of the *aurora infernus*.

'I believe my garden's still there because I found a water pipe leading into the salt dome—the salt dome in Turkey that is the gate to Hell. I think Lucifer built the pipe, and probably a distillery too. He always was something of an engineer. Of course he waited until I was gone before he took over my garden. He hadn't shown any interest in it before. And he'd had two thousand years in which to show an interest.

'Shortly after Christ had preached in Hell, Lucifer came to see me. I was in the garden's unfinished dome, up to my ankles in a slush of scoria, lichen and water, trying to make soil. Lucifer asked me what I was doing, I told him, and he flew off again. I'm certain now that he'd come to kill me. Because he'd worked out that I was a copy of Christ, and that *that* had to mean more than what my lover Sobran said he thought it might mean when I told him about it. Sobran thought that maybe God had a template for treaties. That if Christ was a kind of treaty between God and humankind, and I was one between God and Lucifer, then maybe that was why I looked like Christ.

'I *am* a treaty between them—the Adversary, and the One who can't be opposed. The treaty consists of three clauses. One: *Xas can go freely.* Two: *Lucifer will share his pleasures and God his pains.* And Three: *Only when Xas is with Lucifer will Lucifer be with God.* You see, God is everywhere but in Hell. Hell is hellish because there's nowhere comfortable to sit down, and because of the heartbreaking bleak vacancy of no God. Damned souls and fallen angels feel it all the time— God's absence. But if a fallen angel flies out of Hell—after burrowing through the salt—they are then with God, as everyone on earth is with God all the time, whether or not they know it. But Lucifer is never with God. He carries God's absence around with him wherever he goes. Except when I'm with him.'

Flora was following this, despite the shock after shock of it. She said, 'So you're not just any old angel?'

'You asked me what kind of angel I was. I'm the kind who is a treaty between God and Lucifer. And I'm a copy of Christ— though that's probably only symbolic, as Sobran thought.'

'Symbolic my eye,' thought Flora. She felt she was looking at the numbers on the reel of a film she had to cut. She asked, 'But weren't you a treaty *before* Christ?' She wanted to add, 'These shots are in the wrong order.'

'Yes. I asked God about that. I may have come first, but Christ is the original. God exists outside time so can make an angelic copy of a divine human before the birth of that human. God said to me that He made a copy of His Son because He wanted to see what His Son would do if He didn't do His duty.'

'God's experiment can't have pleased Him then, since you're a fallen angel.'

'I'm not really,' Xas said. 'I wasn't cast out of Heaven. I only followed Lucifer to Hell. I was interested in what he'd been saying. He didn't get to finish, so I followed him to hear the rest. I chose interest over happiness. But I was free to go back. Then, as soon as I tried, as soon as I was out of Hell and on earth and on my way to Heaven, they caught me and made a treaty out of me. They signed me—God and Lucifer. First I was a copy, a *test*. Then I was a treaty, or something like a telephone, or two-way radio.'

'Wait,' said Flora, holding up her hands. She was still trying to put the story in order, and had run up against something unexpected. 'Did you just say that the war in Heaven was only *hundreds* of years before Christ?'

'Yes,' said Xas. He looked impatient. 'The churches have got it wrong. They talk about the truth of the Bible but keep reading it more like a myth than a history. In the churches' readings there has to be an agent of good and an agent of evil. But the *malak*, the clever messenger angel in the Old Testament, the one who tests people—like Job—that's Lucifer, working *for* God.'

Flora, hearing this, had several thoughts. A first and a second and so on, each thought revealing itself to her as a succession of shining faces, like the girls of a chorus line peeling off girl by girl, to finally reveal the star. First she thought, at last feeling it as true, that, yes, Xas was an angel. He didn't have wings, but the shape of his life was angelic, epochal.

Her next thought was a memory. She recalled the moment just before she'd met him. She was crossing Mines Field, carrying Cole's bow tie and a bag of turkey sandwiches. She was whistling a tune and listening for her whistle to echo, as if the twilight was a soundstage. That moment had been one of a certain kind in Flora's life. Flora—the film editor, who sometimes, when she was alone, thought she could sense an alteration, as if in time itself, something like the soft click of a splice passing through the gate of her editing machine.

She could feel that now, and she was positive that what she was feeling, and had felt at other times throughout her life, was God, God's personal attention turned to her, Flora McLeod. Because if God lived outside time, then when, as a girl, Flora had sat in church beside her grandmother— passing on the collection plate because she hadn't a purse of her own—*God was there*. God, Who had all the footage. God, matching shots for meaning as well as logic. He was there in the church, He was there on Mines Field, and He was here now in her kitchen.

Flora considered this thought, then asked Xas, carefully, tentatively, why he'd come back.

'I came back because you asked me to. Because, like Sobran, and unlike God or Lucifer or Conrad Cole, you make me feel I have the power to please you. I came back despite having met Lucifer on your paper road. Despite having become available to him and not wanting to. And despite Cole's attempt to kill me.' He added, emphatic, 'Being invulnerable doesn't make much difference to the horror of having someone try to kill you. It's the hatred that's horrible. Or it's the desire—the desire with emptiness as its object, yourself harmed, then emptiness where you were. Cole wanted the world without me in it. That hurt me.'

Xas was breathing hard.

Flora tried to make her stiff, incompetent body get into a position where she could embrace him. She couldn't, and let out a sob of pain and frustration. Xas jumped up and took her in his arms. Her satin robe was the only thing between his skin and hers, and his more-than-human warmth was pouring into her.

He was shaking. 'People die,' he said. 'I've been afraid of that since I first cared for one. But *he* showed me his power, and that was even worse. He made part of me disappear. He made me afraid of dying.'

Flora had a suspicion that Xas's 'he' was Lucifer, not Cole. She was too afraid to ask him what he meant—what exactly Lucifer had done to him. God in her kitchen was one thing; Lucifer, as she imagined him then—out in the fog, wings mantled, standing on the cold clotted sand of the track by her back gate—that was more than she was ready for.

She held Xas and whispered 'Sweetheart' and 'Darling'. She said, 'Hush now,' and, 'It's all right', and he buried his face in her unwashed hair and took deep, gulping breaths of her probably none-too-clean human smell, as if he were smothering and she was oxygen.

Later, when the light was fading, Flora and Xas were lying on the sofa. O'Brien had settled on their legs, where, even if he slept, he'd get immediate notice of any promising movement from either of them. Flora was hungry, but she was also very comfortable. It was rare for her to be so comfortable. Xas had a superlative, gentle dexterity. Holding her, he was as pliant, and yielding, and strong, as water.

Flora had been talking to Xas about what was important to her. She'd finally told him about the fire—what she could remember—the heat against her ankle and the first streaks of flame she had looked down at past her own raised arm, and then, suddenly, the flames enfolding her upper body and head like the petals of a carnivorous flower; all that, and then how she'd run and the fire had streamed back from her face and arms and chest so that she hadn't inhaled it; that, and how the people had scattered before her, except for Cole, who had stood in her path like a matador, his cape a curtain he'd torn down; all that, and the long terrible weeks in the hospital. She told it all in a rush. And as she did she began to feel that the story of the fire, the story that was the centre of her life and made her *Flora*, even more than her work, wasn't the centre any more, that maybe the centre of her life was *this*, herself lying in a dusky room in the arms of an angel. She felt that she and Xas had, in effect, been saying to one another: 'This is the use the world has made of me so far. What do you think it means? And what am I to do now?'

Flora told Xas about the fire, and John Weber, and what Cole had done to John. She said, 'Con killed John out of indignation. He got indignant on my behalf and had to do something about it. He hates to feel helpless.'

'Yes,' said Xas. Then, 'Are you going to show me your scars?'

'Not right now. I'm too comfortable to move.' She gave a sigh of happiness, then slipped her fingers under the cushion of the window seat and felt for the paper she'd stowed there. As she did she had a moment of feeling mythological, as if she was Psyche, lamp in hand, creeping toward the couch where Eros lies sleeping. 'Someone came asking after you. He wrote me notes. This was the last of them.'

Xas took the paper and read, then dropped his head back against the window frame. He closed his eyes and said softly, 'I knew I was a copy but I hadn't really considered what that meant.'

'What?'

'It means I'm not like—' he hesitated, then began again. 'Perhaps it doesn't so much matter who I'm like, as who I'm *not* like.'

'Your brothers?' said Flora.

Xas nodded faintly, but kept his eyes closed.

Flora thought of snuffed candles—fire starved of air. He was dampening himself down, more angry than sorry, and trying to hide it from her. 'The note says God made angels, but didn't make people.'

'That's Lucifer's heresy—that God didn't make the world, only found it. And that when He made angels it was an attempt to discover how people worked by copying them.'

Flora felt dazed, but this was her chance to get answers and she wouldn't let it go by. She could sense Xas clearing all these considerations away, and hiding himself from himself. She said, 'When I was a child in church the preacher would talk about fallen angels as demons who tempted people. But the note says that fallen angels aren't demons.'

'Lucifer maintains that, like earth, Hell was there already, inhospitable and ugly, but a whole real world. He says he first went to Hell about the same time God started to store souls there—and that he took to going there to be alone with his thoughts. Out of Heaven—its colour and clamour—he was able to think, he said, and he came up with his heretical ideas. Then he aired them in Heaven and argued with other angels—not with God. I guess with God by proxy, but he never seems to acknowledge it.'

'So there are no demons?'

'Yes, there are. Demons are the oppressed native people of Hell,' Xas said. 'Fallen angels are their colonial masters. Demons are low creatures, and impossible to like—but I do think they deserve something better.'

Flora laughed. 'That's a remarkably Christ-like thought.'

*

Xas buried his face in Flora's hair and closed his eyes. He wouldn't say anything further. The things he'd kept from Sobran he'd keep from Flora too. For Flora would understand, like every other Christian, that humans had earthly lives and immortal souls and God rewarded each soul for its life. And how could it matter to her—whose daily life was one of pain—whether God made the world or not, since He took care of human souls once they came home to Him? That's all she needed to know.

Xas had his own heresy—his very own. His heresy was that God didn't just sort individual from individual but *within* each individual, at least all those He let near Him, so that souls in Heaven were not the people they'd been on earth. Xas had believed this since the death of his first human friend, the bee-keeping monk, whose soul he'd sought out in Heaven, and found greatly altered. Xas wouldn't show Flora the fine print, because what all the old songs had to say was true—in Heaven there was no trouble or sorrow or pain.

He opened his eyes and gazed at her pale, sleepy face. He kept his lips shut tight. '*Who are you? Who are you?*' he thought, as if by concentration, and questing will, he could keep her, all of her, alive forever and out of the happy conglomerate good that was Heaven—that was her best hope.

Intermission

# Los Angeles

## 1932 1938

In 1932 Xas was settled in Venice with Flora. He got a job. A friend, Tram, sent Xas to talk to some people he knew at Lockheed, where they'd signed him up as a test pilot. ('Tram' was Frankie Trumbauer, an old friend of Millie's, and a saxophonist of elegant and otherworldly sounds. He was also a pilot who knew test pilots, and later became one. Tram was flying for fun, and haunting the after-hours clubs on Central Avenue. His collaborator Bix Beiderbecke had finally drunk himself to death, and Tram had rather lost his way.)

In '32 half the country was out of work and yet Xas and Flora found themselves in well-paying jobs. They bought new beds, a new sofa, rugs, and a phonograph. They had the house painted and papered. Then Xas borrowed a truck and drove the furniture they no longer wanted out to a refuse tip on the edge of the desert where—he later told Flora—he sat watching animal and human scavengers, and a dust devil churning this way and that, full of rags and yellowed paper. Then he drove off again and took everything to some Hooverville and invited the people there to take what they could use. (And when Flora told him she was glad he'd thought of it, he'd just stood there sadly shaking his head and saying, incomprehensibly, 'So many *things*. Things burying things.')

The years passed. Prohibition ended. Every year the Los Angeles River flooded. In '35 there was a crisis at Flora's studio when Monroe Stahr died in a plane crash in Ohio. Stahr's funeral was the last time Flora spotted Crow's ex-wife (Crow and Edna had divorced in 1932). Edna attended the funeral because she was Stahr's late wife's sister. Crow and Edna stood together in the demonstratively weeping crowd, Edna clutching the hand of a woman in a very plain hat and coat who Flora thought must be her nurse.

With Stahr gone Flora worked on a film Crow was doing for Warners. She drove further every day—Burbank again instead of Culver City. She saw less of Xas. She'd come home to find a pot of chilli on the stove with heating and serving instructions and maybe cornbread on the kitchen counter wrapped in a dish towel. Xas's cooking had improved, she supposed, till he told her that the food was a gift from the Mexicans he'd befriended and was helping. ('Helping' meant he'd dug them a well.) Or she'd come home to find a note saying where she could find him. Usually at a jazz club. He'd have put on his suit to go to the Alabam, and then would follow his musician friends to the black clubs where, around three a.m., they'd lock the doors and the black and white musicians would play together. Flora did sometimes go out and join him. She'd knock on the door and say, 'I'm Huss Hintersee's friend.' (One of his Mexicans adopted a Spanish pronunciation of Xas, and it caught on in the jazz clubs and at Lockheed too.) Flora would join him up on the balcony where he'd be sitting with his arm on the rail, looking down on tables and guests, and the floor covered in cigarette ash, trodden in and smeared into clouds. They'd listen to Nat Cole then drive home singing.

Conrad Cole set a new airspeed record. He wooed this and that beauty. But Xas was the only one to share Cole's sovereign darkness, those rooms from which all light was excluded, where he holed up and was at peace, or sweating with fear.

Cole bought, then eviscerated, a great studio, and both Xas and Flora were party to many discussions—while sitting with movie people in the velvet banquettes at the Trocadero, or in the dappled light of the Clover Club— about whether Cole had terrible taste in movies, or just supposed the 'general audience' must have.

Then, in 1935, Cole met the vivid and brainy Sylvia Seaton, and fell in love. They set up house together. He was happy and in good health. Xas was surprised to discover how relieved he felt. It was as if he'd carried Cole to the far bank of a flooding river, and could now set him down. Xas had been afraid of the future—Cole's future—but could now tell himself that the man was in better hands than his own.

Flora's back lawn was by this time carved up into flower and vegetable beds. Xas fed her out of his garden. She didn't put on much weight but, over time, felt better, had more energy, was more supple and resilient than she had been since her accident. She was both grateful and resentful to be the object of his care. His reaction to loving her seemed to be a desire to make her last. He didn't want to lose her, so looked after her. He worried about Cole's mental state, and her material one.

After they'd been living together for a couple of years Flora finally let Xas inspect her scars.

In her accident Flora had suffered first-degree burns around her knees and ribs, the places where the fire had touched only momentarily, first where the dry fronds of the grass skirt were hanging, and then where the burning material floated up around her like an opening flower. The fronds had been consumed quickly, and Flora was already in flight, so the flames and smoke had streamed away from her face. Her halter top hadn't caught fire so her breasts were protected.

The burns to the tops of her thighs and patches of her stomach under her navel were, however, second-degree. The fire had burned down to living skin, but it didn't destroy her nerves. Instead it left them raw, scorched, and reacting in a weeks-long scream of pain. Those burns had healed under shiny, thinned skin, pigmented alternately in patches of red and purplish pallor. This skin was not as pliable as normal skin, its give as far from normal as that of pigskin work gloves is when compared to kid evening gloves.

But the second degree burns were not the worst of it.

Flora's grass skirt was decorated around the hips by butterflies made of celluloid. When the skirt caught fire the celluloid ignited, shrivelled, melted, then clung, fiercely hot and molten, to her skin. When Cole caught Flora in the curtain and carried her to the floor the flames had gone out, but the hot material of the decorations went on scorching its way deeper into the flesh that it had adhered to. Flora had sustained four third-degree burns in spots—the largest the size of the top joints of three of her fingers. The molten celluloid had seared its way down through fat to muscle, destroying nerves, leaving pits in her body full of eschar, scabs of dead hardened flesh surrounded by living flesh starved of blood.

It was these burns that made Flora's doctors fear for her life. Two days after the fire she'd swelled up to twice her normal size and, for some hours, was producing only a tiny amount of nut brown urine. But she had no inhalation injury, and since it was the height of summer she didn't succumb to cold, as burns victims often did. The doctors kept her on a saline drip, and her kidneys slowly recovered and, miraculously, no infection ever found her wounds.

Flora's scars marred her beauty—gave her pale figure the look of a foxed photograph. But it was the four pits of scars around her hips that gave her most of her problems. They were like rivets driven into her flesh connecting layers of skin and fat and muscle that should normally be able to glide against one another. They pulled at the less seriously damaged skin around them, wouldn't bend or stretch, so that if Flora squatted, or spread her legs, at least one of the four would crease right across in a hard fold, then split and bleed lymph.

Flora showed Xas her scars on an occasion when one had ruptured and was weeping clear matter from its pale pink interior. She was in the bathroom, with a bottle of iodine in one hand and a cotton ball in the other. She was feeling very sorry for herself and called out to Xas, asking him to come and help her dress her wound.

Xas came in, and stood for a moment studying the scars. Then he crouched and licked the oozing fissure. His tongue was warm and soothing and, after a minute, Flora began to feel light-headed and indifferent, as though she'd taken a couple of Nembutal. Xas left the wound wet with his spit then fetched her nightgown and dropped it gently over her head and lifted arms. He put her to bed and, in the morning, the wound was much better, sealed under spit, a thin glaze like gum Arabic.

When the wound was quite healed Xas took to rubbing lanolin into Flora's scars—something that had been recommended to her by the doctors who had followed up on her case when she returned from Brawley to Los Angeles, a treatment she'd given up for tequila, taken internally. Flora was embarrassed by these attentions. They were too intimate for her simply to accept them as more of his husbandry—like the meals he cooked her, and her bedding changed twice a week, no matter how busy they both were—all his efficient, unstinting, inexhaustible care. Xas would apply the lanolin and then hold her for a few minutes. He'd catch her after her shower to treat her or, if he came in late and found her still awake, he'd appear and would burrow in her bed clothes and pull down her pyjamas to apply the lanolin. She sometimes suspected him of wanting something—some sexual recompense. He was so tender it was like worship. He wasn't brisk and businesslike. He'd stay under the covers, his arms wrapped around her, his palms against the top of her buttocks and face pressed into her belly. Sometimes he'd go to sleep like that, or they'd go to sleep together and she'd wake up a while later—because the light was still on—and would look at the lump he made under the covers and would worry, stupidly, that he wouldn't be able to breathe.

Xas's attentions worried Flora, but she didn't stop him or confront him or interfere with whatever trajectory he had. After all, he never had imposed on her in any way. And he made her feel good, made her aches and pains fade, made her sleep better. And he kept his clothes on, and stayed with her for only an hour or two and, eventually, she came to think of his visits as equivalent to O'Brien's.

Her cat always spent part of the night with her. He'd come in through the bathroom window—adding each time to the river of claw marks on the paintwork. He'd saunter into her room, jump onto the end of the bed, circle her, purring, then settle down behind her knees to give himself a long, vigorous, bed-shaking wash.

They were the same, the cat and the angel, warm presences that shared her bed. And sometimes, when Xas was lying next to her, Flora would slip her hand down the collar of his shirt to sink her fingers into the feathers on his back, and actually let herself think of him—the smooth-skinned, springy, shapely body beside hers. Flora never let herself feel anything more than wonder, for she was too fragile and inflexible to imagine herself asking for something more than warmth and closeness. The feelings she had for Xas weren't answerable, there was nothing she could do with them. Besides—she told herself—she only considered what she might ask because he was benevolent and earthly, like his own garden. But she must never forget that he was also like his brother—his brother the Devil. So whenever she found herself feeling infatuated with the warm, affectionate, sleepy angel who nursed her scars and then stayed for a time under the covers embracing her, she'd just shake her head at her greed for pleasure. How forgetful and arrogant of her to be greedy for pleasure, after all those years of pain.

Third Reel

# Venice, Los Angeles

## May, 1938

Flora was awake when Xas looked in on her. She was trying, with her schoolgirl French, to puzzle her way through his copy of Saint-Exupéry's *Terres des Hommes*.

'There you are,' Xas said. Then, 'I saw Crow.'

Flora laid her book down. 'How is he?'

'How do you think?'

'Busy? Too many irons in the fire?'

Xas studied her face. 'Is that a euphemism?'

'The railroading film, I mean, and that Sabatini property.'

'He's moving on from MGM, he said. He had a fight with Sam Goldwyn. So that's Bill Fox and Jack Warner and Goldwyn he's fought with so far. He tells a good story, though, doesn't he? Actually, we stopped on Larchmont Boulevard and had a bite to eat.'

Flora was surprised by this. Crow always gave her the impression he was being forbearing about Xas, keeping his lip buttoned on the whole subject of her sharing a house with 'Cole's special friend'. 'What do you suppose that was about?' she said.

'I think he was buttering me up.'

Flora waited for him to say more. They stared at each other for half a minute, till Flora realised that he was fishing, that he thought Crow's friendliness related to some change in their relationship—her and Crow's.

'Why would Connie butter you up?' Flora said.

Xas gave the abrupt abbreviated nod he used when he'd guessed right. It got so that she could interpret these not-quite-human tics of his. 'Other people joined us,' he said. 'Crow might fight with the heads of studios, but everyone wants to know him. I sat back and watched them. Eventually Crow sat back too and we monitored each other's reactions while this stupid bunch tried to hustle one another, and one woman struck meaningless poses in order to show off her figure.'

'Because Connie's in the market?'

'Is he?'

Flora could see that he was imagining a secret dalliance with Crow. She kept her eyes down and flicked through the book looking for illustrations. 'So, that was it for the evening?'

'No. The hopped-up crowd took their leave, and Crow pinned me down by buying me a very fancy dessert—without asking. Then Dudley Nicholls came over and they had a good-natured scrap about the writers' strike. Crow said the strike breakers had "shown admirable professionalism". So—is Nicholls supposed to be writing Crow's comedy?'

'I doubt it. Is this comedy something quite apart from the railroad thing and the Sabatini?'

'Don't you know?'

'He hasn't asked me if I want to work on any comedy.'

'Better comedy than tragedy,' Xas muttered. The remark was just audible and Flora was pleased to have heard it. Not only did Xas think she was involved with Crow—he was feeling protective. She smiled at him.

He said, 'I'm going to bed,' and took himself off.

# Beverly Hills
## Late July, 1938

Crow came to the gate himself, opened it, and followed Flora's car up to the turning circle before his house.

'My phone isn't off the hook, you know,' he said to her. 'You could have called.'

Flora shook her head and stayed in her seat. He leaned over and kissed her on the cheek. 'Sorry to sound unwelcoming, but if you've turned up because you think I'm in trouble, then by all means *do* feel unwelcome.'

'I've never been here, Connie. To your house.'

'Is that so?'

Flora got out of her car and gave Crow her hand. He tucked it under his arm and walked her up the curving flight of fieldstone steps that led to a terrace under a pergola covered in white wisteria. It was cool there, and Flora would have been happy to stop, but Crow seemed to want to give her a little tour—of the exterior, anyway.

There was a stone terrace and asymmetrical pool at the

rear of the house. By the pool were chairs, and loungers with white cushions and fringed canopies. There was also a drinks trolley, typewriter, piles of pages.

Beyond the pool was a strip of lawn, then a hedge of aspidistra, and then olives at the edge of the property. Beyond *that* Flora glimpsed two surveyors climbing the rocky slope of the canyon. One was carrying a theodolite and the other a surveyor's pole.

Crow said, 'Yes, they are about to build houses in a dry wash. I expect it'll all come down on me one day.'

'Isn't there something you can do?'

Crow laughed. 'Move,' he said. He picked up a whisky bottle and shook it at her invitingly.

'Just a small one. With ice.'

Crow poured. Flora looked longingly at a lounger and then sat on a chair. She removed her cheaters to admire the colour of the pool. In a breeze coming up the valley its ruffled blue surface caught the sunlight so it seemed there was a school of white fish there, hanging still in some impossible current.

'I wonder that you've never been here before,' Crow said. 'Surely you've had an invitation?'

'There were invitations to parties, I believe,' Flora said.

'Seems you always come to find me when I'm somewhere else—avoiding people.'

Flora sipped her drink and looked about her. 'So, this is your life,' she said, then, 'You never came to my house either.'

They were silent for a time and the wind changed direction. A whiff of chlorine came off the pool. The chlorine seemed just as inviting to Flora as the colour of the water. She used to swim in the ocean, and at the hot saltwater baths in Venice. She might still swim if bathing costumes were as modest as they'd been when she first came to Hollywood.

'Cole used to come to my house,' Flora said. 'And Gil.'

'Gil was there the night before his accident.'

Flora scrutinised Crow. 'How do you know that?'

'Myra.'

Flora frowned. She couldn't think how Gil's wife had known, unless, that night, Gil had gone home to Myra and happened to say something. Flora hoped it hadn't been anything beginning, 'Flora McLeod thinks ...'

'You never said anything, Flora.'

'It was a private conversation, Connie. And Gil wasn't the pilot, so his state of mind had no bearing on the accident.'

'It wasn't good then, his state of mind?'

'Myra was seeing Cole. You must know that whole story by now.'

Crow nodded.

'Well,' said Flora. Then, 'It's all so long ago.'

'You believe that? You believe it's all water under the bridge?'

Flora looked at her friend. He was wearing cheaters and she couldn't see his eyes. She could see only his stubborn, reticent mouth and slightly weak jaw. It occurred to her that Crow's character had begun to make its alterations on the architecture of his face. She thought that since she occasionally had conversations where someone, speaking from personal experience, said, 'Before Christ', then actually she shouldn't claim that anything was 'long ago'.

'I'm sorry. I don't mean to fob you off, Connie. But the conversation I had with Gil was about me and him. Mostly.'

'Fair enough,' Crow said, and leaned back in his chair. 'So, you're here because someone has given you the task of checking up on me. Since I'm not working, or off at the racetrack, or hunting, or on my boat, there's some cause for concern.'

Two months before Crow had finished a film of which he was rightly proud, a film that found favour with audiences everywhere except that vast somewhere, the Midwest, and therefore hadn't in the end returned the studio's investment to its satisfaction. After that he'd lost the Sabatini project, his kind of film—martial, masculine and fun—and one he knew would have made him money.

When Flora had seen him in June, at the opening of the racetrack at Hollywood Park, Crow had been his usual self-congratulatory, big-spending self. Then, only a month later at a party at Buster Keaton's old mansion, Flora hadn't arrived fashionably late, but had caught Crow on his way out. It was a party the host had put a lot of effort into. There were paper lanterns all around the pool, and over the top terrace an awning made of yards of white silk. Flora had come with Avril, who was recently divorced and defiantly dateless. She'd found Cole there, with Sylvia Seaton, as he always was these days. Cole was enjoying himself, and was even relaxed enough to remark to Flora in a whisper that one reason he *was* enjoying himself was because the low-slung lights made it easy for him to lip read. Xas was there, with the band, Lee Young's Esquires of Rhythm. In their break, he introduced Flora to Lee. Later Flora had spotted him in the middle of a noisy group of guests having what appeared to be a very earnest discussion with Sylvia. Then she'd bumped into Crow again, who was looking displeased. He said he was leaving. And she said, 'You're *still* leaving, are you? Why don't you just stand here for a wee minute and talk to me?' He scowled, and didn't talk. She was a little drunk, and nerveless, so she just stood near to him and stared up at him, waiting to hear him complain. Connie's complaints were always so imaginative. But then he twined his fingertips with hers and came nearer, so that they were standing hip to hip, or rather his hip was touching her waist. Flora was very surprised. Crow wasn't a physical person, and he had his pick of beautiful girls. He only had to say, "Are you interested in being in the pictures?" and they'd come running. But he was holding her hand. After that he had conducted her to a curved stone seat, and they'd sat together, still holding hands.

It was Flora who let go. She removed her hand from Crow's when she saw Xas coming their way, walking down a flight of steps in his not-quite-competent way, his gait careless, as if he was expecting at any moment something different to happen than his sole meeting the next step and his leg having to support him. He looked coltish and inebriated—but what Flora knew she was looking at was an angel walking downstairs, his steps a series of falls, each one commemorating his former power to refuse gravity.

Crow said to Flora, 'Is he worth it?' Then, before she could respond or even think through what he'd said, he was gone.

'Was that Crow?' Xas said.

Flora gave him a scathing look. His eyesight was too good for the pretence.

'It's what people say,' Xas said, apologetic, and sat beside her. 'I'm getting away from Cole. He and Cary are having a conversation about how everyone is out to diddle them.' He pulled a face. 'Did I interrupt something?'

Flora looked into the schools of white light that seemed to hover just under the surface of Crow's swimming pool. She took a deep breath and filled her head with chlorine and the scent of honey mesquite blowing down the canyon.

'Would you like a swim?' Crow offered.

'I don't,' she said. She'd just been about to admit that she was here because he'd held her hand.

'But would you like to, anyway? There are costumes in the pool house. And, if you like, I can go indoors.'

Flora contemplated the pool for a little longer then said, yes, she'd like that.

It was a long time since Flora had felt weightless. She swam and floated from end to end of the pool, suspended in blue, liquid sunlight. The cypress trees surrounding the pool looked impossibly tall and black, etched against the still sky. Flora trod water at the deep end, gazed up at the cypresses and imagined she was looking up from her own grave, through transparent earth and stone, at time passing so fast that every hour was empty of people. The people were moving too fast for her to see them. The clouds were passing too quickly to mar the largely cloudless southern Californian sky. Flora remembered the cypresses at Forest Lawn Cemetery, black beacons, burning for decades. She thought about Gil, and Millie, and how much time had passed.

After half an hour she climbed the curving flight of steps at the shallow end of the pool, and shouldered her own weight again. She went into the pool house and stripped off the wet bathing suit. She put on a thick towelling robe and fastened its belt.

Flora went to the pool house door and put her eyes to one slit in its wooden louvres.

Crow was back. He'd lit a cigarette and poured another drink and was rolling the frosty glass back and forth across his bared breastbone inside the opened top of his shirt.

Flora left her clothes and shoes in the pool house and went out to him.

The hair on Crow's chest was grey, his skin damp with the condensation transferred from the sides of his glass. Flora touched his chest. He touched her neck; said her skin was still cold. Then he moved his hand, parted the robe and ran his palm down her flank. Flora followed his touch, losing it as it passed across a deep scar, where there were no nerves in her skin. She tilted her face up to his and he kissed her. Then he flicked his cigarette into the pool and took hold of her face between his long, dry palms and kissed her some more.

*

They were in his bedroom, both undressed. Flora showed him her scars, the deep inflexible ones. She raised her leg to demonstrate how, if the scars did bend, they folded. She stopped before the fold became a sharp crease. 'If I do that, it splits,' she said. 'Do you see? I'm sorry.'

Crow brushed her nipples with his thumbs. 'Have you ever let yourself get carried away?'

'Yes,' she said. 'Then there's afterward. And I'm always alone with that.'

'Really?' Crow was dubious.

'I haven't let myself get carried away, and be hurt, for a long while.'

Crow tucked the knuckle of one thumb into a scar and the tips of two fingers into another. 'Now try,' he said.

Flora raised her leg. The scars moved, but didn't fold. Their waxy surfaces were braced against Crow's fingers. Crow smiled at her, smug and lascivious. She laughed.

'I have an idea,' he said, and went into his large walk-in wardrobe, emerging with a white silk flier's scarf, of the sort popular during and after the war when cockpits were all still open to the air. The scarf had yellow marks on it—possibly old bloodstains. Crow held the scarf by one end and twirled it, so that it wound into a rope. He caught its end before it could unwind, and then tied it around Flora's hips, where it slotted into two of the deep scars. 'Ah-ha!' Crow said. He set his long thumbs carefully into the two remaining scars and walked her backward toward the bed. He said, 'Let's think of my grip as a dead man's brake. I must not let go, no matter what.' He sat Flora down, then lifted her up the bed and lay down over her. 'It's an interesting challenge,' he said.

Flora stayed at Crow's house most of that week. The following week they holed up together at the Furness Creek Motor Inn in Death Valley. Then she went to Palm Springs with him and they were seen together, on the golf course, at a table for two.

In the kind of company Crow liked to keep—that of hard-drinking, tight-lipped tough guys—Flora passed as a good sport, someone who could hold up her end in any conversation, and who did not require the careful handling or gallantry more ornamental women would naturally expect. Crow would introduce her as 'my friend, Flora McLeod'. As Flora McLeod she was known for her work, and Crow's 'my friend' explained that they were intimate and, everywhere they went, she was silently acknowledged as Crow's chosen companion.

Their affair had happened quite naturally. She was his confidante. Besides, for Crow, sex was idle and unceremonious. If he wasn't avid or passionate Flora could assume that that was because she wasn't beautiful or difficult. She didn't expect him to be faithful. She didn't expect the affair to last. She accepted it as an interlude, part of the long varied story of their friendship. Often, at the end of an evening, they'd retire together and sometimes Crow would grin, and produce the old flier's scarf, and twirl it while she laughed.

When they left Palm Springs she made a point of

remembering to pack the scarf but, just as pointedly, left something else behind. When she was checking their rooms she went into the bathroom and saw that she'd left the rubber diaphragm she'd only just got sitting on the side of the bath. She looked at it for a long time. She thought about the maid's embarrassment on finding it—which was silly, because surely those people eventually saw it all. Flora considered the maid, and she considered how *mad* she was to think of leaving it. And then she left it.

# Venice, Los Angeles

## August, 1938

Xas, coming home late through the waste ground of the paper road, saw his brother waiting on the track near the back fence, a looming shadow against the southern horizon where, beyond Washington Street, the pumps of the Venice Peninsula oilfield hunched under the oily light of the lagoon.

Xas sat near the archangel and waited for him to speak. After a time he became aware of a muffled buzzing. It was O'Brien's snoring purr. Xas reached out, fingers punching through the crust on the dry sand, before finding the cat's soft vibrating body.

It hadn't rained for over a month. The wind was blowing across the parched country, and Xas could smell sage, wild mustard and manzanita in the canyons. Between gusts of those dusty scents, he smelled the thick roux of muddy water in the nearest canal, Flora's orange trees and, finally, his garden, the fatty stink of squashes, wilted lettuce, herbs, flowers, laundry soap—for he'd been reduced to watering with greasy suds he bailed from the washing machine.

There was a carpet of cornflowers and poppies spilling down from the open gate—self-seeded from plants he tossed away when he thinned his flower beds. The moon was full and the poppies were partly open, their petals as crepey as the wings of newly hatched butterflies. The stars were bright and close and the night so still that Xas could actually hear the oil pumps' pushing heartbeats.

Though sunset was hours ago, the house would still be hot. All its windows were open, so Flora was home. She hadn't been home for days. She'd been with Crow. Xas didn't like coming home to an empty house, but he always did, to feed O'Brien. Xas hoped that Flora was fast asleep. He resolved to submit; to get whatever it was the archangel wanted over with quickly. Flora must not wake up, come out, and discover them.

After a moment Xas said, 'Since you're not speaking to me I suppose you're making yourself known to God.'

'He always knows where I am,' Lucifer said. 'Whether or not you're near me. After all, it isn't a very big blind spot I'm in. I'm sure that when the sun is low in the sky He can see my shadow moving far ahead or far behind me as I fly.'

Xas listened to the oil pumps, O'Brien's vibrant circular breathing, and the contented creaking of ducks nesting in the congealing marsh. He practised patience.

After a time Lucifer said, 'I am thinking of proposing to God that Hell gets a copy of every film.'

Xas shrugged. He looked at the open windows. The interior of Flora's house was as black and hot and uninviting as the insides of a carbon-coated oven. He kept an eye out for Flora, and continued to practise patience. It wasn't as if he was sleepy. And he had nothing to do the next day.

Lockheed had asked him to take a leave of absence in order to recover from an accident. Some weeks before he and his co-pilot had had to bail out of a burning plane. Whenever Xas was flying with someone else and had to bail out he'd always wait to see how the other person was before opening his own chute. That was his policy. He and his co-pilot had left the plane together but, because Xas was lighter, the other man was a little below him by the time they reached terminal velocity. He looked down and saw his co-pilot's parachute pack on fire, the flames pale and smokeless in the blue air. The man deployed the chute, and it didn't even have time to open before it was fully alight. Xas rolled himself into a ball and tried to race the man down. He uncurled now and then to steer himself nearer. He could see that the man was conscious, hanging onto the cords, looking up, and going down in a spiralling trail of sparks and smoke and fragments of burning silk. Xas finally caught the ends of the trailing cords. But he hadn't been watching the ground and he'd only seconds to think— maybe only one second to do the *right* thing. But he was thinking like an angel, so once he caught the man for a moment, by reflex, he tried to open his wings. He tried to open his wings, and felt all his muscles move and his scars smarting and only then remembered to pull his ripcord. Xas kept hold of the man, but they weren't going slow enough when they hit the ground.

Xas understood what had happened, understood it thoroughly. He didn't have any quarrel with the facts—he just didn't seem to be able to come right afterward, so Lockheed stood him down.

Lucifer abruptly started speaking; explaining the origins of his plan. 'That woman you live with once wrote me a note that mentioned a "Conrad Cole". I was curious, so I found him in a movie magazine. I read some of those magazines. Then one of our brothers gave me Sergei Eisenstein's "A Dialectic Approach to Film Form" and "Methods of Montage". For some years I read about film— though most of the printed matter on the subject is merely gossip and advertisement. I didn't see a film till 1934, when they opened the first drive-in.'

'I guess for you it was more of a hover-over,' Xas said.

Lucifer was quellingly still and quiet for a time, then he began to talk to God. Xas listened to his brother's end of the negotiation. Lucifer asked that Hell receive an eleventh copy of any film copied ten or more times. Xas could tell that his brother supposed ten was a negligible number. Xas thought of various people in the Hollywood colony making movies of their parties, picnics, and tennis matches. Ten was too few. Hell would eventually drown in children's birthdays and pool parties, beach barbecues, beauty contests, and beloved dogs begging and rolling over and playing dead. But Xas didn't say anything to warn Lucifer. He just let his brother make a mistake—he even enjoyed it.

Lucifer concluded his negotiation. He stretched, adjusted his wings, but didn't get up. This subtle but thick rustling roused O'Brien, who made a melodious chirping noise, before resuming his blissful purring.

Xas frowned at the cat, and his brother remarked, 'Your forehead looks like sheet music, without the music.' The light was behind Lucifer's head, so his smile was audible rather than visible. 'So,' he said, 'to return to our conversation of seven years ago—why did I cut off your wings?'

Xas tried to get to his feet, and Lucifer put out a hand and held him down. 'Shall I help you?' Lucifer said. 'You went to Heaven to find the lost page of Jodeau's brother's suicide letter. Jodeau's wife had burned it because it accused her of murder. She burned it, and therefore sent it to Heaven, where all destroyed originals go. You went to Heaven to find it. To steal a tiny bit of lost truth.'

Xas was very surprised that his brother knew this.

Lucifer took note of his surprise and explained that, of course, Leon and Celeste Jodeau were in Hell. 'Where I spoke to them,' he said.

Xas had known his lover's brother only through Sobran's stories about him—stories, worries, and a profound and puzzled grief. But, some ten years after he'd lost his wings, Xas had entered the Jodeau household as a tutor to Sobran's younger sons. He'd lived under Sobran's roof—though only shared a bed with his lover when Sobran was away overnight in his room at Château Vully. Xas had known Celeste Jodeau. He'd been careful with her, and kind to her. He hated to think of her soul in Hell and under interrogation, her thoughts and acts examined, all of them irredeemable, not in themselves, but by virtue of her damnation. Everything Celeste was had been thrown away whole—her cruelty, her selfishness, her duty, her generosity, a whole murderous, motherly person excised from the future, from God's promised Kingdom, if not from the story of the world. Lucifer had questioned Celeste and, no doubt, had judged her as God had. Judged differently, for he was the Devil after all, but judged nevertheless. Xas imagined the interview. He imagined Celeste's despair, and Lucifer's cold, angelic certainty.

'Why would you want to talk to them?' Xas said. 'Celeste and Leon?'

'Well—I had time,' Lucifer said. 'I'm only letting you know what I already know so that you won't leave anything out.'

Xas shut his mouth and remained stubbornly silent. He stared at his brother trying to make out his expression in the moonlight. Lucifer didn't prompt him again, but neither did he lift his restraining hand.

Xas said, 'I knew Celeste Jodeau. I keep wanting to ask after her, to say, "How did she look?"'

It wasn't a real question, but Lucifer answered it. 'She looked like her homeopathic self; like the memory of a remedy. She looked how damned souls look when they remember their mortal lives.'

This was apt and cruel, and Xas found himself saying, 'There really isn't any afterlife, is there?'

'Are you asking the Governor of God's prison whether he actually has any inmates?'

'I don't mean "actually". Actually there is an afterlife. But there isn't in the way that mortals suppose there is.'

'Hell is Hell,' said Lucifer.

'You know what I mean. I don't mean just that Hell is hopeless.'

'I know that you have your own heresy. That God doesn't after all save everything.'

'Yes. But imagine—' Xas began. He caught the haughty, quizzical expression on his brother's face and turned away from it. 'Imagine the atheists are right,' he said.

'Why would I bother to imagine what isn't true?'

'To discover what is—the spirit of the promise.' In trying to explain himself, Xas came out with a parable. 'Let's say that human bodies are planes. The purpose of a plane is flight. A soul is a flight; it is the purpose of a body. But what is it that flies? I don't think you can separate a thing and its purpose. But that's what God does, He winnows things from purposes and keeps only purposes. Which makes me wonder—what was it God lacked that He called for light? And what kind of lack couldn't be satisfied by *all this*?' Xas gestured around him at the welcome mat of self-seeded garden flowers, and silver billows of moonlit lupin.

Lucifer said, musingly, 'Although you now seem to believe once more that God made the world—called for light—I think you may still be more of a heretic than I am.'

Xas waved this away as an irrelevancy, then said, eager, 'Okay—imagine the atheists are right. It's easier to see how the world works for atheists when the world is bad. So— imagine the bad world.'

Lucifer laughed. 'All right, I've got that, the *bad* world,' he said. Then, 'Go on.'

'An atheist who lives through evil times must try to make sense of things without recourse to the idea of God, without a comforting authority, a fixture in the sky from which to suspend their final judgments. Without anyone to blame, *history* is the monster in their stories. History— immortal, capricious, remote, present everywhere. At best what they're left with—those atheists—after their struggles with history, are their hopes. Their hopes like some cross between a coffin and a boat, a vessel to carry their treasure away somewhere. But if I say "coffin" it sounds as though I'm talking about the ceremonial afterlife of interment and memorial. I'm not. All the hopes are for is that moment of passing—to be there, *singing something.*'

'Did you sing to Sobran when he was dying?'

'No,' Xas said. He felt tired and discouraged. He'd supposed his brother was paying attention, but Lucifer had only listened, alert for the appearance of a gap in his defences. Xas sighed, and patiently finished his thought. 'We should imagine there's no afterlife, because there is none for angels.' Then, 'I can't trust God with my treasure.'

'Because He let me cut off your wings?' said Lucifer, sly and persistent.

When Xas didn't respond, Lucifer made a sound of exasperation and got up. This startled O'Brien, who turned into a stiff, barbed fury, and sprinted away toward his basement bolthole. Lucifer's hand, which had only weighed on Xas, and held him in place, closed into a pinching grip.

The archangel picked him up, and clasped him close. Lucifer's scent—clean sunlight, spicy apple and fennel—was extraordinary. It made Xas feel weak, and a little crazy.

The archangel took off. His wings were loud and his progress was a series of pauses and accelerations. Then he caught a current of air several thousand feet up, and began to glide.

They flew along above the paper road as far as it went, down toward Playa del Rey, then turned out to sea. The archangel swooped and plunged, and once he banked, leaning against gravity as though barrelling around a solid and nearly vertical wall made only of air.

The wind was blowing from the southeast. It was a dry wind, a dirty wind, even several thousand feet up. Xas saw that they were flying in a pinched patch of clear air under a thick, flat-bottomed thunderhead.

Lucifer began to climb toward the cloud. Closer to, it was less defined, its edge filmy. But still it seemed strangely inert, not an airy thing full of water and electricity, but only a shadow, like its own shadow.

Xas knew that Lucifer was climbing toward the cloud as a precaution. For, though it looked passive as they passed along underneath it, the cloud suddenly ruptured, not with lightning or rain, but with a spray of fine particles of ice. The ice burst out and dropped onto and around and past them, then, hundreds of feet below, it hit the hot, dirty wind and evaporated. Xas felt the temperature change and pressure fall below them. He also felt Lucifer's lungs expand. The archangel sucked in an apparently endless breath, clasped

Xas even closer to him and locked his six rowing wings into one. The hands on Lucifer's two lower sets of wings seized the one above them, and closed like louvres to make two long instruments of coordinated muscle. Until that moment Xas had always thought the multiple wings were only for show—to make archangels look bigger and fiercer. But he learned then just how much redundant strength his brother actually possessed.

If Xas, back when he'd had wings, was hit by a downburst from a thunderhead, he would simply have resigned himself to being pushed into the sea. But Lucifer fought back. His wings locked, his wing beats slowed, but his wings described wider circles. He raised his face to the cloud and closed that final fifty or so feet to its underside, just in time to meet the blast of wind that erupted into the patch of lowered pressure directly beneath them. The wind hit them, and pushed them down. Lucifer's wings laboured, locked, powerful, but the downdraught slammed them into a straight plunge toward the sea. The archangel tucked his head in so that his chin touched Xas's crown. He was breathing hard, and his skin heated up, till it was hotter than human flesh, but still dry.

As they fell, Lucifer fought his way forward. Xas could see the sea below, rushing closer every second. A few further seconds went by, and the howling of the wind abated some. Then the sea was less than twenty feet below them, flashing past, but not coming any closer. Xas looked back under the archangel's wings and saw the blurred air below the cloud. The cloudburst was quite confined, and behind them now.

Lucifer headed in toward the coast, unlocked his wings, slowed almost to stall, and floated up on a thermal that rose against a bluff above the sea. He dropped Xas on to a grassy cliff top, landed beyond him, then whipped around and with a single soft wing beat was back beside Xas and pressing a foot on him.

'Don't tell me you don't remember,' he hissed. 'Don't make any more of your abortive parables. And don't tell me again how *things* have come between you and the sky. I know you remember all our words for air, for weather, for the sensations of flight. Where are the human words? Do they have a name yet for that fall of fine ice?'

'No,' Xas said. Then, 'Get your foot off me.'

'Angels never forget anything,' Lucifer said, vehement, then lifted his foot, sat down, and replaced the foot with a hand.

Xas had planned to slither off the cliff and perhaps that way escape. But he found himself caught again. The grass against his cheek was as dry as last year's hay. Their scuffles had raised a cloud of dust, which hung around them, for there was very little wind on that headland, despite the downburst out to sea. There wasn't a human habitation anywhere in sight, and they were in some place where the coast highway looped away from the sea, probably because the cliffs were subsiding. There was a stand of pines nearby, one tree with its roots bared and lying like glossy embroidery against the crumbling cliff face.

'Shall we continue,' Lucifer said, and gave Xas a good hard shake. 'You went to Heaven to read the destroyed page of Leon Jodeau's suicide letter. Someone objected to you being there, and injured you.'

'Why do you want to tell me this?'

'Perhaps I mean to tell God, not you.'

Xas shut his eyes for a moment, and gave in. 'It was Michael who injured me,' he said. 'It wasn't the first time. In 1819 I stole into Heaven to see Sobran's daughter, Nicolette. She was only seven when she died. I promised Sobran I'd visit her. Michael caught me when I was leaving; coming out of the crater lake of the volcano in Antarctica. He carried me down out of the sky and onto the icy granular dust of the dry valleys, where he battered my head on the ground till it bled, all the while promising that if I ever trespassed again he would break my skull open and eat anything he found there.'

Lucifer gave a faint chuckle, possibly amused by Michael's use of 'anything' as a qualifier.

'Michael tried to damage the signatures on my side, the entwined names, yours and God's. I suppose he objected to the treaty. Anyway—when he caught me again in 1835 he did what he'd only tried to do the first time. He put his hand into my side.'

'And you think that, in 1819, God stopped Michael because you were at that time still chaste?'

'What makes you think I was still chaste in 1819?'

'I'm only guessing.'

'Then you must think it's true that God let Michael half kill me in 1835 because I was unchaste.'

'I think God can't prevent His great archangels from murdering their brothers. He didn't stop *me*. Or not soon enough. But even if God didn't stop Michael from hurting you, He might easily have mended you, Xas.'

'I know that.'

'Once you were injured, why did you go to your lover?'

'You mean, why did I go to Sobran rather than seeking help in Hell? I wanted to see him. I was dying and I wanted to see him once more.'

Lucifer nodded. Then he asked, again, 'Why did I cut off your wings?'

'God wanted me to live, but out of His presence. He grounded me. This is supposed to be my Purgatory. I'm supposed to repent. Repent loving Sobran.'

'And Conrad Cole, and who knows how many others— since it's chastity God requires from you, not that you withhold your heart.'

'God *asked* you to cut off my wings.'

Lucifer said, 'You think I'd do what God asked me to?'

Xas stared sullenly up at his brother.

Lucifer removed his hand and sat back. 'Your lover did help you,' he said. 'Remember the book fountain?'

For the last two and a half millennia Hell had been getting a copy of any written document copied more than ten times. Xas had heard Lucifer describe the arrangement as, on God's part, something like the prosecution letting the defence know what evidence it has—a courtesy, and a legal formality. In Hell there was kind of *spring* where books and papers appeared. They appeared in one place and pushed away what was already lying there, so that it looked as if books were bubbling up out of the rock. Fallen angels were always at the spring, waiting for news and entertainment. They took turns looking at newspaper headlines and pamphlets and playbills and sheet music. They kept up with what was going on.

Lucifer said, 'In September of 1835 one of my brothers brought me a sheet of paper, printed on one side only, a rush job. It read: *"Father, Xas—once your servant—is sorely injured and will die, if he is not already dead. Father, all things are possible for you. Save him. If he has sinned or led me to sin let him at least live to make amends."* The message was signed *"Sobran Jodeau"*, and under it was an address: *"Xas is at Château Vully near the village of Aluze, on the banks of the Saône."*

'I gathered then that you had told your friend how human writings found their way to both Hell and Heaven, how what's reproduced goes to Hell, while only destroyed originals go to Heaven. Because an address was included in the notice I reasoned that *I* was the intended recipient of the page. God wouldn't require directions.

'I'm sure Jodeau had prayed over your bleeding body. I'm sure he petitioned God, no matter what he must have believed about the sin of a man lying with an angel. And God didn't respond. So Jodeau sent a letter to a printer in Chalon-sur-Saône, perhaps the person who made labels for the Château's wine bottles. The printer's name and address appeared in fine print—a single block in the composite—at the foot of the notice.

'Jodeau knew enough about your history to know that you were as much mine as God's, and that if God didn't seem to want to help you, then perhaps I would.

'When I got Jodeau's message, several days after you were injured, I immediately went where I was directed, to Château Vully, near the village of Aluze.

'The Château had many outbuildings, but the trees were dying around only one of them, a coach house with a long gallery above it, a perfect place for a man to wait for an angel to visit him. When I saw that room I understood that you had a life together—you and Jodeau. God must have been with you, seen, known, not interfered. But of course He wouldn't interfere, for the first clause of our treaty says that you can "go freely".

'God hadn't interfered, but nor had He mended you, for when I arrived you were lingering at the point of death and trying to live. You had a hole in your side. I could see that your attacker had pushed a hand in there, perhaps seeking to hold your heart, to hold it still. But you're so small—for an angel—and your ribs are close together, and well knit. Perhaps Michael's hand didn't fit. Or perhaps his violence was half-hearted. I don't know.

'Your heart had stopped beating because you had no blood left to pump. But you weren't yet dead, and you were struggling to live. That's why the trees were dying. Jodeau had wrapped himself about you. He was semi-comatose with exhaustion and grief. Around the bed where you and he were lying I found a dozen dead and dying sheep and goats. The animals were tethered to the frame of the bed. There was a woman sitting on the stairs down to the coach house, a friend of Jodeau's, a clearly intelligent woman who, observing how the life was draining out of everything around you, had supplied the sheep and goats hoping you'd drain them instead of her friend.'

'Aurora de Valday,' Xas said, 'Sobran's employer. She was extraordinary. She found her friend clasping a dying angel and acted intelligently and collectedly.'

'That's why I gave her my pearls,' Lucifer said, then laughed and added, 'Also to make her feel compromised and uneasy.' He went on, 'Aurora, though shaken, was helpful. When I asked her to, she brought me candles, and knives, and needles and thread. Jodeau was useless and irrational— though I confess I didn't command him to be calm. I let him feel his natural terror. He seemed to think I meant to carry your corpse away with me.

'Before I laid a finger on you, I had a word with God. The double doors of the gallery were ajar. They opened on to empty air about twenty feet above a pit of sand, and hot cobblestones, and young lindens with dying foliage. God was there, but because you were nearly dead there was a kind of cloud over God's presence, like a cataract.

'It was over a thousand years since I'd been in His presence. You see, I'd kept away from you. Even in Hell, where God wasn't, I'd kept away. I was unused to God, and I—' Lucifer broke off and shook his head. 'I hurried. When I spoke to God I was in a hurry to get out of His presence again. I thought we were having a consultation, and failed to hear Him telling me what would happen. That's what God deals in: *What will happen*.

'I said, "Do you mean to let Xas die?" And God said, "I mean to have you save him." And I imagined that it was a test. God hadn't lifted a finger to save you, but I was to raise myself to the task. I'd have to sew up the wound in your side, tell you to live, and stay with you for a time to make sure the telling would take.

'And that is what I did. But I believed that God meant to make me feel that if I kept you alive then that was proof I wanted to keep you near me—a table at which He and I could one day sit down together. And because I believed that, I cut off your wings so that you couldn't come near me again. I crippled you. I left you in the world of surfaces with only the remainder of your body.'

Xas felt numb and stupid. He thought that Lucifer was lying, not about what had happened, but why he was telling the story. Lucifer had said 'He' of God and 'you' of him. Lucifer had been talking to him, not to God.

But, as it turned out, Xas was mistaken. For as he sat there on the cliff top, trying to fathom his own new understanding, at least enough to come up with a question, God began to talk to Lucifer. Xas heard his brother's response. Lucifer sounded very tired. He said, 'It does me no good to be good to me.' And then he broke off, looked at Xas, and reached for him. Lucifer clapped his hands over Xas's ears, and pulled the angel toward him so that Xas's face was buried against his chest. Xas was unable to hear his brother, or read his lips. He could feel the vibrations of Lucifer's voice in his chest, and his ragged, shallow breathing.

The consultation took only a moment. When it was over Lucifer shoved Xas away from him.

Xas shouted, 'Go away!' But Lucifer was already in the air.

The archangel tore straight upward, rapidly dwindling from sight. The sound of his wing beats grew softer and seemed to spread till they were coming from every part of the sky.

When Xas walked back into Flora's house two days later, he found her suitcase by the door. She was in a sparkling kitchen polishing cutlery. 'Where were you?' she said. 'I called Cole and he was cagey. He really is putting all that behind him, isn't he?'

'All that?'

'His wild past,' Flora said. 'Look—Connie's calling every hour now. I've been putting him off, but I don't want him to think I'm reluctant to go away with him.'

'Where?'

'Palm Springs again. But I didn't like to leave O'Brien.'

'I'm here now,' Xas said.

Flora closed the lid of the caddy and put it, and the polish, away. She left the rags for Xas to deal with and washed her hands at the kitchen sink. 'I'm sorry to sound brusque. It isn't as if you're unreliable. But I couldn't think where you'd got to. I even called Tram and Lee Young.' Flora ran through a list of jazz musicians. 'And Lockheed, in case you were back there and somehow managing double shifts, though I didn't think it likely.'

Xas said, 'Why don't you just ask me where I've been and whether I'm all right?'

'I'm afraid to.' Flora fell quiet and fidgeted. She flipped up the edge of her wavy bob, and fiddled with her beads. Finally she said, 'Well—you're in one piece, so...'

'Have a nice trip,' said Xas.

# An airfield in Texas

## September, 1938

It was when they were in Florida, where Crow was meeting with a writer about a book he planned to film, that he finally fell out with Flora. Or maybe it was less a falling out than a series of exclusions. Whatever, Flora had seen it coming. In Miami, after a few days, she noticed that whenever she'd say something—her ration of conversation in a room full of men—Crow wouldn't look at her. Instead he'd purse his lips and wait for her to fall silent. She'd review what she'd said. Had she said something silly or slight? Or something that 'called undue attention' to herself—as her exacting grandmother always warned her a girl must never do.

By the end of the trip Flora was reduced to pleasantries in company, and Crow was always out late, and tired or inebriated by the time he came to bed.

*

Flora and Crow had sleeping berths on the airliner back to California. Flora turned in early, hoping to avoid any argument with Crow. He was annoyed with her, or disappointed in her, and she judged that it was better she didn't seek to know why. Not just yet. Back in Los Angeles she'd be at her house and he'd be at his and they could resume contact when it suited him—go on as they were, or as they'd been before their affair.

Flora turned in, got into her pyjamas, and climbed into her bed. A little over an hour later a hostess shook her awake. She was told she had better get up and strap in. The pilot had decided to put down ahead of a storm in a little airfield in Texas.

The plane was already descending, gunning its engines against gusting winds. The craft was jostling, its lights dim and bright by turns. Flora got up, put on her coat over her pyjamas, then pushed her slightly swollen feet into her shoes. She returned to the seat opposite Crow and buckled up. He nodded to acknowledge her, then continued to peer out the porthole beside him.

Rain was washing the glass, rain and slushy snow. Beyond the raindrops the world was black. Then it appeared—the sky around a thunderhead lit up within by lightning flashes. The plane vibrated as the thunderclaps pushed through it. Flora couldn't hear the thunder over the engine noise, but she felt it in her teeth, and in the bones of her skull. Her ears popped.

For a short time the plane passed out of the rain and the coach was quieter, then the engine sound grew as the plane accelerated before touching down. The plane came in to land and ran, tilted nose up and back down, fast, then slowed in spurts, pushed by the wind.

Flora cupped her hands by her eyes and pressed her face against the glass. She saw hangars and a huddle of Quonset huts, one showing lights. The plane taxied to this shelter, rocked by wind gusts. Yellow dust drifted in waves on to the edge of the tarmac. The black front of cloud Flora could see from her side of the plane bloomed with light one more time, then blurred. The rain hit the airstrip, washed the dust down out of the air so that, within seconds, sand-filled rivulets were running across the tarmac, and the hard-packed earth was filmed and shiny with fallen water.

The plane came to a standstill. The hostess reappeared and told them they would be all stopping a while to shelter in the building just to the right of the door.

Crow went down the steps ahead of her, waited to help her, then let her hand go and dashed for the hut. A hostess came after Flora with an umbrella, but they were only under it for a moment before it turned inside out and was torn from the woman's hand.

Flora struggled into the building. Crow had waited at the door, and drew her inside. The other passengers were there already, panting, shaking their coats. The building had a tin roof, no ceiling, only beams from which bare bulbs were suspended. Under the deluge the room was roaring. The hostess arrived, without her umbrella, apologised on behalf of the airline and invited them to make themselves as comfortable as possible. She gestured at a shy looking man who seem to be saluting them with a steaming coffee pot. He retreated behind a counter and began to pour coffee. Most of the passengers kept their coats on and stayed standing to drip dry. Flora accepted a cup of coffee. She followed Crow to the window.

The room faced east. It was flat country, the nearest range of hills only a low stickleback at the edge of the world. The sun was coming up, but it didn't appear. All that showed over the silvered ground and in the thick silver air was a bright oval like the view through an antique Claude glass, an eighteenth century optical instrument that concentrated and isolated a view so that it could be painted.

Flora saw that there was a bird just beyond the window. It had been beaten out of the air by the cloud burst. Its drenched wings were spread, its beak gaping as if it couldn't catch its breath. It fluttered about, kicking up water, then stopped struggling and drooped. Its breathing gave a little hitch.

Flora hurried back outside. She got down on her knees to retrieve the bird. Her coat trailed in the puddles. When she got up, clutching the bird one-handed against her silk pyjama top, she put her other hand on the windowsill in order to keep her balance, and it came away covered in flakes of sun-blasted paint. She went back in. One of the other passengers opened the door for her.

Someone emptied a wastepaper basket and, when Flora put the bird down on the floor, they placed the basket over it. Flora stood over the basket and watched the bird collect itself, blink, shake its wings, then shut them. 'It'll be okay, I think,' said the person who'd found the basket.

Flora's pants clung clammily to her shins. Her coffee was cold. Crow wordlessly brought her another. He watched her drink it. He was wearing a cool, blank expression. 'Are you cold?' he asked.

'Only very wet,' she said.

'That was a little sentimental, you know.'

'If it was filmed it would be sentimental.' She sipped her coffee. It had been stewing and was shockingly bitter.

The world beyond the waiting room was now only that lozenge of yellow light. A waterfall dropped in solid splashes from the gutter by the door. The water made so many sounds it seemed to be different kinds of water, softer or harder, colder or warmer; dense and misty, clean and dirty. It came from everywhere, fell straight down from the sky, then in cascades from the building, then rebounded from the ground to thump the clapboard walls.

'This is biblical,' Flora observed. She was feeling drowsy, uncomfortably damp, but comforted by something—something she couldn't quite figure out, about the bird, about her decision to scoop it up, and bring it in out of the storm.

She had always liked animals. 'Too soft for farming,' her grandmother had once said. That was twice in one night she'd thought of Grandma McLeod. Did it mean anything? Was that why good people shouldn't go to Heaven? Because—as Xas had once seemed to hint—they couldn't go whole? And, if they didn't go whole, was that because if they were good and beloved they left useful bits of themselves behind them? Things that their loved ones had to keep in order to live. To live well. To know that a bird being beaten to death by the rain is like a woman on fire and running in panic through the horrified guests of a café.

Sometime later Flora woke up. She was propped against the wall. There was a space beside her on the bench, yet Crow was on the other side of the room, straddling a chair, his arms across its back and head hanging. There was a scattering of cigarette butts beneath the chair, one smoking faintly; it had been pinched out halfway along its length, yet Crow had lit another and already its tip was a fragile inch of ash.

The rain was quieter, the radio audible again. Flora's neck hurt. She thought that Crow might have considered lying her down and bundling his jacket beneath her head. Or he might have stayed by her and let her head rest on the cushion of his arm.

She got up, went to the window, and wiped a clear circle on the misted glass. She cupped her hands around her eyes and peered out. There was the plane, its propellers strapped. There were several other planes, the Quonset huts, one illuminated, and a hangar. There was a sign above the door of the hangar. It read: *Millie Cotton Memorial Flight School*.

The glass squawked as Flora's hands dropped. She leaned against the window, her damp coat blotting the glass in clear furry-edged patches. 'Connie,' she said.

Crow didn't respond.

She called him again.

'Uh-huh.' He got up slowly as though he was having trouble with gravity. He dropped the cigarette and ground it out. Did all this with an elaborate show of effort.

'Look,' Flora said, once he was beside her.

Crow gave a grunt of surprise. He said, 'Her friends must have got together and done it anyway. Then named it for her.'

'Don't you think it's strange that we didn't know?' Flora said.

Crow shrugged. 'Different worlds, I guess.' He knocked on the glass with his knuckles. 'Now *that* would be sentimental if it was in a film.'

'Yes,' Flora said, 'it would be sentimental because it would be supposed to mean something.' She paused, then said, 'It might mean something anyway.'

'It means her friends found money to start a school and named it for her.'

'But we're here.' Flora touched her own chest, and then his arm. 'We're here by accident.' Then, 'What's wrong, Connie?'

'Must something be wrong?' Crow said.

'No, but—I thought that it all went well in Miami.'

'It did.'

Flora moved her hand from his sleeve to his hand, she wrapped her fingers around his. Crow let her hold his hand but didn't reciprocate, didn't close his grip.

'Though I did spend some time on the phone arguing with Cole,' Crow said. Cole was to produce this next film.

She said, 'Con's feeling his oats. Since flying around the world he's the world famous Conrad Cole. No one is his equal when he gets full of himself like that.'

'I couldn't ever be his equal, Flora. He always had me at a disadvantage. You understand that, don't you? You understand that our friendship was founded on compromise.'

'In what way?'

Crow turned his head to examine her. 'Oh—come on!'

'I don't know what you mean.'

'Flora—I obtained film stolen from him and cut it into my own film. It was dishonourable of me.' Crow turned away and looked at the white glass, for the condensation had closed Flora's window again. 'Don't you have any idea of the kind of position that put me in with him?'

'Are you saying,' Flora began, then hesitated. 'Are you suggesting that *I* put you in that position?'

'I'm not *suggesting* anything,' Crow growled. Then changed the subject. 'Do you think your friend's failure with Millie is the reason he takes such good care of you?'

'Xas?'

'Yes, your friend, Cole's powder puff.'

'I don't know.'

'Though it can't be too much trouble—taking care of you—what with one thing and another, like his advantageous relationship with Cole.'

It sounded to Flora as though Crow was accusing Xas of being involved in some kind of lucrative blackmail. What *had* Cole been saying?

Crow asked suddenly, 'Whose idea was it?'

'What?'

'Stealing Cole's film?'

'It was unwanted footage.'

'Apparently there *is* no unwanted footage.'

'It was my idea,' Flora said. 'Xas had nothing to do with it. I'd only just met him.' Flora wanted to deflect Crow's hostility from Xas. It was silly of her to want that. Crow was saying she was a thief—that *she* was if 'Cole's powder puff' wasn't. It was herself she should defend, but she couldn't see why Crow had suddenly found the need to blame her or, if he was in fact blaming her, why he'd given her an out, why he'd offered her someone else to blame instead.

But Crow had always been like this. She shouldn't kid herself. Crow was prepared to respect what people could do for him. People like Xas. Crow would pay for work. He'd offer praise. He'd offer the largesse of his company, his approval. But he'd not alter one of his prejudices, so that everyone had to eventually remain where he'd first filed them, under 'a good sport', or 'fake', or 'fag', or 'traitor'.

Crow said, 'You have to be able to trust people.'

'Meaning what?'

'I don't like this,' Crow said. He sounded uncomfortable, fastidious. 'I don't like having to give anyone the air, Flora, but I think I have to tell you that I don't want you editing this next film.'

Once Flora was able to react she only shrugged. Crow was firing her before he'd in fact hired her. They had no agreements, no contract governing the terms of their work, or their affair, or their friendship. Flora was ashamed of his behaviour. Whatever had prompted it, boredom with the affair, panic about her being some burden to him— whatever—his behaviour was shameful. She found she couldn't look at him. He was letting her go. She loved him, and he was letting her go.

At that moment Flora understood that she'd be all right. In a day or two she'd feel indignant, scornful, straight in her head. 'Life goes on,' she thought. 'Life goes on and you find you can't even control which way you turn your head. You refuse to look at someone, then lose sight of them for good.' She made herself look at Crow then. She met his pale blue eyes and made herself imagine a time, months or years from now, when they were over this, and were sitting together somewhere having a drink and chewing the fat. In her head Flora turned the knobs of her Moviola, and let the film run on. She shut one gate, let the loop of film appear, shut the other, and made a cut. She pushed the unwanted footage aside. She'd forget this, then she'd forgive him.

She looked out the window again, at the sign: *Millie Cotton Memorial Flying School*. She said, 'Cole gave Xas some money back in 1930. Xas invested it in a funeral home, the Madill Brothers in Santa Monica. They have branches in Long Beach and Pasadena now. The brothers send Xas quarterly reports. I always imagined he reinvested his dividends. But perhaps some of it comes here. That would be like him; to do that and not mention it.'

'And we set down here by chance and discovered it,' Crow said, 'It *is* almost a Hollywood story.'

# Venice

## October–December, 1938

Xas noticed a new smell in the bathroom after Flora had been in there. It was one of her smells—he knew them all—but altered.

On the morning he registered the change he left the bathroom and followed Flora into the kitchen where she was toasting bread and brewing tea, wandering from sink to refrigerator to table. She was taking small careful steps. It was her normal indoor gait, but had something of the restraint Xas had noticed in her movements when he first met her.

Xas observed Flora for a few minutes, then finally passed his verdict. 'You're pregnant,' he said.

Flora went on buttering her toast, pushing the butter, now black with crumbs, to the edges of each slice. She was steeling herself. In a moment she'd take a bite. Her stomach was empty. She felt sick with emptiness, but too sick to eat.

Xas asked, 'Have you told Crow?'

'Not yet. Connie and I had a falling out.'

'But you are going to tell him?'

Flora finally took a bite of her toast. She was so hungry that she felt the fat in the butter go to her head, then some letting go in every cell of her body. She said, 'You never told me about the Millie Cotton Memorial Flying School,' and resumed eating.

Flora didn't tell Crow. Didn't tell him, or see him. Her acquaintances had become accustomed over the years to her patterns of inactivity and retreat. It was understood that she wasn't robust. Closer friends knew Flora retreated when she was in pain, or depressed. They respected her disappearances. Besides, Xas would take care of her.

Xas did take care of her. He waited patiently for what he expected—an early miscarriage, followed by a slow return to health and happiness. But the miscarriage didn't happen and he was left waiting, uneasy.

What he told himself was this: Flora loved Conrad Crow, and Crow was worthy. Flora, finding herself pregnant, would naturally want to have the child of the man she loved. Besides, terminations were almost as risky as pregnancies. Continuing the pregnancy was a good, sane, loving thing to do, Xas told himself. And all *he* could do—he told himself—was be kind and vigilant and unfailingly there.

Xas gave up his job, temporarily, he supposed. He had money in the bank, and the Millie Cotton Memorial Flying School no longer needed his profits from the Madill Brothers. He cut out another oblong vegetable bed from the lawn, composted, planted more. He watched Flora round out. And, assiduously, every day, he rubbed lanolin into the scars on her abdomen, and the soft flesh that began to puff out around the pits of scar like pastry rising around a moist halved peach.

As for Flora—she never announced her intention to have the child she was carrying. She kept her plans to herself— became quiet, dreamy, tentative. She took up reading, picking up one in fifty of the books Xas brought home, reading five pages at a time, a reading that involved a lot of staring into space lost in thought and, in the first months of her pregnancy, sudden naps of narcoleptic intensity, naps she'd come out of feeling as heavy as the stone statue of a swooning saint, as warm as sun-heated stone.

After ten weeks the tiredness relented and time came back, time and her interior; the future, and an evanescent sensation, like a tiny bait fish flittering inside her.

No one knew what she was thinking. She was silent and she was cunning. No one but Xas was to know about her pregnancy till it was four months on, and too late for anyone to talk her into a termination. Several times she was speaking to good old friends—Wylie and Avril—but didn't mention her pregnancy. Wylie would call wanting the lowdown on her quarrel with Crow, Avril to ask whether Flora—or Xas—had seen Cole.

Avril said that, apparently, Cole wasn't seeing Sylvia any more. Sylvia was on tour with a hit play, and phoned him every day, but had been turned away from Cole's Westwood place when she tried to visit on the one night she was passing through town.

'I haven't seen him,' Flora said. 'Nor has Xas. We've been keeping to ourselves. Con's doing that too, probably, just keeping to himself. You know he does that on and off. I guess he's unhappy that what he had with Sylvia didn't last.'

'But he made sure it didn't. I talked to Sylvia. Cole changed—she said. It was after he ran down that man on Wiltshire back in July. He bought himself out of trouble, as usual, then, Sylvia says, just started sleeping in another room, and gradually moved rooms away so that every few nights there was another closed door between them.'

'You know how he comes and goes,' Flora said to her friend. 'He pulls the curtains, lies about, lets himself fester a bit. Then he expands his business, or starts shooting a new film, or courting some beauty, or a whole brace of beauties and, before you know it, he's on the front page of the papers again.'

'You're probably right,' Avril said, then, 'And how are you? I heard that Connie moved on—the louse.'

'Did he move on?' Flora asked.

'Darling! Don't you read Lolly Parsons any more?'

'No. Tell me.'

'Connie went back to Florida to make his hurricane film, and met this girl who was on holiday in Miami. On holiday with her mother. One of those girls brought up on tennis and swimming and horse-riding lessons. Twenty-one years of age, and elegant. I'm sorry Flora, but I can't at this moment recall her name. A whippy, sporty girl. Apparently Connie even took her out big-game fishing with Papa Hemingway.'

'I see,' said Flora.

'They're engaged.'

Flora listened for a time to Avril's commiserations. Then she said she had to go. 'I have something on the stove.'

'All right, darling. But do call me when you finally feel like talking. You know *my* feelings on the subject of Conrad Crow.'

Flora put the phone down and gazed at her own ankles, which were swollen. O'Brien padded into the room, took a careful look at her, and deposited himself on her feet, smiling, one eye slitted, chest and chin turned up invitingly. The cat rolled all the way over to offer his woolly ginger belly and all four paws, their dirt-scuffed pads sunk in tufty, colourless fur with the same texture and gloss as asbestos fibre.

'I'm going to be all right,' Flora said to her cat, very determined.


Flora's belly grew rounded. She had a peaceful period when the fog of tiredness dissipated. For several weeks, whenever she went to bed, she lay on her back for a time. The baby hated that, and would kick her. She loved to feel it kicking. She'd go to bed early. She wasn't exhausted but had an apparently unappeasable appetite for sleep. She'd fall asleep quickly and wake up in dreamy increments. Xas would have opened the curtains. He knew she preferred them open in the morning.

The morning sun whitened the bedroom. Flora rolled over onto her back. The baby woke up and began to kick, little volleys of kicks. The only thing in Flora's mind was her body and the baby, its intermittent, intimate ticking, kicking, quickening.

Whatever she did Flora felt she was returning the baby's signal.

She ate. She got in the bath. Her belly floated above the waterline like an island, the dry part of her.

Everything she did, every small act of everyday life, was like a loving murmur, an echo of the baby's heartbeat. It was a beautiful time.

Then, at around six months, Flora's happy unthinking lassitude changed to fear. The belt of scars began to close its grip on her. Before long her swelling belly developed a discernible ripple where the skin wasn't just tight, but constricted. She could still walk on the level, or on a gentle slope, but if she raised her leg higher than the position where thigh and shin make a right angle at the knee, the distressed skin between the pits of scars would stretch, and part in small splits. She could no longer step over the rim of the bath to shower. Xas had to lift her, and lower her into the bath. He'd wash her feet and hair, then stand her upright, run the shower to rinse her, and lift her out. He began to boil all the towels and sheets. He washed Flora and her bedding every day and, several times a day, sealed the ruptures on the surface of her skin with his spit. Flora surrendered to all these ministrations. She hung a coat over the full-length mirror on her wardrobe door, for what good would it do to watch the progress of that hernia-like pregnancy, the bulge above the belt of scarring? Her womb would not drop. The baby couldn't grow into her pelvic cavity; instead everything pushed up against her diaphragm, so that she felt short of breath, at first only when she was kicked, then all the time. She had constant heartburn. Bile was always in her mouth. She ate very slowly, and all day. Xas would carry her out into the backyard and leave her to amble about between the beds of his garden. It was a still, sunny winter. O'Brien was old for his age and kept close to home. Flora would wander about, her steps slowing gradually. She'd eventually come to a standstill staring out over the fence at the long view to the mountains. O'Brien would come and flop down at her feet. He'd heave a sigh, and eye the few little blue moths flitting over the seeding chard. Flora would stare at the mountains and think that they had somehow ceased to look real. It seemed to her that there was too much *feeling* in the view, as though someone had painted it, perhaps with an eye to selling something. The landscape looked less like her old, familiar view, than like the label on a box of Comet Premium Lemons, picturing mountains, lemon groves, a column of smoke from a smouldering pile of prunings, a comet, and big white and yellow splashes of stars.

Sometimes Flora would find herself muttering, 'This isn't real,' as if she was gently informing someone—the someone behind the view—that she wasn't fooled by any of it.

Xas would come out to check on her. He'd pat the cat, pull a few weeds. He'd never ask her what she was doing. If he had asked she'd have said only that she was occupied— yes—she was occupied, and shortly she'd be vacant, and what more was there to say?

By the middle of January Flora had given up standing in the garden. Her feet were swollen all the time. She couldn't sit with them up, because sitting now was guaranteed to split her scars. And, when she lay down, she was acutely uncomfortable. There was a constant pressure on the base of her throat, as of some mass improperly swallowed. She slept only in snatches. For a time hunger would wake her and she'd call for Xas to help her get up. He'd ease her straight body off the bed and tilt her onto her feet—a feat impossible for any human of his size. He'd use his body like a board to brace her own. He was always touching her.

Sometimes Flora would feel she had a number of bodies: a distorted body of unevenly stretched skin, her belly and fat fluid-filled feet, and her own scarcely altered body of bone and muscle. Then there was the baby. The baby wasn't her, but it was there all the time. And then there was the angel, capable, gentle, warm and as wholly savoury as the sunlight. He was there, and was like the sun touching her. He was there and as animal as ever, but, as the weeks went on, he seemed to dissolve, or Flora's whole exterior world blended with the angel and became something indefinite in which she was immersed—she, her pains, the baby's small hard back resting spine-out to the right of her navel, its rummaging movements, the vertiginous rollercoaster lurches she felt when its rummaging displaced her intestines. All these sensations took place inside a fine fence of pain made from the weeping splits in her scarred skin. Beyond that was the world, warmth and nourishment, bathwater, the springy, sweet-smelling body that cradled her own, and the tongue that numbed the sting of air on her exposed flesh, and briefly dissolved the barrier between her body and her world.

# Venice

## Late January, 1939

Xas got Flora up and helped her to the toilet. Her feet were so swollen that her steps reverberated in her bones, and her skin prickled with the vibrations. Her bladder felt full, but there was very little urine. What there was of it was strong and stung. When she stood up she saw the water in the bowl was dark yellow.

She'd lost her appetite. Xas asked her if she wanted something to eat, but she shook her head. She took a few mouthfuls of water, but then felt sick. She lay down again and drifted. O'Brien came and lay under one of her arms, against her side. Whenever she woke he was still there, purring furiously. Once she woke to hear the cat's purring and a murmur, too, of incomprehensible speech. Flora couldn't understand what Xas was saying but his words came down like rain and seemed to thin her muddy thoughts and make them fluent again. She opened her eyes and said, 'Are you praying? You don't need to pray.'

'I'm not praying.'

She went to sleep. She dreamed that she was carrying a vase of flowers toward the end of a long corridor. It was night. She'd been asked to remove all the flowers from her grandmother's room. At night, she was told, there would be a competition between her grandmother and the flowers for the air in the room.

Flora woke up. She was cramping, and the bed was wet.

The baby came quickly, and easily, because she was very small. Xas held her in his cupped hands. She was motionless, covered in Flora's inner oils and her own waxy coating of vernix. He watched the cord pump. He set her down on the sheet between Flora's legs and touched her chest with a fingertip. Flora tried to sit up, but couldn't. Xas put his wet hand on Flora's chest and pressed her back. He bent his head and took the cord in his mouth. It was still twitching minimally. He bit the cord in two, held the severed end upright, pinched it closed, picked the baby up and put her down between Flora's breasts. Flora strained to raise her head, looked, gave a little moaning sob and dropped her head back on the pillow.

Xas saw that his hand was trembling; he paused a second, his fingers an inch from the baby's tiny, pale, secretive face. He made his hand be still, then gently pinched the baby's cheeks so her mouth opened, her thin lips forming a small beak. He put his mouth to hers and sucked gently. A quantity of salty fluid flowed into his mouth. He touched her ribs with his free hand. Three fingers spanned the entire length of her rib cage. He felt the baby's chest depress faintly, and blew, or began to blow, but spoke instead, spoke into the sepal of her open mouth. He told her to live. Said, '*Live*,' in his own tongue, his fingers and lips immediately feeling the effect of his word as the tiny body flashed with warmth, and stirred. Then his instruction seemed to come back at him like an echo, not from the slight depth of that body, but from the future. He had a moment of panic, and his throat hardened with it. He knew he'd done something extraordinary, something unreasonable. He couldn't take it back, all he could do was come up with something to mitigate whatever it was he'd done. He whispered, with nothing like the same urgency or certainty, 'For a hundred years, at least.' There was blood in his mouth. His throat was bleeding.

The baby was wriggling now, her face screwed up. She was crying. She had his blood in her mouth and seemed, between complaints, to be savouring it, her lips rubbing together and cheeks sucking.

Xas sat up and pulled a second pillow under Flora's head. He picked up Flora's arms and placed her hands over the wriggling baby. Flora opened her eyes and stared. 'Oh—look!' she said.

Xas waited for the contractions to begin again, gentler this time. The placenta, glistening, deep red, slipped out between Flora's legs. Flora seemed scarcely to register this. She was frowning at her baby. 'Is she too small?'

'She is very small.'

'She can't be two pounds,' Flora said.

'No.'

Flora's gaze drifted beyond the baby, past Xas—not to stare into space, but at the corner of the bedroom. She smiled. 'You can keep her alive,' she said.

'We can,' Xas corrected. He rolled the placenta to the foot of the bed. The sheet dried its surface and it was very sticky by time he had it out of his way.

'What's that?' Flora said. 'That's not my insides?'

Xas laughed. 'No. It's the placenta.'

'Of course,' Flora said.

'Let's wait a moment. I'll get more pillows in a moment. Then maybe you should try to see if she wants to suck.'

'Her mouth is so tiny.'

'It can be done. I saw her swallow.'

Flora sounded peevish. She said, 'How come you know so much?'

'I don't. But I've seen babies this small before. When I came back to the States on *Lake Werner* I went to Coney Island and there I happened to see premature babies in warm ventilated boxes—incubators—in Courney's exhibition. Babies at an amusement park. People were coming back every week to see how they got on.'

'She doesn't need an incubator,' Flora said. 'Does she?'

'Well—we don't need the charity of an amusement park. We can afford to get her cared for in a hospital,' Xas suggested. 'Hospitals have incubators for those who can pay.'

'If I'd wanted a hospital I'd have gone to one already.'

'You've been asleep for months. In a way. You haven't been thinking. You haven't actually declared what you want.'

'I made you marry me.'

It was true. Three months back Flora had dragged Xas in to apply for a licence. The application took a while because he wasn't a citizen. But, eventually, they did get their five minutes at City Hall. Xas had been surprised by Flora's insistence—he hadn't thought she'd mind so much, either on her behalf, or the baby's, about its illegitimacy. But now he did understand. Flora, her hair tangled, face and body puffy and striped by fissures of split skin, some weeping lymph, some blood as well—this battered woman, less than an hour after giving birth, fixed him with her gaze and said, 'We'll register her birth as soon as possible. And you will be her father.' She was glaring at him.

'All right,' Xas said.

'She's yours,' Flora said.

'Ours. All right.'

'We don't need a hospital. She'll live if we stay together. If I feed her, and you hold her.'

'All right,' he said.

'You must hold her all the time,' Flora said, her face set and determined.

He nodded.

Flora relaxed. She took a deep breath and her eyes wandered around the room, once giving off a happy flash of light, as though her gaze had struck a spark off something. She said, 'Find me more pillows. I'll sit up now and try to feed her.'

Xas got off the bed. He fetched the pillows from his own room and arranged them behind her. She could sit, but was too tired to support the weight of her own arms. She needed another pillow to put the baby on. He went to get the cushions from the cane chair that sat in the corner of Flora's room. He was a little confused when he reached the chair. It had been pushed back into a pot plant, though he didn't recall there being a pot plant in the room. He grabbed the cushions and extracted them from the greenery, brought them to the bed and arranged them. He asked, 'Is the room warm enough?' When Flora had gone into labour he'd carried the living room heater into her bedroom. It was a cylindrical heater with four elements, it had been on all night and was giving off heat like a stone garden brazier heaped with coals.

'The sun will come in soon,' Flora said. Then she began to weep at the sight of her breasts, globes of white flesh netted with blue veins, each much bigger than the baby. Her nipples were huge. 'How can I do this?' she wept.

'She's asleep now anyway,' Xas said. 'Don't try till she wakes up.'

Flora drooped, she warmed the baby between her breasts, her fingers cupped over the tiny skull.

Xas saw that the baby's ears were still attached to the skin of her head, like the ears on a partly finished sculpture. He saw that she had no fingernails. He saw the blood vessels in her fingers, the continual faint flashing of red. He bent to the baby and sniffed her sticky scalp. She smelled new and familiar at the same time. Then her scent blasted into his head and wiped out everything, momentarily but utterly, every interest, desire, loyalty.

The baby stirred and gave a cracked, complaining cry. Xas started speaking to her again in his own tongue. He said, 'You cry and I'll comfort you. I'm here. I'm the guarantor of all your needs, if you need me to be. Right now you don't even need to be vigilant about your own life. I'm here. It's all right. If it's what you need I can be the world, the beginning and the end.'

Flora's tired voice interrupted him. 'You should stop that,' she said. 'You have blood on your chin. I think perhaps you're not enough of an angel to keep that up.' Then, 'She's awake, I'll try to feed her.'

# Los Angeles

## March–August, 1939

Six weeks later Flora and Xas took the baby out to register her birth. She was thriving, but tiny still. The shells of her ears had separated from her head and her fingernails had appeared from behind the horizon of their quicks. But Xas had done a little reading—once he dared to put the baby down long enough to go out to the library and borrow books on infant care. He realised that Flora and he should perhaps prevaricate a little about when she had appeared. She was doing much better than she could be expected to for a baby so premature. Of course, the clerk at City Hall wasn't a paediatrician and while he helped Xas and Flora complete their paperwork he didn't even glance at the quiet little bundle Flora was carrying.

Alison McLeod Hintersee.

Flora's house had a modern mangle washing machine, not an old copper. As a girl Flora had sometimes sat in the wash house and watched her grandmother fish clothes from the soaking tub—grey concrete with the tide mark of soap on its sides. Grandma would lift them into the copper then, after stirring them in boiling water, transfer them from the copper into the rinsing tub. Flora had admired her grandmother's hardy strength. It was just as well she didn't have to think how to manage any of this herself. Xas did it all. He washed everything in the machine, with detergent, then put his big chilli pot on the stove and boiled one sheet or five diapers at a time. And, once, one of the neighbours was intrigued to see 'the young pilot', as he was known in the neighbourhood, out at the washing line after midnight, lifting wet diapers bare-handed from a pot that was billowing steam into the cold air, wringing them out and pegging them up, all while the cloths fumed hellish tendrils of steam.

Flora called Avril, who was on location in Hawaii, and then sent a photo of Alison, smiling one of her early, toothless, open-wallet-shaped smiles. Avril was full of questions; she promised to visit as soon as she was back.

She appeared several weeks later, with flowers, and a christening gown of Brussels lace. Xas fixed Flora and her guest tea, then got out of their way. But, late that afternoon, Avril found Xas out by the clothes line, pegging out washing. Avril picked her way across the lawn, walking on tiptoe to prevent her shoe heels from penetrating the turf. She was carrying Alison. Xas upturned the empty laundry basket for Avril, and she sat down, Alison on her knee. 'Baby is only halfway through a feed,' she said. She rubbed Alison's back to raise a burp. Alison slumped, sleepily. She grizzled, her pouting mouth red and wet with milk, her hair darkly curdled with perspiration.

'It seems to me that Flora's a little touchy, even for someone so tired,' Avril said. 'But it's hard for me to judge. I really haven't any experience of babies.'

Alison produced a burp, and Xas caught a whiff of the breast milk's sweet fennel scent.

Avril looked disconcerted. 'I guess that's the desired result,' she said.

'Yes.' Xas smiled at her. 'Keep going, there might be more.'

'And, surely, Flora's feet shouldn't still be swollen,' Avril said.

'I have suggested we get a doctor to look at that.'

'And?'

'Do you think she's against doctors because of her long stay in hospital?'

'No. Flora's far too sensible for that.'

Xas nodded.

'But right now she's too tired to think straight. So you should just decide for her. Make an appointment. I can make some recommendations if you don't like your current doctor.'

'We don't really have one.'

'Are you telling me she didn't see a doctor at any time during her pregnancy?'

'She was very reluctant. I thought she must be afraid of them.'

Avril stared at him for a time. Then she asked, 'Do you always let her get her own way?'

'I always let everyone,' he said, then, after a moment, 'That sounds worse than it is.'

Avril got up and put Alison over her shoulder. She lingered a moment longer, swinging her weight from foot to foot, as people do by instinct when they're holding a baby. 'I fixed us some crackers and tomatoes before, and I had to ask Flora where you kept the salt shaker. She said you don't salt anything, and it occurred to me that you already had her on a diet. That you'd read a book.'

Avril had noticed all the books. From her expression Xas thought that perhaps she disapproved of them. 'Yes,' he said, 'I think it's better if she has next to no salt now.'

'If you know that much, then why haven't you made her go to a doctor already?'

'I don't make people do things.'

'You mean, you won't be responsible.'

'I once gave someone bad advice.'

Avril frowned at him, and looked set to linger. But Alison was yawning, squeaking, smacking her lips, clearly ready for more milk, so Avril carried her inside.

Xas fetched his hoe then went around his vegetable beds scraping the tender green flush of weeds from the soil around his young tomato plants. He thought about the bad advice he'd given Sobran. Perhaps not so bad in the balance. Celeste, the woman he had encouraged Sobran to marry, had never been wholly sane. And at times she had been insane. But they'd had seven children and those children had brought

Sobran great happiness. Was it really a sound policy never to offer advice? And, Xas wondered, was that really his policy? He had also offered Sobran advice on viticulture and winemaking. He'd offered Cole advice on the design of planes. He'd had many discussions with Flora about film, and some of that might have amounted to a form of advice, for their talks must have helped Flora form her tastes. Was it only the big things which he abdicated any responsibility for? The big things—love, and the acute mortal risks that often followed on from loving: children, illness, all the consequential trouble of the ravelling and unravelling of separate human lives. Had he been telling himself that, since the people he cared for died, it didn't matter when they died? When or how? Did he suppose that it was his business only to make those he loved comfortable?

Xas sat down on the ground. The bean frame was between him and the house, and he was hidden behind a filigreed screen of scarlet-flowering tender green runners. He put his hands over his face. Whatever he'd been thinking, he had to change. For this reason. Whenever he heard Alison waking up he'd come to look into her bassinet, and she'd smile at him. She already knew who belonged to her. She knew that he did. She'd smile and begin to kick, and wave her hands, as though hoping to clamber up through the air into his arms. She'd yawn, and the bud of her chin would sink into a socket of soft fat. Her tongue would curl around coos and ahs and she'd sing, or seem to sing, in her melodious milk-thickened voice. To *him*.

Xas wondered what Sobran would have thought of all this. He wished he could speak to him—for once wished not just to see Sobran and speak to him about their shared past, but to show him something, Alison, to share her, like great news that it should be possible to broadcast back in time to the beloved dead.

O'Brien came through the open back gate and, strangely, didn't trot toward Xas. Instead he plodded, apparently footsore. Xas picked the cat up and cradled him. He stroked O'Brien's rough fur, his these days tangible spine. He gathered the cat's sandy paws in one hand and kissed him on the tips of his warm ears.

Xas found Flora a doctor. The doctor sent Flora to a specialist at Cedars-Sinai. Xas waited outside the specialist's office during the consultation. When Flora came out the specialist said he wanted to speak to Mr Hintersee alone. A nurse would wait with Mrs Hintersee. One of the nurses offered to walk Flora to their car. She took Alison's carrycot from Xas. Flora and she took hold of a handle each and set off down the hall.

The specialist invited Xas into his consulting rooms, and asked him to sit down.

'I don't know your wife,' the specialist said, 'but one would think that her line of work required sharpness, perspicacity?'

Xas nodded.

The specialist made a thoughtful humming noise. He fingered the papers in his file. He looked up. 'Your wife is already showing some changes in censorium,' then, 'Oh, excuse me—'

'I know what you mean,' Xas said.

'She's irritable, her concentration is impaired, she is suffering from fatigue, and insomnia. We might be able to put all that down to motherhood. But she also told me that there are times when, hearing herself, she thinks she sounds drunk.'

'In the past week once or twice she's slurred her words,' Xas said.

'She told me that she noticed, and was distressed that she couldn't correct it. She also complains of itching. And is occasionally nauseous. She said that you could give me a more comprehensive description of her diet.'

Xas did that. The specialist kept nodding. He seemed grave. He then said, 'I can't see any adjustments you need to make. I did tell your wife that I'd like to admit her and she only said, "To do what?" I do appreciate that she doesn't want to be separated from the baby.'

Xas nodded.

'We discussed weaning the child. I've given Mrs Hintersee a book about infant formula—

'And what did she say?'

'She agreed. Can you handle all that? Hygiene and sterility are very important.'

Xas nodded.

'Your wife said you could. She has a great deal of confidence in you.'

'All right,' said Xas. He wanted to walk away, join Flora and Alison in the car, drive them home, get back into his routine—with whatever 'adjustments' were necessary. He wanted to be private, to watch Alison at Flora's breast for a little longer, her small hands patting and pressing, her eyes flicking back and forth, as though she were reading her mother's breast. He wanted the hours to stretch—for a little longer. 'All right,' he said, again.

The doctor got up, came around his desk, and put a hand on Xas's arm. He sought Xas's eyes—caught his gaze, held it. 'You do understand?' he said.

Xas nodded.

'Your wife didn't have kidney disease, but her kidneys have been fragile for a long time, almost certainly because of the burn injury. The pregnancy was too great a strain. She is now showing several signs of acute renal failure.'

Xas nodded. He remembered standing with Flora on a set watching a rehearsal. It was cold on the soundstage, and the actress was wearing a leotard and cotton tights under her satin robe. He remembered how Flora had turned to him and said, 'Jean's a gorgeous girl, but you can see she has a problem with her ankles. They swell up now and then, like mine.' Flora had had an example before her—young Jean Harlow's puffy ankles, and her own. When Harlow died surely Flora hadn't believed any of those myths about the actress having accidentally poisoned herself with too much peroxide from bleaching her hair?

The specialist said, 'Your wife's system might—*might*—right itself. But if it does not there's very little we can do.'

'Yes,' Xas said. 'Thank you.'

'When your wife has weaned the baby I'd like to see her again.'

'All right,' Xas said.

The man released him.


Xas called Crow and told him he should visit Flora. Crow said that he had a lot on his plate: he was getting married the following day, then flying to Hawaii for a honeymoon.

Xas said, 'I understand that you and she argued. And that the argument was about honour.'

'We didn't argue,' Crow said. 'And I don't respond to emotional blackmail. I know what *you* want. I can see how minding a baby wouldn't sit with being a test pilot, and being out at all hours at clubs on Central Avenue. Or any of your other pursuits.'

'Gardening is my main pursuit, now that I've quit Lockheed.'

'Look—I'm starting afresh,' Crow said. 'It's rare for a man my age to get the kind of chance I have now with Grace. Grace is a once-in-a-lifetime girl.'

'You're supposed to say you're in love.'

'Any sap can say that.'

'So love's an opportunity? A stroke of luck?' Xas said, then, 'You're an idiot, Crow. A great artist, but an idiot. You're a couple of years shy of fifty and you've still not worked out how long life can be, and how your seventy-year-old self will require certain things from the man you are now and, if you fail him, if you fail that old man, he'll disown you.'

'Good God! Whenever you do open your mouth you sure say a mouthful. Look—I'm not liable for Flora's decisions. Flora is a big, grown-up girl. And, I have to say that, while you're telling me off, taking the moral high ground, I notice you're still hedging your bets with compliments. That tells me a lot about you.'

'What it tells you is that praise comes to me more naturally than criticism. That that's the way I was made,' Xas said, 'you benighted animal.' He hung up the phone.

Cole said yes, he would come and visit his friend. But he didn't appear. Instead, he sent three dozen red roses. Xas put the flaring mass in one bucket, rather than several vases, and carried the bucket into Flora's bedroom. He told her who they were from, and she said, irritable, 'Oh, don't tell me *that's* going to start up again?'

'That?' Xas shook his head. 'No.'

'Where's O'Brien?'

Xas promised to find the cat. He gave the roses one last tweak. He said, 'It's summer, so he's pretty busy in the waste lot.' As he spoke he felt lightheaded, and injured inside, as he did whenever he lied.

These days O'Brien would often only sniff at his food, lick up a little of the meat juice, take a few laps of water. Then he'd go outside to lie in the crosshatched shade under the rosemary bush, and sleep.

Xas went out, and found O'Brien exactly where he expected. As he picked O'Brien up, the cat gave a little, exhausted complaint, then began to purr mightily, a loud sawing that shook his whole body, and reminded Xas of a person rocking themselves around a pain. Xas cradled the cat, carried him indoors, and put him on Flora's bed.

The men who came to the gate of Cole's Westwood house wore pressed brown pants and button-pocket shirts, clothes suggestive of uniforms—not police or studio security, rather of municipal workers in some wealthy, self-respecting small town. They wanted to know what business Xas had with Mr Cole. Their questions were startlingly personal. They seemed not just protective, but possessive of their employer. Xas tried to satisfy them, then spotted Cole's chauffeur, Carl, and called out to him. Carl strolled down to the gate. He explained that this was Huss Hintersee, an old friend of Mr Cole's. The gate was opened, and Carl walked Xas up to the house. When they were out of earshot Carl looked at Xas and said, 'Those people—they're like gophers. There's one, then two, then the lawn's gone.'

'Who are they?'

'The help, like me. Except they're all related—you know—there's a man, and the man's cousin, and his brother-in-law. Related. Mr Cole is a family business now. Only it isn't his family.'

Carl left Xas on the porch. He said, 'No one answers the door because no one comes to the house.' He pushed the door open, then headed back to his garage.

The house was shut up, as if unoccupied. Curtains were drawn. The only light came through a porthole in the door of a below-stairs kitchen.

Cole was in bed. The bedroom smelled dank, yeasty. When the door opened he reared up and called out, fearful, 'Who is it?' Then he said, 'Oh, it's you,' and slumped back down.

Xas approached the bed and Cole shrank away and drew the sheet up over his mouth. 'Are you clean?' he said.

Xas sniffed his hands; smelled milk and mild baby bile. 'Would you like me to wash?' He could tell by the expression in Cole's eyes that the offer wasn't adequate and that Cole would not believe he'd washed unless he watched him do it. And Cole wasn't about to get out of bed.

There was a fireplace in the room, a neat mound of pine cones on its grate. The cones, frosted by dust and spider web, had probably been there since the previous summer. Since Sylvia's time. Xas knew the decorated grate was Sylvia's doing. He remembered an evening, several years ago, when he'd driven Flora up to a hotel in Colorado to visit the set of a movie Crow was directing and Cole producing, a movie in which Avril starred. Sylvia had been visiting too. She hadn't liked the hotel. She thought it grand, but cold. Xas remembered her saying that there were things that should never be empty, 'Like a fireplace or a fruit bowl.' And then everyone else had chimed in:

'A cradle. Or a heart,' said Avril.

'A wallet,' said the leading man.

'Or a bottle,' said Flora.

'A threat,' said Cole.

And Crow, falsely earnest, 'A future.'

And then they all looked at *him*—the only one who hadn't volunteered anything. He'd forgotten he was there—

except to listen. Besides, when he did come to consider it, there were no emptinesses, only unwelcome silences, like listening to someone out in the woods at evening calling a child and going unanswered. But whenever the longed-for voice failed to answer the silence was still God. It was God saying, 'No,' but God nevertheless.

Crow had interrupted his thought. 'He's going to ask us to define emptiness,' he said, and everyone laughed.

On the mantelpiece of the fireplace in Cole's bedroom Xas found a silver canister full of wax matches. He struck one and held its flame to the dry scales of a pine cone. It caught, and the fire trickled up through the kindling. Xas waited till the cones were fully alight then put his hands in the flame. It was too hot, and it hurt him. But it made no difference to his skin, only streaked it with soot. He heard the springs in the bed complain as Cole sat up.

As he was laving his hands in the fire, Xas realised that he'd done this before. He had coaxed a fire back to life by stirring its embers and rearranging its logs. He'd crouched at the grate in a room above the Cuverie in Château Vully, his wings screening the rest of the room from what little heat there was to be had from the dying fire, chilling the man standing behind him. The man—Sobran—who'd got out of his warm bed on a snowy night because an angel had knocked at his window.

It was on that night that Xas finally took Sobran in his arms meaning also to take the man as his lover. Xas remembered putting his hands into the fire, making practical arrangements to revive it, then making his decision. Remembering, it occurred to the angel that *that* was perhaps the only occasion in his life where he'd chosen. Deliberated, then made a choice. 'This disaster is my future,' he'd said, and then lay down over the man. Responding to an offer wasn't a choice. Coming back when called wasn't either. The gardener who broke new ground was choosing; but to hoe and harvest and *keep on* was not a matter of choice.

For a moment, as he crouched at Cole's hearth, bathing his hands in flame, Xas wondered what after all he'd done with his life—as if he had a life, and was a person.

He removed his hands from the fire. He shook them to cool them. He turned to Cole, who lay back down, no longer fearful or shrinking, but languorous.

Xas climbed into bed with and lay over the man. It was a commemorative act. He cupped the back of Cole's head with his hot, sooty hands. He kissed Cole, whose mouth was sour and teeth velvety.

Xas told Cole that he must visit Flora.

Cole shook his head. 'I don't like to be looked at,' he said.

'Since when?' said Xas, 'When you broke the long-distance flight record everyone was looking at you.'

Cole nodded. He looked perplexed. 'That's right. And it didn't trouble me straight off, then. Though I did have qualms. I tried to land beyond the crowd. I landed as far beyond them as I was able while still being on the airstrip. Then they all rushed toward me. The men were tossing their hats. It was night and hats were going up like black bubbles, as if the air was dark champagne. I had to grin and bear all the attention, and the yelling. The crowd made a sound so loud that my good ear just decided to quit and not let anything in. It was the same during the tickertape parade. That was like a silent film—the tape coming down slowly like dry snow. I was sitting up on the trunk of a car with the Mayor of New York and he kept chattering to me. I couldn't hear a thing he said, I had to keep looking away from the crowd to read his lips. It was a grand occasion though, and it's strange to think how I went from that to...' Cole trailed off. He began to weep.

Xas brushed at the tears with his thumbs, kissed one damp temple, and then the other. 'It's a short walk to my car,' he said. 'The hallway is empty and so is the lobby. It's past midnight. Someone has watered the lawns and they smell good. The aspidistra are all out along the drive. My car is at the gate. The city is as quiet as Easter Sunday. I can have you back before the sun comes up. Get out of bed and come with me now.'

Cole did get up, and Xas put him in the shower and washed him. He dressed Cole, clipped his toenails, and pushed his bony feet into a pair of loafers. Then they went out.

Cole sat with Flora and hid his fear. He was mild and gentle. And when they eventually left her sleeping and walked out together, Xas took Cole's hand and said, 'Thank you,' and 'I love you, Con.'

'You say "I love you", but I hear, "Good dog, good dog".'

'Still,' said Xas.

'I shouldn't have to do those things,' Cole said.

Xas opened the passenger's door for Cole then climbed into the car himself and started the engine. Cole said, 'I won't forget you made me do that.'

He was silent for the rest of the drive. But when Xas had delivered him home, and they reached the foetid and lightless hermitage of his bedroom, Cole made an effort to meet Xas's eyes. He said, 'She's very sick.'

'Yes.'

Then, 'Can you save her?'


Xas called Avril, who visited again, brought more gifts, and sat with Flora. She held Alison and remarked admiringly on how she'd grown. When she left, Avril told Xas he should have called her right after Flora had seen the specialist.

She asked Xas to walk her out to the road where her chauffeur was waiting in her car. She introduced them. She said, 'This is Robert. When Flora has to go into hospital, you call me and, if I'm working, I'll send Robert to collect Alison. I'm sure that, between us, me and my girl Betsy can take care of the baby.' Betsy was her maid.

Avril gestured at Robert, who got back in the car and closed the door. Avril took Xas's hand. 'Alison is Conrad Crow's daughter, isn't she? I can see now that she has his eyes.'

Xas didn't respond.

Avril said, 'None of us was sure.' She waited, then added, 'That's all right, you don't have to tell me.' She squeezed his hand, kissed him on the cheek, and blotted her eyes with the knuckles of her gloved hands, skilfully, so that her mascara was barely smudged.

Xas opened the car door for her, said, 'I will call. Thank you.'

Flora was sitting in the cane chair, which Xas had carried outside and put in the shade by the back steps. He had pegged out diapers, and was now picking beans. Alison was lying on the lawn, on a rug, grasping her own feet and singing to herself. The day was so lovely that, to Flora, it seemed possible to leave only if it was impossible to stay. She tried to imagine leaving. She imagined that her body was asking her to leave.

She wasn't in any great pain, the kind of pain she'd known for years, the kind that was a goad, and issued commands like, 'Move! Do something!' The pain that would sometimes, as if whimsically, instruct her to stay still, for stillness was like movement too, was something she had to *do*.

Dying wasn't like that. It seem to Flora that the only way to go was not to be able to stay.

Flora raised her eyes to measure the sky. She knew she was only trying to imagine dying. And she knew that her failure of imagination didn't mean she'd live. She thought, 'Perhaps the one who leaves isn't even an "I" any more, the "I" who can measure the sky.'

She looked back at the garden. Xas was brushing the dirt from fingerling carrots. He had given Alison a wooden clothes peg. Alison had the peg in one fist and was staring at it with cross-eyed intensity. The garden was still there for Flora, whether or not she was able to fix her attention on it. Maybe—she thought—to imagine leaving she'd first have to imagine that the garden wasn't there. She tried to do that, subtracted the garden beds, the busy angel, the baby, the small wilderness of the waste lot, the distant mountains. That left only herself, in a kitchen chair, Flora McLeod, using her imagination and failing to imagine being gone.

When Xas held Alison on his knees, facing away from him, he could look at the back of her head and see that it had just as much personality as her face. She was face down in her character already, and it had closed over her head. The fingerprint pattern of the hair on her crown was her biography. It said she was delivered, it said she consented to breathe, and to suckle, apparently bewildered by her mother's breast, this first surface. It said she learned how to send herself to sleep, comforted by her father or mother's breathing. It said she slobbered in pain with colic and was walked up and down the house on her father's shoulder. It said she learned how to talk to the wind in the cornflowers, how to sleep outdoors. It said she'd learned to manage to get food into her, and show she liked it by smiling at her father from under a froth of mashed carrot. It said she was given toys she first flung helplessly from her. It said what she'd do, given time. Her turned head said, 'I'm by myself' and 'I might just take off any moment now.'

Flora wasn't sleeping well. When she fell asleep she'd jerk awake, her arms and legs jumping up off the bed. Xas knew this was a symptom. He called the specialist who said there was nothing that could be done about it, short of sedating her, and, 'It's not time for that yet, is it?'

Xas heard the specialist's 'is it?' and knew he was being asked to make a decision. He couldn't think what to say.

Eventually the specialist broke the silence: 'It would mean admitting her. That's the decision I'm asking you to make.'

Xas said, 'I think she's more comfortable at home.'

'Can you manage?'

'Yes,' said Xas.


Xas sat in the chair in the corner of Flora's room to feed Alison her morning bottle.

Flora was in bed, propped up on pillows. O'Brien was asleep beside her, curled in a tight ball, his ribs plainly visible whenever he inhaled.

Flora said, 'When did that chair lose its leaves?'

Xas looked over his shoulder at the cushion behind him. It was covered in floral fabric, faded by its many recent washes. The cover had shrunk, so that the cushion was fat and distorted. 'I'm afraid the pattern has faded. I had to boil the covers, back when Alison was small and I was sterilising everything.'

Alison was still small at six months, but was doing everything that could be expected of a six month old, according to the book produced by the Children's Bureau of the US Department of Labor.

Flora said, 'I seem to remember the leaves on the floor.'

'The cushions?' Xas was puzzled.

'The leaves.'

'There was a pot plant there,' Xas said. 'Someone moved it.' Xas frowned at Flora. Her eyes were distinguishable only as slits in swollen flesh. She'd lost most of her eyelashes. The puffiness was like a mask. It disguised her expression. Xas stared at her, and supposed her mind was wandering.

'It was the chair,' Flora said, dogged. 'It had leaves. You did it.' Then, 'I hope you'll be all right.'

'You know I will. And I promise that Alison will too.'

Flora nodded. She rested her head back on her piled pillows and gazed at the ceiling.

Alison had drained the bottle. Xas carried her to the bed and sat beside Flora, set Alison on his knee and began to jiggle her gently to dislodge wind.

'Don't do that,' Flora complained.

Xas stopped jiggling and rubbed the baby between her shoulderblades instead.

Flora said, 'I don't need Alison to admire me—'

'But I'll show her your films,' Xas promised, eager.

Flora waved an impatient hand at him. 'Never mind that. Alison is going to see this differently from everyone else, but you mustn't let her think she lost me because of what I did. She *is* what I did.'

'The movies are what you did too,' Xas said.

Flora heaved a sigh. She looked exhausted. There was a film of sweat on her face. 'Stop changing the subject. Why did I choose to have this baby?'

'You loved Crow,' Xas said.

Flora stared at him and waited.

'You loved me,' Xas said.

Flora nodded. 'Yes, I do love you. And I love Connie. But, listen. You've spoken to him, haven't you? And after you spoke to him you changed. You became quiet. Quiet and deliberate.'

'I only spoke to him on the phone.'

Flora looked pained and impatient. 'No,' she said, 'Not Connie. Your *brother*.'

Xas didn't know what to say.

'You told me he'd found you. That time when Millie thought you'd been bitten by a snake. He came back again, didn't he? I mean *after* he'd written his notes.'

'Yes. I spoke to him. He spoke to me.'

'I thought so.' Flora closed her eyes. 'What did he offer you?'

'Nothing.'

'But he will one day.'

Alison managed a burp. Xas wiped the baby's chin with her bib. He stared at Flora. Her head lay in the socket of her pillow. Her face was lifeless, and closed.

'Flora?'

Her eyelids stirred, as if she were dreaming. She said, 'When she's grown I want Alison to see that I didn't make a stupid decision. It wasn't all about Connie. It wasn't all love.'

'But it was,' Xas said, wounded, puzzled, plaintive.

'Not all. I didn't hear anyone say, "Build an Ark", but I have built one. "A shady bed in the whirlwind of mysteries."' She fell silent. Several minutes went by and Xas supposed she had finally fallen asleep. He waited for one of the things that always woke her now: a myoclonic jerk, her restless legs. Then she said, 'She's beautiful, anyway. Time always runs forward, but the reasons for things sometimes go back. She's beautiful, and *that's* why I had her.'

After that conversation Xas didn't get any sense out of Flora—only responses. She wanted the toilet. She didn't want another sip of water. 'Take that baby out of here if she is going to cry.' 'Where's O'Brien?' 'Could I have another pillow under my legs?'

To his relief she wasn't ever as incoherent as she had been about the 'leaves' of the chair.

And then one morning there was blood in the toilet bowl. Flora couldn't answer his question but, by the smell, he guessed it was from her bowels. He cleaned her up and changed her nightgown and carried her back to bed. He restored her to her nest of pillows. For the last week she'd slept, when she'd been able to, propped up. It helped her to breathe, particularly in the early hours of the morning, when breathing was a real struggle for her.

Xas sat down on the edge of Flora's bed and stroked her earlobe till she looked at him. He said he thought he should take her to hospital.

'It's too early,' she said, and he didn't know whether she meant it was too soon or thought they shouldn't bother anyone until a more reasonable hour. Then she said that she didn't like hospitals.

'Perhaps I should call Avril to take Alison.'

'Let her sleep,' Flora said, and Xas couldn't tell whether she meant Alison or Avril. He decided he would phone Avril. Then he'd wake Alison and bring her in to her mother. He got up from the bed. 'I'll be back in a minute.'

Flora was holding his hand. She let it go, then when he began to move away she reared up and snatched at him. 'Where's O'Brien?' she gasped.

Alison was fast asleep in her cot, so Xas went out to find the cat for Flora.


Xas first checked under the rosemary bush, then walked to the top of the nearest rise, where the track to Flora's back gate branched from the main path. The sun wasn't up yet. There was just enough light to colour the closed poppies, and the tangles of bramble, and club-like flowers of the bulrushes.

Xas called. He walked away from the gate, calling. Minutes went by, then tens of minutes. He knew he should go back, should call Avril, shouldn't leave Flora alone. He looked over his shoulder. The neighbours' houses were quiet, windows still sealed by blinds or curtains. The only light showing was at their own kitchen window. He saw this, as he always had, as a sign that Flora was home. It was as if he'd been out late, at a jazz club, or with Cole, and had come home to find that Flora was up and might call out to him, so that he could go in and give her the news—what he'd heard, who he'd seen.

Xas walked on. He continued to call. He listened—heard nothing much—as if everything on the wasteland had fallen silent to make sure his voice was heard.

Xas sank down then, he sat on his heels. He dropped his head and said, in his own tongue, to God, to Whom he had feigned deafness for nine years, 'Father, let me find this cat.' He prayed, and then lifted his head and waited. God was there—always there—as unconcerned and unhurried as the morning.

Xas waited. Then he gave up waiting. He turned back to the house and made for its homely light. At the gate he did stop once more to look back. And there was O'Brien, coming over the crest of the low dune.

The cat trudged, slowly. Xas could see mud and leaf litter clinging to his draggled belly. As soon as he saw Xas, O'Brien flopped down.

The cat had walked—had come back—as far as he was able. Xas knew that O'Brien had been walking for as long as he'd been calling, and for as long as he'd prayed. God might have heard and understood his prayer, but O'Brien had come himself, out of the trust of his own tired heart, from love and from graciousness.

Xas went to the cat and scooped him up. He carried O'Brien indoors and put him down beside Flora. He placed Flora's hand on the panting cat and, his hand covering her own, they smoothed O'Brien's matted fur.

At what she thought were intervals of only a few minutes, Flora made an effort to open her eyes. She was waiting for the sun to come into the room. For the sun to come, and another night to be over. O'Brien was pressed against her leg, purring so fiercely that his exhalations shook the bed.

Xas brought the baby in. Alison's warm, wispy head brushed Flora's cheek. Then the baby gripped Flora's hair and gave it a tug. Flora felt Xas extract Alison's fingers. The bed moved as he sat down, the baby on his lap. Alison had her bottle, she was slapping it as she drank, the formula making a musical splashing.

Flora opened her eyes. No sun yet. She closed them again.

Xas said something.

The air in the room was as cold and wet as fog, thicker than air, hard to manage. Flora remembered being in the lit capsule of a streetcar on a very foggy night, the mist fuming through the seams of its doors. She had been talking to someone that night about how to make sense of a story, and the difference between the audience watching a character do something—say, a woman burning her gloves—and another character observing the same thing, unseen themselves, say a man in the room the woman has come into. Was it Connie she'd been talking to? They'd often talked about things like that. Often, all of them, Connie, Carol, Wylie, Con on occasion too, and different cameramen, Pete, Jimmy Chan, and Cole's editor, the woman who'd taught her how to cut film.

Flora opened her eyes. Why was the sun so slow in coming? It seemed a thousand years since she was well.

Alison was making baby music in her milk-thickened voice, the happy singing with which she began every day.

So it was morning.

Flora closed her eyes. 'Oh, Connie!' she thought. It was so funny, the way he gave away his real ambition every time he called the audience 'the audience' instead of 'the mob'.

Connie always loved to say that, for the audience, it was the story that was the thing, whether crafted by a novelist, or thrown together by a newspaper copy boy or an opera librettist. Connie and his 'story'. Flora remembered him, in the middle of one of his expositions of his method, saying to Xas—also party to some of those discussions—'Pretend you're in the story.' Of course Connie hadn't known that that's what Xas was always doing, and that the pretence pained and embarrassed him. Xas was always more comfortable off to one side and serving other people's stories. Always happier providing some business in the background, keeping moving, like a fake multitude, the column of soldiers that seem to go on forever but are only marching around behind the live area to enter the shot over and over. Xas was like that. He was back there, behind things, a thunder and shining that made everything seem real.

Flora opened her eyes. The room was still dull. Perhaps it was an overcast day.

Alison was lying against Xas, her head on his chest, sucking her fingers. She stared at her mother, sleepy and solemn.

'When I go into hospital, if I do say anything odd, they'll put it down to the psychosis,' Flora said.

'You've been reading my book,' Xas said. Then, 'Would you like to hold the baby?'

'No. I can see her,' Flora said. She stared at her daughter.

'Tell me what to do,' Xas said. 'Tell me the rest of it.'

Flora closed her eyes. She couldn't understand what he meant. 'The rest of it'—as though she was halfway through telling him a story. Then she heard him say, 'I mean—tell me what you want for her. For Alison.'

'I can't imagine,' Flora said. Then, 'It's all right, Xas, sweetheart. Pretend you're in the story.'

The world turned peach-coloured. The sun was shining on Flora's eyelids. O'Brien was shaking the bed with his purring, Xas was weeping, while Alison's puzzled complaints came and went in counterpoint.

Flora opened her eyes.


Xas went with Flora in the ambulance. The specialist had a room ready, a private room, so Xas could sit by her bed.

She'd lost consciousness shortly before the ambulance came, and didn't revive. Her admission form said, 'Uraemic Coma.'

Xas sat beside her and held her hand. Flora's fingers were so swollen they felt rigid and boneless at once.

He had phoned Avril and she'd come, with her chauffeur. Flora had rallied enough to squeeze her friend's hand, but hadn't been able to find words. Then, once Avril and Alison had gone, Xas called an ambulance. He'd left O'Brien lying on the coverlet. Perhaps the cat would be too tired to stir again, but the back door was open, just in case O'Brien's animal needs drove him out again into the wasteland, to whatever bush he'd been hiding under before he was called. The ambulance had arrived, and the attendants were very gentle with Flora. They'd moved with dispatch, but without urgency. Flora had gone behind her body by then, was unreachable beyond her own face.

Xas didn't take his eyes off her face. He hoped she might surface. He didn't even blink. He sat by her stretcher in the ambulance, then by her hospital bed. He raised his voice over the sound of her laboured breathing to sing her the songs they'd both loved.

The nurses heard him singing—the young man with the much older wife. They looked in from time to time and did the little they were able to, took the patient's pulse and made notations on her chart.

At these times some spouses would watch all such activity with resentment or anxiety, while others were reassured. The young husband seemed oblivious. He seemed to notice no one but his struggling, comatose wife. One nurse thought this touching, another thought it rude.

They advised him to rest, to have something to eat. But he wouldn't stir. They didn't know how he managed it. For twelve hours he kept his seat and held his wife's hand. The doctor was in twice, at nine in the morning, shortly after the patient was admitted, and again at six in the evening, before going home to his dinner.

Then, at two in the morning, the young husband appeared at the ward sister's desk and said, 'She's dead.' Just that. He followed the ward sister and a duty nurse back to the room, stood against the wall while, for a minute, they were busy by the bed. They whispered to one another, in deference to him, not the poor woman, the patient who, comatose on arrival, was a blank stranger to them. They closed the patient's mouth and drew the covers up under her chin, the sheet rolled to hold her jaw in place. Later they'd cover her face. The ward sister moved the chair—its rubber feet squawking on the polished linoleum—to suggest to the husband he sit again. Sit awhile longer.

Xas resumed his seat. He put his palm on Flora's forehead, felt her cooling, but still elastic skin. Her soul was invisible to him. Invisible on earth. On earth—he thought—it was easy not to believe in souls.

The nurses had gone and he sat in silence. Time passed and, in time, he saw the bridge of Flora's nose sharpen, become stark. She was immobile, but sinking somehow, sinking perceptibly.

The noise in the corridors gradually increased. A cart was wheeled by. It paused at the door then went on, leaving behind it the smell of steamy unsalted eggs, butter and bread.

After a good while the doctor came in and said some practised, apologetic things. He glanced at Flora's chart, and made out a death certificate.

The muscles on Flora's face were firming up again. She looked starved, but resolute.

The ward sister returned and she and the doctor conferred quietly. Then the doctor bent over Xas.

Xas said to the doctor, 'She didn't wake up again.' But he was thinking, '*Who was she? Who was she after all?*' The question expanded to fill all the space around him. All the space and all the time.

The doctor slipped a hand under Xas's elbow and helped him stand. The ward sister took his hand and they led him to the door. She said, 'There must be people you need to call.'

Xas turned, wrenching the sister's arm, and scraping her hand against the sharp bevels of the doorframe. He looked back at the figure in the bed. This was it—the last time he'd see her.

*She peeled an apple, washed her hair, chewed a pencil, fiddled with the tuner on the wireless, rolled an orange against her cheek, patted O'Brien, peered into her Moviola. She always left the kitchen light on when he was coming home late.*

The face on the pillow was as closed, still and secretive as Alison's had been the moment she arrived in the world. This wasn't Flora; it was a relic. But Xas wanted to stay with the relic. Shouldn't he stay? Shouldn't he stay and see what could be done?

They were coaxing him—the doctor, the ward sister, the nurse who'd come hurrying along the hallway. 'Mr Hintersee,' said the doctor. 'There must be people you need to call.'

Mr Hintersee hesitated and, to the doctor, it seemed that everything paused with him, the noises of the world, the dust in the air. Then he said, 'I'll call Doug Madill, who is an undertaker.'

It appeared that the young husband had anticipated this moment after all. For some reason the doctor found this shocking. He released Mr Hintersee's arm. The nurses did too. Their hands shunned him.

Mr Hintersee asked, 'Where is the phone?' And the ward sister pointed the way.

# Flora's Paper Road

## November, 1941

On a crisp fall night, two years after Flora had gone, Xas heard a subtle but unmistakable sound, a deep, soft crack of wings braking the descent of a winged body through the air above the house. He left the couch, where he'd been sprawled, wearing pyjamas and reading by the rosy light of a lamp draped with an old silk scarf. He hurried through the house, and out the back door. Beyond the back gate he saw the archangel's bulky shadow.

Xas went to his brother and took his hand. 'You came,' he said.

'You asked me to come,' said Lucifer, and produced a folded and sand-chafed copy of the bill Xas had had printed seven weeks earlier.

Xas said, 'The printer was happy to be paid, of course, but was unhelpfully helpful about the size of that "XAS". He said the letters couldn't be read once the bill was wrapped around a power pole. He imagined I was printing something to paste on power poles and billboards.'

'So—you used Jodeau's method of communicating with me. Very clever. What do you want?'

'My friend Flora is dead these two years,' Xas said. He released his brother's hand and stood poised.

The archangel remarked that he looked like someone about to levitate.

'Highly unlikely, without wings,' Xas said. Then, 'You wait right there. I have to get candles and a torch.' He eyed Lucifer's wing hands. 'I'll only be a minute. There's something I want you to do for me.'

'Something which requires illumination?'

'It'll help,' said Xas, then reached out again and stroked the archangel's forearm softly with the backs of his fingers. It was all he could think to do, it was instinct, it was what he'd do to calm his daughter or call her attention to him.

Lucifer simply stood still, looking down his nose. He raised one eyebrow.

'Wait,' Xas said. He hurried back to the house. He found several paraffin candles, a box of matches, and a torch. He pulled the rug from the sofa, and went back out.

'That's a lot of paraphernalia,' Lucifer said. 'I can't think what you plan to do with it.'

Xas spread the rug on the ground.

The track had been narrowed in the hollow by the profusion of self-seeded flowers, and the blanket lay humped over lupin bushes and canterbury bells, daisies, and wild mustard. Xas lay down on the rug and rolled till the foliage was flattened. Lucifer stood by and watched. 'I'm intrigued,' he said.

'We're very lucky it's a windless night. These candles should stay lit, so long as you take care not to make any sudden gestures with your wings.'

'I'll bear that in mind,' Lucifer said.

Xas thrust the candles upright in the sand, and lit them. The flames soon stood tall, little spires of light that turned, at their tips, from threads of flame to threads of smoke.

'Have you been following this war?' Xas asked.

'Yes. I don't like it.'

Xas straightened and met Lucifer's eyes. He had been very relieved that Lucifer had come—in time to do the little good he was able to—but when he looked at the archangel Xas felt more than mere relief; much to his surprise he found he felt pleased to see Lucifer, pleased to look into that grave, arrogant face. Xas smiled at the archangel—who waited, unsmiling, then prompted, 'Yes, Xas?'

Xas put the torch down. He adjusted one candle, the only one making any noise, a fiery whisper, perhaps chewing its way down past some impurity in the paraffin. As he did so Xas talked. 'I have a correspondent, August Hintersee, a man of substance and influence in Germany. And I had a subscription to a German newspaper, though I cancelled it several years ago.'

'Because you didn't like the war?'

'Because it wasn't really possible to work out what was going on from what was reported. Cancelling my subscription was something I could do. And I gave up August. But when I filled out my census forms, I had to write that I was a German citizen. Apparently my marriage was of too short duration, or—I'm not sure—I've been talking to a lawyer, but he's prevaricating. Then the there's the *Alien Registration Act*. I had to register. I was photographed and fingerprinted.'

'You *married* her?'

Xas stepped away from the candles and took off his pyjama jacket. He balled it up and tossed it through the gate and onto the lawn. He said, 'I'm interested to hear you say that you don't like the war.'

'Why? Do you expect me to like it?'

'I don't know.'

'Xas?' Lucifer said, 'Why have you taken off your shirt?'

Xas turned away from Lucifer, then looked back over his shoulder. 'I want you to pull these feathers out,' he said. 'Only you can do it. I can't reach, and no human can alter an angel. I just want to be able to pass a bit more than casual scrutiny. Say—if a doctor wants me to remove my shirt so that he can put his stethoscope to my back to listen to my lungs.'

'Are you planning to enlist?'

Xas bit his lip. He didn't want to sound irritated. He looked down at the candle flames which were all standing straight again, though he had the impression that a cold breeze was playing on his bared skin. He said, 'I want to take whatever precautions I can not to be separated from my daughter.'

'Oh,' said the archangel. 'I see.' Then, 'So you want me to pluck you?'

'Yes.'

Lucifer raised his wings, slowly, so as not to blow the candles out. He lowered himself onto the ground at the edge of the blanket. His huge top wings made a pavilion above them, and he stretched the bottom pair out before him, between the candles, so that they formed a kind of ramp. The middle wings he closed, so that the pinions folded behind him, and the top joints bent before him. He reached up to Xas and pulled him down onto the ramp of his joined wings, turned him over using the four hands he had free.

Xas held his breath. He felt the calloused fingers, two hands softer and bare-skinned, and two finely feathered and tipped with hard nails. Lucifer's fingers sifted through the down, tracing the channels of the scars. Xas took a deep breath—smelled warm anise, and cold apples—and his mind went away from him for a time.

There were several tugging sensations, beneath his shoulderblades, and on either side of his spine. Tugging, then sharp, specific pain. Lucifer's hands smoothed the stinging spots. 'There'll be some blood,' he said. 'And it'll take time.'

'That's all right. Just try to get them all.'

Lucifer leaned forward and one of his gritty plaits slithered across the back of Xas's neck. The tugging resumed. 'Tell me what happened,' Lucifer said.

Xas told Lucifer what had happened to Flora. By the conclusion of his story the candle flames had almost crept into their sockets of sand. Xas's back felt hot and flayed. Trails of blood were drying on his sides. The tacky, pulling sensation of his own blood was as unfamiliar and uncanny to him as the pain. Lucifer had listened to his story, but hadn't made any comments or asked any questions. And he hadn't asked about Alison. He did, however, ask about Cole—and then said, as if explaining his interest, 'I keep reading about him. He's an interesting character.'

'I stopped seeing him,' Xas said. 'But it wasn't one of those rational estrangements where someone decides that they're just not themselves any more in the other person's company.'

'You mean that's happened to you in the past?'

'No. But I've seen it happen to other people.'

'Other people,' Lucifer said. 'So you're people now?' He dug his fingertips into a channel of scar to pull the stubborn feathers there. 'I've always supposed you were more tenacious than *people*.'

Xas gritted his teeth and breathed through his nose. When the worst had passed he said, 'I was so sad about Flora that I forgot to be sad about Cole. And I'm not entirely sure why I gave him up.'

Lucifer said that he'd seen Cole's western, *Miscreant*, which had been released earlier that year, then withdrawn shortly afterward because—Xas knew—Cole wanted to re-cut it. *Miscreant* was Cole and Crow's last joint project, a movie Cole fired Crow from.

Cole was practically nocturnal by 1940, and filmed most of *Miscreant* in interiors, or outdoors taking night for day. If, in the film, a door was open, showing supposed daylight, that daylight was icy, false.

Lucifer said, 'I saw it at an ozoner in Arizona,' using the slang for drive-in to make his rhyme. Xas could hear the smile in his brother's voice, could hear Lucifer enjoying the idiom. 'It's an odd film,' Lucifer said. 'With its hero and heroine who smoulder at each other from different corners of rooms, their romance made of looks, and dumb double entendres. And the camera keeps tracking in toward their faces—in reverse shots—first him, then her, then him, then her, till it's impossible to tell who the camera is standing in for, who it *wants*. The actors seem clumsy and sulky. They look like they're immersed in clear oil. And I was particularly struck by the way the hero talked, in a drawl, but his voice light, with a slight quizzical lift at the end of each statement and, at times, a passive, almost narcotised delivery.'

'Uh-huh,' said Xas.

'I decided he was playing you—that actor, Birch. Cole obviously gave it a lot of thought. And then there was the way Cole chose to light Birch, to get that *spectra*, that solar halo look, where everything is darker around the source of light.' Lucifer sounded intrigued and amused. 'Odd film,' he said again. 'Within the censor's limits, but still beyond the bounds of good taste.'

He was down to the last few feathers now. These were slippery with blood. He was having to pinch them between his nails, to get any purchase. It was delicate work and he was concentrating. Xas could hear his brother holding his breath for minutes at a time, then, when he exhaled, he blew white down everywhere. 'Do you want to know what this looks like?' Lucifer said.

'I'll check it in a mirror later.'

The archangel volunteered a description anyway. He spoke with relish. 'It looks like pimpled chicken skin,' he said, 'with big, bloody pores.' Then, 'You have no business caring for a human child,' he said.

'Who else...?' Xas began, but Lucifer set a palm flat against his greasy skin, pressing so that the breath was forced out of his lungs.

'Don't answer,' the archangel said. Then, 'I should just carry you to Antarctica and throw you into that crater lake. Heaven is where you belong.'

Xas heaved in a breath and said, 'You wouldn't have bothered to spend the past several hours pulling feathers if you intended to repatriate me forcibly to Heaven.' Then, 'Have you got them all?'

'I have.' Lucifer raised his hand and Xas rolled off the silky ramp of wings. His back burned and smarted. He sat on his heels facing Lucifer.

The archangel folded his bloodied hands on his bloodstained bottom wings.

One candle went out, snuffed by the sand. But there was light in the sky now. The sun was just below the rim of the mountains.

Xas said, 'I do know I shouldn't be looking after a child. I know that I'm not a good parent. I'm vigilant, but I haven't any instinct for it.'

And then Xas told his brother about the woman on Venice Beach.

He and Alison often went to the beach. One morning in July of that year, he said, they were there, on a weekday, with only the sparse weekday crowds. He'd taken Alison in to the low surf for a paddle, holding her hand. Then they went back up the beach and he read while she pottered about with her spade and bucket. He peeled a mandarin for her, tugged at the frill of her sun bonnet to get her attention, and fed her the fruit segment by segment, she smacking her lips to show him when she wanted more. She was distracted by a dog barking and chasing a stick, then sneezing as it breathed in seawater between barks. She kept twisting back to tap his arm and point to make him look too.

A woman came and stood over them. Xas recognised her. She was often at the beach, lived in an adjacent house. She was a hardy woman in late middle age, with short grey curls and an intelligent face. 'Excuse me,' she said. 'This will probably seem prying and impertinent but—you're not deaf, are you? Either of you?'

'No,' Xas said.

'I had thought you were. Or she was.'

'Why?'

Alison got up and came to sit on his lap.

The woman didn't answer his question, only went on, 'Then I saw her turn around when that dog started barking.'

'Yes?' said Xas again.

Alison frowned and put her chubby toddler's hand across his mouth. He removed the hand to ask, 'Why would you think she was deaf?'

'I'm sorry,' the woman said. She may have been blushing beneath her deep mahogany tan.

'I'm not offended. Only puzzled,' Xas said. He moved his head to avoid his daughter's sandy fingers.

The woman nodded at him. 'See,' she said. 'She doesn't like you talking. Do you live alone? Does she never hear you talking? Do you never talk to her?'

Xas was astonished. The woman was right. He had not been out of Alison's presence—except when she was asleep—since Flora's funeral. He was hardly ever more than an arm's length from her. When he wanted her attention he'd touch her—and he'd always known what she wanted. When as a baby she'd cooed and gurgled and made word noises he had never hung over her mimicking the sounds she'd made. He'd never talked to her, narrating what he was doing, as he'd heard mothers do—as Flora had done when Alison was tiny, saying things like, 'I'm just going to change this diaper,' or, 'In a minute, baby,' or, 'Yummy, *mmmm*,' when spooning mashed banana into her little mouth. He'd done none of that. He'd been silent.

'How old is she?' the woman asked.

'Two-and-a-half.'

'Do you suppose she doesn't have any thoughts to share with you? And have you none you'd like to share with her?'

'None that are useful,' Xas said. 'I mean my thoughts, not hers.'

The woman looked impatient. 'If you don't talk to her she won't learn to talk. Just imagine her first day at school—the poor girl standing like a ghost at the edge of the playground. Besides, I can't see how you manage to anticipate what she wants.'

'I'm with her all the time.'

'But she's not an animal, for heaven's sake!'

'I know. I'm just not cut out for this.'

'Well, if you think it isn't your place to tell her that *that* is a mandarin and *this* is a beach—'

'Yes, but—' he began, and Alison made a determined effort to pinch his lips closed.

'See,' said the woman. 'Now she thinks you're not quite yourself. Are you always silent? Are you always alone?'

Xas fished another mandarin out of the paper bag and began to peel it. He looked at his daughter and said, 'Here, Alison, do you want some?'

She climbed off his lap and stood before him, mouth open.

'That's better,' said the woman. 'You keep that up.'

Xas said, 'If we chance to be here again would you please come over and talk to us?'

'If you like.'

Xas nodded.

The woman raised a warning finger.

'Yes,' he said. 'We'd like that.'


'So,' said Xas. 'I'm not the best father. But I am her father.' He didn't want to say anything further. It should be obvious to his brother why he had to stay. He did add, 'It no longer matters to me that God didn't make the world—because He has the raising of it.'

'I see,' said Lucifer. He got up, and the last two guttering candles went out. He stood for a moment, utterly still, with his head bowed. Finally he said, 'That woman—your friend Flora—gave you a clock to watch. The child is a clock. Angels are good at keeping vigils, so I guess you'll watch that clock till it finally winds down.'

Xas caught the sound of a querulous calling in the house, the bang of the swing door to the kitchen, the slap of small feet on the linoleum, padded heels and toes, the childish bounty of fat not yet pressed away between her slight weight and the surface of the world. He quickly gathered up the main mass of feathers in the bloodied blanket. He grabbed his shirt and pulled it on. When he glanced behind him he saw that Lucifer had gone.

Alison stepped onto the back lawn. She pressed her toy bunny to her face. Bunny was a lop-eared velvet rabbit whose straw stuffing sprouted like hair under the arm Alison always hauled him around by.

Xas dropped into a crouch and stretched out his arms. Alison ran across the lawn—and Xas saw her bare foot fall right beside the day's first browsing bee. There was danger everywhere, but she wasn't aware of any. She ran into his arms, giggling, still hot from sleep. Xas straightened and raised his daughter up into the air, over his head. She shrieked with happiness. Xas spun, flying her about, holding her up between himself and Heaven.

# Epilogue

# Route 66, the Mojave desert

## 1975

Conrad Crow hated flashbacks. He preferred to get at a character's back story this way: he'd introduce a guy into a group, some guy they'd all heard a story about, the kind of story that makes people look at a man with mistrust. We, the audience, watch the way the group treat the man. We hear them talking about what he's supposed to have done. We observe what we think is his unrepentant defensiveness. And we have to work it out. We have to judge for ourselves. We're not shown what happened in the past. We don't get a flashback.

I haven't offered any. I've told the story in its proper order, and, were I able to, I would even have told it without me in it.

I made a call to Xas's message service asking him to phone me on a certain day at a certain time. I gave him a number.

At the appointed time—2.30 a.m.—I was waiting by a phone in the forecourt of an all-night gas station on Route 66. The place was open, but the attendant was asleep, his head down on the counter by the cash register. I had instructed him to sleep.

While I waited, a car pulled into the forecourt. I wandered over, unhooked a nozzle from a pump, and offered to help. The driver declined my assistance and drove off, his car's rear end fishtailing as he hit the road.

After that I decided it would be better to close the place down. I considered pulling the power lines from their ceramic insulators, but I wasn't sure whether the phone needed power to work. I hadn't used a phone before, and didn't know much about them—to me they were just a noisy prop in movies, a plot device. I thought about the mobile Army switchboards in war movies, and how the operator would wind a handle to raise a charge. I reasoned that the phone must need power, and finally decided that the safest way of making the gas station look shut was to stuff myself through its doors and find the light switches.

It was a cold night and once the lights were off I could see that the moon had a halo. A big rig approached, and the shadow of the pumps and high awning swung away and back as it went by.

The phone rang.

I picked up the receiver and put it to my ear. There was nothing—well—there was his voice, familiar, saying an unfamiliar tentative hello. But apart from that there was nothing. God didn't join me when Xas spoke.

I've lived a long time, and I've been unhappy, never in any simple way. Most of my feelings are mixed feelings, but at that moment I was happy. It was uncanny to be happy, it was strange and more painful than misery.

'Is that you?' Xas said.

And I said, 'Hey. It's a funny thing. It seems I'm alone with you.' I pressed the phone to one ear, inserted a fingertip in the other, and closed my eyes. Another truck rolled by and when it had gone I was able to identify the tune playing in the background. Duke Ellington's 'Solitude'.

Xas said, 'I'm picturing you crammed into a phone booth like a hatchling in an egg.' Then, 'You got this number from Cole, I guess.'

'How long have you had a message service?'

'Alison told me about them in 1959—so that we'd always be able to keep in touch, wherever I went. So—did Cole give you the number? I know he had it because he left a message several weeks before he died.' Xas was silent for a bit, then said, 'I've been avoiding the obituaries, and the clips on TV. I don't want to contemplate all that black-and-white grandeur.'

Behind me, out in the desert, a coyote began to yip, an anxious calling. The mouthpiece of the gas station phone had a smell. It smelled of what it was, and of the more pungent things breathed into it—plastic and gingivitis.

'Was he surprised?' Xas asked.

'To find himself in Hell? How surprised do you think he could be after a life of promiscuity and paying bribes and interfering with political processes.'

'And murder.'

'Yes—taking it on himself to seek someone else's vengeance out of nothing more than boyish indignation.' I listened to Xas's silence then said, 'He was surprised—as they all seem to be—that it was too late for him, and that his remorse was pointless, since it no longer served any civilising purpose.'

'I forget,' Xas said.

'What do you forget?'

'What Hell is like.'

'Angels never forget anything, Xas, but there are always things we don't know. Perhaps you would like to know what Cole said about you? *I'd* like to know what happened to you. What happened after I came back to your house in 1942 and found the windows were broken and boarded up.'

But Xas wouldn't bargain. He wouldn't ask for anything. Instead he told me what had happened when he last saw Cole.

In 1957 Xas sought out Cole who, rumour had it, was holed up in an old theatre, from which he'd had all the seats removed, except his own special chair. Cole was shut away in the dark watching movies.

Xas finagled and elbowed his way in to Cole through the dimwitted yes-men Cole had around him then. By the time he reached the door of the auditorium he had two men hanging off either arm, trying ineffectually to haul him away. Several others rushed ahead of him, to surround their boss, and perhaps carry him to safety. They pulled open the door and stumbled into darkness. A dank, combustible stink came out of the room and enveloped Xas and the men holding him. He heard the film, a good sound system, but cranked all the way up so that it took him a few seconds to recognise John Wayne as a booming sideshow god. After a moment the sound cut out, the speakers emitting a wounded popping and squawking. Then he heard a voice— rough, frightened and thready: 'What is this? What's the problem?'

He yelled, 'Con!'

He heard murmurs, explanations, apologies. He heard, 'Who is that?'

'It's Xas!' he called. 'I have to see you.'

More murmurs, measured, reasoning, then one of the men reappeared and said, 'You can let him go,' to those holding Xas. To Xas he said, 'Mr Cole agrees to speak to you, but you have to stay there.' He pointed at a spot only a pace on, in the doorway to the auditorium.

Xas stepped into the doorway. The men shuffled up behind him. They put their hands on him, and held him in place.

The room beyond the door was huge and dark, and filled with a thick sour smell. In the wedge of light Xas could see that there was another carpet of dust on the carpet, like the soft fur that forms on a rotting lemon.

As his eyes adjusted, he saw Cole, enthroned in a grubby lounger, bearded, and completely naked. Cole's shins and forearms were bony; his knees had ripples of loose flesh above them, where his muscles had begun to waste from disuse. There was a drift of white around the chair—used Kleenex.

'Con,' Xas said, 'I want to ask a favour.'

Cole made a wheezing noise. He was laughing. 'I knew you would one day.'

'Yes, you were right,' Xas said.

'I was right. It's all commerce. Everything. Even for you.'

'Yes,' Xas said. Then, 'Con.' He said his former lover's name with tenderness and ownership. His mouth began to water. He wasn't disgusted. He wanted to walk into the dark room and lift Cole's bony body out of that greasy chair and carry him away somewhere. He wanted to repair Cole.

'Go on,' Cole said. 'Tell me what you want.'

'You have this theatre. And I imagine you have copies of the films you and Crow made together—the films Flora edited. And all those early ones of yours she edited. I want Flora's daughter to see them. I want Alison to see where she comes from and what's possible for her.'

Cole was silent.

'It wouldn't take too long,' Xas said. He peered into the foetid darkness.

Cole laughed some more. 'You want to bring the girl here and show her what's possible for her?'

'Weren't you ever curious about her?'

'I was,' said Cole. 'And several years back I had a detective take some pictures. So I've seen her. A tall, skinny, flat-chested girl.' Cole lifted his grey, ropy hand from the arm of the chair and waved Xas away. 'Sorry,' he said. 'I can't help you.'

One of Cole's cronies immediately stepped between them and closed the door. Xas let the others conduct him out the nearest exit. He found himself on a fire escape. The sun was bright, glaring off the freshly painted wall behind him. He went slowly down the stairs and around the front of the cinema to his car. He got in behind the wheel and sat staring at the building, its clean white paint.

He had read about Cole's seclusion. He'd heard talk of Cole's 'mania for privacy'. He had always supposed that Cole would call if he'd had any further use for him. He'd been busy himself. Their estrangement *had* been a rational one. It was just what happens to people.

'To people,' Xas thought, and closed his eyes. He remembered Cole standing by the trestle table in the hangar at Mines Field, saying, 'I'm not *people*. Not *folk*.' Youthful, brilliant, as proud as an emperor, a man whose keenest feelings were for himself.

Cole had helped Xas discover that he couldn't teach someone to love just by loving them. It was something he had needed to learn. It was a hard lesson, but Xas didn't think that Cole was ever hard. To call him callous would be to claim that people made more impression on him than they had. He wasn't callous, only remote, lost in his cloud of habits and hobbies, hobby horses and phobias, and a loneliness as ordinary to him as air.

Xas sat in his car outside the sealed cinema and thought that he had been right when he'd deduced, a long, long time ago, that souls in Hell were more like themselves than souls in Heaven. But now he understood that, although this was true, it didn't matter, because the souls that came to Hell were already spoiled. Insufficient or, like Cole, having somehow never worked properly, as though there were people given to the world—and to those who had to love them—broken from the start.

And then Xas thought, 'I did love him, after all.' Sure, he'd made a mistake with Cole, and had given his heart where he stood to lose it. But that was good, it was right, it was what should happen, it was the way faith worked, it was the proper use of love.

When Xas had done talking, the record playing in the room behind him had long since come to an end and, in the ensuing silence, I heard church bells: old, deep, and mellow.

I said, 'Cole filled himself with drugs, and surrounded himself with attendants who handled everything with rubber gloves but were properly reverent of his personal filth. He regarded "the herd" as deadly and diseased, so shut himself up, and lay in bed like an invalid, wearing nothing but his sour skin. And you say he was damned from the start because he was born broken.'

Xas said, 'I'm not on your side, Lucifer. I'm not going to say, "What kind of God does that?" like people do. There's another way of thinking about all this, only I haven't found it yet.'

'You're not going to find it on earth, Xas.'

'Don't start that again—offering to restore me to Heaven.'

'All right.' I took a deep breath. The frame of the phone box creaked in complaint. I made my voice casual. 'What are you calling yourself these days?'

'I'm not going to tell you. I haven't forgotten that Hell has phonebooks. And soon the number you called won't be any good. My message centre is winding up its business, because everyone is buying answering machines.'

The desert was a dusky Martian-red already. There was a bullet-battered Joshua tree near the highway, and others further out, appearing against the red light as feathered blots of spilled ink.

The gas station attendant came out and leaned in the gilded aluminum frame of the door. He rubbed his groggy face. His cheek showed the clear print of the coins he'd been counting when I told him to sleep. The windows of the gas station threw back the soft fire of the first sliver of sunlight. The attendant blinked, dazzled, and put up his hands as if he was trying to part a curtain between him and what he could see. Then he saw me and staggered back.

I shook my head at him. I pointed at the door.

He ran back inside.

A car went by, slowed, wobbled, accelerated again. It drove on for a short distance then pulled over and braked hard. Its driver wound his window down and craned his head out.

'I'm getting looks,' I said.

Xas said, 'In a few days I'll be able to go to the newspaper reading room at my library, and look for news of you.'

'The *foreign* newspapers,' I guessed.

Xas said smoothly, 'The LA newspapers. Your area code is a giveaway. I think you're in the Mojave. There'll be something in the *LA Times*. In their whacko spot. They won't report an angel though. No one ever sees angels now. Now it's all aliens.'

A couple more cars had stopped by the first. I tried to ignore the excited consultation between the people there. I listened hard to the room at the far end of all the lines and the undersea cable. 'Xas?' I said. 'Where are you?'

He was quiet. Then, 'No.'

'There's a gathering of people here now,' I said. 'The attendant is on the phone inside, no doubt summoning the police. The sun is up.'

'How problematic for you.'

'Yes. I'm visible,' I said. 'And the cities are huge now, Xas. The skies are always light, and full of planes. There's radar. *I* can't go freely. I can't *pass*, I can't walk around and take my time till I find you.'

Xas made a small noise, possibly of amusement. 'Perhaps you'd like me to cut your wings off?'

I didn't answer, and after a short silence, he hung up on me.

I didn't fly away from the gas station, but walked through the little crowd of vehicles, pausing a moment to formulate a sentence in my native tongue, one that would make the film in the camera I could see spoil, but would leave the people and machinery unscathed. I worked out the command, uttered it, and the woman holding the camera dropped it and doubled over, while everyone else clapped their hands over their ears.

I kept on walking. A snake fled ahead of me, making a cross-stitch pattern in the sand.

When Xas's first friend the beekeeping monk died, he came to believe that God didn't after all save everything. That Heaven didn't want circus acts with circus performers. I offered to return him to Heaven, but he, Godlike, wanted more. He wanted back the people he loved. He wanted to call, and have them answer. He wanted them to be themselves forever. Godlike, he wanted that.

When I spoke to him in 1938, he talked about souls, and what God does with them. He came up with an abortive parable. He wasn't sure enough of what he thought, and his parable turned into a question. What he said was this: 'Let us say that human bodies are planes. The purpose of a plane is flight. A soul is a flight; it is the purpose of a body. But what is it that flies? I don't think you can separate a thing and its purpose. But that's what God does, He winnows things from purposes and keeps only purposes. Which makes me wonder—what was it God lacked that He called for light? What kind of lack couldn't be satisfied by *all this*?' And he had gestured around him at the moonlit flowers of Flora McLeod's paper road.

When I was far enough from the highway to judge that I couldn't be seen, I pushed off from the ground. My wings laboured till they caught the weak upward tendency of the new day's first thermals.

I would go back to Hell, and our cinema. I'd move its main projector, the DP70 Todd-AO I stole from the Newsreel Theatre in Los Angeles by carrying it off through a skylight one night in 1957. I'd wheel out the older projector and put on a silent movie—*Dance Hall Daisy*. I'd watch the young Flora McLeod checking her hair and waving hello.

There was a highway now on Flora's paper road, and an industrial park spreading on the airfield she'd crossed shortly before dawn one morning in June, 1929, whistling, and listening for her whistle to echo as if the twilight was a soundstage. Flora the film editor, who understood transitions, and understood time, and who once said to Xas that, when she was alone, she would sometimes sense an alteration, something like the soft click of a splice passing through the gate of her editing machine.

I put this story together from the testimony of the damned, and I used my imagination. I will continue to run it, listening for clicks. Angels never forget anything. There is no unwanted footage.